THE VILLA ROUGE

Also by Maggie Ross

The Gasteropod
Milena

Maggie Ross

THE VILLA ROUGE

MACLEHOSE PRESS
QUERCUS · LONDON

First published in Great Britain in 2015 by

MacLehose Press
an imprint of Quercus
55 Baker Street
7th Floor, South Block
London W1U 8EW

A CIP catalogue record for this book is available
from the British Library

ISBN (HB) 978 0 85705 322 0
ISBN (TPB) 978 0 85705 323 7
ISBN (Ebook) 978 1 84866 578 1

10 9 8 7 6 5 4 3 2 1

Designed and typeset in New Baskerville by Libanus Press Ltd
Printed and bound in Great Britain by Clays Ltd, St Ives

THE VILLA ROUGE

CATHCART

O nly later, when the New Year celebrations had passed, did somebody in the Three Graces pub say that the body of a man had
been found on the railway line over the road.

Cathcart Brodick did not tell anyone, least of all his wife. There had
been a minor altercation in the snug, towards the end of an evening's
drinking. He could say nothing. Afterwards, on the other side of the
road where the railway parapet was low, he and Kermalode had grappled in the dark.

It had happened a few days into January, during that time when
regulars were reluctant to face the thought of spending entire evenings
at home worrying about the future.

In the saloon the noisy group from Cathcart's office had been
extracting the last ounce of seasonal goodwill, in the face of what might
prove to be a problematic year. All agreed that 1939 might yet be peaceful, if the Prime Minister could be believed, although sandbags in the
streets, gas masks distributed, were not reassuring. Kermalode had said
that Britain should welcome the friendship of Adolf Hitler, with his
organisational skills and brilliant army. Look at Austria, taken without
bloodshed. Cathcart's repeated interruption was that one should be
wary of dictators.

And since only Kermalode knew where the Sudetenland was, agreement went mainly with him. "If Hitler says it is his, then let him have it
and good luck!" Another drinker said, "If our government doesn't give
a ha'pennyworth about Czechoslovakia, why should we?" An old soldier,
trying to intervene on Cathcart's behalf, insisted that the last war must
not have been waged in vain. The arguments were hopeful, for there was
an unspoken fear that these convivial get-togethers might soon be

7

history. Banter became circular and sillier, ending on the question of whether the Führer's moustache could "knock spots off Chamberlain's".

All evening Ronald Kermalode's voice had been an irritant, as it had been since the man joined the department. There had never been any direct confrontations until the revelry in the pub. True that Cathcart, who had already been in the architectural section when Kermalode joined it in 1936, had not expected to be sharing an office with him. Their initial handshakes had been as enthusiastic as one would expect in the circumstances, given that they were potential rivals for promotion. Kermalode reminded Cathcart of his father, only too proud to call a spade a spade. Civility in the office was not beyond them, but each knew that Kermalode, senior in years, might be chosen over Cathcart. That is if political upheaval did not get in the way.

Cathcart began to notice how competent Kermalode was. He admitted to Morgan that he hadn't liked the look of him from the start: something about the challenging stare. She suspected there were other reasons her husband hadn't liked the chap, but asked only did they share the same sense of humour.

Even at school Cathcart had been considered the witty one. Not for him the whoopee cushion or the firework in the lavatories. His jokes had been admired and often quoted as he made his way to the sixth form.

He brought to his job the humour that had served him so well at school, finding it a useful distraction from any inadequacies. It had not taken long for Cathcart to see that his rival's humour was of the basic kind.

Kermalode's comments and innuendoes had in no time assumed a sexual tone. Some passing female had "a nice pair of pins", or the boss's wife was "a right piece of skirt". These were not to Cathcart's taste. Nor did he appreciate having to listen to dubious stories of how the chap had spent his weekends. Bent over their drawing boards put them into a false camaraderie, too close for Cat's comfort.

There had been a sort of argument on 3 November 1938, the date

retained with bitterness and a rancour Cathcart did not like to acknowledge. How could he tell Morgan that such a man could get under his
skin with a few paltry statements? She might have questioned him. And
Cat secretly needed his wife's accord in everything.

By the end of 1938 Cathcart was given his own space. This had little
effect on Kermalode, who constantly aired his political bias towards
fascism. Admiring Benito Mussolini's exploits in Abyssinia, he said he
could see how much could be gained from taking over a country run by
golliwogs. Cathcart was infuriated by this admiration for land grabbing.
Kermalode's loudly expressed view was that the last war had been a
mistake. He personally had no intention of putting on a uniform. His
unwanted opinions, often presented in a joking manner, increased
Cathcart's suppressed hostility. He felt only he was capable of making
light of a serious situation without harming it.

For hadn't his skilful sense of humour been the deciding factor in
winning Morgan? Whether she agreed with this he never questioned.

Cat's father's views on the match were clear and nothing to do with
jokes tasteful, clever or dirty. Morgan was too grand for his son.

"Out of your class, lad. Them good-looking women's special," he
had said. "Women like that have expectations you won't be able to live
up to." How his father had arrived at this notion was baffling.

"She may be one of 'em that hides a lot of feelings under them
looks. Makes 'em skittish, like a horse. If you want to marry her, you'll
have your work cut out." Particularly since money was involved. "With the
way things are going – fewer jobs, more strikes, mark my words – you'll
be one of the lucky ones."

Cathcart, unsure, had replied, "I may marry her. I may not. Haven't
decided yet."

"Your mother was one of them thoroughbreds. I found out too late.
Secrets never spoke. Cleared off one day. Bolted." His father had never
talked like that before.

"You told me mother had died."

"Might just as well. Now you're grown you can have the truth. You must be tough enough if you're willing to take on the Perincall girl."

The conversation had left Cathcart wishing his father had not opened up so frankly. All it had done was leave him with a greater sense of insecurity.

Worries about an errant mother subsided slowly, decreasing the disquiet over Morgan Perincall. They continued to fluctuate over the three years of their courtship, right up until the autumn of 1927.

Morgan's father, Montague Perincall, had stated her suitor was "steady". Cat was certain he'd heard it, just as he'd heard the Perincalls' housekeeper, Rhoda Swell, reply, "She'd do best to marry that Brodick chap. So, Morgan being Morgan, she will not! She'll lead the poor fellow a merry dance." Her employer's reply was carried off on the September wind rattling the chestnut trees. There and then in 1927 Cat decided he would have nobody but Morgan Perincall, whatever the challenges or the rumours.

His new wife rapidly dispelled any doubts about her desire to be wed. She enjoyed sex as much as he, "within the bound", as she first expressed it, "of careful management".

A nagging thought persisted that women should not be so eager in bed. Nor so spirited out of it. Cathcart's private feeling was that married women should present no further problems, but should live in gratitude for having been saved from spinsterhood. He knew this was wishful thinking, for he was not a fool. But the breadwinner's word should be law, he having forgotten that his new wife had brought with her a dowry. And an unspoken independence at odds with her husband's expectations.

Morgan merely acknowledged that Cat, five years older, would be more conservative. Her need to "take herself off", without giving any details, caused him much irritation. Within the first weeks of marriage she had gone exploring London. No hard words could bring his new wife to heel. So Cathcart slowly learned that lighthearted reprimands were the best means of control. As Morgan's need to explore diminished, and Cathcart retained his sense of humour, the marriage settled.

There were shared interests in food and books, art and music. Cathcart's preferences were for galleries and museums rather than concerts. Churchgoing continued as it always had at the Villa. Morgan's behaviour improved gradually over their thirteen years. The arrival of two children contributed much to the change, until theirs became a routine as fixed as any in the neighbourhood. Habit became the blanket covering their lives, under which she sometimes struggled to find breath. But she continued to try, and overtly succeeded, in devoting herself to her chosen role.

Sex continued to underpin the marriage; her sometimes violent lovemaking the only sign of any inner turmoil. If an unspoken fear of pregnancy resulted in quieter conjugal habits, it did not prevent her from dreaming.

Her husband seldom wanted to discuss much that was intimate. Cathcart's father's words about women like her remained with him for a long time. He had not wanted to be proved inferior, therefore rarely did he question her deeply. So both managed to maintain an outward, admired calm.

His acknowledgement of his wife's housekeeping abilities diminished with time and familiarity, although occasionally he complimented her on her skill with a dish, a frock or hat. This happened less and less, and Morgan gradually came to care less about her husband's disinterest.

For her their alliance had been the end of a chapter. For him the start of independence, the job in the architectural section confirming him in his role as provider and father. When his father died in 1930, leaving him the house in Tufnell Park, Cathcart felt he had achieved his goal.

Their London life was all important since their connections with their own families were limited. By deaths, in Cathcart's case. In Morgan's, by a reluctance to connect with her old home. But whenever the word "home" was mentioned, she always took it as referring to that childhood villa by the river, and not the house in Tufnell Park she was to inhabit for thirteen years.

On various occasions Cat had heard Morgan telling this or that visitor to number twenty-eight how she loved the flat lands, the beautiful countryside around the Villa Rouge, the river in all its changes.

"If you miss the place so much, I'm surprised you don't want to go back more often," he said. Her replies were unsatisfactory: it was a long way to Lodford; buses and trains were irregular; children became fractious.

"Next you'll be saying you want me drive you there. I can't buy a car without promotion. If there's a war, we may be lucky to get sufficient contracts. Soon they will be building nothing but bunkers."

Her excuses varied: a professed dislike of her father's housekeeper; Cathcart had not seen eye to eye with her relatives. It was true he found his wife's brother, of whom she rarely spoke, full of resentments he couldn't fathom. Near the start of the marriage, Morgan's dramatic reaction to Charlie's accident had been a surprise. She had left Billy, their newborn, and rushed off to the Villa in a panic. To do what? She had come back fast enough, saying Rhoda Swell was fussing over Charlie with no room for anyone else.

Cathcart had known from their first meeting how little he was liked by his potential brother-in-law. Charlie not been won over by later invitations to come to London. Morgan seemed to have regarded her young brother's rare visits as irksome. Yet she kept his ill-written cards and letters taped and tucked in a drawer. Visits from her father Montague Perincall were treated with the same vexation, her explanations being of the busy housewife variety. But her husband saw only a wife who found time to sit reading or gazing into space.

Only since Kermalode's death had he begun to wonder, while he stood unseen watching her, what she was thinking about. He hoped she might be daydreaming, not pondering what secret her husband was hiding. About the killing he dare not utter a word, least of all to her.

At closing time that January night the revellers had left the pub together, saying long farewells as if they were going overseas. One of the last to leave, Cathcart found himself confronted by Kermalode leaning against the railway parapet. Kermalode, whose lack of sobriety had intensified in the night air, began a freewheeling criticism of Britain's armies past and present.

They were alone. Cathcart's intake of alcohol had freed him to counter Kermalode's rants forcefully. His forefinger had at times connected with his adversary's shoulder. But he convinced himself later that he had never lost his temper, even at being called a twerp.

This was the way Cathcart liked to remember the quarrel: he would never have hit the man over the matter of British versus German patriotism. Yes, he had exaggerated his father's heroic role in France, for Brodick senior had been behind the front lines feeding the troops. And Kermalode had tottered and swayed, muttering derogatory words that Cathcart swore to himself were blasphemous.

In retrospect it was clear that this man had always had a dangerous temper. For hadn't Kermalode's fist bounced off his drawing board, in anger at not being believed, when he claimed his father had received the Distinguished Conduct Medal? And when somebody in the office had raised the subject of the Spanish Civil War, Kermalode had been unnecessarily confrontational, openly questioning why Brodick the patriot had not volunteered in the autumn of 1936. Or that is how Cathcart wished to remember events. No, not after the catastrophe of the Somme. Cat knew he was being made to look cowardly in front of the office. He had felt intimidated enough to retire to the lavatory for a smoke.

He knew only too well it was not about who had fought whom, or who was going to fight this time. No, it was about Morgan, and had been ever since the start. On those occasions when Kermalode had talked of seeing her – in the street, in the park on Sundays, during rare visits to the office – a lascivious expression had been all too apparent. At the Christmas party that look was on Kermalode's face when he had greeted Morgan, holding her hand too long. And she had allowed it.

In the dark by the railway parapet, through Kermalode's drunken mutterings, her name had come out clear. He had definitely kept repeating that Cathcart's wife was "a cracker". And it was not the first time. It was about all those long-endured innuendoes that had come flooding back as they stood locked and swaying in the gaslight. It was the way in which Kermalode had mouthed insufferable things about Morgan's partialities.

But it was not just about her. It was Kermalode diminishing the status of Cathcart's father. Back and forth from father to Morgan and on. Intertwined. Disjointed. Soldiers . . . War . . . Morgan . . . insults . . . swear words. The wrestling. The backing off, the pushing, the fisticuffs. Then it was dark, the lights from the public house suddenly snuffed. The gas lamp barely colouring the pavement where they tussled above the railway.

He must have hit Kermalode then, the man's saliva was on his cheek, so close were they. How many minutes or hours had passed? There was no sense to the stop and start of the punching, the cries. The last word he heard coming from the bloody mouth was "knucklehead".

Had Kermalode leaned too far over the parapet to vomit? Why had it gone so quiet? Surely Cathcart had left the scene before the fellow disappeared? As he stumbled away, his self-questioning perished unanswered in a haze of alcohol. By the time he reached number twenty-eight all his concerns were on keeping upright, in case Morgan had decided to stay up and wait for him.

In the two months that followed, if Cathcart had sometimes been kept awake by the thought of Kermalode, the next day he could spend moments unobserved, bent over his drawing board, eyes closed. The trouble was that when he shut his eyes visions of the man's grimace, close and bloody, arrived to extinguish sleep.

On into February his fight to maintain a night's untrammelled sleep became harder. The police had been to the office with questions, and had gone. Their uppermost concern was how many of them might soon be called up. That they had not bothered to question Cathcart at home made him more nervous. Why had they accepted so easily everyone's statements that Kermalode had left the pub alone in an inebriated state?

That this was not rare? Telling himself that an oncoming war was of more consequence than the death of an architect, did nothing to calm his frayed nerves.

After the killing, the joking had stopped. Given the political situation, this quieter Cathcart was regarded with new respect by his colleagues. Events were turning dangerous. Building plans were put on hold, air raid shelters given priority. Gas masks were again slung across citizens' shoulders.

Although Morgan noticed the change in her husband, at first it was not of the utmost importance. She was focused on what might happen to them all if bombs and gas attacks came as predicted. She kept her worries to herself, for eight-year-old Billy, and Teresa, only five and attending her first school, were too young to be made anxious. But as March came, she began to question whether this silent husband cared about his family at all.

She could not pinpoint the day on which Cat had become so remote. She too, like his office colleagues, put it down to ongoing concern at a political situation deteriorating daily. His talk, such as it was, was becoming bleaker. When he spoke he was more likely to bemoan the fate of Europe, quote her father's warnings that they must be prepared for war.

But nothing prepared her for the news that came early one Wednesday afternoon. With just one sentence Cathcart removed all doubts about his objective. He told Morgan he had joined the army as a volunteer.

Immediately she thought her husband had grown tired of them all and had found an escape. Whatever his explanations about protection or patriotism, or following in his father's footsteps, she felt a betrayal that continued from then on.

For Cathcart departure could not come soon enough. Allied to his fear about his crime and its exposure was guilt at leaving his family to face a London at war. Now it was impossible to talk much at all, in case she might mention that his duty lay with those at home. As April came and with it conscription for young unmarried men, and real war loomed larger, his only admonition to Morgan was to think of her responsibilities.

He saw her becoming complicit in this, as if her own needs were unimportant. He took to watching her, afraid of what she might be thinking. Watching how she sat staring into space, supper neglected. When he looked away did she turn her gaze on him? Whatever he said to her, his words, he felt, were filled with new meaning, as if a simple request to pass the butter would bring on some reprimand. Or some question about a certain New Year's night.

One morning when he risked saying, "In the night you came close to me and you were cold," had she given him a sharp look as if fearful of intimacy? She did not ask if he still loved her, as she might once have done. When they first married she had wanted to discuss feelings. Now it was he who worried whether she would support him or side with the law. It had been a long time since they had had intimate conversations and he could ask nothing.

Both had long since tacitly agreed that two children were enough. But on the night of his leave-taking there was a wild sortie into unprotected lovemaking that left him drained and irresolute. Had her mad attack been directed at him, or at the unknown man she had called out to in her sleep? He would never know, for there was nothing humorous anymore in which to cloak so dark a question.

With relief Cathcart had gone away with other younger men, happy to put on khaki in defence of a country more and more likely to need him.

Only in August had he reluctantly returned home on enforced leave, from which he ran back to camp as fast as he could. What neither of them knew was that this leave would be his last for a long while.

For Morgan's part, her escape had come equally as suddenly. On the morning of 1 September, 1939, she had taken the children to the railway station and watched them go, with hundreds of other children, to the promised safely of the countryside. That night her decision was made. She too would depart.

Throughout her thirteen married years she had longed for and been afraid to return to the Villa Rouge in equal measure. On 2 September she had collected her suitcase, coat and gas mask, locked the front door of number twenty-eight, boarded the bus to the main station and caught the train back to her childhood home.

The problem was there was nothing overtly sufficient to lift her out of the protection of her home. No war had begun, only threats, warnings, Nazi advancements. And no Cathcart to make choices for her. Not until the children had been snatched, almost without her say-so, did she see what to do. Then there was no choice at all. Justifications for leaving could come afterwards. For now it was the Villa drawing her back.

On the train, huddled in a corner of the carriage, she eyed its occupants. Unlike her husband, they were so young, these soldiers with their nicotined fingers, whose kit-bags threatened her feet. They knew nothing about what she was enduring: her losses, the shock of the speed of it all that was pushing her forward. Pushing her back.

Her reflection in the carriage window revealed an impassive face flawed by the striae of passing vegetation. The hat with the flower made doubly ridiculous by its double reflection. A fleeting memory came of someone – of course a boy, his name subsumed from long habit – who had grabbed at the flower as if to eat it, then grabbed at her.

Those had been the mad days, for which she had been feeling resurgent longings, suppressed with increasing difficulty. It was Cathcart's fault, with his chilly manner and silences. It was his fault for neglecting her in bed. Then deserting her altogether. The children too must have suffered under his aloofness. It was not surprising that neither Billy nor Teresa missed their father when he went into the army. Home on leave, his attitude to them had not changed, so neither had theirs. Morgan was grateful that her children could face life as it came, good or bad. This was an attitude she would try to adopt.

But as she watched, through a haze of cigarette smoke, the country-side passing, rising feelings of dread continued to compete with the thrill of going home. On her lap her book lay unread. She closed her eyes, trying to shut her ears to the conversations around her. Eventually she managed to drift into a hot, half sleep filled with images of elm trees and children and windswept grasses. Of Lodford. Of Charlie.

CHAPTER ONE

It was imperative to escape. It had to be to the Villa Rouge. She was born and had grown up there. It was the centre of the most momentous events of her young life. It held her secret. But she had given scant thought to the consequences of going back, or how long she might stay. Although in such disrupted times there was little chance of knowing what might lie ahead.

Someone had said that genuine war was certain, for the Nazis had already marched into Poland. What to believe? She tried hard not to think of her children in their new home. Thoughts of her husband continued to fade.

It was a long time since she had been home to Lodford. Hardly had she stepped from the train into the familiar smell of coal dust and walked a few paces down Station Hill, than the doubts surfaced. Would she be recognised as the girl no better than she ought to be, back to offend this hidebound town? What would her father say? And Rhoda? What about Charlie, so needy, so disquieting?

The steep incline sent her rapidly down to the bottom of the hill where it crossed the brook, the suitcase banging her silk stocking. It was still hot. The coat and gas mask felt leaden. The brook looked abnormally low for September. Charlie, in the infant school, had been forbidden to climb down into it. But no small child could resist its lure. The braver ones would wade up to their knees as far as the tunnel under the Plumberow Road. At seventeen she had done it with one of the Lucas boys. The thrill was to enter the dim hollow arched with moss and kiss, with the water dripping onto them. To slip was easy; that was the excitement.

The Lodbrook was her river, downstream from the North Sea

estuary, flowing salty and fast, until it was tamed by the floodgates of the Perincall tidal mill.

In thought she followed it from the mill, picturing it as a slow-moving stretch of freshening water, gradually narrowing into a brook between scrubby grass banks. Passing between the town's cottages and gardens, it ran in a deep gully between West Street and Long Alley. It flowed over stepping stones behind Willams the grocer's where the old village pump stood.

She could see how diminished it was as it went under the railway road bridge, reappearing as a rivulet over the pebbles. Many generations of children had tried to follow it back to its source in Ironside Lane, only to find a disappointing trickle emerging from a hillock.

She had been contemplating the Lodbrook in reverse. Cathcart had always accused her of backward thinking.

The sound of horse's hoofs, but no traffic. She hoisted the suitcase and set off towards the town centre. It was as dusty and depressing as if the war had already begun. From Whitley's garage a mechanic waved. He might have been one of her classmates from the junior school, who had waded the brook with her. She acknowledged him briefly. Coming back was not easy. There was bound to be someone to recognise her, to want to ask questions: where were her children, her husband? To want to go down memory lane.

The usual knot of boys staring into the depths of the blacksmith's. A horse tethered. Smoke, the clang of hammer on anvil accompanying her along West Street. No signs of change yet. Shops just as empty looking. She reached the market square without stopping, before the heavy suitcase and coat forced a rest by the cattle trough. She dipped her hand in the water. She and Beebee, the son of the piano teacher and the rag-and-bone man, had done more than that in 1924. The shocked saddler's wife had berated them from her bedroom window.

Somebody in the butcher's shop raised a hand. It was Alice Dance from grammar school, leaving at sixteen to chop chops in her father's shop and gossip about matters that she shouldn't. "Hello, Morgan!"

She raised a feeble finger in response and ducked through the alley, past the cobbler's into North Street. That particular street she crossed at speed, avoiding a glance at the post office – it was bound to be there still. She chose the Co-operative store route that held no such disturbing memories.

Only a mile to go, but a long mile, traipsing around this corner and that, seeing little that was new. She had a terrible thirst. A man on the train had offered her a beer that she had refused, aware of disapproving looks. She glanced longingly at the Tall Ship, but without an escort she would not have dared go in. At four o'clock the pubs would likely be closed. Shops with their blinds down looked abandoned. Everywhere so quiet. It was dispiriting seeing it again.

It must have been four years since they had been back to Lodford, she and Cathcart, son Billy and the newborn.

The visit to Grandmother Perincall's house at Great Gormson she remembered best. It was to show off Teresa, who had, by her constant mewling, prevented critical comments. Hints on child rearing were proffered by Aunts Harriet and Maud who, as teachers in the Little Gormson infant school, felt they had the authority. Winifred did her worst to calm the infant by rocking her violently. Being spinsters, none of them had actually raised a child. It was said that Harriet had been engaged to a Prittend solicitor, who had returned from the war and never been heard of since. This accounted for Harriet's often gloomy demeanour and tendency to sarcasm. Morgan's father warned her not to be too dismissive of her aunts.

Everyone seemed out of sorts on that visit, including Charlie who kept sliding down the arms of the horsehair sofa, until Montague threatened to take his belt to him. So Charlie had hidden in the outdoor privy until going-home time. No gifts for anyone, except a cot blanket of Winnie's meticulous crochet. It was a relief when Cathcart cut the visit short.

Morgan's luggage was forcing her to walk slowly. Seeing the landmarks of her youth made her uneasy. She passed the surgery of Mr

Starling the vet, her father's friend, with whom he often played cards. And probably still would, unless the war changed things. He, Dr Chilling, her father and Charlie had often gone coarse fishing on the River Brod. Rhoda would have it they spent most of their time in the Smugglers at Blytham, and bought the fish from a vendor. The housekeeper once declared it was well named since Charlie, under age, had to be smuggled into the pub by Monty.

Starling's job was to see to the welfare of the pigs, whose aroma drifted on the west wind into the Villa's windows. Morgan's mother had complained about it for years. Next to the vet's was the dairy: green-tiled walls with pictures of cows. It looked empty. All Morgan could see was her distorted reflection undulating, the hat atop the dark fringe. The dairy yard was deserted save for stacked churns. No sound from the stable. For a moment she considered asking Mr Boxley for a lift on his milk float. An unseemly idea for a respectable woman. She would have to continue by foot.

All the houses, their curtains drawn against the sun, looked vacant. Had everybody taken fright after Munich and gone into hiding? Panting in the heat, she walked on. Was she doing the right thing? At least Charlie would be glad to see her.

Overhead the roar of an aircraft startled her. It vanished in the direction of the estuary, over the mill and the Villa Rouge. It was a long walk even on a cool day. At the British Legion she refrained from sitting on the war memorial steps. The sight of a lone woman lolling in public view might not be the best of ideas, people might remember her. She could not help being remarkable. Mr Phledge had told her she was as pretty as an alstroemeria. She had early recognised the susceptibility of males and used her looks relentlessly. Now she accepted them for what they were, still satisfactory.

It might be wiser to stay as inconspicuous as possible. Before marriage to Cat, being seen in compromising situations with numerous boys earned her a reputation, and her family's reproaches. Nobody knew how one loss following close on another could send a girl wild. Only later did she see it herself. For five years she had tried to escape from blame and pain in the arms of any youth who would risk her. Until she had turned to Cathcart for rescue.

A quivering heat haze lay over the far stretches of the Gormson Road. She could make out the thatch of a cottage, the sparkle of a dew-pond. Beyond, there were fields and farms that had once been as familiar to her as the road she was now considering.

The Gormson route home, despite its good pavements, would have added at least another half an hour to the exertion. She would risk her good shoes along Morn Avenue.

The heat felt more intense. Her underarms were damp, energy ebbing fast. A man on a bicycle came towards her. He called her name then slowed to a wobbling halt. He was one of the boys she had danced and flirted with and rejected. She called hello and hurried across the road. "Staying for the duration, Morgan?" he shouted back before riding off. He was wearing khaki.

Morn Avenue with its familiar houses, whose occupants were probably the same as when she had left in 1927: the Borrell family, all eight of them crowded into number seventeen; Percy Rough at number twenty-one whose mother had rejected the prospect of Morgan as a daughter-in-law. So what? He had been no catch. The Lucas boys at thirty-nine, with not an ounce of conversation between them, but an awful lot of sex. Not much choice in a small town. The fatigue of fighting them off when they tried to go too far.

Perhaps she was still being watched. When young that suspicion had engendered defiance. She had held her head high, daring anyone to probe her secret. What a relief it had been to marry Cathcart and move to London. Whether it had been right or not was another matter. Why had Cat gone so soon? Where was he now? She shook away plaguing thoughts and walked on.

Towards the end of Morn Avenue she was forced to stop, remove her hat and wipe her sweaty fringe. Her earrings hurt. The frock was beginning to cling, the suspender belt felt tight. Not a breath of a breeze. No reviving clouds. So quiet, apart from her breathing, the sound of bees, the rumble of lorries or thunder. A summer storm? She had left her umbrella in Tufnell Park. Her shoes were not waterproof. There was a ladder in her stocking. She muttered, "Botheration!" The worst part of her trek to the Villa Rouge was to come.

The road was narrowing and ridged, the surface full of dusty potholes. No trees. She thought she remembered trees, less neglect. The houses here were older ones, with tiny gardens. Now they looked even smaller. Her mother's friend had lived in one. There had been interminable afternoon visits. And iced biscuits to compensate for the long waits while the two women discussed ailments Morgan did not comprehend. Their graves were not far apart in Little Gormson church-yard.

She passed the Peculiar Chapel, where her mother's friend had worshipped. A mysterious place she had often lingered by. Charlie, too young to understand the fascination, would tug her to move on. The chapel was closed, yet it was Saturday. Had those worshippers been evac-uated too? There was some criticism of their ways by the aunts – no hymns, no vicar in vestments to lead the service. Morgan's father said the Peculiars could do as they liked as far as he was concerned. Rhoda agreed.

Captain Perincall had no truck with religion after the death of his wife Berenice. It had left him at loggerheads with the rest of the family, especially his mother.

Dividing the chapel from the senior school was a tiny plot of land. Next to it a red-brick building in a tarmacked playground, where Morgan and the other children had scraped their knees. By the time Charlie went there, she had already left the sixth form at Prittend Grammar. It looked as forlorn as everywhere.

The road ended suddenly at the playground. Ridged cement dipping into earth and twitch grass. She knew well the house standing at the end, beached by a builder who had run out of ideas. In its garden lay an assortment of scrap metal, thirteen years of it. The man who lived there was a rag-and-bone merchant. What fun Morgan had had with Beebee, the eldest. His wife had tried to teach Charlie the piano. Coming from the house was the faint sound of "Apple Blossom Time".

Ahead were familiar fields, through which lay the final stretch home. Encumbered as she was, she would have to negotiate this part with more than usual care. There was a stile to climb with luggage, thorny bushes to be avoided.

But something new was standing in her way, a concrete platform as high as her head, sprouting pipes and wires. Around its base, open bags of sand and cement. Planks of raw wood lay scattered, a leaning mixer half full of cement still wet, yet no sign of workmen. She circuited the emplacement, careful not to do more harm to her stockings. She nearly fell clambering back over the stile to retrieve her suitcase. "Damn!"

On the other side, the path ran between a pea field and a ditch with an unruly hedge. The pea haulm was giving off a familiar, sweetly mouldering smell. Sometimes there had been potatoes growing in that field, sometimes broad beans. On the other side of the hedge she could see the last stubble of the wheat harvest, awaiting the plough.

If he had been there, her father would have told her the exact species of wheat, how many bushels from that acre, what colour the grain, the number of grains to the ear, whether flinty or mealy or plump or bearded, whether to mill for biscuits or bread. It was evidence of her father's obsessive nature that he had nicknamed Charlie "Little Josh". "A variety of wheat sown in autumn!" Montague had once said with heavy irony.

She drew a deep breath. At last, away to the south through hazy trees, she could make out the mill's solid silhouette, almost cathedral-like. A noisy dirty place that her father had often reminded her was the source of their daily bread. And, just visible, the ribbon of the River Lodbrook, its provider of power. She had walked this bourn in heat, rain and snow and always felt the same thrill at those glimpses of silver water that meant she was approaching home.

Now it was just a question of reaching the oak tree, certainly still standing the end of the path and marking the penultimate stage of her trek.

The grass along the ditch was brown, the hedges bedraggled, exactly as she felt. In the blackthorns a few desiccated sloes still hung. No sign of the rose hips her mother had once wanted her to collect. Did Rhoda send Charlie foraging for berries? She had always pickled, bottled and dried everything in sight with frightening competence. Rhoda would be in her element if rationing came.

Montague Perincall had mentioned in one of his postcards that there might be food shortages. *"Waste nothing"* he had written, forever sending instructions. Cat was amused, saying they at least contained some sense. *"Eat less yourselves but feed the children well for they will need all their strength. Never go to bed on a full stomach for it increases anxiety on the morrow . . . Listen carefully to the wireless every day . . . Remember the last war and prepare for the worst. If it comes, get out of London."*

After Cathcart went into the army, the postcards were confined to the back of the mantelpiece. Now she was coming home to face her father's formidable presence. And the nearer she got, the clearer she could make out the sounds she always associated with him and home.

The low hum, the rattle of hoists, the whirr of the water wheel, the gear wheels grating a rhythm on the wind. These were the background to her youth. At times one could hear the hissing of water when the floodgates were operating, a noise akin to the sound of grains tumbling into the chutes. The smell of it. The very taste of the clouds of chaff. These sounds and smells were an inescapable part of her young life, only missed when they had gone. After marriage, without the sounds of traffic in the streets of Tufnell Park, she might have gone home sooner.

The turn of the path. The oak tree. In its shade she dropped the suitcase and coat. She looked down Mill Lane, along which the grain lorries came from far wheat fields. From the mill they returned laden with flour for the cities. She hoped the barges that used to glide past the Villa Rouge were still operating.

Nobody was moving about in the mill cottage gardens. She had forgotten how private people were. In the garden of Mr Talbott, the mill manager, a Union Jack was dangling from a pole. He had not been her favourite person. One never knew what such a closed-in sort of man was thinking.

She heaved the suitcase onto her hip. The same smell of pigs in the air, still there in their pens not a hundred yards away across the lane. To reach the Villa grounds it was best to hold one's nose, scurry past the sties towards the old turnstile. She ran as best she could, calling hello to them out of habit because Charlie always wanted it.

The turnstile a final hurdle, forming a bridge between the two ponds. More lakes than ponds – natural barriers at the lower end of the Villa estate. Her father's story was that they had once provided monks with trout. All Charlie ever caught there were sticklebacks. The gate was new. It was difficult to manoeuvre herself and her baggage through it. Hard too to find enough energy to climb the grassy slope, but good to look up and see the Villa shining between its trees.

Why it was called the Villa Rouge was a mystery that the present occupants had long since ceased trying to solve. It was just a house, plain and unprepossessing in a few acres of land.

Morgan thought perhaps those Victorian Perincalls, builders and modernisers of the ancient mill and the Villa Rouge, had retained its exotic name in the hope it might transcend its commonplace location. They evidently did not consider their surname exceptional enough to re-christen the house with it. Centuries before, it might have begun as a mere hut, Saxon or earlier, built on a salient spot beside the Lodbrook, one of the many tidal rivers that penetrate England's eastern coast.

Over the ages the dwelling had been rebuilt and rebuilt until, by the early part of the nineteenth century, it had become the present house: a confusion of styles not large enough to qualify as a mansion, overlooking the river whose waters flowed by means of floodgates into the proximate flour mill.

Morgan's father would tell whoever would listen that the term "villa" might once have alluded to an entire medieval village, the land farmed over the centuries by tenants owing allegiance to the lord of the manor. Its size and influence dwindling over the centuries, it had passed into single ownership and eventually into the hands of the Perincalls. They had handed it down to succeeding generations of the same family. She was tired of the telling.

Montague, the one male Perincall to have survived the trenches of the Somme, had taken over the mill after the death of his father Nicholas. Having no training as a landlord, Montague employed an agent to oversee his tenants' farms and cottages, as few previous Perincalls had done. Morgan wondered whether the house was still littered with photographs of those deceased Perincalls: whiskered gentlemen, soldiers on horseback, severe ladies, and children in starched garments all framed in silver.

She knew she was not to inherit. Her father had made it clear. That would fall to Charles as the direct male heir of the family. He was the one who might be ready, in time, to follow her father's demanding dreams. Not a mention of her son William. Sometimes she cared, when the unfairness hit her. Generally she considered herself lucky to be away from the responsibility, the dictates. Cathcart always claimed she could not think beyond her nose, but his was a critical nature.

At the top of the grassy mound she glimpsed the cricket pitch, the strip of defeated earth, the wooden pavilion, windows boarded, looking less pristine than she recalled. Much kissing had gone on there. Much fending off of a too importunate fiancé.

Outside the Villa everything under attack by the sun. Dry grass at the edges of the chicken run. She greeted the scattering hens, surprised at their numbers and the size of the enclosures. She was forced to go around them to gain the garden. But where the garden proper began was puzzling. Part of the fencing was missing and the gate had fallen.

It had not been much of a garden when she had last seen it, though back in her mother's day it had flourished. But the extravagance had disguised an underlying order. Morgan had loved her mother's garden. Now a few parched roses still clung on. Hoed weeds lay under maimed, once precious shrubs. The lawn was parched, one corner half dug, the spade still stuck there.

She could see Rhoda's hand in this, just as it had been since she first came in 1922. But was the vegetable garden, Rhoda's pride, still in existence at the back of the house? The greenhouse? And the potting shed, where her father spent summer evenings smoking Old Holborn away from complaints?

What an ordinary sort of place it was. For in that part of the county where river and land merged, where fields of wheat were interspersed with meagre hedgerows, there was nothing dramatic to admire. Sea walls, saltings, mud and water were not to everyone's taste. Morgan's father had often spoken about the hopes of local families who, in the aftermath of the last war, had struggled to recover from a cruel slump. They wanted no more changes other than the alternating seasons, and the chance to continue working their land. Now it was September 1939 and he was telling everyone this would be an even more cataclysmic war, brought about by a belligerent Nazi dictator intent on annexing other people's acres.

The cricket pitch and pavilion, the drive, were almost hidden by trees. Bordered by chestnuts on one side, on the other a deep ditch, the drive was shut off from the Gormson Road by iron gates. From there it ran past the house towards a strip of pebbled and sandy beach that changed to mud at low tide. She wondered whether, between beach and water, the old moorings were still rotting among the saltings.

No-one knew exactly how far downriver the family land actually extended. One could walk along its protective wall for miles, almost to open sea without hindrance, save for an occasional stile. The dyke had been Morgan's favourite walk, testing herself against the distance, smelling the salt, hearing the skylarks. The memory of lolling under a wide sky had been one reason drawing her back. She had taken only special people there. Now it was its isolation she needed.

The garden fence would no longer keep out rabbits. They had been on the lawn. She had yearned for a gazebo, from where she could see across the river. Why she wanted to look at this inaccessible no-man's-land, a marshy area of hawthorn thickets, elder and weeds, was beyond her father. With customary irony he said she might like someone to bring her refreshments. But he had provided a bench. He said her mother's plans for that part of the garden had included a pergola and statuary. The greenhouse was still there. The D'Arcy Spice apple tree too – thirty-two years old, planted in the year of Morgan's birth.

She knew her father might gain financially if war came. A shortage of imported grain would increase the price of home-grown wheat and the flour he milled. Think of the army's need for biscuits, his sisters said. His thoughts were more on what the army might face. The narrow band of the Channel between England and France would be less of a barrier now than it was before. The river on which they relied would put them in danger. It flowed directly into the North Sea, from which would come the enemy as surely as had the invading Vikings, Danes, Normans. Then there were planes, those newer sources of terror. He could envisage Nazi aircraft using his river as a guide to London. If they failed to reach that target, he imagined them dropping their load on his mill, his home.

Morgan thought the house, like the garden, looked more wrecked than in 1935, possibly due to erosion of the paintwork by salty winds. But she wanted to believe it was the long absence of her mother taking its toll.

The knocker on the front door was shiny enough. She waited for footsteps.

Charlie was at the door, staring.

"Hello, Charles." Handing him her suitcase, she pushed past him into the hall. "I had to walk from the station."

Seeing her was a shock. "Which way did you come?"

"Is that all you've got to say? Not a soul to meet me!"

"Which way?"

"West Street of course. The square. East Street. British Legion. Where else? I'm so thirsty. The avenue, then the short cut. Did you know there is a huge concrete thing at the school?"

"Yes. Did you see the pigs?"

"The smell!" She fanned her face. "Charlie, you cannot believe how exhausted I am."

He dropped the proffered coat and gas mask. "Did you come through our new turnstile? It stops Asher's pigs escaping onto our land. Did you see how low the ponds are?"

"Get me a drink of water."

When Charlie returned she was looking around. "It's like a morgue in here. Not a soul at the station to pick me up.

"Where is everyone? I've had the most ghastly time getting here." She drank the water in one gulp. "No trains to speak of, and soldiers hanging out of carriages calling impertinent things." With a thud her handbag and hat joined her things on the floor.

"Anyone would think there's a war coming!" Charlie said, trying to adjust to her presence. "You were lucky to get here. Most trains are being commandeered."

"You're always so dramatic, Charlie. The rest of my luggage is still at the station. Why was nobody there to pick me up? Where's Pa?"

"What are you doing here anyway? He's at the mill. Where are the children?"

"Oh, they've gone." She was not wanting him to know her feelings. "Evacuated. So I couldn't stay in London, could I? And be blown to bits." When she moved to sit on the stairs, the light from the stained glass window carmined her hair. "But I really think they're just trying to scare people. Absolutely nothing has happened in Tufnell Park."

He was still staring, having forgotten how beautiful she was. "How could I meet you? We weren't expecting you. How long are you staying?" Her shrug could have meant anything. "Do Billy and Terry know you've come home?"

She beckoned him to her side. Obediently he came. "Morgan, why didn't you let us know you were coming?"

She took his hand and stroked it. "I sent you a card. Of course I did." He was not believing her. "Oh, Charlie, everything was so rushed. One minute the children were there, the next I was tying labels on the poor dears and telling them to stay together. At the station, hundreds of them. Like ducks at Christmas. I cried when they waved from the train."

"I expect they cried too." He took his hand away. "How long since Billy and Terry went?"

"What is today?"

"The second of September! 1939, for your information!"

The irony was lost on her. "They must have gone yesterday. Yes, Friday. It has all been so horrible." She began smoothing the creases in her frock, running her hands over her thighs in a way he wished she wouldn't. "Ever since Cathcart volunteered for something called the B.E.F. and left us in May. Apart from a bit of disembarkation leave. There was no need for him to join up at all. He is exempt, I found out. But off he went without a thought for his responsibilities. It's not fair.

"I wrote to you, remember? But you didn't come. I was so lonely, Charlie. You can't imagine what it was like in that house alone. You wrote you were busy. With what? It has been months since he went."

"You had the children."

"Then when they went, I was totally on my own. No street lights. Black as your hat! Last night I hardly slept a wink." She was facing him. "See my eyes? Bloodshot."

He looked into her green-flecked eyes and saw his reflection. "How long will you stay?"

"You could have come when Cat left. But you didn't."

"I was working. Helping father."

"Oh, you're so grown up now."

"Eighteen. Old enough to volunteer, like Cat did."

"Don't be silly, Charlie, you know they won't have you. And it's not as if there's anything going on, whatever that Alvar Lidell person says on the wireless. But I tell you, Charlie –" she was grasping his arm – "no gas attacks. Not a Nazi in sight. People can scare-monger about Russians making pacts. They just like wearing tin hats and looking official. Now we have to put strips of paper over the windows against the blasts. Send our children away. Hide in shelters. Not do this and not do that. What-ever Cathcart believes, it is a storm in a teacup. Mr Chamberlain has been telling us so for months and months.

"That is what I'd say to Cat, if he has the good grace to let me know where he is. All I have had is one mouldy card saying he is not allowed to tell his whereabouts. Me, his wife! I ask you!" She paused for breath.

"Do you know where they've gone?"

"Who?" She was massaging one silk stockinged foot. "Oh, the children? Somewhere in the West Country, I believe. They'll be back soon, I know it."

"Somewhere! Don't you know where your own children are? Teresa is only four. And Billy can't be more than—"

"Eight. Charlie, you don't understand. What was I saying? It's typical of Cat to treat it as an adventure."

"And the children?" Charlie insisted.

"Yes, the evacuation notice came. The next day everything was topsy-turvy. No time to get them looking decent. The next day, or was it the day after? Anyway . . . I was *informed* they had to go to the station. Chil-dren, hundreds of them, piled into this train. Mothers everywhere crying like fits . . . Then we were *informed* they were going west. Possibly Gloucestershire. But I told Billy not to leave his sister under any circum-stances."

"Sounds odd to me. How will you know where they are? Are you certain you weren't told where the children were going and you have forgotten?"

"How could I forget my own children! Sweet Terry was hanging onto Billy's hand for dear life. They had huge gas mask boxes. Hers was a Mickey Mouse. But no tears. I was quite proud of them."

"It might have been better to stay put, waiting to hear from them." He could feel the heat from her body. He did not know why it was disturbing. Another thought: "How could you have sent us a card if you didn't know until the last minute they were being evacuated?"

Morgan sighed. "Oh, Charles, you're not going to be horrible to me already, are you?" She leaned her head on his shoulder, and her special smell jolted him. It was always the same when he was near her: inhale her, be touched by her, then they were more than brother and sister. Twins perhaps or, he thought, she the lizard and he her dismembered tail, ever craving reattachment. He smiled at the thought of his sister a cold-blooded invertebrate.

She asked what he was smiling at, but it would not do to tell her. It had not taken him long to learn that permission for closeness had to be granted. She was too mercurial.

When he was five she suddenly married Cathcart Brodick and went to live in London. One minute she was there for him, the next gone away with a stranger. Before that, ever since he could remember, she had treated him as the mood took her, sometimes dismissively, even cruelly on occasions. There was as much desolation in her presence as joy.

Sitting beside her, he was trying to comprehend why she had always been so . . . unpredictable. Because of the difference in their ages? When he was born she was already, he counted fingers secretly, fifteen. A grown woman to a child. Someone whom he had toddled after admiringly, until she shooed him away. Or gathered him to her with hugs. Impossible to predict or understand.

When she married, she promised not to leave him behind with Pa and Rhoda. But the promise had been false. It had taken only a few days for him, the child, to understand that adults lied.

Now she was beside him, the difference in their ages didn't seem so great. She hadn't changed at all since that fateful leave-taking, despite having had two children, her skin smooth and translucent, the hair as dark. She looked well nurtured and that was something new. Cat must have done as he had promised Pa and got a good job. But what now?

He glanced down at her painted nails, the wedding band, the other ring that glistened green, and wondered about housework. About whether fireworks would recommence between her and Rhoda.

It had happened before, a ruckus that had gone on for days because Morgan had told Rhoda she was nothing but a hired help. Four and a half years old Charlie was at the time. From his hiding place in the pantry he heard the raised voices. But it was he who, while finishing off the last jelly cube, had been the recipient of Rhoda's resentment.

Not long after this he had thrown a spectacular tantrum of his own, because his beloved sister had announced she was getting married. Down by the river he had howled at the waves with grief.

"I had to get away, Charlie," she murmured. "But I left this address at the offices."

She had seemed to pick up his thoughts. No use asking why she had deserted him for Cathcart. He was afraid she would say she loved her husband.

"Aren't you hungry?" he asked.

They went into the kitchen. Beef was roasting in the oven. They lifted lids like co-conspirators, peering at raw potatoes and cut greens, at batter waiting for the Yorkshire pudding. In the pantry were towers of tinned meat, fish, and fruit, rice and pulses. On the floor, firkins of wine frothing at the neck.

"Pa and Rhoda think there might be food rationing. You should see the coal bunker!"

"When can we eat?"

Not until Pa and Rhoda were back. Their father always had his Saturday lunch promptly at half past one. If she liked, Morgan could make the gravy. She refused to on the grounds of exhaustion. It was women's work, he reminded her.

"You'll have to get used to our ways all over again," he said. "Be some help." He told her as nicely as he could, knowing that she wouldn't like it.

They stood staring belligerently at one another. She said he had changed, adding, "Not for the better!" and stomped off into the garden. He followed.

One or two swallows were still flying high. There was the scent of hay mingling with the salty smell she had so missed. It was a few minutes from garden to shore. A few more to reach the start of the sea wall. By the first stile their irritations had already cooled. It was one of the walks they shared, right up until she was twenty and he a disappointed five-year-old.

They sat down on the side of the dyke. The river sparkled in a slight breeze. She could see, upstream in the dock, a red-sailed barge. The noise of the mill was a low humming sound which, when they lay flat, blended with the sounds of sawing grasshoppers, bees and flies, a skylark's song overhead.

"You will stay, Morgan, won't you?"

"Not if I'm to do all that work and be bossed about," she said lightly. "Rhoda doesn't care for me. Never has."

"There's our boat," Charlie said hastily. "Cabin cruiser. See her?" He was pointing downstream, at a vessel turning like the others towards the incoming tide. "Brown. Green lines? We bought her last year. Remember I wrote about the old one that I helped caulk? That was a job and a half. This one's not clinker built. More powerful engines. She cruises at eight knots." He was tapping her arm. "See? Over there—"

"I see it. I see it." But she didn't. "Stop it, Charles or you will bruise me."

"Thirty-five footer. Her draft's two foot nine. Thorneycroft engines. Sometimes we go fishing right out to sea."

"Who is 'we'?"

"Father and Mr Talbott and Ronnie. And me."

"And I," she corrected him automatically. She was staring across the water, as if the other side had become of great interest. "What about her?" She was too casual. "Does she go fishing too?"

"Who do you mean?"

"You know who I mean."

"No Morgan, I don't know who you mean."

"Charles," she said, "don't play games with me. I'm hot and I'm tired and I'm . . . getting really hungry." She had almost mentioned her children, but did not want to be criticised again for her seeming neglect of them. "Has her cooking improved?"

"Her name's Rhoda." Charlie snatched at a piece of grass. "And no, she doesn't."

"Doesn't what?" She began to watch him warily. The sun was burning her forehead. She could hear waves splashing. A single bird flew east west. Pa would soon be home for lunch, covered with the usual patina of white dust.

"Go fishing." Charlie paused. "Her name's the *Berenice*."

"Whose? What are you saying now?"

"The boat! Mahogany and elm with some oak. Mr Talbott's boat is over there." Charlie was pointing in the direction of a group, swinging at anchor. She's the *Clara*. But I don't know if that is *her* name or not."

"Whose name?" She was barely listening.

"Mrs Talbott's. I think the tallyman once mentioned she was a 'Grace'. Perhaps her husband called her after Clara Bow, the film star?"

"What are you saying now, Charles?"

"Ours is called the *Berenice*. There. On her side. There!" He was pointing more urgently. "The *Berenice*. Our mother's name. Don't you remember? You can't have forgotten that!"

She got to her feet, and grass fell from her frock. "Mother was always called Bunny," she said grandly, "but you wouldn't know that." She was releasing an earring. "I am a bit surprised that Pa didn't tell you Mama was always called Bunny."

"He might have done. When I was younger." Charlie was blinking in the sunlight. "I wish I remembered her."

"Of course you do. You must remember *something* about her."

"I can't. I was too young."

"No, you were not." She was positive. "You were more than a year old when she died."

"My first memory is lying in bed next to a woman. But I thought it was you."

"Why on earth would it be me?"

Crestfallen, Charlie scrambled up. He followed Morgan back along the sea wall, aware that she was not bothering to see how he was managing the stile and slope.

On the gravel path he nearly caught up with her. "It would sound silly to name a boat *Bunny*." Morgan kept striding on. "Only rabbits are called *Bunny*!"

Rhoda found them in the smaller sitting room, huddled on the sofa as if they were cold. She pretended not to be surprised at the sight of Morgan.

"I wondered when you'd turn up. Bombing London already, are they? How are you getting on with this blackout business? Monty says we'll soon have it here too." She sounded cheerful, although her smile did not reach her eyes.

"Come here for light relief, have you?" Rhoda was unpacking her basket on the *chiffonier*. She looked hot. "Not much here. News pretty dreadful. Poland's caved in. We've bought a new map of Europe –" pointing towards the kitchen – "I bet you don't even know where Poland is." She slapped a newspaper down. "Watch out for Holland and Belgium. Us too, if we stand by them and the French. Ask your father. It'll soon be all hands to the pump, mark my words."

Morgan rolled her eyes at Charlie, who was trying to hide his concern.

"How's your hubby? Kicking his heels in some army camp? Not for long, I'm sure." Rhoda was at the door. "Did anyone think to feed the stove? Of course not! Charlie, I'm surprised at you."

She was looking around. "Where are the children?" She was perplexed. "Don't say you've left them behind. Who is looking after them?"

Charlie explained quickly that Billy and Teresa had been evacuated to Gloucestershire. How Morgan had come home the next day because of gas scares in London. How they were announcing that war was definitely possible, like Pa had foretold. And Morgan had thought it best to leave, because she couldn't sleep and the streets at night were dark and dangerous. He was talking too fast, trying to cover the silences that would fall between the two women if he stopped. They looked at him without pity, knowing well what he was trying to do. And knowing he was bound to fail.

"How long is she staying?"

"How can she know? Nobody can know that, can they? War might be declared at any minute. Pa said so himself." Charlie wished he were somewhere else. He wished his father would walk in. He wished he were not already looking at Rhoda through Morgan's eyes, at her bony body in its frock with sweat stains. He was wondering how two women could make similar frocks look so different.

Morgan, trying to put some warmth into her tone, said, "I shall stay as long as you'll have me, I suppose." It would do no good to antagonise her so early. But she could not help adding quietly, "I did live here once, even before you," to Rhoda's departing back.

The clock over the fireplace chimed. "The clock's wrong." Sunlight sent dust motes over the room, lighting their faces silver.

"Well –" Morgan was crossing her arms – "I lived here fifteen years before she came." Charlie was saying nothing. "And five years after that too. I have been here five minutes and I am expected to watch the stove. Those Gormson Road girls, they come and clean and such? The one who is a bit simple? And her sister with some sort of flower name?"

"You know them – Myrtle and Thelma Retchen. Usually both come."

"There you are then!"

The rattle of pans in the kitchen, cutlery and plates. Rhoda was setting the table.

Another clock chimed the half hour. Charlie was still huddled on the sofa. "I never had a mother. Only Rhoda. She brought me up."

"Oh! Thank you very much, Charles, for all my efforts." Morgan tossed her head. "So I did nothing, is that it?

"Somebody has a short memory. I can remember dragging you to the recreation ground. The sweet shop. School. Wiping your horrible little nose. I really shouldn't have bothered with you at all."

Outside car wheels were loud on the gravel. "You were a miserable brat." She wanted him to argue. She heard the Rover door slam and hid her apprehension at the imminent reunion. The rush of longing to see her father was tempered by the knowledge she would be instantly reduced to that immobilising state of childhood she knew so well. Would they ever right the fragile balance of power between them without the inevitable friction?

In the hall Rhoda's noisy greeting, her voice lowered as they discussed Morgan's arrival. Montague's footsteps through the kitchen, not coming to his daughter, but going on up the stairs. The bang of the bathroom door. Nobody had ever told him he should wash in the lobby or the boot room.

"Well, you did too," Charlie said.

"What?"

"Brought me up. And don't say 'what', it's rude. You were always telling me that." Her laughter was arrested by her father entering.

Montague, heading for the table, turned and came back to his daughter. He pulled her towards him in a clumsy embrace She tried to kiss his cheek, but he recoiled as if she had bitten him.

Lunch was not a pleasant affair. Her father looked old, hunched. It entered her mind that she might have come to live with not one, but two cripples.

"Where are the children? Evacuated, are they?"

"It was very quick, Pa. No time to prepare much at all."

"Little Teresa too? Why didn't you bring her home here?" Before she could reply he added, "Not safe at all. Not for any of us. Or you." He began to carve the roast.

"I thought you might come." In the same breath, "I read they are sandbagging official buildings. Bombs dropping on London, they told us on the wireless. No doubt we'll be in for some too. Have there been bombs in your district?"

"No, Pa. Just a lot of people running about like chickens."

Her father laughed and helped himself to cabbage. "More of that to come, you can be sure." He was looking around. "Where did you say the children are?"

"Evacuated, Pa."

"Ah. Somewhere safe?"

"She says she doesn't know where they—" Charlie was stopped by a kick on his shin.

"Gloucestershire, Pa," she replied.

Montague wasn't satisfied. She had to explain why she had let her children go. He could not understand the folly of a mother coming eastward, rather than choosing to go west to safety with them. In protecting her own person, he said, she would be protecting Cathcart's heirs. And where exactly were they billeted?

"An official letter is sure to arrive on Monday." It was no use trying to say she had suffered a sort of panic. That it had not occurred to her to think beyond the farewells.

Charlie tried to explain that evacuating London's children was only temporary. After all, war had not even been declared. There was still hope. He was told not to be foolish. To try to live up to his eighteen years.

Morgan asked about her luggage. Ronnie Talbott would fetch it, her father said, but his mind had moved on. "Mark my words, there might be war as soon as tomorrow."

The others knew better than to contradict this. Rhoda kept nodding. "We shall all have to put our shoulders to the wheel. And that includes you, my child." He was pointing his fork. "You will be another mouth to feed. So you will have to pull your weight." He speared a slice of beef.

"As far as the mill is concerned I may, or may not, have to intercede on behalf of some men. I will be exempt because of my age, unless this war lasts. The same for Talbott, I think, classified as doing war work. Josh –" he was pointing at Charlie – "cannot go for obvious reasons."

When Rhoda tried to intervene, saying Charlie wanted to wear a uniform, she was brusquely told not to interfere. During the peaches and custard she hardly uttered another word.

Late that night in Montague Perincall's room voices were raised. Morgan and Charlie in their separate rooms heard them, although neither came onto the landing to listen. He did not want to hear Morgan whispering, "I told you so," nor hear her conspiratorial talk about the possible threat to his heritage which Rhoda, as his potential stepmother, might pose.

Of course he had thought about it, and it did not seem so awful. Rhoda had virtually raised him from when he was five, but she had always seemed more of a pal than a mother. She was Rhoda, who could never take his mother's or Morgan's place.

Charlie had always accepted without question Rhoda's efficiency. In her care, after Morgan's marriage, life had become less hectic, more ordered, duller.

But it was not to Rhoda he went for emotional comfort after his accident. Even if it had happened closer to the Villa, he knew he would not have sought her out. The nearest person after his fall, the one who staunched the bleeding and called the ambulance, had been the mill manager Bernard Talbott, who had done as well as his nature would allow in the soothing department. His wife Grace, too, had shown Charlie prompt kindness.

Rhoda's best role was as the sickroom organiser. Charlie had wanted only Morgan. And Rhoda was the one who brought his sister from the station, preparing her for what was to come, and staying until Morgan's hysterics had played themselves out.

In the beginning Morgan, who had found it hard to sit in the sick-room, brought Charlie soup and calf's foot jelly. Yet she could barely stay long enough to watch him eat. It was unbearable seeing him lying with his splinted leg in the air. She was already telling him he would be well again in no time. It was her second experience with the bedridden, the first so deeply implanted in her memory that she had no way of coping with this new one. Her stay had lasted two days.

Then Rhoda took over. As Charlie improved she chivvied him to get up, not allowing him time for self-pity. She insisted that boys with damaged legs still kicked balls. She encouraged him to take up football again. Charlie refused. All he wanted was to be able to play cricket, and he was secretly afraid he might never be able to run.

Rhoda didn't berate him, as Morgan and his father had, for having jumped into the waters of the lock while the floodgates were closing. He was only copying the older boys who used the mill as their playground. They had treated Charlie as an equal only because his father was the boss. He blamed them to their faces for what had happened to his leg.

After the accident, the rift between them and Charlie was as bad as the scar. "It'll take time," Rhoda had said. "Time is a great healer." These banalities were all she could manage in the face of his isolation.

The night of Morgan's return, hiding behind his bedroom door, Charlie imagined what Rhoda was saying to his father. He knew that what went on in his pa's bedroom was not his business. This time it was different. There had been raised voices before, but not like this. One or two incomprehensible words were shouted. If one of them was "marriage" it would not have surprised him.

Of course his father should have married Rhoda. Any fool could see how much she adored him even if, as an embarrassed boy, Charlie had tried to avoid noticing it. In his teens he could see that Rhoda, with her small bosom and scrawny frame, did not inspire desire. With her strange accent and lack of education she was no catch. He could almost hear his father saying the same. It was upsetting to see both points of view. He knew that his father was fifty, and that was very old to be getting married again.

Charlie could not guess Rhoda's age. She wasn't half so bad when she put on a bit of lipstick and combed her hair to go to the pictures with him. Of late he had even tried envisaging her naked to help him masturbate, but it never worked. He usually ended up thinking of someone like Louise Brooks the film star, who more closely resembled his sister. Morgan was considered beautiful by most people, with the curious exception of Grandma Perincall, who always said, "Handsome is as handsome does", with no elaboration.

It was entirely understandable that Rhoda wanted security. She wanted people not to gossip about her, as did the Gormson aunts, Harriet going so far as to accuse her behind her back of being a scarlet woman, living with two men.

In the bedroom, his father's low tones were interspersed with Rhoda's higher volume. Charlie heard the words "power" and "possible", of which he could make little sense.

Were they discussing Morgan's arrival and what that might mean for the Villa's peace? Whether to let her stay. And for how long? It worried him. What if Rhoda was delivering an ultimatum that either Morgan must go or she would? He could feel panic rising.

So Charlie did something he had never done before. He ran along the corridor to his father's door and banged on it.

There was a moment of silence in which he could hear the tiniest of sounds emanating from all around: the wood panelling creaking, a window rattling, the wind whining like a forlorn dog. He even thought he could hear, deep inside the distant mill, the plop plop of flour onto the meal floor.

His father's voice called, "Go away, child!" evidently thinking it was his daughter outside. "We all need sleep. That includes you! Tomorrow is going to be a very long day. Be off with you!"

CHAPTER TWO

Mr Chamberlain's announcement at 11 a.m. the next day that a state of war existed between Great Britain and Germany was enough to sink the strongest spirits. But life and eating had to go on, Rhoda said.

Berenice Perincall had adhered to the biblical injunction not to work on the Sabbath. After her death Montague saw no reason to change this, and Rhoda was glad of the rest. So cold meat it was.

Throughout lunch Montague talked with his mouth full, something his wife would never have tolerated. He wanted them to understand the implications: they were not to think that Austria's capitulation last year had been the beginning. No. He could see what was coming in 1918 soon after the armistice. Rhoda kept nodding in agreement, as if he and she had been party to this hypothesis all along. He talked of Hitler's seizure of the Sudetenland as only the preliminary to further annexations. "I have seen it before." He was speaking like an eyewitness. "If you've got land, you want more."

Recently at the cinema Charlie had seen columns of German troops marching with banners. Seen British tanks in Belgian towns; flotillas of warships promised to protect a nation in peril. Could he, with his damaged leg, be accepted into the Royal Navy? Or would that new service, the Royal Air Force, take him? But no, the sea always quieted him. He had hoped to go out on the *Berenice* with his father before the weather turned.

Morgan, unsure what she was doing in this house without her children, watched the beetroot on her plate bleed into the mashed potato.

Her father said, "This war will be longer than the last, God help us."

"Haven't the Nazis got what they want?" she said hesitantly, aware that her father was addressing her. "The land was theirs anyway, wasn't it?"

This had been Cathcart's summary of the situation. Or perhaps he had said the Sudetenland was *not* part of German territory. And where exactly was Austria? She wished she had paid more attention to European history.

She used to be able to recite fairly convincingly the list of Britain's kings, from Canute to the present George VI. Geography had consisted mainly of drawing maps of countries that were never adequately joined. Had Cat said it was a good thing that Britain had come down on the side of Poland? If so, his volunteering for the army would make more sense. But she could not get over his choosing to leave her and the children.

Now her father was lecturing them about Chamberlain, saying that anyone with a grain of observation could have seen that signing a treaty with Hitler was futile. "That dictator was intent on war," he said. "And now he's got it."

After the jelly and custard Morgan made to leave, but was followed by Rhoda suggesting she might like to help with the dishes. In the kitchen Rhoda asked what her plans were, which duties she would be taking on, what would be her financial contribution? Morgan said she would consult her father, adding that Rhoda was not to worry, for with war imminent she would soon have too much to think about to bother with matters that should not concern her.

All afternoon Montague kept his ear to the wireless, while Rhoda brought him cup after cup of tea. Charlie, restless, went outdoors. He could be heard in the garden clapping his hands at pigeons on the cabbages.

While she had still lived at the Villa, Morgan's father had insisted it was her job to guard Charlie. Home from school she was instructed always to watch him. "This place is a death trap to a child." She was told never to let the infant beyond the garden fence. "Keep Little Josh away from the river. Don't let him near the ponds." And that was when the child could barely crawl. It was as if Bunny's death had induced in him terrible insecurity. Morgan was to make sure he was not scratched by the chickens, or he might catch a mysterious illness called "Pip". Charlie had never caught it and neither had the poultry. In fact he contracted very little other than mild measles, that she was not there to catch. "Mind you stay with Little Josh all the time," her father would say to her during school holidays. "Don't you go scattering off again."

There was Rhoda, and what was Rhoda's job but to look after Charlie? Montague trusted his new housekeeper and never understood his daughter's needs. So Charlie had five years of Morgan's haphazard care and Rhoda's attention. After that there was only Rhoda. Montague gave her a free hand from the time she arrived at the Villa Rouge in 1922. On paper she looked young for the job of housekeeper to a widower with two children, and one only seven months old. He told her his daughter would help, not divulging that Morgan, at just sixteen, was proving unreliable if not downright difficult.

Everything about Rhoda was quick. That was what Montague admired. Her mind, like her person, darting here and there. No need to tell her twice. In no time at all she had everything in the household under control. With the exception of Morgan. Soon she was calling her employer Monty and tapping him familiarly on the chest. His daily instructions became briefer and briefer, before he was off to the mill and the work that was sustaining him.

In a few months Rhoda had arranged the running of the house to both their likings, with minimal help from Mrs Retchen the elder and her daughter Gladys. She reorganised the kitchen, the larder, the chicken runs, even the books on Montague's shelves. While Morgan went to school she saw to the daily needs of Charlie, on whom she doted. That she could cope so well was a marvel. Montague told her so. Unfortunately he praised Rhoda too often in front of his daughter who, without doubt, felt sidelined. Morgan's only defence against Rhoda's ferocious efficiency was to upset the apple cart in minor ways. She managed now and then, when her wanderlust temporarily abated, to sabotage the household arrangements, to her satisfaction and the other's chagrin.

This time, having been home for only a day, Morgan could already see that Rhoda's competence had its limits. The kitchen had been a place where the alignment of saucepans and dishes took precedence over the meals cooked in them. Now it looked disorganised.

The rest of the Villa, like the garden gate, had an air of neglect at odds with Rhoda's love of order. In the sitting rooms magazines, sewing, the odd cup and saucer, lay haphazardly where they would have previously been tidied away. There was a vase of dead flowers on the landing. The bathroom, Rhoda's favourite cleaning goal because it produced dazzling results, had lost its gleam.

In Morgan's old bedroom, her suitcase already looked aged with dust. Her ancient doll, with the snarled hair and glassy eyes, was still on the dressing table. Only because Rhoda had wanted to throw it away had Morgan insisted on keeping it. From the window she looked onto the back garden where, on the line, garments hung contorted by a previous wind. Washing out on a Sunday! It had never been heard of. Her father was getting as lax as Rhoda. The whole house, to Morgan's eyes, had the same weariness as that hot September afternoon. Never one for house-work, she ran her finger over skirting boards and architraves. In a corner she detected the yellow ball of a spider's nest. This wasn't like Rhoda, always so neat. She would look at her more closely and try to discover the cause.

Conversely Morgan thought Rhoda over-attentive to Charlie. She fussed over him at lunch. Why wasn't he eating more? Was he poorly? Gave him another helping of beef and pickles when he said no. Told him that soldiers always ate their greens. Picked up his napkin when he dropped it. Charlie allowed this with some display of petulance. His eyes, with their deep lower lids, gave him a babyish expression. Morgan could see there had been changes. He was taller, with a sort of coltish elegance despite the injured leg. Perhaps his looks were against him. For with his thick hair and feminine mouth he certainly appeared less than his eighteen years. Eighteen. It made her feel depressingly old.

That afternoon Aunt Winifred paid them a visit, unusually without her sisters. She told them that hardly anyone was at St Margaret's at Little Gormson that 3 September. Only those who, like her perhaps, had been afraid to wait for Mr Chamberlain's announcement and had gone early seeking spiritual consolation.

For Aunt Winnie this was quite a mouthful, for she seldom spoke much unless pressed. Her brother Montague did not like the way Winnie was treated at home, and made an effort to welcome her at the Villa. She had always been the quiet spinster who had become, Montague claimed, part of the furniture to Harriet, Maud and his mother. He knew that Winnie was looking for reassurances, for the empty church had frightened her. So he seated her in his favourite chair, rolled her a cigarette and explained that he would not, unlike the last time, be required to serve his country.

The evening was different. In all the local churches from Prittend-on-Sea to Struttleigh inland, from Lodford to tiny Blytham, worshippers came to kneel and pray. So many people crowded into St Margaret's for the evening service that vestry chairs had to be brought in for the overflow. Even Portland Threw, Montague's land agent and a notorious agnostic, was there with his daughter. The heat from bodies was intense. Morgan, packed between her three Perincall aunts, two of them astonished to see her there, was afraid she might faint.

The hymns were rousing, the prayers fervent. The national anthem was sung. The Reverend Dorby, from a pulpit draped with the Union Jack, urged everyone to be of stout heart, for the hour had come. He quoted from Jeremiah 10: "*Thus saith the Lord, learn not the way of the heathen and be not dismayed at the signs of heaven; for the heathen are dismayed at them.*" There was a special prayer for the safety of the King, the Queen, and the two princesses.

Montague, who felt duty bound to be there because of the serious situation, thought the sermon weak, since the best way to win a war was to Know Thy Enemy. He had sung the hymns earnestly, in an effort to bolster lowered spirits. The older parishioners had all too recent memories of the previous war. The names of their loved ones, like those of his two brothers, were memorialised on the sides of the Lodford cenotaph. These monuments had risen like dragons' teeth all over the country.

All three of his sisters would never, in his opinion, find husbands, for eligible men continued to be outnumbered by women. Maud had walked out with a boy in the Yeomanry, dead at Verdun in 1916. Harriet's loss had been more cruel, for her returning soldier had chosen not to renew his acquaintance. Montague feared that, as in the last war, women might be needed to do men's work, giving them revolutionary ideas.

After the service, while the children ran in and out among the gravestones, he stood with the men, joining in with their concerns. There was discussion about the recent excellent harvest and potential government interference, who would be called up from the farms and who might be exempt. This time few appeared as eager to volunteer as they had in 1914. This would be different, although Montague's own son-in-law had enlisted early. During the last war there had been Zeppelin bombing raids. A relative of a Gormson farmer had been killed in Yarmouth. But this would be a war of modern machines. Having seen on the Pathé News how lethal Nazi planes were, no-one doubted that a new power would be unleashed.

Dr Chilling cited Guernica in Spain. Where were our aircraft? Ronnie Talbott said the flying club at Lodford aerodrome had been disbanded and was being refitted by the Royal Air Force. There were planes on the runways under camouflage nets. Rolls of barbed wire lay about the perimeter. Charlie confirmed this. His Uncle Nails, the ironmonger from Prittend, had got the contract for extra cable.

Cedric Brodir, a farmer from Iverdon, claimed he had seen more than usual activity in and around the camp that was being built on his village's football field. Why would anyone want to build on that site in the first place, least of all enlarge it, taking over the hill and putting up masts? It had been derelict since the demise of the football team in 1914. It was remote, the roads poor.

His neighbour, whose fields had been commandeered by the minis-try – he did not reveal the compensation – announced that the site sloped to such a height the summit was visible from as far away as the River Brod. Spotted by an enemy in minutes. Nothing secret about it, although it was being well and truly fenced. He had seen for himself the gates double padlocked, a new sentry box, pillboxes already in place. Men in air force overalls were building solid wooden huts within, he said. The villagers suspected it was to be some kind of radio transmitting station. But very hush-hush. Many of those in the churchyard had noticed the increased traffic to Iverdon along the Gormson Road. Lorries, not the usual mill trucks, were coming and going in greater numbers.

Aunt Maud Perincall said that, as early as last spring in '38, she had noticed that vehicles passing their house had trailers carrying quantities of metal rods. These were for the construction of four enormous masts. She said they had been raised at speed and could be seen for miles, dominating Iverdon at well over three hundred feet each. Whatever their exact purpose it must be serious, although nobody discussing them in the churchyard that evening could guess what.

It was unusual for Aunt Maud to be given an airing, Morgan thought. Generally women were aware that men never listened to them. She sometimes felt that in their presence they were invisible. Except when it came to sex. In the churchyard wives and mothers stood apart, voicing to one another fears about food shortages and the safety of their chil-dren and what might be in store for their menfolk. What they thought of Morgan, a young mother in city clothes, accompanied by neither husband nor children, they kept to themselves. After all she was a Perin-call, whatever rumours about her had once circulated.

She would have liked to join the discussion with her father, now conversing with Threw, his land agent. Somebody was talking about the Maginot Line. She remembered that Cathcart had said that it ran right through France from Switzerland to the Belgian border and was impreg-nable. But before she could insert this opinion, other male voices were agreeing that with such defences France would prevail. Her father was doubtful. The Maginot Line, once broken through, would be powerless to stop a well-equipped invader. And anyone who had hunted wild boar in the forests of the Ardennes, as he had done on leave, would understand that tanks could find their way beneath trees.

As his tenants' landlord, Montague Perincall was respectfully listened to. He was convinced that Britain would do well to prepare for the worst. He had read newspaper reports, knew his history, had a map. With Nazi troops moving eastward, it looked as though events in northern Europe might be happening with speed. The Belgians and French were looking nervous. Perhaps after the horrors of the last war they had no stomach for this one. Starling the vet warned him not to be so pessimistic. After all there were few signals yet that England was anything but peaceful.

They were not to take this as a sign of peace, Montague replied. Not for no reason had war on Germany been declared by England and France. After the collapse of Poland, the British government had had no choice. It was facing a warmongering nation. Starling thought that lessons might have been learned. In Montague's opinion the calm was merely an overture to the main symphony, which would be loud and long.

Rhoda muttered to Charlie that she had never heard his father crowing so convincingly, like the cockerel back home with the hens.

Eventually the unofficial meeting in St Margaret's churchyard broke up. Goodbyes were said more earnestly than usual, with much hand shaking and wishing one another well. The shared sense of lurking danger had raised spirits, so that many went home more cheerful. The Reverend Dorby departed with his wife and five children, satisfied he had reassured all and sundry. Mr Starling got on his horse and trotted off. The Perincall aunts walked back to Great Gormson to tell their mother of the excitement at church. And how their niece Morgan Brodick, all done up in a fitting frock with smart hat and gloves, had come alone.

As the last stragglers were leaving, a farm hand sidled up to Morgan and whispered, "Cheerio, pretty thing! Wouldn't mind having you on my side."

"Watch out, or you might get more than you bargained for!" she replied.

Laughing, he joined his wife and children at the lych gate.

Montague, Rhoda, Morgan and Charlie walked off in the opposite direction. Montague had insisted they travel the half mile to St Margaret's by foot. Shank's Pony was good practice he told them for when petrol would become scarce. The mill lorries would be given enough fuel to for the job. He still needed the Rover for work, but was uncertain of civilian needs being fulfilled. Charlie's suggestion to dig a petrol tank in the Villa grounds had little appeal, and was possibly illegal. His father said his other idea of storing combustibles in one of their barns was foolish and dangerous. They would have to get used to staying at home and, if necessary, be ready to defend it.

It was long after supper that Charlie remembered Granny Dorp. "We must pay her a visit." It was already dark outside, the river flowing flat and metallic. A few birds homing across the moon. Thin trees bending in a light breeze.

He could see Morgan was hesitant. "We must," he insisted. "Granny Dorp hasn't seen you for ages. And she may not have heard about the war."

This brought smiles. "Does it matter?" For everyone knew that Granny Dorp suffered, or some said enjoyed, a state of mind known locally as *the Doolally Tap*. Their maternal grandmother had days good and bad.

Pleading with Morgan would do no good. She had disliked going to her tiny cottage in Hatts Lane ever since Granny Dorp had once tried to interfere in her grandaughter's life.

Charlie could never explain his fascination with his grandmother. By the time he was eleven and allowed to visit her on his own, she had already beguiled him. Her wandering mind with its fanciful flights had always been of intense interest. As a child his imaginings had often chimed with hers. In the past, on the best of her flightier days, Granny Dorp would take Charlie into another universe colonised by mysterious entities: chickens that conversed with frogs; worms with wings; termites so large they could consume the very chair underneath him. Her descriptions had thrilled him with their sweep. Long after the telling, he could see the soldier ants advancing up the walls, the crazed eagles mobbing them. He had struggled against many a whirlwind that whipped the thatch up in the air, over the brook and Ironside Lane. With her he had leaned into these metaphoric winds as if they were both in mortal danger.

In recent times he might find his grandmother in her corner, plucking at the skin on her arms. He was intrigued by the way she would shrink from him, unspeaking. On another day she would want to examine his cheeks, his eyebrows, hair. And there were days when she would sit watching him for a long time. It was no use asking her why, for there would be no reply. Tired of the long silence, he would speak rudely to her and leave.

On a lucky visit Granny Dorp might be sitting on her chair by the brook, or under the moss rose outside her door. She would nod permission to approach. The ritual would begin, the looking back and forth, back and forth. Was she fearful of her invisible creatures invading her tiny space? Calmed, she would ask after his health, advise him on the prevention of pimples, how to keep hair glossy, or avoid flannel tongue. Perhaps launch into answers to questions unasked, answers so elliptical he was left none the wiser afterwards.

He thought of her as his private witch. Over the years her times of madness, if it could be called madness, intensified and Charlie welcomed this. He came to recognise that in her stories lay the kernels of her experiences, transformed and, in his eyes, beautified. If she beckoned him he hoped she would impart some secret, naughty information; that it would be the first time she had voiced it, and for him alone.

He wanted Morgan to experience Granny's wild words, the blank withdrawals. Could not someone like Morgan appreciate another's temperamental highs and lows? His sister told him not to listen to the ramblings or they would make him as daft as she.

She refused to go with him down Hatts Lane, claiming it was always greasy. The houses were wooden, nothing more than shacks with verandas.

Granny Dorp's cottage was brick built and sound, with a thatched roof and a chimney. Exactly the right size for a two-year-old boy. If he stood at the shallow sink in her kitchen he could reach right over the draining board. There was his footstool, covered in something she called *moquette*. On her shelves countless jars of herbs. Upstairs was a room accessed over a sill from her bedroom, where hung a portrait of her second husband. Mr Dorp's Christian name was never mentioned. On the walls of this secret room were cuttings from *The Quiver*, pasted there during her earthbound days. It was apparent to Charlie she had appreciated things that others might spurn.

He had once shown her a striped snail, discovered under the rhubarb beside the privy. His Granny had let it wander over her hand and laughed. She had cried when he threw it into the brook, but he did not tell Morgan that part.

"You always made excuses not to visit her. But we really should. We could drive the long way round."

"No driving." Montague would not have it. The old lady might be in be in bed, but who could tell? "A lot less trouble now," he added. "In her right mind she used to drive my dear Berenice wild with her maxims and herbs."

Enjoined by her mother to care for the less fortunate, as the Bible proclaimed, Morgan the child had reluctantly carried to Granny Dorp her mother's gifts: boiled puddings in cloths, a fresh loaf, an occasional skinned rabbit, mushrooms in the season. It was a long walk past the piggery, along Mill Lane, beneath the towering bulk of the mill, across the floodgates' bridge. Then along her grandmother's slippery route, so overhung in autumn with apple and bullace branches there was danger of being concussed.

Danger too of Granny Dorp asking her granddaughter to fetch the water. "I had to lug a bucket to that standing tap in Hatts Lane. It was a big performance for a seven-year-old," Morgan told Charlie. "You had to open the door in the wooden pillar with a key, turn the tap, fill the bucket, then lock it again. And remember not to drop a drop."

Charlie said he had done the same dozens of times since, when the man from the Three Tuns pub forgot. Granny Dorp had always been grateful. In the pocket of her pinafore were dubious lemon drops from the mill sweet shop. He never refused one, spitting out the fluff afterwards. "No more tap in the lane now. They've piped her since." For some reason this caused the others to laugh. But that evening nobody went to see if the old lady knew about the Declaration of War.

Charlie went two days later and found Granny Dorp unable, or unwilling, to comprehend the message.

By that time minds were more taken up with the announcement that all men between the ages of eighteen and forty-one were liable for conscription. Charlie told Rhoda he was ready to go. She said he wasn't to build his hopes too high. His war work would be at the mill, helping to feed the nation. In any case nothing much was happening. A lorry driver had heard stories of bombs being dropped on an airfield up north. His mate had told him of a factory in the Midlands that had had a direct hit. No reports of men being forced into uniform, which she thought was a shame.

To fight for one's country, in one way or another, was to Rhoda the finest of ambitions. Charlie should pay more attention to the goings-on in Parliament.

Grandma Perincall told Charlie that young men were getting married before they went to the Front, just as had happened in 1914. Aunt Maud said she had read that an expeditionary force was already in Belgium. Was that not far from Verdun? Privately she told Charlie she was glad he would not be put into that kind of danger.

Some boys who had been at school with Charlie were volunteering to join up. The seemingly fit ones had, at their medical examinations, been rejected. So Charlie gave up trying to enlist. His father, occupied at the mill with new regulations and directives, ordered his son to take on more responsibilities.

When Simon Arpent, the first of the local Air Raid Precaution wardens, arrived at the house, it was Charlie who was detailed to comply with his instructions. Gas masks to be checked, windows and blackout curtains inspected for leaks of light. Buckets to be filled with sand in case of incendiaries. Fines were threatened for non-compliance.

Morgan's view was that Simon Arpent, with whom she went to junior school and had later been kissed by, was a busybody who was a warden only because his surname began with A.R.P. He had once tried to steal her school sandwiches, for which she had never forgiven him. When Rhoda invited him to lunch, saying he might as well have Monty's share now he was spending all his life at work, Morgan had words with her.

Charlie found it exciting listening to Simon's tales: twelve miles inland from the coast had been designated a danger area; London was in a state of emergency, although it was reported that people were dying mostly from accidents caused by pitch-dark roads; there were already wardens on street patrols in the West End. Arpent said A.R.P. posts were being set up in London's private houses. So why not at the Villa Rouge? Rhoda and Charlie thought it thrilling. All Morgan could think about was her home in Tufnell Park.

Before leaving, Simon whispered in her ear that the toy factory at Prittend was being moved over to war work, but she was to keep it to herself. She did not like his intimate breath. More hush-hush, he claimed, was the special nature of the new camp at Iverdon. Its transmitting and receiving masts could send signals right across the Channel. Had she seen the swarms of airmen, and strangers in civilian clothes, going in and out at will? There were bunkers, like those being built on the far side of the Lodbrook and along the dyke towards the North Sea. One day, he told her, he might be sitting in one with his binoculars trained on this very house. She dared him to snoop on her, and sent him home to his wife with the ham bone he had noticed, claiming it was for the dog.

There was a visit from the postman, Eden Dufrene, who arrived whistling "Tipperary". It was his way, Rhoda declared, of telling the world his brother Roy had gone off with the British Expeditionary Force. Roy was somewhere getting the French out of trouble, just like the last time. Although the name Dufrene might sound French, Eden was not so keen on his brother being killed to save them. Rhoda said everyone should do their duty. She kept to herself the fact that Cathcart Brodick had gone with the B.E.F., just in case Eden might turn out to be another of Morgan's admirers.

Eden said that bringing the post right to the door might soon be a problem, due to the petrol. The postmistress, Miss Kymmerly, had hinted that it might have to be left at the main gates. There might come a time when he would use a bicycle instead of the van, and that would be the finish, due to his bad back. This was why he could not go and do his bit for his country. He ought to be put in the deferred category.

Morgan's letter was postmarked Gloucester. She was pleased it was from Billie, written in his best handwriting on exercise book paper, the address clearly printed at the top:

Dear Mummy,

We live next to the village green with geese. They are not nice becarse they bite your legs if you dont run. Mrs Timmobold gives us bacon for tea and samwiches. Mr Timbold is a myner. They say to tell you we are allright. Terry wants her pink ribbon and Pammy.

Love Billy

"It seems a happy letter," Morgan said. "And now we know where they are."

"What's 'Pammy'?" Charlie asked.

"Epaminondas, Terry's favourite doll."

"Why didn't she take it with her?"

"Oh, it's a great raggedy thing, all arms and legs. She has had it since she was born. I had to stop her trying to stuff it in with her gas mask."

"Where is this Pammy now?"

"At home, of course."

"Here, do you mean?"

"No, silly. Number twenty-eight." She was turning the letter over. "Fancy Terry remembering that pink ribbon. But I know she is fond of the doll."

He could see she was pondering something. Was she already considering going back home? "You aren't going to go and get it, are you? It's only a doll."

"Simon did say London is dangerous." She was frowning. "Perhaps he meant only the West End."

"There won't be many trains," Charlie said. "All crowded with soldiers. Buses too." He reread Billy's letter. From the envelope a drying fern leaf dropped, the kind that grew between stone walls. "They seem settled enough where they are."

"I suppose so." There was nothing in the letter's few lines about missing their mother, for which Morgan was relieved yet disappointed. "They must be homesick."

Charlie was watching her carefully. "The bombing has got much worse. They say north London will be hit. Then they cordon off the streets. Your water and gas will be cut off." No more reasons for her to abandon him came to his rescue. Morgan, after a moment or two, pocketed Billy's letter and said no more about going anywhere.

It was the second letter, an official one, redirected from Gloucestershire, that was the surprise. It informed her that in the absence of her husband, Sergeant C. Brodick on active service, she would, as temporary head of the household, be required to pay two pounds per week towards the upkeep of her children, namely William and Teresa Brodick, presently in the guardianship of Mr and Mrs Timmbold in the village of Barmford in Gloucestershire. She tucked it behind her mirror for later consideration.

In the evening she rescued her old bicycle from the garage, pumped up the tyres and rode off. Not knowing why she was going added to the pleasure. She took the road towards the Gormsons because, once out of the main gates, the choice was simple: in one direction lay the town of Lodford, in the other a few villages tucked away in miles of open countryside. And what she wanted was the breeze on her face, the return to strength of long-dormant muscles. She needed air, not people.

The next day she might regret the ride. For the time being there was the satisfaction of not knowing her destination. It was like the old days, speeding between hedgerows alive with birds alarmed by her passage. Already she had passed St Margaret's, where her mother and her friend were buried. She cycled on through Little Gormson between the alley of tall elms that had always darkened the brightest of days. Then rapidly into the glare of late sun. The evening was still light enough for cycling to be agreeable. And there was no-one to ask what she thought she was doing alone at that hour.

At the sight of the Shepherd and Crook, the pub where she and Cathcart had spent many an evening like this, she felt a twinge of nostalgia. It looked the same, its thatch still askew. Two men on a bench whistled at her as she passed. She pedalled on, thankful for good speed on a flat road.

Into Great Gormson, nothing more than a few rows of houses and workers' cottages, to be passed at pace. A glimpse of the church tower of St Wynfrith's behind its thickets of yew. Her wheels sent up a shower of confetti. Then another pub called the Hectoring Mason, whose name nobody had ever managed to explain. A person lolling on a wall outside called out to her. She did not respond, unsure whether man or woman, and whether she knew them.

The Iverdon crossroads came quickly. Averting her glance, she sped past the house of Grandma Perincall, hoping nobody was looking out from the windows. For that she would be reprimanded by her father. Her aunts would have been welcoming, would have commented effusively on her modern look. But Grandma Perincall, with her accusatory expression and her acerbic words, was not a woman Morgan willingly faced. A flash of colour from the banked aubretia, growing over the ditch outside, was all she heeded as she flew by.

Where to go next? East to Blytham might be possible, although it was a long way, and her legs were beginning to feel some pain. Blytham was wonderful, secret, special. It was where another river, the Brod, flowed, where there were bigger boats and bigger tides, oyster beds and repair yards which smelled of salt and tar. An ancient village, composed randomly out of necessity, of cottages and shacks all packed close by the water. A few fine Georgian mansions. Not one but two ancient churches were pointers to a prosperous past. And it had the Smugglers and the Wherry, cosy, dark pubs where nobody asked questions about one's age or looked askance at a woman in the bar. Where she had often spent her father's money long before she married Cathcart and spent his. Blytham was reputed to have been a smugglers' haven. Stories of brandy and tobacco hauled on night wagons through the lanes appealed to her adventurous spirit.

She stopped and turned left at the crossroads, leaving Blytham for another day. With a flood of happiness came the realisation that she intended to stay a long while, despite Rhoda's protests. Or Cathcart's, if ever her husband contacted her again.

She belonged in this seemingly bleak landscape that hid its secrets from all but the most perceptive. She loved its skies, the fact that if she wished she could go as far as the sea that one knew was always in finger-tip reach. Yet she deliberately turned left, in order to leave for another day the satisfaction of going where she most wanted to. There would be time enough.

The masts towering over Iverdon had decided her. They were clearly visible above the tallest elms. Closer, she was still a quarter of a mile away, their height and dimensions were not like any masts she had seen before, excluding the tower at Blackpool. But that was only in a newspaper photograph. These four towers seemed tougher, built with curious double crosstrees. Were they wood or metal? Whatever they were, they looked menacingly military, as if the authorities were anticipating something serious.

She reached the corner of a double linked fence. A notice read: PRIVATE WAR MINISTRY PROPERTY PATROLS. Behind it were brick buildings stretching into the depths of the site, where people in air force blue were coming and going.

The last time she was at Iverdon was no later than 1921, when there were dances in the village hall and this site had been nothing more than a field for weekend football.

The changes were greater than any mentioned at St Margaret's that morning. It took minutes to cycle along half the length of one fence. Behind it uniformed men, and women, were hurrying, shouting. Noisy machines breaking the Sunday peace. She wondered what the inhabitants of the council houses opposite thought of this intrusion.

The main gates swung open, forcing her to stop. Another barrier raised, releasing a lorry load of airmen in leather jackets. Their shouts were loud. She wished she had worn her hat. The attentions of men, particularly *en masse*, made her feel more like a specimen than like Morgan Brodick, married woman of thirty-two with two children and a (probably) loving husband. If it was her due to be admired, she wanted it on her own terms.

Behind the lorry came a blue Morris motorcar, open topped, driven by a man in R.A.F. uniform. Beside him a woman. He was wearing an officer's peaked cap. The woman, to Morgan's eyes wonderfully dressed in a smart blue cape with matching hat, stared at her and continued to stare as their car passed. Instead of driving off, it stopped only a few yards away. She heard the door slam and waited, knowing that the driver was going to walk back. Under her breath she muttered, "Botheration!" thanking goodness she had not come bare legged. The approaching man, middle-aged she decided, was wearing a uniform too small for him, and a cap that was indenting his forehead. Morgan guessed by his demeanour he was a person of authority.

At close quarters the thin moustache above full lips did nothing to reduce the heaviness of his face, red in the evening light. His eyes, blue, were not smiling. He saluted. "Madam, d'ye know you're trespassing?"

No, she did not. In a voice like that of the Lodford bank manager, who had an intimidating manner, he asked if she knew there was a war on. Yes, she did. The woman in the blue hat was turning in her seat to see what was going on. Morgan replied that this was a public road and anyone could use it. But with a smile, eyes lowered, that often in the past had proved disarming. What she did not know was that this officer was as insecure in his posting as he was of many things, which led to anomalies in his behaviour. His uniform, she could see, was new, and guessed it had been tailored by request.

When he asked her less menacingly if she was a spy, she imagined the smile had been justified. Did she live nearby? She said she did not. How far had she come? What was the reason for her journey? The questioning continued. What exactly was she doing in Iverdon? There was in his speech an underlying accent that made him less threatening. Morgan always knew accurately enough the class of person she was dealing with. It was inbuilt from childhood. Her mother had not liked impostors. Her replies were concise, although she had no desire for an argument. If he could think of any reason why she should not come out for an evening ride, then he should feel free to disclose it. Perhaps *he* was the spy. The officer laughed.

Hearing the laughter the woman quit the car and started walking towards them. Together they watched her slowly negotiating the path, in heels not made for country walks. Her outfit seemed unsuitable for this isolated location. Her expression was severe.

"What is it Flossie, darling?" She was talking in a low-pitched voice whose accent immediately set her socially above him.

"Got a bit of a problem here, Coral," he said. "This young lady's off bounds. Don't quite know the solution."

"What is her name? Where is she from?" The woman spoke as if unable to address Morgan directly. She looked several years younger than her companion.

Morgan, who hated being spoken of in this manner, replied that, since they had not been introduced, she had no way of knowing whether they too had any right to be there. Now it was the woman's turn to be suspicious, frowning as if this might be a ruse to deflect them.

The two women stood staring at one another for several seconds before the man held out a damp hand. He was Floster, group captain. He flourished the name. "My lady wife, Mrs Coral Floster", had no alternative but to present to Morgan her own hand, limp in a crocheted glove.

Feeling somewhat intimidated by Mrs Floster's clothes, Morgan introduced herself too grandly as the daughter of the owner of the tidal mill on the outskirts of Lodford. She emphasised that the Perincalls, and the Villa Rouge, were well known far into the county. She had, with her mother's encouragement, long since jettisoned her regional accent caught from local children. She put herself on Mrs Floster's level by speaking in the same measured and haughty tones.

They stood for many minutes on the roadside while status was established: assessing one another, touching on such subjects as what might lie in store for a people unprepared, what changes the region must endure, the current state of the Nation. As stiff as their stances, the conversation soon petered to a halt. Meanwhile the light was slowly failing, the western sky deepening into shades of apricot. Finally Mrs Coral Floster, taking the decisive role, told her husband they must return to the motor and get on.

Their destination was an hotel on the sea front at Prittend where, if Flossy did not hurry and crank the engine, they might miss dinner. She told a surprised Morgan, unused to personal confessions, that she suffered from a colicky condition brought about by irregular meals. If the war became serious, which they had been privately advised was likely to be the case, her digestive juices would be under threat.

Ignoring this, Group Captain Floster said it might be dangerous to leave the young lady in oncoming darkness so far away from home. "Who knows who might creep up behind and attack her!" His wife merely shrugged.

So Morgan's bicycle was perched over the back seat of the Morris, Mrs Floster telling her to keep a firm hold on it because her husband had a tendency to speed.

There was no evidence of it on the journey back to the Villa Rouge. They crept along at a snail's pace, the group captain sounding the horn at every curve of the road. Finally at the Villa gates, in near darkness save for the strip of silver sky above the river, they stopped.

Again nobody knew how to proceed. This time Morgan solved it by asking him to unload her bicycle while she opened the gates. At an even slower pace he followed in Morgan's cycling wake towards the house, keeping his attention on her legs, pedalling white in the headlights' glare. His wife complained that because of this diversion she would suffer from stomach cramps the next day, for which he would be to blame.

The Villa presented a picture of gloom. Morgan had forgotten that blackout curtains had reduced it to nothing more than looming silhouettes. Their shadows lay faint across the lawn.

Coral Floster said, "Do you have dogs? I sincerely hope not," as she was helped to alight. She needed all her husband's assistance to negotiate the uneven approach to the front door.

Morgan's intention in bringing these strangers was to divert her father's wrath at her late arrival. She knew he could not give voice to his inevitable ire at her going off and not returning until nightfall, as she had often done when single.

Her family seemed delighted with the visitors, especially Charlie who, on seeing the air force uniform, began to ply the group captain with questions. He was presented by Montague as his "son and heir". And Rhoda, with a flourish, as the Villa's housekeeper, Mrs Swell.

Morgan went upstairs to change, aware that by calling his housekeeper a married woman when she was not, Montague was demonstrating there was nothing to hide. That even someone as lordly as her father would prefer strangers to be assured that there was nothing unseemly going on in his house. Checking the state of her dress in the cheval mirror, Morgan began to wonder if Rhoda really was married and was concealing a secret past.

When she returned, the atmosphere in the sitting room was one of conviviality. Montague had produced a bottle of single malt whisky and was toasting "our brave servicemen", saying only the best was good enough for them. Charlie had, she supposed, been detailed to sit beside Mrs Floster. They were deep in conversation, discussing dreams. But how they had arrived at this point was impossible to tell. In the lamplight both their faces had taken on the pensive look of their subject. She thought Charlie particularly handsome, and, to judge by her proximity to him, so did Coral Floster. Her mouth near his face moved with careful words that were indistinct. What she was telling him was mostly lost. Her husband, too, occasionally sent an admiring glance in their direction.

Although her looks could not be described as pretty, with her thin lips and sapphire eyes Mrs Floster possessed an attractive quality that Morgan understood. She wore her azure outfit with effortless elegance. Her hat with its fascinator was as charming to Morgan as, she noticed, to her father.

The others were seated around the table, whisky bottle at the centre, cigarettes to hand. Conversation was loud. Rhoda, all animation, was joining with the group captain and Montague in trying to unravel the complexities of international alliances: Russia's part in the war, the failure of the League of Nations, why Czechoslovakia had been left in isolation to fend for itself. At one point Rhoda shouted excitedly, "The consequences!" as if she had been waiting for this chance to let off steam. How did she know, Morgan thought, that Britain was bound, *bound* to succeed in a war that was so unjust? "Everyone should be proud to do their bit. Everyone!" Rhoda cried. Morgan thought her ridiculous.

It was three-quarters of an hour before a lull in the conversations. By then the whisky had done enough of its work for Montague boldly to ask Floster what was actually going on at the Iverdon camp. The room went quiet.

The group captain, his face serious and flushed, pursed his lips and looked at his wife. She was shaking her head. "Top secret, old man."

The reply was sufficient for both men to nod wisely, and for Montague to change to his favourite subject. "Do you know anything about wheat?"

It was getting late. Rhoda had noticed that Montague's and the group captain's speech was slowing. However her offer of tea was met with a cry from Coral Floster. They had forgotten their dinner appointment at the Pier Hotel. She leaped up, startling Charlie who, settled nicely beside her, had been anticipating further queer revelations.

No tea. Nothing. Could Flossie kindly use the telephone to delay their booking? Unfortunately the mill possessed the only phone in the neighbourhood, Montague said. It was obvious that no Villa inhabitant was willing to go there in such darkness, merely for the sake of a meal.

So the Flosters must leave immediately, without hearing his discourse on native wheats suitable for wartime growing. He had hoped these seemingly cultured visitors might prove more receptive to his lecture than many previous visitors.

They left in a flurry, the group captain promising as he exited backwards, to come again at Monty's particular request, not only to discuss crops, but to inspect the cricket pitch that he thought he had detected under the trees. For he, like his host, loved the game.

"A bit late in the year for cricket, Pa," Morgan said as the front door closed on the Flosters.

"He could be a good contact, appearances to the contrary." Her father looked satisfied. "I've come across them before, odd characters like that. Doesn't do to dig too deep. But they can often fight with the best of them." He tapped her on the shoulder. "Never know when you'll need help. But he'll be the one to know where to find it."

"What sort of help, Pa?"

"The kind with two arms, two legs and a strong back. Preferably detailed to us by someone in high-ranking uniform! Some of the chaps I'm relying on now will soon be called up, mark my words. This is only the beginning."

Charlie, who had followed them into the hall, stood listening. He was excited. "I know something about the Iverdon camp."

"And what's that, dear Josh?" The whisky had mellowed his father's response.

"He knows as much as I do." Morgan was tired. "Maybe less, since he has never been there." It had been a long day. Her legs were beginning to ache. "Who told you about the camp?"

"She did," Charlie was pointing in the direction of the night. "Though she doesn't know much about aircraft."

"Who is *she*? The cat's mother?"

Montague, sighing, had pulled out his watch, the normal signal for bed. "Don't start bickering now."

"Alright clever one, what did that woman say that was so special?"

Rhoda could be heard washing glasses in the kitchen. Charlie hesitated. "It's a password into the camp, I think."

"You think!" Morgan waited. "So? What is this famous password?"

"Chain. That's exactly how she said it to me. C-H-A-I-N. I know I heard it right."

Morgan snorted. "Of course you did – you were almost sitting in her lap!"

But Charlie, instead of wilting under attack, merely replied, "She's nice," and followed his father out of the hall.

CHAPTER THREE

Autumn was brief. The swallows had gone, crops harvested, winter wheat sown, roots clamped and animals brought into shelter. "A battening down of the hatches", as Montague Perincall called it, in the last quarter of a year that they might, he warned, look upon with some nostalgia. Trees had lost their gold in weeks. There was a clarity to the skies which to local farmers warned of harsh weather. Barn owls were quiet. Migrant birds were arriving from colder places. For Morgan, London began to feel far away, her children even further.

The Villa Rouge was isolated no longer. Lorries were depositing rolls of barbed wire along the beach, their barbs rusting fast in the salt air. Great coils were dumped beyond the floodgates and along the pathway to Hatts Lane. Metal spikes were put into the ground at intervals, ready to repulse Nazi tanks. Since Hatts Lane was only wide enough for a single pony, minus its cart, its residents became sceptical of their council's, not to mention their government's, ability for sensible organisation.

Remonstrations were futile. The Lodbrook, the mill, the Villa and environs were strategic. An officer from the Pioneer Corps informed Monty the plan was to run defences right along the dyke, downstream as far as the estuary. It was confidential that invasion was imminent. Concrete pillboxes were appearing all along the North Sea coast. Charlie told Rhoda it was the government playing war games.

Men came armed with maps and pencils. They wandered the dyke, pointing out to sea or at those mysterious marshes on the far side of the river. Charlie asked them questions they answered with another "Don't you know there's a war on?" He did not like the way they trained their binoculars specifically on the *Berenice*.

There were meetings at the mill amid the deafening noise of

machinery and the sweet smell of flour. Montague was instructed on what to do in the event of fire. He explained that in his line of work there had always been the danger of explosions or spontaneous combustion. They already had pumps etcetera for such emergencies. His concern was a sufficiency of wheats in order to meet his quotas. The officials seemed not to understand the difference between heavy croppers at more bushels per acre and light croppers providing the reverse.

Hs worry over shipments from abroad engendered little attention. The officials were eager to leave as soon as they could. He had wanted to show them his museum of wheat samples. The grains had been set in glass-fronted boxes labelled SQUAREHEAD MASTER, RED STANDARD, RED RIVET, LITTLE JOSH and so on. But very few visitors showed genuine interest.

One evening, on the lawn at home, he found fourteen sheets of curved corrugated iron. With them came a weighty rail, metal bolts and instructions on how to join them together into an Anderson shelter. To be completed within an allotted time, the cost seven pounds, payable at the council offices. Another bureaucratic intrusion. Yet he took it seriously, detailing Charlie and the mill manager's son Ronnie Talbott to dig the shelter's foundation to the required depth of four feet, in the back garden close to the kitchen door.

The two young men struggled for several evenings to join the corrugated halves together. Extraneous earth was shovelled onto the shelter's roof. Due to the omission of a metal shield and a blast wall, they constructed a door instead. Nobody was keen to go into the shelter after the initial inspection. Rhoda thought it damp. Morgan refused to get her shoes muddy. Montague said he would prefer to die outdoors and Charlie agreed, insisting that not one enemy aircraft had been sighted from Prittend to the far north of the county.

Simon Arpent the A.R.P. warden came, he claimed, on official business to see if the Villa's blackout measures were sufficient. It was clear his real interest was in Morgan with whom he tried, unsuccessfully, to renew old memories. All she remembered, with distaste, were his wet lips. Charlie and Rhoda looked on these visits with suspicion and refused to offer Arpent even a cup of tea. He told them there were fighter planes at the Prittend aerodrome. People in the town were being asked to take in airmen as lodgers. Only Rhoda understood the implications of this and began to count empty Villa rooms.

In October the *Royal Oak* was sunk at Scapa Flow. Stories began to emerge of shipping, bringing food supplies, being attacked by U-boats. Rationing was a real possibility, Montague warned.

He was not wrong. All persons, young and old, would be required to have a ration book, each page divided into points, so many points needed for each item of food or petrol. In November Morgan queued at the council offices for the Villa's books. After some argument about her status – was she visitor or permanent resident? – the youth in charge, bewitched by her green eyes, capitulated. After this she pleaded that her grandmother Dorp should not be forced to collect her ration book in person. These successes cheered her for the rest of the week.

November days were getting colder. Fires were lit only in rooms in regular use. Charlie had to break the ice on the chickens' water pots. The Rover refused to start, forcing Montague to trudge on foot to work. The ponds beside the turnstile had begun to freeze. Charlie stoned the icy patterns and went to look at the pigs. One day Esher the pig man, busy packing straw over the sties, told him that something bad had happened in Finland.

A few weeks later it began to snow. Nothing much. Late afternoon some flakes drifting in on a northeast wind. By morning the whole estate was covered in deep white, trees bent under the weight of it, grasses combed by it. Roads narrowed, high snowcaps on hedges, shrubs, barns, pigpens, outhouses, rooftops. Charlie went down at six o'clock to look at the river, feeling intrepid as he kicked his way through the snow-piled paths, thrilled that his and the foxes' were the only tracks around. The rolls of barbed wire along the beach had overnight become fretted sculptures with a look of permanence.

The river was yellowish like the sky, slow running, boats made big by their coverings of snow. Everything in silhouette. He looked downriver, unable to decipher whether they were whirling snowflakes or small birds, like a murmuration of white starlings. It would be good to use the gun, make big bangs and watch the snow explode in great flurries. Before the thaw he would go out and have fun.

He rowed out to the *Berenice*, uncovered her from snow-filled tarpaulin that froze his hands, filled his boots and left him drenched. Through the haze, beyond the boathouse, the furled ochre sails of a wheat barge meant it was going nowhere. Visibility lessening by the minute, he tidied the cabin as best he could, disengaged the fuel supply, covered her, checked all ropes and reluctantly left the *Berenice* at her moorings. The *Clara* was similarly trussed.

Soon the most difficult of tasks was trying to keep warm. Charlie ventured out each morning to clear paths that had piled with snow overnight. He fed the chickens, fetched vegetables from the outhouse, then tramped to work along his father's tracks.

The path from the oak tree at Mill Lane to the senior school had been closed off by wire and War Ministry signs. The concrete plinth, that Morgan had had to negotiate in September, was now a fully fledged gun emplacement. It was sandbagged and manned by soldiers, although nobody had as yet heard the guns. Their billet was the school, now filled with bunk beds. The playground had become a lorry park. Nearby, in the playing field behind the school, was a searchlight.

This information came in part from the Retchen sisters, Thelma and Myrtle, who arrived as usual oblivious of the snow. In previous years it had been their mother who had daily worked at the house. Before that, their grandmother. Whatever the weather, the girls were cheerfully prepared to do any job they were given. Both sisters were fond of Charlie, often arriving early to waylay him before he left.

On the first day of snow they cornered him in the lobby. Sock in hand he had to listen to "There'll Always Be an England". They were sixteen, with little difference in looks but, as Rhoda privately remarked, "only one brain between them". Their mother, having the job of cleaning the police station, sent a warning that the Villa was in line as a billet. "Ask for the air force, not the military." Army boots would ruin the parquet floors her daughters had to spend much time polishing.

The picture houses in Prittend, reopened after brief closure, were now inaccessible to the snowbound. Charlie already felt deprived. Morgan, too, had been looking forward to her weekly films, as she had in London. She, like Rhoda and Montague, spent most evenings listening to Home Service reports of happenings elsewhere.

Charlie had been trying to follow the shipping news. In December the scuttling of the battleship the *Graf Spee* in Montevideo harbour brought some cheer. Montague was not so sure that battles were going to be confined to distant oceans.

Prompted by her father, Morgan wrote to Cathcart, care of an army clearing house. Huddled in one warmed sitting room, there was scant privacy. She could put little real feeling into her letter. She told of the weather, of the Villa that was big and cold, of the barges trapped in the ice. Wracking her brains for anything else to say, she found herself describing a Plymouth Rock due to be killed for the Christmas roast. Embarrassed by her diminished lack of feeling, she would have torn up the letter, had it not meant going through the torment of writing another. Perhaps she, like a long-term prisoner, was going slightly crazy.

To the children in Barmford she wrote simply, *"Keep warm. Wear your liberty bodices."* Billy's replies, happy enough, gave no clear picture of their circumstances. She could divine little from *"we ate a lot of plums and got stumich ache"*, a memorable event for him retained since the autumn, reassuring her that their lives were peaceful. All she could expect from Terry was her usual big *T* at the end of her brother's letters.

On one particular evening of wireless pessimism, Morgan expressed her longing to have the children back. Montague tersely told her to be grateful they were safe in Gloucestershire. "They wouldn't do much good here."

Charlie and Rhoda spent evenings poring over seed catalogues. Merchants and products were compared, lists made and rewritten. There was much discussion about how many potatoes to plant, which bean would give the best yield, whether both onions and shallots were needed. And whether marrows would grow on top of the Anderson shelter. Seeing them talking so intimately irritated Morgan, who suspected Rhoda of provoking her somehow. Charlie went on with the annual ritual of seed selection, oblivious of the undercurrents it was causing.

The dark days ahead, which King George had warned of in his first wartime broadcast, had arrived, for now there were food shortages. Although meat was still in reasonable supply, other items were becoming more scarce. Perishable provisions in the Villa larder were diminishing. The women were forced to spend time going from shop to shop in search of butter or ham. It was hard work in the snow.

Rhoda was disgusted that the price of candles had gone up to one and sixpence. She had been assembling supplies for the Anderson shelter – candles, matches, an oil lamp, a first-aid box, toilet paper and a chamber pot. The latter Charlie promised to get from Granny Dorp's cottage as soon as the weather improved. She still had two.

Meanwhile she was being cared for as usual by the Coreys, who ran the Three Tuns at the end of Hatts Lane. Montague paid them for this, and regular reports about her welfare: "The old lady doesn't notice the weather." "We have to stop her trying to go out. And without her shawl." "She was her old self today and spoke my wife's name." "Did Mrs Dorp throw something in the brook? She wants us to dredge it. Today, mark you!"

Trips to the shops were improved by using Morgan's old sledge from the attic, more sensible than trying to push bicycles through churned-up slush. On the other hand the snow lightened the landscape into mirror-like radiance. At night snow light outshone the glimmer of shop windows. It supplemented reduced headlights of the many vehicles travelling between the aerodrome and the camp at Iverdon. By day the snow lit up all roads narrow and wide with an intense blue.

The sky became a deeper version of the same azure, with its tracery of skeletal trees and silhouetted spires.

The entire winter of 1939 was bad. It brought with it biting cold to underline the fact that war, bombs or no bombs, had truly arrived.

The Perincall hopes that the war would be short-lived were pinned on letters that Morgan finally received from Cathcart. Reading between the bland lines, she deduced that his regiment was somewhere on the other side of the Channel, not fighting but waiting, bored by inactivity. He wrote that he was longing for some action, sent his love and asked if the children and the house were safe.

"It's alright for some!" Morgan was finding life at the Villa Rouge onerous, with no escape from daily chores. It was no use explaining to Rhoda that darning and mending did not excite her. Or that dusting was a low priority when there was so much cooking to do. What was the point of having the Retchen sisters do the housework if more was required thereafter? In Tufnell Park there had always been a local woman to help clean and iron.

So what had she done with her time then? The question had circled in her mind since Charlie, one busy morning, had asked it. If he had been satisfied with her reply – "Cooking. The children, of course, they take up a lot of time" – it was not perceptible. He had thought himself lucky that Morgan had not dismissed him with some biting observation about his own laziness. He was not lazy, neither was she, only cast adrift onto a sea neither could yet negotiate. The luck of having his sister returned to him was tempered by his fear of losing her.

That winter everything once so familiar had acquired a newer, stranger quality. The Villa, the only home Morgan had known when young, apart from Aunt Pandora's in Hackney, had become something akin to an hotel of faint memory. She felt she should by now be losing that sense of being a temporary inhabitant, yet it persisted. But without the children was it not inevitable?

Her old room, with the silvery light that dappled the walls at high tide, was part of the strangeness. Items were missing, but what? The china doll with the ragged hair, still staring into space, had never pleased her. Had there been other favourites lined up along the pillows as well as Epaminondas? Were they now in Teresa's hands?

The bare walls of her bedroom had lighter patches where pictures had hung. There had been a portrait of her mother, painted by an itinerant who had camped by the Lodbrook in the summer of 1920. Her mother had taken pity on his poverty and commissioned it.

On those nights after her mother's death when Morgan couldn't sleep, she had stared at the image through her tears, trying to vitalise the wan cheeks and wonky eyes, to redraw the dun hair as it once was. Afraid to take the portrait down in case she forgot to remember its sitter, she had been equally fearful that it truthfully represented her mother. Now it was gone, consigned to the attic by Rhoda, she felt secret relief. On another wall there had been an etching, a gift from her mother when she was fourteen: a view of the old pump next to Willams the grocer's. A curious choice, but one she had cherished. Where was it now? When she hung her clothes in the wardrobe its familiar cedar perfume, not the bedroom's chill, made her shiver. In the linen cupboard there lingered the aroma of woodruff collected by Granny Dorp on the fringes of Plumberow Wood.

Morgan kept coming across reminders of her childhood with her mother: the embroidered pictures on the landing, the cushions in the sitting rooms, the tablecloths of drawn thread work still in use at meal times. These were small islands of remembrance in a sea of unfamiliarity.

Each day's work should have reminded her that she was not just a visitor, although that was how she felt. She was aware that her welcome was dependent on what use she was to the household. Her father's unwritten rule was that to earn one's right to stay, one must be useful. That was the way he had always run things. Charlie had known no other regime. If he went along the dyke, for instance, he must return with agrimony or a few elderberries. It was no use admiring the view from the shore if the driftwood at one's feet went ungathered.

Before her mother's death Morgan could remember a different father, much less obsessed with work and tide, who strode along the Lodbrook's edge, his young daughter straddling his shoulders, pointing out the May trees clouding the far banks. Or the rooks building high. There were summer evenings on the old boat, eating curling sandwiches and drinking ginger beer.

One Sunday afternoon while her father taught her how to skip, her mother, claiming shortness of breath, had had to sit down. The Villa lawn, immaculate then, was not the easiest of places on which to turn a rope. Despite his bulk her father had performed his jumps and bumps with a grace Morgan remembered with a smile. It was he who had taught her how to swim too. In the shallows he had shown her how to float, breathe, move frog-like. He had towed her on a rope behind his dinghy in mid stream until she had lost all fear of drowning.

Mother confined to the house. Pa not so talkative, not so ready to join in a game, more concerned to direct. Get everyone else "down to work". Pa spending more and more time away from the mill, worrying over the wife upstairs. It was better then to escape, leaving the invalid with just the baby Charlie in his cot by her bed.

Charlie was four and mother dead by the time Montague found the heart to teach him to swim. Morgan had looked on, amazed at the speed with which he had learned. "Watch me! Watch!" were his cries over challenges conquered just to impress her. He had never required more of Morgan than a few words of praise, which she knew often came too late, or not at all. Had anything changed?

Rhoda was still there causing disquiet. There was, and had always been, something intolerable about Rhoda. Was it her habit of darting about as if the Villa were on fire? Was it her skin, scaly from the cold, her hair awry? Her strange scent? Or the way she denied that she bit her nails when the evidence was incontrovertible? Lists of Rhoda's inadequacies would be endless if one did not acknowledge that, without her, the family might never have held together at all.

If only, Morgan thought, when Rhoda had first arrived she had had the sense, no, the decency, to wait a while before imposing herself upon the household. It was as if, in confronting Morgan on that first afternoon, she was saying, "Here I am, seven years older than you, chosen by your father to take your mother's place. So that is what I will do, whether you approve of it, of me, or not."

Too late to know the truth. All Morgan could be certain of was that she did not want a proxy mother giving her instructions in housewifery.

Knowing her skills, her father had designated Morgan as chief cook, much to Rhoda's disgust and Charlie's delight. She must, with Rhoda as assistant, produce their weekly dishes in regular rotation, given current restrictions: Saturday roast meat, Sunday cold roast, Monday leftovers with pickles, Tuesday cottage pie, Wednesday offal of sorts, depending on Dance the butcher, Thursday steak and kidney pudding, Friday fish. It was no use Morgan exclaiming that it was beyond her. To Rhoda's delight she was expected to serve these dishes with two vegetables and some pudding, often of the suety kind.

Morgan loved to eat, but after a month's inexorable round of cooking, allied to the anxieties of a diminishing larder, her appetite lessened and she grew thinner. When Charlie asked if she had not always cooked like that in Tufnell Park, she told him occasional pot luck made diners more appreciative.

Both women had sworn to Montague they would make the enforced partnership work. He told Morgan not to rile Rhoda, who had seemed on edge lately. Rhoda was counselled to treat his daughter carefully. He left them alone to sort it out.

The kitchen thereafter was not a happy place. There were a hundred ways of causing aggravation by word, gesture, look: Rhoda scrutinising the way Morgan was cutting the vegetables she had personally grown; Morgan throwing down the knife, saying, "You do it, then!" If Rhoda's gravy was lumpy, Morgan would be too ready to offer the whisk; Rhoda standing at Morgan's elbow to point at a speck in the mashed potatoes. After a bad argument, one or the other would absent herself and vent her fury by punching a mattress or kicking the lavatory pan. The greatest sufferers were the china and cutlery, the noise level reaching as far as the topmost bedroom. Montague came down one Sunday afternoon, his nap cut short by a din he compared to the *Boches* attacking the Allies' trenches. Morgan's murderous thoughts were unloaded later on Charlie. Rhoda told him that his sister was worse now than she ever remembered.

Charlie kept out of the kitchen as much as possible. He trod carefully, having made one bad mistake. Saturday's Yorkshire pudding and roast beef was a favourite meal. There was no doubt that Rhoda's puddings were superior to Morgan's, and Charlie had foolishly stated this. After that Montague detailed Rhoda to make the puddings. Morgan served them in silence as icy as the snow outside.

At work Monty strained to fill in myriad forms about his business. How many personnel? How much grain milled? What quantities of flour produced and of what qualities? The idiot who had devised these forms, he commented, would be better employed winning the war than tying him down in red tape. Time had to be spent claiming deferment for his male employees, whom he privately considered unpatriotic. Many of his men had already told him they would never be hoodwinked by cunning generals into fighting, as their fathers had.

Montague left much of the day-to-day running of the operation to Bernard Talbott who, working best under guidance, gave no indication he would rather be in uniform. Mrs Grace Talbott was instructed to take over the tiny sweet shop, built in the shadow of the mill, that had served generations of visitors' children. Dora, their daughter, the previous shop assistant, had left to join the Women's Royal Naval Service. The day before she departed, she told Charlie she had good reasons, but did not elaborate.

Before the war it was Charlie's pleasure to sneak to the sweet shop in search of liquorice toffee. Without telling Morgan or Rhoda he had recently bought himself a supply of blackjacks and cached them in the his bureau. Everyone knew the shop would be closing. The only hope was that it would not happen until after Christmas and the thaw.

Eden Dufrene, still trudging through snow with the post, said that the Prittend pier had been closed for the duration. Along the whole sea-front shops and houses had been turned into barracks. Pillboxes were sprouting like mushrooms all along the esplanade, sailors, police and soldiers everywhere.

But the most amazing sight for Eden was, for the first time in his life, the sea frozen solid. Charlie, arriving with armfuls of holly, verified the fact that there were triangles of ice forming all along the edges of the Lodbrook. Only a narrow channel in the centre of the river was still free flowing. All moored vessels, including the *Berenice* and the *Clara*, were trapped by green slabs. "It's incredible! Big spikes pointing sideways!" Everyone went to look and was amazed.

Advent came and went. Nobody struggled to church, even though the Gormson Road, freed of snow by traffic, had become the only working artery. Attempts were made to keep the Perincall driveway sufficiently clear to allow wheels to negotiate its hazards.

One afternoon, when the sun's orange rays appeared by magic, a motorbike and sidecar emerged from between the trees. It came to an enforced stop on the drive at a solid pile of snow forked there by Charlie and Ronnie Talbott. Driving the motorbike was a young R.A.F. man in helmet and goggles, wearing a leather jacket. Clinging on behind him was Mrs Floster, enveloped in a greatcoat. Fitting snugly into the sidecar was her husband, Group Captain Floster. He too had on a leather helmet and goggles. The snow forced them to dismount and plod the rest of the way through the sludge.

On the Villa doorstep, Rhoda did not recognise them. The group captain took off his helmet to reveal his identity. They were on their way to Lodford aerodrome he told her, but weather conditions were affording them time for a "flying visit", a joke she failed to get. The other airman, introducing himself (in a posh voice, Rhoda thought) as flying officer Peter Parclay, endeared himself to her with his politeness.

The group captain and his wife had come with presents for the ladies of the house, in appreciation of previous hospitality. Charlie looked with covetous eyes more at the pilot's leather jacket than at the cigarettes and chocolates. The airmen's eyes were on the whisky and sherry on the *chiffonier*.

It was three thirty in the afternoon, the snow's reflection still lighting the faces in the room. Flying officer Parclay looked young enough, Charlie thought, to be his schoolmate. The same thought was going through Rhoda's mind as she seated them round the dining table, explaining that the other rooms were too cold for comfort. Knowing much about the art, Morgan suspected Rhoda of flirting with him. She wondered why this flying officer was responding so gallantly.

As she went in search of glasses, she wondered yet again how Rhoda's intimacy with Montague was progressing, and whether he was aware of this change in her behaviour.

Charlie followed Morgan and found her squatting in front of the drinks cabinet. "How old do you think he is, that Barclay chap?"

"Probably the same as you. A babe in arms by the look of him."

Charlie bent and hissed in her ear. "He pinched your bottom."

"No, he did not."

"I saw it! I saw his hand come out and . . . You are lying."

She put the glasses on a tray, shoving him aside with her elbow. "If that is who is going to win the war for us, we had better start praying for grown-ups. Let us get out of this morgue. It's freezing in here."

"You let him! You let him!"

She was already at the door. "Turn off the light, Charles, and do not be stupid." He was close behind her. "Anyway, it was the other chap." Not for the world would she tell him she was already feeling kinship with the young flying officer.

For the rest of the visit Charlie watched the airmen closely, noting she was right. It was not Parclay who attended more to Morgan than to Rhoda, but Group Captain Floster. How he positioned himself next to her at the table. How once he had flapped his handkerchief too long at some speck on her sleeve. He also saw Mrs Floster's displeasure.

He seated himself beside flying officer Parclay. Here was someone who could explain the mysteries of flying. The pilot was happy to describe the advantages of the Spitfire over the Heinkel. The Stuka too for that matter, its range, manoeuvrability, firepower. He would have given more details, had not the group captain hushed him with an admonitory finger and forced a change of subject.

Group Captain Floster's relationship with his men, or at least with this one pilot, Charlie found inspiring. He too longed to be under a leader so evidently devoted to them. So thrilled was he with this conversation, he did his best not to show it by behaving as seriously as possible. Mrs Floster, trying to renew their talk about her dreams, found him unresponsive.

Montague came home early, not displeased with familiar visitors brave enough to tackle the weather. He was unusually affable, sympathising with Coral Floster about the lack of social life in Iverdon, listening to what the airmen had to say. The group captain's subject was antiques, of which he said he had a few, including his wife. To Charlie's delight, Rhoda proved capable of a witty exchange. "Which wife?" she asked. Morgan suspected her humour was disguising a dislike of Floster.

The laughter grew louder, the group captain's jokes more *risqué*. The penultimate single malt whisky was liberally shared. His face grew bloated, reminding Charlie of the Gloucester Spot in its sty. He had ceased to calculate at which airman Morgan smiled the most. By half past six, after darkness had long descended, when all the sherry, plus most of the whisky, had been drunk, the party broke up and the visitors departed.

"Not before time." Montague had missed teatime by an hour and a half. On the whole he thought the delay had been worth it, because of the good that might come from the visit. "Connections are all important, especially these days," he told Rhoda and Charlie. "That pilot Parclay seems a first-class chap, probably close to government. Cultivate people like that and you've got a potential network."

To Morgan he said, "Be nice to the Flosters. Get the wife here again. Pretty little thing. In need of distraction by the look of it. Give her a tour of the property. That should impress her. Show her the cricket pitch when it thaws. I have had the whole county here for matches, including second teams, tell her. The husband is interested. Tea in the pavilion." He was beginning to ramble. "Upper middle class, I would say she is. Was that your opinion, child?"

So unused was Morgan to being asked her opinion by her father, or for that matter any man, she was momentarily tongue-tied. It did occur to her that the R.A.F. camp might be a source of stockings or chocolates, should the future prove dismal. She said she thought the young pilot genuinely nice. Whom she would like to get to know, she kept to herself.

No more visitors came to the Villa other than tradesmen. Mr Boxley wanted permission to deliver three times the usual bottles per day, so that difficult journeys would be cut. The milk would last an age out in the cold. He asked after Morgan's children and said what a coincidence that his boys, like Billy and Teresa, had been evacuated to Barmford in Gloucestershire. His littl'uns were living in what he guessed was a dodgy billet. Did she think it would be safe to bring his children home? This was the second man who had asked her opinion. Was it a sign of the times?

As Christmas approached and the cold continued, all they could do was block up the cracks through which the wind whistled, pile on more clothing, go out only when necessary, keep the minimum of rooms warm and go to bed early.

"We're turning into Eskimos," Morgan told Charlie.

"But they live on meat, not offal." Charlie had started to complain about the diminishing quantity on his plate. Hard work at the mill was making him hungrier. Rhoda told him to tighten his belt, or go out and shoot a pheasant or two. Daily her temper worsened. Relations with Morgan were snapping.

It was a domestic war, set to intensify like the one in Europe. The warning signals, coming from a distance, disturbed only those closest to the action. In this case Charlie, who elected each breakfast time to leave the battleground as swiftly as he could.

Things came to a head one morning, when the wireless announced that conscientious objectors would be exempt from military service, if they could prove sincerity of purpose. This so incensed Rhoda that she began a tirade against cowards.

"They're not cowards." Before she argued this, Morgan had never given a thought to the subject. Now she was preparing to do battle on their behalf. "Conscientious objectors are probably just as patriotic as you, Rhoda Swell." She was juggling plates. Charlie looked anxiously from one to the other, then at the spatula in Rhoda's hand.

"What do you know about anything?" The words were out. "All you think about is yourself, Morgan Brodick." Rhoda slapped Charlie's egg over. "Selfish cowards should be locked up." The bacon was starting to smoke.

"What did you say, Rhoda Swell?" Morgan's face had turned red.

Knowing the most effective reply, there was only a moment's hesitation before Rhoda went into proper battle. "I said, 'All you think about is yourself', ever since I've known you when you were going on sixteen." The smoke was beginning to swirl. "Hair. Nails. Boyfriends. Creeping off at all hours to drink in pubs. I heard. Under age. Look where your children are now. Abandoned."

Morgan turned, tears welling. "Do you hear this, Charles? Should she be allowed to speak to me like that?"

At a loss, he could do nothing but escape.

Sitting in the office he knew he had done the right thing, even at the cost of his breakfast. All morning he chewed a few handfuls of wheat grains until they turned to gum, wondering what would greet him at midday. Whether there would be any lunch at all.

Montague said the women would get over it. Rhoda often had a go at him too, he remarked, as if it amused him. "Come Christmas, everything will be as right as rain." Charlie thought he had seen Pa more in a state over his lack of tobacco than at what was going on under his nose.

The coalman came with a message from Grandma Perincall that

everyone at Great Gormson was well and managing. What school there was had been suspended. He handed over four parcels blackened by fingerprints, to be opened on Christmas morning.

That evening they had a fine fire that Morgan and Charlie stoked to blazes, while Rhoda and Montague were out of sight.

"Stop it, Charlie." It was Christmas Day. Morgan was still in bed despite calls from the kitchen. He was pinching her ear. She opened her eyes.

His grinning face was close. "Happy Christmas." Something heavy dropped onto her chest. She did not look. "Go away. It's too early."

"Rhoda says she's going soon."

"Where?"

"She's going soon, and you've got to get up and look at your present." The parcel slipped from the quilt. "My present." He was rescuing it. "I got you a present. Morgan!" Shouting now.

Finally she sat up, tetchy. "So you gave me a present. That is a novelty."

"You never gave *me* any presents."

"Yes I did." Charlie's thank-you notes were always so fulsome it was as if she had given him the moon every time. She was recalling two or three years when she had forgotten his birthday completely, or left it too late. "What did you say about Rhoda?"

"Open it."

She knew already it was a book: *The Daily Herbal.* "Where did you get this?"

"Don't you like it?"

She could see by his expression that he knew she knew.

"This book is Granny Dorp's. She used to make recipes for us. Cough mixture – paregoric and laudanum and . . . something or other."

Charlie had turned his face from her.

"You didn't steal it, did you?"

"How can you steal from someone who doesn't know what she's got?" Head still down, he muttered, "I thought you would like it."

She got out of bed and reached for her dressing gown. "Well, it's not really a present, is it? More of a passed-on theft. You will have to take it back."

"Didn't you ever steal anything?"

"What has that to do with it, Charles?" She was cold. "Go away, I want to get dressed."

At the door he lingered. Her face, he thought, looked older in the harsh light. "You stole Cathcart from Emily Whatshername."

It was a jolt. "Who told you that?" Then she knew. "It was Rhoda, wasn't it?" She was grabbing her hairbrush, ready for flinging. He left her bedroom in a hurry.

On his breakfast plate was a five-pound note, a present from Montague. The same for Morgan. What Rhoda received she was not disclosing.

Montague left for work as if it were not Christmas morning. Charlie went to feed the hens, their numbers reduced by one, which he had killed and plucked the previous day. Rhoda removed herself from the kitchen speedily, leaving Morgan to clear and wash up.

An apparent domestic truce had arrived in time for the preparation of Christmas lunch. Unusually Morgan left Rhoda to choose which vegetables, what kinds of sauce to accompany the bird, which dinner service. Rhoda did not seem to care about this honour. There was a slow sullenness in her actions at odds with her customary speed. Nevertheless the meal was prepared on time, ready to be served immediately following the national anthem and the King's speech. Everyone sat down to listen.

The speech over, that only Morgan felt moved to criticise for its hesitations, the meal began. Although the Plymouth Rock was tender, the vegetables well cooked, the bread and Bisto sauces tasty, the Christmas pudding "better than good", there seemed to hang about them all an air of failed yet unspecified expectations.

Afterwards, in the dying afternoon light, they sat looking at one another as if wondering what to do. Morgan remembered card games played on the cleared table without a thought for dirty dishes. Yet Rhoda went to the kitchen promptly to wash up. Charlie, wearing his overcoat, escaped upstairs to his room. Montague in his armchair slowly went to sleep, watched by his daughter with dismay and a great feeling of loneliness.

Boxing Day was no better, except for the roast pheasant. Morgan, followed by Charlie then Rhoda, ventured into the snow to throw a few snowballs. But its quantity and depth defeated them. They came back chilled and barely speaking.

Later, joined by Montague who had suggested a bracing constitutional, they went along the drive towards the road, impeded by the mounds of snow that had blocked their visitors' motorbike. There was nowhere to go for a real walk.

Through the wrought-iron gates fixed open by ice, Charlie slid into the centre of the Gormson Road and stood there. No lights in the Redwood pub opposite. The road empty in both directions, its startling whiteness cut into by four diminishing parallel lines of black. Hedges twice as high with snow, fading into a misty distance as the road turned out of sight towards Lodford. Nothing but receding elms, rooks corresponding, the spire of Little Gormson church, to which surely only the foolhardy had gone for Christmas services.

Montague stood on the drive, banging his hands against his sides, his breath steaming. He called to Charlie, "See them? See?" pointing north across the bleached expanses of the opposite fields, beyond the trees bent almost to the ground with the weight of snowfall.

Charlie thought at first he meant the rooks' nests in the elms, black and insecure. Then he saw the Iverdon masts, so tall their tops were clearly visible through the white distance. "What do you think they're doing there?"

He swung his gaze round towards the rising smoke from Great Gormson chimneys, thinking he could smell it. The aunts were doubtless sitting as close to a good fire as Grandma Perincall would allow, the oil lamps already lit. Every now and then a small eruption of snow dropped from some bough. He thought of bombs. Morgan and Rhoda were stamping their feet, complaining.

There was no option but to return to the Villa, feed the hens, stoke the boiler, secure the blackout curtains. Nobody wanted to go outside again to check light leakage from the windows.

High tea, bread and butter, jam, trifle and cold Christmas pudding, was eaten early and in the kitchen. Classical music on the wireless cold comfort, since it had been preceded by threats that the New Year would bring further food rationing.

Afterwards Rhoda took Charlie to one side, instructing him on how to prune the roses in March, and how to manage the vegetable garden. This was unusual, but he could smell alcohol on her breath and wondered if she and Montague had shared a private tot or two.

Rhoda began to talk about her position as housekeeper, the attitude of Grandma Perincall and the aunts. "You'd think after all I've done, after all this time, they'd see things different."

"You can't expect it," There had been rare occasions in the past when Rhoda had treated Charlie to intimate revelations, as if they were the same age. A few scraps about her home, her troublesome brother. He did not mind as long as she refrained from talking about him as a toddler or, God forbid, when he was in nappies. This time she seemed to want his opinion.

"Why not?"

How could he tell Rhoda that differences of class could never be overcome? Instead he said, "They're set in their ways," realising with a rush that if Rhoda deserted them, his life at the Villa would be very much more difficult. Then he began to hate her a little for whatever she might be going to put them through.

It was entirely understandable that Rhoda wanted security, people not to talk about her behind her back. There had been occasions when Grandma Perincall had spoken in her particular oblique way, about the need to keep up appearances. Although she had never actually told Monty he should not be living like that with Rhoda, the hints were there.

Charlie could picture what it must have been like the first time his grandma and aunts saw Rhoda – sizing her up, her clothes, fingernails, grammar, the accent. They must have asked her where she came from. Rhoda probably tried to endear herself by helping serve high tea and doing the washing up, at speed of course. It did not occur to him that his aunts might have already been wary of Rhoda's ambitions. To divert her, Charlie mentioned the surprise everyone would have when they produced their first crop of early peas. Her clever invention of mulching with seaweed should be kept a secret until the last minute.

"You'll do it for me, Charlie," she said. 'I'll be gone by then."

Montague found Charlie and Morgan sitting together on the sofa. It was several days later. Between them lay the open pages of the *Telegraph*, which they were studying deeply.

"So, what are you two doing in here? What's the secret?"

"What secret, Pa?" Morgan's reply was too quick. Charlie's head went down.

"When I see you two like this, I know something's brewing." His shadow was covering them. "Come on now, I haven't got all day."

Reluctantly Charlie stood up. "I did tell you Pa, before New Year." He was looking to Morgan for support and she was nodding.

"Tell me what?" Montague was becoming irritated. "What is this big secret that neither of you can say?" He was taking out his watch. "I have work to do and I'm not playing games. Understand?" There was a pause. A sudden fall of snow from the roof sounded loud in the room.

"It's Rhoda!" Morgan said it in a rush, her face pale.

"Rhoda? What about Rhoda?"

"I did tell you she was going," Charlie had again shrunk into the sofa, "when we were hanging the pheasants."

"Pheasants? What pheasants? Did you say 'going'?"

Morgan rose and edged close to her father. "Gone, actually." She was touching his sleeve. "Rhoda has gone, Pa. She's gone."

"Is this one of your puerile jokes?" He was looking around as if

Rhoda might be hiding somewhere. "I hoped you'd grown out of them."

"Come and see for yourself." Charlie left the sitting room, Morgan close behind. It was so sudden that Montague was left still staring at the door.

The sun, pouring through Rhoda's window, was lighting up the counterpane, sending a shaft across the cupboard where she kept her clothes. They were still there on hangers, hooks neatly facing inward: one cotton house frock, one day frock of beige wool, her blue cardigan for gardening, one afternoon frock of flowered crêpe, one navy summer coat with pointed pieces on the sleeves. Two pairs of shoes with trees, lined up below. Morgan pulled down a suitcase from the shelf. Charlie tried to stop her, but she opened it, crumpling tissue paper.

Out came a cloche hat. Then a long frock that shimmered as she shook it. "She's got an evening frock here!" Another one edged with blue feathers was in her hands. Morgan held it against herself. "When did Rhoda ever wear anything like this?" Charlie's surprise was at Rhoda's desertion.

Montague came into the bedroom. "What are you doing in here? Get out, children." His voice was stern. "This is private property."

Morgan dropped the frocks into the suitcase. "We were only looking for Rhoda," her voice taking on her little girl whine. "We told you we think she has gone. We are worried about her."

"So you think she might be hiding in that portmanteau!"

Morgan at the dressing table began pulling out the drawers, revealing nothing but hairpins, a mothball, a single stocking. "She has left this," she said holding out a hand mirror.

Montague peered over her shoulder. "She never had much." He fingered a ruched lampshade.

"And now nothing but those peculiar frocks."

"I can see that for myself. Where are you going, Charles?" Charlie was sidling out of the room.

He reluctantly came back and stayed leaning against the open door. He could not make out his father's mood. "Rhoda used to have another suitcase." Montague was looking around as if in a foreign place.

They began to search, aware that possibilities were few. Under the bed nothing but a chamber pot. In the bedside drawer only a pencil, a pad of notepaper and a packet of Swan envelopes.

"What about the attic? Her case could be up there." Charlie had always liked the attic, where trunks and boxes lay undisturbed, and the smell of the rafters stirred the imagination. "So could she," he added. This remark was met with contempt from both Montague and Morgan.

He finally had to admit what he knew. "Rhoda went out yesterday, about eleven in the morning. That's the time she usually goes to market."

"Did you see her go?"

"No, but Ronnie Talbott saw her getting on the Lodford bus."

"With a suitcase?"

"He didn't say. I didn't ask."

Montague sat down on the bed. As he did so the counterpane slid sideways, revealing a bare mattress. "When is wash day?"

"Not Fridays." The truth, although lately Rhoda's routine had slipped. After visits from officers looking to billet soldiers, she had become less interested in routine, causing Morgan more exasperation. So far not one soldier had been assigned to the Villa.

They went downstairs. Morgan's father ignored the tea she made. At the kitchen table, his head supported by his hands, he was apparently studying a stain on the tablecloth. Charlie and Morgan sat for several minutes looking at this new phenomenon.

Putting out a tentative hand, Morgan said quietly, "Rhoda probably wanted a holiday." Adding, "Last week she did say she didn't like the dances being moved to the Women's Institute."

Montague raised his head. "Dances! What on earth are you saying, child?"

"She . . . We all went to the Senior School for the dances before I got married. It's full of soldiers now. There's a searchlight."

"The ack ack gun battery's there too," Charlie added.

"What are you both talking about?" Now he was getting angry.

"She had a permanent last Tuesday."

"What?"

"Hair. A permanent wave. At Maison Dringley, on West Street."

"I know where Dringley's is. What I don't know is what this has to do with Rhoda Swell deserting the ship."

Morgan gave up. It was no use explaining that when a woman is going somewhere, perhaps for a certain length of time, she has to make sure her hair is in good order. Rhoda's stringy hair would need attention. No man would understand this, least of all her father. She patted her own smooth bob and kept quiet.

"How could she do this to me?"

"And me too, Pa." Charlie spoke meekly.

It wasn't until Montague went upstairs to his bedroom that he found Rhoda's note. She had hidden it under his top sheet, so that when he turned it back the note was revealed. It was typical of her, he thought, to make him wait until night. Suddenly he was remembering times when she had kept him waiting deliberately, because he would not do something or other she badly wanted. Would not respond to her eternal hints about marriage.

It was a note, not a proper letter in a sealed envelope. This was disrespectful. She had written it on shopping list paper, as if it was an afterthought. Revolving thoughts began. Had this really not been a last-minute decision? What in the last few days had changed her? Had she been planning this for long? Was it Morgan's arrival that had sparked it? How could she do this to him after so long? How dare she!

Montague studied the note – the recognisable and childish handwriting that had always dismayed him, the big print in capital letters. Was she trying to annoy him even in her absence?

It was short. All she had written was *"DEAR MONTY AM GONE TO JOIN THE WRENS LOVE RHODY."*

CHAPTER FOUR

Grandma Perincall, when told of Rhoda's defection to the W.R.N.S., asked, "What do you expect, Monty? She did not want to stay a skivvy all her life. What woman does?"

Montague glanced at his sister Winnie, moving about the room, duster in hand as always.

"You will have to manage, my son. Tell Morgan and Charlie to buck up their ideas." She looked for his reaction. "How is it with those two? Behaving herself, is she?" She thought she knew the answer. "See how she copes on her own. Should be interesting. Get the boy away from her and married off, Monty."

He didn't like her speaking in front of his sisters. "He is barely eighteen, Mother."

"So how old were you when you wed?"

"There was a war coming."

"So what is this upon us now?"

His mother was a determined woman. Widowed in 1906, she had moved herself and her three daughters to a double cottage on the crossroads at Great Gormson. So she was able to see in three directions, westward towards Iverdon, eastward towards Blytham, and north to Little Gormson. To see all roads pleased her greatly, more so now the war would mean an increase in traffic.

In 1907 she had informed Montague there would have to be changes. To Harriet, Maud and Winifred she declared it would be better for all concerned if Monty were left rattling about on his own in the Villa, since it would decide him to marry quicker. Never a woman to heed others' feelings, she once told Montague that, since a man covered in flour was not to every woman's taste whatever his acres, he had better make haste.

Better to raise one's children early. She had been trying to impress upon her unmarried daughters too, the necessity of finding husbands in the face of much competition.

So she and the girls had moved. She claimed she had never liked the house's proximity to the river. That the miasma coming off it had contributed to Nicholas' death. What she never said was that the Villa Rouge held too many memories of her other two sons, killed in Picardy.

What everyone knew was that any references to the mill, other than its income discussed in private, offended her sensibilities. Her husband had been forbidden any mention at home of wheat, sieves, hoists, grinding stones, turbines, tonnage et cetera.

Out of old habit Montague continued his working life in this way, keeping commercial matters away from his mother, then his wife, only opening up to Charlie after he began working there. For he still had an unstoppable need to talk, with anyone willing to listen, about his attachment to grain.

So Montague had rattled about alone in the Villa. Mrs Retchen's mother and a series of helpers saw to his needs, until he married Berenice Skeffingley, a local beauty, of whom his mother said that what she lacked in robustness she made up for in breeding. It was agreed that she had been the right choice, since she had so quickly provided Captain Perincall with a daughter.

"Now Rhoda's gone I shall need Little Josh more than ever, won't I, Mother?" Montague's remark had taken some thought. "Until she is back, that is."

"Perhaps Rhoda will marry a Jack Tar in bell bottoms!" Her sisters smiled at Harriet behind their hands. Their brother told her not to be snobbish.

Maud said, "What is the world coming to? Soon women will be wearing trousers."

"They are already wearing them in munitions factories. And look at Katherine Hepburn." He knew this reference would be beyond them.

How Harriet and Maud could manage to instil in their pupils a comprehension of the universe was something he could not imagine. If this war, so slow in building, impinged upon their existence, he hoped it would make them see beyond their noses. Not that he wished them harm. But his love was for Winnie, into whose meekness he tried, unsuccessfully, to foster some of his grit.

She took him through the snow to the greenhouse, to show him the spinach beet seedlings and ask his advice about Jeyes Fluid for the brassicas. Would she be considered unpatriotic if she continued to grow cinerarias that needed heat? He replied that plants, like everybody, would have to become hardier. As usual Winnie delayed him, asking what to do if bombs fell, or the weather stranded them and they ran out of food, safe in the knowledge that her brother would not try to belittle her.

He left as soon as he could, after checking the blackout curtains, filling the oil lamps and securing the door bolts in case of a Nazi invasion.

A new year. 1940. January. Conscription for men between the ages of twenty and twenty-seven. Only Charlie was cheered. More restrictions, sugar rationed, then bacon and ham. For Morgan this was some relief, having wasted hours haggling over purchases with unsympathetic assistants. She could not understand why he wanted her to stop shopping in her London clothes. Or tone down her lipstick.

The cold, dark evenings meant listening to the news then retiring to bed. Montague could not resist Lord Haw Haw's nightly propaganda broadcasts. Some had a sympathetic tone he found worryingly persuasive. There were B.B.C. bulletins about carrying gas masks, remaining watchful and optimistic. The newspapers provided little cheer: brief reports about Russian forces infiltrating Finland; about brave fighting in Europe that Lord Haw Haw scoffed at.

It was not difficult to read between the lines of a Fleet Street hack claiming that, despite the savage U-boat campaign, the German Navy was doomed. It was clear to Montague that the Royal Navy was bearing the brunt of submarine attacks. The numbers of ships sunk in the Atlantic fuelled his suspicion that this war might not so easily be won without the Commonwealth's contribution. In December, had the Canadians come with a shipment of wheat? Would British grain suffice? Could Mr Churchill, once again First Lord of the Admiralty, be believed that, if Britain survived this winter, the first campaign would be successfully achieved?

Nothing much about the British Expeditionary Force in Belgium, where Cathcart almost certainly was holed up. All Montague could guess was that unabating freezing temperatures across Europe were preventing much enemy action. Cedric Brodir, the farmer from Iverdon, rang to ask if Monty was having problems retaining his workers. Women were promised as replacements for conscripted men. "And anyone with an ounce of sense can see where that will lead!" He sounded sanguine.

Without Rhoda, Morgan was kept busy. It was no use complaining that fire lighting, meals, shopping, washing, ironing, mending, knitting, sewing and snow clearance were more than three women could cope with. Her father did not listen.

Thelma and Myrtle Retchen worked longer in the house, with an enthusiasm she found touching. Their infectious good humour helped a little to alleviate the daily round. If some of these jobs were not done to Rhoda's standards, the house did not fall down and no-one went hungry, so far.

The girls took delight in counting the remaining tins of Nestlé's Milk, baked beans, Ovaltine. They reported the finished Bovril and Camp Coffee as if they were casualties of war. These items were still in the Lodford shops, if one queued indefinitely. Morgan believed her father, that they would become as rare as diamonds.

She could not discourage the Retchen sisters from whitening the doorsteps, Brassoing the doorknocker and blackleading the grates in unused rooms. Pleading with their mother to restrain them, Morgan came to understand that, without these familiar routines, Myrtle and Thelma could not function.

Their preoccupation with Charlie amused her. She would stop and listen to their conversations. "Charlie's socks have holes in them . . . Mum says her mum said that Charlie walked before he could crawl . . . Charlie doesn't like tapioca on a Wednesday, just like me . . . Friday is Charlie's day for a haircut. It is wavy."

Charlie blamed Mrs Retchen for her daughters' lack of education, ignorant of her efforts. She had married one of the Villa gardeners who had not, as she discovered, the best of characters. For his children he had no time. Widowhood came early, when the girls were small, and with it lack of money. When her mother had become too old for Villa work, Mrs Retchen had taken over. Her duties gradually narrowed to that of nurse to Mrs Berenice Perincall until she died.

She had answered Montague's pleas for help by sending her daughters to the Villa, preferring to find employment for herself elsewhere. Thelma and Myrtle came to work with obvious enjoyment. After Rhoda's desertion they settled even more cheerfully into their unwavering ways.

By Ash Wednesday the longed-for thaw had arrived. Montague warned that with it might come unwelcome events. Russia had overwhelmed Finland. Between them lay neutral Norway and Sweden, still in the grip of winter. Such small distances to conquer.

The River Lodbrook was running higher. Trees were dripping and cracking. Everywhere sodden. For days water ran from roofs, gutters and gullies. The air was filled with such moisture it felt as if they were inhaling clouds.

The roads had melted into black slicks that froze again at night. Morgan once more could cycle into Lodford, if her father refused to drive her. It was hard enough ignoring the whistles of men leaning from vehicles, trying to attract her attention. She hated the way her legs and coat were splashed. If this went on she would not have a decent thing to her name.

One morning as she was passing the Retchen house, a man shouted,

"Hoy, Miz Prinkle! Hoy!" He too was on a bike, passing close enough to hit her with his foot.

It was Gideon Jensen, "Hopalong", well known for his ability to cycle with one leg, the other being wooden. It was the wooden foot, rising and falling stiffly above the unused pedal, which had struck her. She wobbled to a halt. He cycled on his way still shouting, "Hoy!" as he went. Some things never changed.

The chain had slipped, as had her hat. "Damn!" Ahead was Jensen, rounding the corner past the ducking pond. In the other direction the Gormson Road, winding away in grey mist towards Grandma Perincall's and Iverdon.

Morgan waited by the kerb, knowing she could walk the few paces to the Retchen home. But this she would never do. Mrs Retchen had not been a comfortable presence in her life. There was something watchful about the woman that Morgan had once complained about. Since her mother thought well of most people, the response was predictable. "What is there to dislike about a decent body, endeavouring to bring up two puny babes on her own?" Morgan had tried asking why Mr Retchen had deserted his wife. The answer was enigmatic. "He interfered with a boy. We do not know the circumstances."

Coming from the direction of the Gormsons was an R.A.F. lorry. She was relieved that it was not some farmer with grubby hands and a mind to match. The driver, who had a passenger, slowed and stopped. Jumping out, he introduced himself, "In case," he said, "you don't recognise me in my blues." It was Parclay, the flying officer who had visited the Villa the previous year. "Looks as if you're in a bit of a bind!" He was already retrieving her bicycle, gauging the damage, looking at her. "I do hope you're not hurt?" His passenger stood watching, hands in pockets.

It was he who held all Morgan's attention. He too was a pilot, his flying jacket collar around his ears. He wore no hat, revealing fair hair unusually long. His chin was buried in a white scarf. His eyes, that to Morgan had a slight oriental slant, were appraising her.

Parclay began to rewind the bicycle chain, saying there was no real damage. She could not concentrate. All her attention was on the other man looking her over.

The moment she saw him, something like a purr had started. The last time that had happened was when she had first set eyes on Cathcart in the council offices. It had been the back of his neck, the way the hair grew, the ears flat to the head. The way Cat had turned and looked. This time it was that same appreciative gaze, the sexual recognition. She managed a smile. He was lighting a cigarette.

Perhaps, like Charlie, she was susceptible to a uniform. And any diversion from dreariness was bound to be attractive.

Parclay was rubbing oil from his fingers. He had noticed her stare. "Meet Flight Lieutenant Woodborne. Commonly know as Patch." He elbowed his friend. His glance between them was keen. The stranger proffered a hand, warm and dry.

It was the same old sensation, the excitement in the pit of her stomach, heat rising from feet to head. All her concentration was on him. She had been deprived for too long, that was it. She wanted this stranger's hot fingers to stroke her wrist, arm, shoulder, her breasts. She longed to emerge from hibernation.

Her thank-yous were brief. No matter how speedily she gathered her shopping, remounted her bicycle, she knew she would meet this stranger again and probably have some kind of disastrous affair with him.

The idea lasted while she queued for groceries, bought middlings for the chickens and carried them home. After that there was only annoyance with herself for being silly. And slight shame for ignoring Parclay.

"What's the matter?" was Charlie's first question. He was waiting for his lunch. She turned on him, demanding why he had not had the decency to set the table. If he mentioned it was woman's work, she would throw his dinner into the stove.

After that she calmed down and told him her bicycle chain had slipped, making her walk some distance. She could see he was sceptical. She wished his intuition where she was concerned were not so acute.

She concluded only deprivation was the cause of her foolishness. She had not, she counted, been touched intimately by a man since Cathcart had left nine months ago. Was she missing more the act itself, rather than any particular man? Parclay too had been kind, yet without kindling any spark.

That evening she lit a fire in a sitting room. Her father did not remonstrate. Neither did Charlie who sat over it, trousers nearly singed by the coals. For a long time they watched it without speaking, only falling slush from the pent roof to break the silence. Morgan's thoughts flickered like the flames: pilot; children far away; husband somewhere; men in uniform; air force blues; lover in a flying jacket; naked lover; fear of pregnancy; contraception; the freedom war might offer.

The air filled with Montague's cigarette smoke. He was reluctant to break the calm. His mind wandered from blame at Rhoda, disquiet should the Scandinavians surrender, worry over pheasants damaging the crops. And whether this new business of changing the clocks to what was called Summertime, would mean going to work in the dark in winter.

Charlie's thoughts skittered between how he would get a rabbit or two, another pheasant if the season were prolonged, whether he'd be invited to a shoot. And what was causing his sister's strange mood.

Morgan was suddenly alert. "Pa, we must get another housekeeper."

"Easier said than done, child. We must all pull extra weight now. And prices are rising a deal." This spoken in a kindly tone, for he was aware of how much she was shouldering. How thin she looked, even in a winter jumper. How nervy she seemed.

"I cannot cope, Pa."

"You may have to, my girl. A billeting officer has been to see me."

"I was thinking," she said, "that if we're to have service people here, we ought to be able to choose them." Montague and Charlie waited. "Would it not be better if we asked for the Royal Air Force? We would not want undesirables, would we, Pa?"

Her father raised his eyebrows. The one thing he had disapproved of in his wife was a tendency to divide the world into those who were, and were not, acceptable. Now his daughter was doing this. The last war had done little to change attitudes, despite the seeming equality of men and officers on the front line. After the armistice the hierarchical system had returned full fold. The one certainty was that only in death were people equal.

"Airmen generally seem to come from better families, don't you think?"

Charlie was becoming suspicious.

"My dear child, I was a soldier. Your husband is in the army. What does that make us? And how does this jibe with our needing another housekeeper?"

"I shall need extra help to look after them." In the past the best tactic had been to produce something akin to a tantrum. All she could say was, "You have no idea what it is like for me here. This house is huge. I cannot be more put upon. Great merciful heavens, is it too much to ask!"

Her father's reaction was unexpected. Very soon the R.A.F. would have better things to do than live so far away from base. Group Captain Floster had said that airmen were already quartered at Prittend aerodrome, where they might be needed in a hurry. The ground staff and such were housed in huts on the Iverdon site, so Coral Floster had told him.

This was new. "When did you speak to Mrs Floster, Pa?"

He wasn't saying. "She tells me there are W.A.A.F.s already stationed there." He did not notice Morgan's dismay. Charlie did. And the way she began to bite at her finger. "Bad conditions. Wind and rain coming in through the windows." With the tongs he grabbed a falling coal. "The bunkers are partly underground, so she tells me. Those huts aren't fit for women. Or even for men in this weather, stoves or no stoves." The fire began to blaze. "I'll see what I can do about a housekeeper. We could ask Mrs Retchen to come again."

"No!" She did not hesitate. "Two of that family is enough already. You wouldn't like Mrs Retchen always telling you what to do, would you, Charlie?"

Montague thought the job might suit his sister Winnie, but he could not see his mother letting her go. Nor Winifred being brave enough to venture out alone with regularity.

Nothing more was mentioned about another housekeeper. And Morgan found no way of retrieving the subject.

As the thaw continued, there was an edginess to life at the Villa that Montague put down partly to Rhoda's absence, partly to an influx of strangers giving advice, handing out ministry leaflets.

At work, official directives continued to annoy him. So did his son's frequent questions that seemed to have no point. Charlie began to ask about the war. Why were our troops manning the trains instead of fighting in Belgium? Why had Scapa Flow been bombed again, when we had fighters capable of shooting bombers down? "We shot down one Heinkel and a Dornier last year." It was his co-workers who spent their breaks discussing such topics with Charlie, fretting over possible call-up; some already worrying that the buildings might be at risk.

Bernard Talbott expressed the view that the lull was the forerunner to another armistice. What problems had the country endured, apart from a few food shortages and a few accidents due to the blackout? In France the Maginot Line would hold, the Nazis be sent packing and Mr Hitler given a bloody nose. "Your grandchildren will be back before the summer," he told his surprised boss, who was not used to his manager trying to compete with the noise of machinery.

Montague's grandchildren seemed to have accepted their life in Barmford with worrying alacrity. One day in early March a letter arrived from Mrs Timmbold accompanying Billy's. The hand was childish, the spelling as suspect as his. But it was apparent there was real affection for their charges.

> *Terry has got over her little moods. Billy loves Rex (our mungril dog).*
> *The forest is where they like to go. Please do not waist a minutes worry*

over them. Me and my husband hope you and your family is well.

Sincerely

Prudence Timmbold

The postscript said *"you are more than welcome any time"*.

Morgan told Charlie she might take up the invitation.

He could see it clearly – she wanted an excuse to escape. The Villa without Rhoda was too much for her. Already her hands were a disgrace, her body too thin. He had seen how she pored over magazine pictures of women in suits and veils. Not the clothes for a country existence. He watched her furtively. If she went to Barmford might she not take Billy and Teresa straight to London instead of back to the Villa Rouge? He hid from her articles in the *Telegraph* about the paucity of bombing raids on her city. In the last month she had already twice mentioned missing the children. She had been enquiring of the coal man how many trains were running.

He couldn't stand it. "Billy and Terry are safer where they are," he had told her several times. "Pa says so."

Needing stamps for her reply to the Timmbolds, Morgan had to go to the post office. She had asked Charlie to go on his free Saturday. He had a better idea – if the two of them went together he could not be asked to help Montague with tax work.

Morgan did not want Charlie. There was the slight hope that she might run into the pilot called Patch, whose surname she could not remember. Charlie, refusing to be put off, came anyway.

Vela Kymmerly had taken over as postmistress, a job that appeared to weigh heavily on her. She was not surprised to see Morgan. Charlie was already well known to Vela, as were most of Lodford's local inhabitants. She enquired after Morgan's children and asked after Captain Perincall. She wondered aloud where Rhoda – a nice person – had got to, not having seen her lately. No reply. Morgan pushed the Barmford letter forward, trying hurry Vela along, but it was no use.

103

Having waited in vain for the inquiry, Vela said sadly, "I'm as well as can be expected." She was looking from Morgan to Charlie. "Mother died. Did you know?" If she did, Morgan had long put it from her mind.

"Everyone around here's getting married." Vela was pulling a face. "It's the uncertainty, you see. They can't risk leaving it to after the fighting." She had lowered her voice. "Fat chance for me, trapped here. Unless I propose to somebody myself." Was she looking at Charlie? Behind him a queue was forming. "Archie going away like that when he needn't have didn't help. A right shame, really."

Charlie glanced at Morgan for details, but none came. Her face had a fixed expression. "When did your mother die?" he asked out of politeness.

"This last twelvemonth or more. She took bad after Archie went. Dropped organs righted, but never the same again. It were December the fifth he left, 1922. Never been back since." She began searching for stamps. "He was up in Berwick-on-Tweed when I last heard. Must be due for call up. Not much of a writer. Did you ever hear from Archie?"

On her face Morgan had an expression that Charlie had rarely seen. It had tightened to a point where it was a mask, one of those *papier mâché* puppets he had made at school, grey before the paint was applied, the lips a stroke of scarlet.

"Mind you –" Vela Kymmerly was stamping Morgan's letter – "it was brave of Archie to go off like that with nothing to his name, don't you think? To make his own way."

Charlie wondered whether Morgan had heard. As he watched her put down the pennies, he could have sworn her hand was quivering.

On the pavement he asked what that was all about. And who was Archie Whatshisname? Morgan said brusquely he was nothing, and walked on.

On their way to the grocer's she changed her mind, and began to explain how Archie Kymmerly had been what some would call a tearaway, always getting into trouble.

"What sort of trouble?"

She took some time thinking. "Once he rode his bike down Long Alley and nearly brained the chicken seller." He was struggling to keep up with her.

When they reached the square, unusually crowded, Morgan slowed. No sign of a pilot in a flying jacket, looking like Errol Flynn in "Dawn Patrol", too handsome for his own good.

They were in West Street. "Doesn't sound so terrible to me, riding a bike like that. I've done it, so has Ronnie."

"Trust you to think so. Archie was fined two guineas." They were entering Willams shop. "There were other things." She was fiddling with her purse.

"What things?"

She didn't reply. By the way she smiled when she raised her head at Mr Willams, and by his enthusiastic response, Charlie knew he had lost the opportunity of discovery. The grocer thrust a packet of tea into her basket, pressing her hand and saying not to worry, he knew the war would be all over in a twinkling.

There was rain in March to wash away the last signs of winter, its chill gradually giving way to promising warmth. Pancake Day came and went and lemons were scarce. Easter meant getting wet going to church and listening to the Reverend Dorby's exhortations to Be of Good Cheer and pray for an end to flooded fields.

The Lodbrook stayed high. Upstream it had become a not-so-tamed stretch of salt water. Morgan, claiming she was concerned that Granny Dorp's cottage might be in danger, went across the floodgate bridge. With difficulty she negotiated the obstacles in Hatts Lane. Her grandmother's cottage was deserted, the river behind it flowing faster than usual, between banks of snow-flattened grass. She followed its course until it became a brook of bubbling fresh water beside the Three Tuns. It then disappeared beneath the Prittend Road, emerging in Lodford, flowing high in its gully behind the shops in West Street. Outside Willams', people were wondering if the water would rise up over the pump steps. Morgan wondered when she would bump into the man who had been filling her thoughts.

At the foot of the railway slope, more onlookers were discussing the likely fate of the old infant school on the other side. It had been flooded before in 1912.

She went as far as the start of the Plumberow Road, not giving up the idea that the flight lieutenant might be looking for her too. Opposite the junior school she lingered, leaning over the parapet where the brook was running in a steady stream. But this was March. She could hear the water rushing through the tunnel beneath the railway line, competing with the train rattling overhead. She saw no children that day willing to risk paddling through it. The water would be over their waists.

But she recalled emerging into the light of Ironside Lane, having struggled through weeds between confining banks. How well she remembered that lane. Overhung with trees, it had once been the main medieval road from ancient Lodford to London. Now it had little purpose other than a haven for couples looking for privacy, or for youths with a taste for mild adventure. For the first time that year Charlie and Ronnie had gone hunting there for rabbits, and eaten their sandwiches on the soggy grass of an adjacent field. Montague had told Charlie he would be better employed buying rabbits for breeding. It would stop him wasting his time gallivanting with the Talbott boy, whose sister Dora had left them in the lurch, just like Rhoda.

With the changing weather a sense of optimism, a sort of skittishness, returned that seemed to infect anyone who came to the Villa Rouge. The insurance man told the giggling Retchen girls they looked like the Dolly Sisters. Mr Boxley from the dairy told Morgan he might drive to Barmford, and offered her a lift. Arpent the A.R.P. warden presented her with a sprig of winter jasmine that she accepted without telling Charlie.

Charlie, on a visit to Granny Dorp, discovered the cottage empty, the moss rose collapsed over the front door. At the Three Tuns he found the old lady ensconced in a corner of the saloon bar, from which she would not be moved. Cory said she had come of her own willingness two weeks since, before the floods subsided. They had wrapped her up nice and warm. The customers seemed to be doing her good, for her mind was a mite to rights. She wasn't at all in their way and was easier to feed. Would Mr Charles please give the reckoning for his granny's upkeep to Captain Perincall, which he did.

The war, so far away, affected them at the Villa less and less. Montague spent less time worrying over remote events. If there was a debacle in Norway he had no details. If there was uproar in Parliament the causes seemed sketchy. His distracted thoughts allowed him to regain some optimism. And there were other distractions closer to home.

He drove Morgan and Charlie to Iverdon because he had promised Mrs Floster and her husband a visit. It was a puzzle to Morgan how long they might have been in contact, and why he was being so secretive. The group captain had been to the Villa on several occasions, lingering long enough for Montague to accuse him, behind his back, of sniffing out an extra tot or two. The cellar was depleting fast. Soon Floster would have to bring more than a couple of small beers, as was becoming his custom. Morgan wondered at her father's tolerance of this man with his off-colour jokes.

Not until the visit to the Flosters did she question her father's motives. Charlie could not see the harm in his father admiring Mrs Floster. He thought she was, in her posh clothes, "an eyeful" and nick-named her "Floral Coster".

"More like Costalot!" Morgan had rejoined.

Montague warned them not to mention the installation across the road. The receiver and transmitter towers were top secret. The country's security might depend on them. They were to stay close-mouthed about everything they might have seen. So the group captain had done more than jest over the liquor on his visits to the Villa. Or was it his wife who had given the warnings?

That Sunday afternoon was bright and windy. Morgan was again discomfited by Mrs Floster's elegance. No wonder her father found her attractive, although, after Rhoda, anyone would appeal. She had the look of somebody in a portrait. There was one in the National Gallery that had fascinated Cat. It was of a dark-skinned woman with a knowing expression. For the life of her, Morgan could not recall why his fixation should have induced irritation in her.

Now she noted with some satisfaction that Coral Floster's stockings were not silk. But there was a fragility about her at odds with her own more earthy charms. When Mrs Floster had placed a hand on Montague's, it set Morgan thinking that here was somebody who could out-manoeuvre any man.

They drank tea from thick white cups, air force issue, Morgan suspected. There were triangular sandwiches with something fishy. Charlie was silently admonished for eating too many. From over the road a series of young airmen arrived, bringing papers for their commander to sign. The telephone rang twice in another room. During the group captain's absence, Montague moved closer to Mrs Floster, keeping a watchful eye on the door.

Morgan had been preoccupied for some time with the camp entrance. Someone she recognised was talking to a sentry. Her stomach lurched. It was her Errol Flynn, in uniform, minus his flying jacket. She waited, willing him to notice the Rover, willing him to come. At last, to her relief, he began strolling towards the Floster lodgings.

He entered the room. She drew a deep breath, recalling the intriguing eyes, pale hair, white teeth. Introductions were brief and this time she committed to memory his full name, Flight Lieutenant Paul Woodborne.

"But we call him 'Patch'. Don't we?" It was this from Coral Floster. The way she arched her neck alerted Morgan to a ready-made problem. Simply that the flight lieutenant and Mrs Floster were possibly more intimate than they should be.

Her father had not guessed. Charlie's need was to get the pilot to talk about aircraft and, as he later admitted, to wheedle a flight. Their stay was not long. The party came to an abrupt end when the group captain, after another interruption, stated that business must come first, and sent them on their way.

April. Nature, released from cold and wet, springing into sudden life. The weather so good that the season's first cricket match was arranged. A group of airmen, sufficient to make up a "tidy eleven with spares", as the group captain told Montague, to play against local men not yet called up or deferred.

Ronnie Talbott and Charlie, part of the home team, rolled the wicket into a playable surface. Nothing much could be done to improve the outfield. The pavilion was opened, cleared of nests by the Retchen girls, folding chairs revived, cricketing gear and tea urn rescued from the Villa cellars. No sightscreens, removed last November to one of the barns behind St Margaret's. Montague said to leave them there. With events so unsettled, there might be no time for cricket in the years to come. So he had invited his three sisters for the afternoon. Harriet and Maud accepted.

Bernard Talbott was selected as umpire, a position he found impossible to refuse, although it meant late nights studying the rules. He ordered his wife to help Mrs Brodick with the teas. She had said little, other than asking whose Typhoo and whose biscuits should be sacrificed. Morgan suspected that Grace Talbott, a woman as close as her husband, might be tedious company. But she was willing to tolerate much if she could meet her flight lieutenant.

On the day onlookers arrived early, many equipped with sacks, for the ground was still damp. No-one was surprised by the turnout, it had been an imprisoning winter. Everyone able to find an excuse was there. Along the drive were parked vehicles predominately military, some private cars, motorcycles and bicycles. Morgan was dismayed at the number of Waafs in their smart uniforms, looking pleased with themselves.

At half past two she could have sworn it was Coral Floster in chartreuse, alighting from one of the air force cars. There was no sign of her husband. Neither could she see Woodborne, for whom she had used the last of her nail polish and dusted her arms with talc. She was sporting her best frock with her highest heels, dangerous on the turf. Morgan's aunts had settled themselves by the pavilion with a bottle of lemonade each.

It was a small field for cricket, requiring little effort to hit sixes. More skill to avoid unwitting visitors, who were being herded from the pitch by Floster and a corporal. Morgan's father had begun an animated discussion with his land agent. He was probably telling Threw, a hunter, as he always did, that too many horses had already died on the Somme.

The air force eleven opened the batting, putting on a reasonable score, being fitter and mainly younger than the opposition. The runs kept coming. By the time Parclay walked out to the crease, the game looked like being a one-sided affair. But after two graceful fours, he was caught out by the waiting hands of Ronnie Talbott. The flying officer, acknowledging the catch, came strolling towards Morgan.

Had he let himself be caught out just to sit with her? He had called her by her Christian name. This she should have found presumptuous, but she was already comfortable in his company. Her attention was on Flight Lieutenant Woodborne, taking theatrical chances at the wicket to an appreciative audience. Parclay asked whether she might have any spare time. Her attention still on Woodborne, she said that sometimes she felt the need to run away.

"Don't run too far," was the reply. His friend's inept performance at the crease was drawing in the fielders. "Rugby is more his game!"

"Have you known Patch long?" Daringly she was using the flight lieutenant's nickname.

That they had met at Oxford meant little to Morgan. "What is he like?"

"He's . . . popular." Parclay was about to say something else, but she sensed by his reticence that she might not want to hear it.

Their conversation, fragmented by the noise of play, drifted into talk of families. He spoke about his parents. She found herself telling him how much she was missing her children. He listened carefuly. She begged him not to stare at her, for people were watching. She was doing her best not to cause comment.

"I think you might have already." He sounded as if it was of no account. "You can't help it!"

Patch was bowled out by a Blytham thatcher, to a cheer from the Waafs. Morgan, covertly observing them, began to wonder about her competition. The R.A.F. side declared with a reasonable score.

At three o'clock, a burst of ack ack gunfire broke the peace. Charlie and Eden Dufrene, opening bats, managed four runs while the fielders were discussing whether the firing was a test.

Mrs Floster was nowhere in sight. Morgan had last noticed her on the boundary close to the Villa, applauding half-heartedly. She hoped she had been imagining her liaison with Flight Lieutenant Woodborne. Or they may have quarrelled. He seemed unconcerned by Mrs Floster's absence, his attention all on urging his team to extra effort. Morgan decided he would not much mind hurting any woman's feelings. Was he married? No ring on his third finger. When he raised questioning eyebrows at her, she deliberately turned away. If ignoring him was what would get his interest, then she would do it. At her side she could sense Parclay's scrutiny.

Her father hit a six that flew high and dropped out of sight, two airmen after it. Onlookers went to help search in the nettles on the far side of the drive. While the field was engrossed, Woodborne turned a long gaze on her.

At tea he came into the pavilion, as she guessed he would.

It was a pity women could not play cricket, he said. "You would make a grand sight in white." It was spoken in a low voice, for Mrs Talbott was listening.

"All men are flatterers." Mrs Talbott's remark startled them both. "At first." She banged the lid of the urn, as if the words had been forced from her.

Ignoring her presence, the pilot closed in on Morgan. She could see a razor burn on his chin. And that his eyes were really the colour of slate. "What do you do all day? Apart from luring men into your cavern?" He was speaking fast, keeping an eye on the door, through which could be heard Floster's noisy bellow, a Retchen girl screaming. Morgan glimpsed Charlie hobbling between the creases. Some applause. A flight of birds darkened her view.

"Methinks you are a witch!" Neither the flight lieutenant nor Morgan acknowledged Grace Talbott's exasperated tut-tut.

"The tea is being served outside," Morgan replied, "where you ought to be." She turned over her hand to reveal the wedding ring.

"What horrible hands you have." He pinched the finger. "It wouldn't do to have everything about you perfect." With that he stepped outside, leaving Morgan and Mrs Talbott staring at one another. Mrs Talbott's look was disdainful.

Soon after tea and resumption of the game, an air raid warning, faint on the breeze, settled closure. The match was declared a draw.

The crowd began to leave, unaware that the siren was a test. Harriet and Maud were looking around for Montague to drive them home. Some local girls hung about the pitch, trying to get Charlie's attention. He ignored them as usual. His only aim was to approach the flight lieutenant, sitting beside his sister on the pavilion steps. It had been bad enough watching her with Parclay, who was now leaning against a tree, staring.

Charlie distracted Woodborne, as he intended. He asked about the difficulties of flying Spitfires at night, the effect of ice on their engines, their manoeuvrability. Morgan listened with half an ear, hoping she might soon be included in their conversation. In the distance she could see her waiting aunts becoming more agitated. She too began looking around for her father. Parclay was gazing in her direction. She mouthed the word "father?" with a shrug. He shook his head twice. Hadn't seen him. Her father had not been in sight, she reckoned, for nearly three-quarters of an hour.

She left Mrs Talbott to clear up, and began to search for her father. Charlie was still monopolising Patch.

With relief she saw an R.A.F. corporal ushering her aunts towards his lorry. Harriet and Maud would be torn between the impropriety of the lift and the novelty. Nobody would hear the last of it.

People were still wandering the drive, but no Montague. She headed for the Villa, between people idling under the trees. Parclay would have joined her had she not refused. He turned aside as if he understood. Strange how she felt as if they had always been friends.

A group of airmen near the river was attempting to prise a gap in the barbed wire, some girls egging them on. Morgan would have sent them packing, but for the sight of Mrs Floster. The group captain's wife, who had exited the Villa by the back door, was hastening through the garden, hat flapping in her hand. Morgan moved into cover to watch her trip, then stop to compose herself. Outside the broken gate she paused, head up. She drew a deep breath and began to run again, her heels lifting divots.

Her husband was strolling by the pavilion in conversation with the two pilots. Although having noticed his wife approaching, he did not respond to her wave. Trees hid them. When they came in sight again the pair were nearing a staff car, the group captain ahead, his wife's hat now dangling from his hand. The pilots too were leaving.

Morgan hurried into the Villa hall. Her father was coming down the stairs. She asked him where he had been for so long. He ignored this. She followed him into the kitchen where he drank from the tap. The side of his face had a scrubbed look. She asked him again. His expression was stubborn. He was not wearing his cricket flannels. Still without acknowledging her, he took his jacket from the peg and went outdoors,

A week later, while feeding the hens, Morgan noticed a man on the perimeter of the cricket pitch. Through the foliage it was difficult to make out who it was. She thought he might be a visitor looking for something lost at the cricket match. A botanist, or some loiterer.

It was Flight Lieutenant Woodborne. She approached him slowly.

After a brief glance he continued examining the ground at his feet.

"What are you looking for?"

"Bits and pieces." His voice, directed over her head, was high, amused. He saw the pinafore bunched in her hand. She wished she had dropped it.

"I have seen a cigarette lighter and a gobstopper. Plus three dog-ends and a button!" He was staring intently at her. "Paltry!"

She would not ask what he meant, believing he was trying to impress her. Even in the shade there was heat, yet he was wearing his uniform. His cap was under his arm. They stood looking at one another.

"Nice cap." He gave it to her. The flat top, curving to the back, looked distorted. The embroidered oak leaves on its peak felt stiff. She ran her fingers over the eagle, the wings. Tried the hat on, then handed it back.

"Suits you, madam."

Their hands touched and she backed away. He stood looking her over, from her fringe to her workaday shoes. Then he resumed his search of the grass.

"What *are* you looking for?"

"I'll think of something in a minute, if you promise to go away a yard or two!"

They wandered in the direction of the road, until they were out of sight of the house. He was causing the familiar sensation.

"I'll tell you what has happened," he said. "This has stopped me wishing I were somewhere else."

"But why aren't you somewhere else? Defending us?"

"Ah! There's the problem. Nothing much to do at present, but sit in an armchair, waiting for Jerry."

"What armchair?"

"Not a Messerschmitt in sight. Just lolling in the fresh air, waiting for 'Chocks away', if you get my meaning. Or playing cricket if we're lucky. And, in my case, being accosted by a beautiful woman who won't leave me alone!" He was keeping pace with her. His glance at the open

114

door of the pavilion was ignored. She wasn't ready, and moved back towards the house.

She wondered how far he would come with her. At the gap of the gate he pretended to open it, saluted and mimed closing it. Laughing she left him, saying she hoped he would find what he was looking for.

"Lord Woolton is Minister of Food," Montague told Charlie and the twins. "That means we must make more of an effort to cut down." The girls, in awe of him, nodded at their feet.

With Charlie they were never silent, telling him their special things: what they had seen, their current favourite songs. He tried to tell an inattentive Morgan they had serenaded him with "We're Gonna Hang Out the Washing on the Sea Free Line", not knowing it should have been the "Siegfried Line".

Thelma caught her finger on the barbed wire and told Charlie it had a limp like his. Myrtle asked him why his mother had not bandaged his bad leg, for it was still poorly.

He told Morgan the girls had been down by the river, where the barbed wire was dangerous, and preventing safe access to the boats. There had been altercation about it at the council offices.

Morgan resolved it in her special way. Charlie watched through the glass partition. The boy in the outer office called his superior, who came from his room and invited her in. She had sat on his desk, lowered her head and smiled, speaking in an animated fashion. It looked so easy – the way she got what she wanted by moving her body in a certain way.

Two army engineers cut a hole in the barbed wire to fold it back. They told Morgan the gap should be disguised. It was meant only for entry to local craft. "Or to collect samphire," Charlie said. One engineer did not know what he was talking about. The other mentioned King Lear, and Charlie didn't know what *he* was talking about.

Eden, with the post, had heard from the constable on duty near the playing fields that Holland might have fallen. Things weren't looking good. His nephew had gone missing in Norway. Charlie was barely listening, for in his hands was a letter addressed to Montague, in Rhoda's handwriting.

He was late for work, but the sight of the letter had jolted him into realising he should be missing Rhoda more.

"I've never known any other mother than Rhoda." He saw Morgan's expression. "And you, of course."

"What do you mean?" Once again he had said the wrong thing. "Rhoda was never your mother. Never."

"All I'm saying is, I can't remember any other," he repeated. He wanted to leave. He wanted to say what had been on his mind for years.

He had to say it. "I probably killed our mother, didn't I?"

She was exasperated. "Sometimes you say the most stupid things, Charles."

"Pa won't tell what she died of. How do you know she didn't die because of having me?"

"You were months old when she died, Charlie. And she had been ill for years."

"What with?"

"We don't talk about that sort of thing."

"Why not?"

"Great merciful heavens, Charles, anyone would think you were still five years old."

He persisted. "How old were you, then, when she died?"

"Fifteen." Reluctantly she was remembering. "As if you didn't know already."

"Do you remember me being born?"

"Yes." She stopped the conversation by pushing past him and clashing the breakfast plates.

Rhoda's letter, dated 1 May, 1940, had to wait until Montague and Charlie came home from work. It had taken nine days to arrive.

Supper was eaten before her father put on his spectacles and opened the envelope. The letter, a lengthy one, took him some time to read. He finished and said, "She's in Weymouth. Dorset. She's had to take Bile

Beans. They're giving them dried egg. Never heard of drying eggs before." Morgan and Charlie waited for more. "She went to Highgate to learn wages and such. She's called Third Officer Swell. Says the uniform's scratchy. Starched collars." He was folding the letter into its envelope.

"What else does she say, Pa? Did she say why she went?"

Charlie asked, "Is she on a ship? It says 'H.M.S. *Boskall*' on the envelope. That's giving away secret information."

"Josh, she is on dry land. She says volunteers are clogging up the roads, setting ambushes, road blocks and such." He was holding his watch, ready for to the nightly broadcast. Rhoda's letter went into his pocket. The three of them sat waiting, hearing a blackbird in the D'Arcy Spice apple tree.

The letter was soon forgotten. Eden had been correct, the unbreachable Maginot Line had been breached. The newsreader said that Luxembourg had been overrun. The German army was pouring into the Netherlands. There was heavy fighting in Belgium and northern France, where the brave Allies were holding back the enemy advance. And, after two days of parliamentary debate, Mr Winston Churchill had been made Prime Minister as leader of a newly formed coalition government.

CHAPTER FIVE

At the beginning of May the weather was fine. Everything had been released into bud by the arrival of a beautiful spring. Bird song was waking Morgan earlier, when the light came through the sides of the blackout curtains. There was no more shivering in an icy bathroom. Doors and windows were opened to let in air. The snowdrops were in bloom, the first bluebells under trees. Plaited hedgerows were stippled with the pale green of young leaves.

Morgan suddenly acquired a taste for afternoon bicycle rides, mainly in the direction of Gormson and beyond. If there were any errands to do, food or messages or instructions to take to Grandma Perincall, she was willing. No, it was not too much trouble to carry a few eggs, some rhubarb, or air raid precaution leaflets. Yes, she could track down the woodsman who was wanted on the Perincall estate.

She badly needed to escape from housework and from Charlie. Since he was kept longer in the office dealing with ministry paperwork, he could not know how many times in a week she went searching for her flight lieutenant.

What she did not know was that he was finding excuses to drive past the Villa gates hoping for a sight of her.

Woodborne had twice attempted to visit. The first time he was halted halfway along the drive by sounds coming from the house. He had parked the Riley and was walking the rest of the way, following the voices. Two girls of sixteen or seventeen were singing as they lugged a basket from clothes line to house. Out of sight he could still hear their raucous tones, attempting "Some Day I'll Find You". What they lost in melody they made up for in volume.

The second time was early evening – a better time perhaps for an encounter with the elusive lady of the green eyes. He thought his friend Parclay had been unforthcoming about his conversation with Morgan at the cricket match. All he had revealed was that the lady missed her children.

He was sitting in the Riley in front of the gates, trying to assess the risks, when he heard the same singing. Seeing the girls approaching, he managed to drive off. All this he told Morgan later. She feigned indifference and never admitted how she had gone looking for him.

Her bicycle rides took her beyond Great Gormson, sometimes as far as the Iverdon camp, despite telling herself to avoid it. She could not hang about in such a high-security area where there was too much traffic, too many watchers. Usually she turned round. Or, feeling optimistic, rode on towards the newly prosperous village of Iverdon, in the hope that Patch might miraculously be there.

On that particular Thursday, blown by a strong wind, she found herself opposite the site. On a whim she knocked on the door of the Flosters' rented billet. The house's pebble-dashed exterior, its front garden full of weeds and sycamore seedlings, looked even less appealing in the bright light. It might once have been the home of a farm labourer, who had cemented the path and combed the front door in imitation oak. Not the sort of place for someone like the group captain's fastidious wife.

Mrs Floster disguised her surprise at her visitor and welcomed her graciously, saying how nice it was to be remembered. Although dressed for company, she seemed to be alone in a room that was hot.

During Morgan's visit she sat, thin legs carefully crossed, showing to advantage a silk petticoat. The frock was sufficient cause for envy, its blues matching the colour of her eyes. The teacups were the same ones she had presented on the previous visit.

"The porcelain has been packed away." Morgan suspected this was not true. They ate egg and fish paste sandwiches. And wafers of Swiss roll on paper doilies, both aware of this demonstration of style.

They sat facing the window, through which they could clearly see the main gates of the camp, the barrier being raised and lowered as personnel came and went. No sign of the flight lieutenant. Now and then a driver in a spiral of dust pulled up at the entrance.

"It's so very quiet here," Coral Floster remarked, as if unaware of the traffic, of a constant humming emanating, Morgan decided, from the four towers on the highest ground. Since her first sight of them there had been more construction. Her thoughts then had been of Blackpool. Now it was Paris. Or was it at the start of a Fred Astaire picture?

The scene was reminiscent of some futuristic film: the vast conglomeration of half-buried buildings, concrete walls, huts, pillboxes. Uniformed men and women were hurrying to and fro. For the first time she understood that real war, right on the doorstep, was a probability.

Mrs Floster was amused. "Large, isn't it? It keeps him busy." Adding for no reason, "Out of bounds to civilians, of course." She helped herself to another slice of cake and ate it greedily without offering any. With wide eyes she stared into space.

Her next action took Morgan by surprise. Practically falling over her visitor, she darted from the room clasping her midriff. From the kitchen came the sound of tap water running, of metal clinking on glass. Morgan waited.

Mrs Floster was in the doorway, traces of white powder around her mouth. "You must excuse me, my dear Mrs Brodick, I have a delicate digestion." She licked her lips. "Flossie is always somewhere else when I want him." She sat down. "But what are 'wants'?" Smiling, she took up the conversation as if nothing had happened.

The afternoon dragged on. Coral Floster revealed more details of her digestive system, saying it was touch and go whether there would have to be surgery. An environment free from anxieties was the best remedy. In the present political climate, with what was going on in the Low Countries, not to mention domestic perturbation, she doubted her chances of survival. "I must not be upset." Responses for Morgan were difficult, the silences between them not of the comfortable kind.

Questions about Morgan's life were idly put. Mrs Floster seemed to know enough about her visitor already, or the subject was of little interest. Morgan's replies, though brief, were polite and as uninformative as she could make them. Her mother's lessons in good manners had not been forgotten. After all she was the uninvited.

She instinctively knew that her rival's seeming fragility hid a flinty core. It was curiosity about the strength of this that kept her seated so long.

"I expect you miss him terribly – your husband, that is? Mr Brodick."

"Officer Brodick. Recently promoted. You are lucky yours is still close to you."

"And devoted. He showers me with gifts."

"And everything so difficult to come by." Morgan kept her voice cool. "Some things are not so difficult. I have always found that if one wants something badly enough, one can get it."

During this desultory exchange neither woman looked at the other, their eyes constantly shifting to the camp entrance.

It was four o'clock when Morgan decided that to remain any longer would test them too much. It was a mistake to have come.

She was pushing her bicycle along the path when Group Captain Floster called a loud greeting. Approaching from either side were flying officer Parclay and Flight Lieutenant Woodborne. Parclay, reintroducing himself with enthusiasm, reminded her of their first meeting, the bike chain catastrophe, the miserable weather. His dark hair and youthful look still reminded Morgan of Charlie. Yet she already guessed that, by comparison, this officer might be the kinder, the more dependable.

Woodborne's looks were as satisfactory as ever. He asked whether the cricket pitch had been sacrificed to invaders. The heat rose again in her throat, repressing her replies. She bent her head.

The group captain begged her to come back with them for "a snifter". To give his wife a bit more company. Things were hotting up, so Mrs Brodick should take advantage of the offer before the balloon went up. Morgan suspected him of showing off.

Parclay stood looking at her in evident admiration. How was she?

Was she well? Woodborne told her she deserved a medal for facing such a wind. What luck it had blown her towards them. She murmured something about being prepared to face anything.

What happened next was simple. The flight lieutenant said, "I shall take you home." Nothing about why he should do this. No excuse, no reasons at all. Grabbing the handlebars of her bicycle he started to push it towards his Riley in the road. The other two men watched, whether in admiration or dismay she did not care, although his group captain said, "Hey there!"

She followed Woodborne, knowing that in the house, behind the clouded windowpane, Coral Floster was looking at them.

He laid Morgan's bicycle across the back of his car, saying she wasn't to worry about its safety. It would be fine. She said that balancing bikes on the backs of cars could be precarious.

He swore he would drive like a snail, which he did, exactly as had his group captain. So carefully that by the time they had reached St Margaret's at Little Gormson he had slowed the Riley to a crawl.

She could not decide whether the lack of speed was due to his wish to be in her company longer, or whether he wanted her to hear him sing "You're the Tops" in its entirety. As it was, the wind and the engine's noise carried much of it away. He had been shouting something else about music.

Outside the church he stopped and asked her if she wanted to go in. "Don't suppose there are many Nazis lurking inside on a Thursday!" She said yes.

As they walked through the lych gate he told her that most of the fighting was happening on the continent. Hurricanes mainly. One of their R.A.F. fighters had shot down a German bomber laying mines over Clacton. No details available. He didn't know if it was a Spitfire. He was hatless again, and she wondered if other pilots had the same casual attitude to the rules. She liked it.

They stepped into the porch where he stopped, and to her amusement began to sing "I'll See You Again" in a low and tuneful voice. The whole song finished, he pushed open the heavy door. She could feel the warmth of his hand on her back.

Inside they stood for a moment, becoming accustomed to the shadows; listening for sounds other than the wind in the poplars. Light flickered through the stained glass, trees moving outside were sending unpredictable colours across the aisles. There was the smell of warm woodwork, of old books, dead flowers from some wedding. He went to look at the hymn board, saying he hoped they were jolly good tunes.

For want of something to say, she told him this was her family's church, part Saxon, the ceiling noted for its eleventh-century wood-carving. The statues of saints in their niches had survived Oliver Cromwell. He seemed impressed. She led him to a plaque on the south wall, above a row of ornate stalls. Each seat belonged to a member of her family. On the plaque were the names of past members of the Perincall clan. With her finger she traced the name of *Berenice Perincall, deceased 1922.*

He told her his mother had died when he was young. His father had had little time for a lost lad. So prep school it was. His tone was cheerful. For whatever reason they kept their voices low, yet both were keenly aware they were alone.

She was looking up at the twin Christs in the east window, wondering about the ages of the children at Their knees, when Paul Woodborne kissed her suddenly before she had time to decide. She knew the kiss had been perfected on others.

She had been waiting for it for months. Wanted more. And more. He kissed her longer. A loud tapping halted them for a moment, until they had decided it was a branch blown against glass. Then they kissed again.

Slowly he was drawing her away from her family corner, away from the light. She went easily in his arms until they were behind a pillar. The stone was cold on her shoulders. He was kissing her on her forehead, her neck. She felt his hands go down to the buttons on her frock. She let him do as he pleased. He took off his jacket and dropped it at their feet.

Then half pulling, half turning her, he bent her backwards, pushing her down into a row of pews.

This wasn't what she wanted, being shoved into a pew. Not there. She was almost underneath the wooden seat, the hessian flooring rough on her palms. Her head had upended a hassock, rocking it against its neighbour with a thump.

She got back onto her knees, knocking over hassocks like dominoes, trying to crawl from the confining space, the pilot crawling after her. Attempting to right herself, she reached for the shelf above. A prayer book fell on her arm with a bang. Another slid over her shoulder as it dropped. Then another.

He was behind her making a grab at her hips, his fingers slipping over the fabric, prayer books everywhere. She heard her frock tear. Still on all fours, she scrambled from the end of the pew until she had gained the aisle. Its tessellations were indenting her palms, her knees, as she crawled towards the altar.

He was standing back. There was no more attempt to touch her. On her feet now, gasping like a fighter between bouts, she was regarding him warily. She could hear trees outside knocking and knocking.

He went to rescue his jacket, came back to stand waiting while she tried to rearrange her frock, her hair, draw normal breath.

"I didn't want it," she said at last as clearly as she could.

"That was obvious, sweetie."

"It won't do. This is my church. My mother is over there," pointing to the churchyard.

He shrugged. "You're lucky to have one you remember."

She thought he would abandon her as casually as he was treating this episode. Leave her standing in the gloom. But he went over to the font, dipped his handkerchief in the water and dabbed a smudge from her cheek. The light in the church was fast fading. She could not see his expression.

He said he ought to get her home before dark. But he kissed her in the porch. And again in the shelter of the yew.

When they reached the Villa gates she recovered her bike from the Riley, bade him a brief farewell and rode home without turning round, not sure she would be seeing him again.

Charlie came home the next day, with the story that Alice Dance's cousin's fiancé, a sailor on H.M.S. *Glowworm*, had been reported missing in action. A customer had lost their son, an air gunner, over France. Lodford people were talking to one another. In the post office a stranger had been telling of a rise in livestock thefts. A woman from Hingdon was being divorced by her man, away fighting in the services, and everyone knew why.

Vela Kymmerly told Charlie he too would soon be called up. She was having trouble recruiting postmen. Sooner or later telegraph boys would be a thing of the past.

"Yet wouldn't you think," Charlie said, "that more and more telegrams are going to have to be delivered? When people die, that is."

Morgan turned up the volume on the wireless.

"What did he say?" Montague was fretting about the lateness of his tea. She said she did not know what Charlie was saying. So Charlie had to repeat Vela's comment about telegraph boys.

Montague's remark, "At least something good might come out of this war!", left Charlie bewildered.

It was Saturday the eleventh. Montague paid the workers' wages early and went home. He said it was no use sitting round the wireless. But they did, hearing that Nazi forces were invading Holland, Belgium and Luxembourg. The resignation speech of Neville Chamberlain had been a dispiriting one. A coalition government under Winston Churchill was utterly unknown. Were Allied troops sufficient to counter German advances?

The arrival at the Villa of a rag-and-bone man exemplified for Montague what was happening: if Britain were unfortunate it would be torn to pieces and some raptor would pick over what little was left.

On the other hand he told Morgan to be of good heart. That not having heard from Cathcart did not necessarily mean he was at the centre of fighting across the Channel. Her thoughts were more on another man who might, from then on, not have much time for her and philandering. Philandering. She turned the word over, enjoying the syllables.

Wireless reports had been droning on into lunchtime. They made little sense. She could hardly concentrate on which countries they were talking about. The news was not good, however optimistically one tried to look at it. Would Patch find time for her if the war got worse? Or even if it did not? Would he be facing danger before they had a chance to become intimate? Was this horrible conflict really coming closer?

The scale of her father's map was puzzling. What were the sizes of all these countries so packed together? If one country fell to the enemy it looked, to her untrained eye, that the others must fall too. One tracing finger could cover the width of the English Channel, a mere ribbon of water too easily crossed by aircraft. Patch and Charlie at the cricket match had been talking about the manoeuvrability of Messerschmitts and Junkers. What about Spitfires? How good a pilot would Patch have to be? How reliable was his plane?

She was standing, saucepan in hand, when Charlie found her. "Do you miss him?" he asked.

"Who?" She was startled. He might have read her thoughts.

"Cat."

"Who?"

"Cathcart, your husband."

Morgan stared into space for a second then said, "Yes."

Charlie found this hesitation heartening.

St Margaret's Church on Sunday, a smallish congregation. Grandma Perincall and her three daughters had not, as usual, planned to walk from Great Gormson, but accepted Montague's offer to drive them. They might as well enjoy it before the order to immobilise cars was put into force.

Morgan looked for Patch, but he was not there. Few airmen were present and only a small contingent of soldiers, marching in early. She thought it callous to make them walk all the way from the senior school. But Mrs Retchen whispered that army lorries were waiting at the Redwood pub. Myrtle said she expected the soldiers would be thirsty for beer after the Reverend's long sermon.

Morgan sat in the usual Perincall pew, trying to keep her gaze from the place where she had so recently resisted her pilot's advances. She was still wondering about her reasons. Was there regret? Words like "sacrilege" and "condom" flickered through her mind.

Genuflecting during the first notes of the organ, her thoughts were flying. Was she still the unthinking girl she was at seventeen, intent on adventure for its own sake? Had she really not altered since her mother had left her, bereft and rudderless? It was not fair to be denied some morsel of life. She would soon be thirty-three. How long before she would lose any man's interest? And Patch looked so young. She raised her eyes to an oriole window, to the sight of a small demon vomiting a glassy red flame.

Her arm was being nudged by Aunt Harriet, urging her to stand for the psalm: "*I sought the Lord and he answered me, he delivered me from all my fears. Those who look to him are radiant; their faces are never covered in shame,*" which Morgan decided could be taken as an augury.

The Reverend Dorby kept them captive for longer than usual, finishing with exhortations to Be of Good Cheer, Fight the Good Fight and enjoy the church bells, for they might soon have to be saved for emergencies only.

After the service Morgan intercepted the mill manager as he and his wife were leaving. Their daughter Dora was in the W.R.N.S. and she was curious to know whether there might have been any mention of Rhoda. She began by congratulating them on having such a patriotic daughter. Mrs Talbott, head down, was hiding behind her husband. "Where," Morgan asked, "is Dora stationed?"

"Ask the wife," Talbott replied. "It's her what deals with that sort of thing." He walked away. Grace Talbott muttered, "Isle of Wight," as she followed after him.

Coral Floster, resembling Mary Astor, intercepted Morgan at the lychgate. Her husband was deep in conversation with Montague, so there was no escape.

"I would be a little bit careful if I were you," was her opening remark. Morgan knew she was about to add something clever. "The wind can be very chilly in May. Especially in an open-topped car." She beckoned Floster, who looked displeased at having his conversation interrupted. "And you were wearing so very little that evening. One must take pains not to catch cold, it ruins one's looks. No man likes a woman who has lost her . . ." There might have been more, but the sight of someone outside the church gate had diverted her. Mrs Floster waved gracefully and abandoned Morgan to her approaching aunts.

Harriet and Maud asked if that was the woman they had seen at the cricket match. And at whom she was waving. Grandma Perincall arrived beside them. "Who is that airman over there, chatting in that unseemly manner?"

Morgan saw Patch, leaning with one elbow on the church wall. Listening to Coral Floster, he was also scanning the churchyard.

"It's flight lieutenant . . . somebody-or-other."

"He seems very familiar with that woman in the green *voile*. Is she his wife?"

It pleased Morgan to inform her grandmother that Mrs Coral Floster was married to the senior R.A.F. officer in the brand-new uniform, currently in conversation with her father. Out of the corner of her eye she saw Patch leave Mrs Floster's side and make his way towards her.

She prepared to greet him. But to her surprise he passed by her, touching his forehead in a brief salute. He was heading for Charlie, in dialogue with Ronnie Talbott beside the Perincall tomb.

She saw how Woodborne took Charlie's arm, drawing him away from Ronnie, talking as he led him back between the gravestones towards her. They stopped, as if Patch had something important to say to Charlie that could not wait. Now they were within earshot.

An overjoyed Charlie was being told that the flight lieutenant might be able to get him onto Lodford aerodrome. "Look at a crate or two. Who knows, even get you up in a Tiger Moth. Or one of the Avro Tutors." Of course Patch would expect something in return. This said looking in Morgan's direction, but jokingly so that Charlie would not take offence. Her pilot was saying he would love to take a trip in Charlie's boat. It was clear from Charlie's eager expression he had not made the connection between the pilot's interest in him and his sister. How clever of Patch, she thought.

The congregation clearing, Morgan went to join her family. The Flosters were getting into a staff car. Parclay had emerged like a jack in the box from behind the platoon of soldiers. He hurried over to ask Morgan if she was alright after her car journey. The Reverend Dorby's wife, herding her children, was waiting for her husband to finish shaking hands. Only Grandma Perincall showed no sign of wanting to go. She was demanding of Montague whether he knew any of these strangers, and if so would he please introduce some of them. She needed some distraction after the horrible disclosure about Holland. Although Dutch was not pleasant to the ear, she wished that country no harm, finding the language preferable to German. Was he aware that the present Royal Family was of Teutonic origin?

Uncertain which way his mother's thoughts were turning, and seeing his son approaching with the pilots, Montague felt bound to introduce the flight lieutenant and the flying officer to his mother and sisters. Harriet and Maud were quick to point out that they had already had the pleasure of meeting them at the cricket match.

The conversation, although on the subject of bad news, had a cheerful tone that Morgan put down to the two pilots, who seemed incapable of gloom. They were looking forward to some real action. Show Jerry what they were made of. Pity they were forced to kick their heels in Blighty. Charlie hovered, storing for retelling the admission that pilots were less than keen to fly Spitfires at night because, as Parclay put it,

"One can't see a darn thing in them." Grandma Perincall warmed to them. The aunts hung on their words. Bystanders stayed listening with fascination to these potential heroes. When the army contingent marched off, nobody gave it a second glance.

It was Grandma Perincall's suggestion that they go back her house for lunch. His mother's behaviour, Montague told the pilots, was so novel it could not be refused. Both pilots cast questioning glances at Morgan. Her nod of assent went unnoticed by her family.

So the Perincalls, followed by the two airmen in their vehicles, drove east to Great Gormson.

The lunch was an exciting one for everybody but Aunt Winifred, who could not cope with crowds. Her mother stated, "We shall have whatever there is in the cupboard!" as if it were the sort of thing she said every day. Winnie stayed in the kitchen retrieving cold cuts of beef, left-over chicken, slices of lamb destined for the shepherd's pie. It was explained that, with no new crops yet, stored parsnips and carrots would have to do. Peas and lettuce were coming along in the cold frame. By next month asparagus and spinach. But next month, the flight lieutenant said with a laugh, was a very long way off.

Around the table elderflower wine, regaining its sparkle from last year, brought spark to the conversation. Harriet and Maud were gratified by the flight lieutenant's attention. Morgan had to make do with Peter Parclay, telling her of his training days in icy Scotland. He was so easy a companion she found herself immersed in their exchanges.

Charlie listened to Woodborne with respect, adding whatever observations he could. It was his opinion that the Allies fighting in Europe could better help the beleaguered Belgians with more air power. He wanted to be heard as a grown-up with a viewpoint. It was well known, he said, that Winston Churchill saw the war coming long before anyone else. He had probably ordered planes and tanks galore. Both pilots crossed their fingers. The aunts did the same.

Nobody knew much about the new Prime Minister, save for his dubious championing of Mrs Simpson and King Edward, but all felt free to discuss him. It did not seem impolite to air one's views on politics, even religion, at the dining table. That this new release from constraint had been brought about by wine, or the novelty of the situation, hardly mattered. As lunch progressed they righted the wrongs of the Abyssinians, relived Guernica, crossed and recrossed Europe, discussed the Sudetenland and disputed Herr Hitler's plans. Grandma Perincall made futile attempts to move talk back to the safety of crops and climate, for she sensed that this shift in her world might again be a prelude to events escaping beyond her control.

After the main course there miraculously arrived tinned peaches and cold custard sufficient for nine persons. It was here that the flight lieutenant endeared himself to Mrs Perincall by telling her, but not so quietly that the others couldn't hear, how noble she was to have raided her stores on behalf of the air force. He personally would make sure she, and her interesting daughters, would not go short henceforward.

Morgan, with whom he had exchanged barely a word, found her role as onlooker oddly satisfying. She could not predict what her pilot might do, but whatever it was it would be exciting.

At four o'clock, an unheard-of time to finish a Perincall lunch, the party broke up. Into Montague's hands his mother put a bag containing a dozen oysters. Alf Reeble, the owner of the oyster beds at Blytham, had sent them that morning. It would have been impolite to refuse, she explained. Being twelve days into May the season was over for the *cognoscenti*, but perhaps one of his workmen would like them.

Her parting words to Morgan were, "Watch that young man, my girl. He requires little encouragement." She was referring to Parclay.

Loath to see the end of this unique event, Charlie made the daring suggestion that the pilots should come back to the Villa and take a trip on the *Berenice*. If real war was just around the corner, there was little time to keep Woodborne to his bargain. Montague told him he did not approve of wasting fuel, but was persuaded by the others into agreement.

Not wanting to lose high water, Charlie, with his father, escorted the pilots to the boathouse. Morgan was left in the house alone.

The air was warm. Lapwings could still be heard in the meadows. But by the time the four men had grappled with the barbed wire, found a way through and trudged along the shore to the dinghy, the tide had turned.

So there would be no jaunt downstream, for Montague had changed his mind. Although he allowed everyone to board he kept the *Berenice* at anchor, saying it would be unpatriotic to put to sea for no reason. The pilots, somewhat perplexed, could do nothing but acquiesce.

Having found there was little to explore on a cruiser her size, they had to content themselves with lolling on deck. There they sat staring longingly in the direction of the estuary.

Heaviness, caused by the elderflower wine, came over them. The descent from jollity was in part due to the absence of admiring women who had buoyed them up all afternoon. And partly having to listen to their host's lengthy appreciation of wheat. This was interspersed with Charlie's laudation of the cruiser's beam and draft, its engine and fuel capacity and reliability at sea. The pilots stretched out and stared skyward.

A light wind had risen, the *Berenice* slowly moving with the tide. Montague thought there might be a squall out to sea that night. The pilots said no, claiming weather knowledge. This started a desultory kind of argument. Not even an argument, more a kind of fractious repetition of each man's opinion on the likelihood or not of storms in the North Sea.

Their voices, to-ing and fro-ing like the rocking boat, lapsed into longer and longer silences, broken at last by Parclay, saying he was feeling nauseous. That was why, he explained, he had not chosen the navy. Montague said it was more than time to get them into the dinghy and back to dry land.

Long before they had approached the boathouse and tied up, Morgan's agitated cries had reached them. She was standing on the beach waving her arms. They did their best, stumbling over the pebbles, each man feeling guilt at having left her unprotected.

It was Granny Dorp, she explained, who had come out of nowhere. Berating his daughter for deserting her grandmother, Montague hurried the party back.

At the front door he decided it would be preferable if the R.A.F. left the family to deal with the situation alone. Parclay, still queasy and apologetic, agreed and said a hasty farewell. Flight Lieutenant Woodborne lingered behind. A few moments later he was following the family, at a distance, into the house.

Granny Dorp was in the second sitting room, a bowl of tapioca in her lap, tapioca around her mouth and on her frock, some on the sofa. To Montague's relief his mother-in-law called him Monty and waved her spoon at Charlie. She considered Morgan for a minute. "She's got her mother's nose. But has she got her nerve?"

Then, "Who's that?" The spoon was pointing at the flight lieutenant stepping out of the shadows. He saluted. Granny Dorp smiled, mistaking him for Cathcart. "So here he is. Thought you were a-fighting."

Morgan's efforts to clean up her grandmother and the upholstery were ended by a flailing spoon.

"What are you doing here, Granny?"

She pointed towards the west. Only Charlie understood that, wanting fresh air, she may have walked into the barbed wire across the top of Hatts Lane. Hence the ripped frock, the scratched arm.

"Would you like me to escort your grandmother home? In my roadster of course."

The others looked at the flight lieutenant in alarm, frightened by the spectre of Granny Dorp in the open-topped Riley impulsively opting for fresher air. Montague said he would not hear of it. He and Morgan would drive his mother-in-law home. But the look on Granny Dorp's face as her granddaughter tried to lift her up convinced him that he would have to take Charlie.

It was a lengthy task persuading her to go home. At last she allowed herself to be taken to the Rover. Woodborne followed them and got into his Riley. They drove off. Morgan watched, dismayed at Patch's cavalier attitude. He had scarcely said goodbye.

She went back indoors feeling spent and morose. Nothing good ever happened. Her life was like this horrible war, getting worse. She would end up like her grandmother, a crazy old woman shouting profanities at all and sundry. She grabbed her apron, collected the chickens' corn and went to feed them.

Patch was standing underneath the lilac tree, its perfume sending waves of sweetness she would remember later as his. His jacket was slung over his shoulder. He pulled a face as if to say he couldn't help being there. She took him back into the Villa, where evening shadows were beginning to penetrate the corners of rooms.

Upstairs in her bedroom the heat still lingered. A bluebottle was battering itself against a windowpane. She pushed aside the coverlet and motioned for Patch to sit beside her. Taking his time, he undid the top buttons of her frock. With light fingers he touched her throat, calling her "sweetie" in a low voice close to her ear. His other hand stopped, hovering over her upper leg where stocking met thigh. She could feel the melting heat of him. Her suspenders were tricky, but he managed them adequately. Now he was rolling down her stockings.

The part of her that was not experiencing the thrill of his touch was assessing this performance with dispassion. Her mind was saying yes, he was doing well. Yes. But her body wanted it faster. On a practical level she hoped the rest wasn't going to be too slow, because there was no telling how long it might take Pa and Charlie to settle Granny Dorp.

"You are dangerously lovely," Patch whispered, which made her grin. Hadn't Tyrone Power said something similar to Sonja Henie? She drew him onto the pillow so that he could kiss her properly, which he did. He was not a messy kisser like Enoch Lucas, nor did he force his tongue into her mouth that even Cat sometimes attempted. A delicious sense of what was to follow came over her, a kind of nostalgia, coupled with that sense of adventure lost since her marriage. This time it was going to be alright.

Patch had toppled onto his side and was struggling to remove his trousers. She opened her eyes. Two wasps were circuiting the ceiling. She wished it could be like the pictures where the lovers lay in each other's arms without uncomfortable preliminaries. It occured to her, as he helped remove her camisole, that one never saw film stars naked. Or, for that matter, in the same bed. One of them always seemed to have a foot on the floor.

He was murmuring again into her ear. Poetical words like "Yonder" and "Velvet". Outside the window a thrush started a loud song. The trees were making a rushing sound, as if the wind had picked up. She thought she could hear the roar of motors along the Gormson Road.

Patch raised his head and looked at her. Her breasts were now exposed, but he made no move to touch them. "Look here, sweetie, this won't do. One must concentrate. Really."

She raised herself on her elbows. "This is a mistake."

"Oh, not again!"

"I cannot concentrate like this." She looked at his erection. "How you can manage it is a miracle to me."

It was enough. He was already scrambling into his clothes, urging her to do the same. In minutes they had left her bedroom, gathering his jacket, her shoes from the stairs as they went.

He led her from the Villa at a run, through the garden's scent, around the chickens, startled and scattering. The thrush, ceasing in mid song, rose in the air. The turf was soft under her bare feet. She was being pulled across the grassy mound towards the chestnut trees, laughing at the adventure. At the boundary of the cricket pitch he carried her through the high grass and weeds, setting her down at the pavilion.

It was still unlocked. The scent of spring gave way to the familiar smell of old wood, heated by days of sunshine. This time there was no demur. As soon as he shut the door they were snatching at each other's clothes. They were on their knees. They were lying side by side, his kisses as hot as hers, his exploring hands as urgent. She knew how little time men needed to fulfill their wants. But time was what she needed.

That he took his time took her by surprise. He was kissing her methodically, on her neck and shoulders and breasts. But in the still centre of his kisses the questions would not stop whirling: why isn't he listening for sounds outside? How can he give such leisurely gratification in these circumstances? Why is his passion not speeding him on? Is this sort of affair customary with him? Does this mean anything to him? Why is this turning out to be almost unsatisfactory?

She was the first to come to climax, which she had not experienced since the early days of Cat. Yet in a corner of her mind, along with the delicious descent, came immediate anxiety. It was there, the abiding fear that had first been fixed in her at fifteen.

Patch climaxed with a gasp. And at that exact moment she pushed him away with such force he gave a cry. His sperm spilled onto the wooden floor. A stack of chairs came clattering down from the wall. Pink faced, he lay panting.

She was sorry. He said it was alright. He explained he had got carried away a bit and apologised. Couldn't think what had happened to his French letters. No fuss about his rights, like Cathcart. No bemoaning the lost final thrill. She thought him noble.

The flight lieutenant stood up with a smile, rearranged his uniform, helped find her knickers. And, as briskly, told her he must go. So that was that. What about the Riley? The car was nicely hidden, he said, parked behind the Redwood.

On their return from Hatts Lane, Montague and Charlie sensed nothing suspicious. The old lady had gone to bed like an angel. If Charlie thought that Morgan looked unusually contented, he imagined she must have been pleased with the way he had behaved on that unique Sunday.

It was with detachment that Morgan faced the following week's reports, which were bad. Mr Churchill's words about "Blood, Toil, Tears and Sweat" had Montague shaking his head. Such stirring sentiments, in his opinion, were always saved for moments of real peril. Unless he was mistaken, or Mr Churchill was more dramatic actor than politician, the country was on the verge of times more terrible than anything so far.

Now, as he read *"Without victory there is no survival"*, there came to him in horrible detail visions of men dying in the mud of the Somme. He pictured again civilians uprooted and left to fend for themselves; aimless wandering bands of women, children, young and old with nothing. If this happened in the tiny islands of Great Britain, where would its homeless people find refuge? Wherever they went, would they not be entrapped by a war that Montague feared would far outdo the last one?

Although he was trying harder to rein in these fears, he had begun to notice how Morgan was changing. His guess was that she too was preparing for what was to come and, for Charlie's sake, was attempting an equanimity she did not feel.

On the evening that Holland's capitulation was announced, she just went on sewing. A feeling of compassion came over Montague. His daughter's losses were already great. Little as she mentioned the children – how thankful he was they were in Gloucestershire – she must be missing them sorely. What mother would not? Added to this was the absence of Cathcart, who might, in the present climate, never return. Montague decided, on 18 May, that from then on he would keep his concerns to himself – especially a new Admiralty directive – for as long as possible.

It was different at the mill. Some of the men were wanting their call-up papers to come soon. They said the building, a vital source of supply, was a serious target. He had already voiced the same thought. There was talk of forming vigilante groups to police the Lodbrook's banks and nearby lanes, the Perincall fields in case of invasion. There had been rumours of deliberate flooding of the marshes.

While forecasts came faster and faster, decision among the mill hands seemed to falter; in some a sense of fatality, even surrender. In others a desire to stand up and fight. Such disparity of views made Montague aware how much his workers were affected by their home lives. His manager's attitude, from the day the Allies withdrew from

Antwerp, was fatalistic. His one opinion, expressed repeatedly, was that they would soon be done for. And he was the one with the Union Jack in his garden. For this, Montague put the blame on the shoulders of both Mrs Grace Talbott, whom he considered a mealy, miserable person, and her daughter Dora, who had deserted them long before it was necessary, just like Rhoda Swell.

Four days later there was genuine panic among the workers when news broke that the Nazis had reached the English Channel. Montague put this to good use by calling on his men to put their shoulders to the wheel to save the country from starvation. He was taking a leaf out of Mr Churchill's book. His exhortations, although not as stirring, had the intended result and the millstones ground longer thereafter.

He was at pains to point out to the pessimists that should wives take over their jobs for the duration, their wages, although reduced, would be shared by their families. This had happened during the last war. His men could take equal heart from the fact that after 1918 women had gone back quietly to hearth and home.

The information that Montague had kept from Morgan was received from the Admiralty as early as 14 May – "*the Admiralty requests all owners of self-propelled craft from 30 to 100 foot to send all particulars within 14 days*". It could only mean one thing, that the forces fighting in France and Belgium were in dire trouble and needed help.

He had shown it to Charlie, who might have grasped its implications if he had not been so excited. This impending adventure was better than any escaped bullock on market day. Morgan had heard the same message over the wireless, had told him there was a crisis across the Channel. That same hour Montague sent Charlie out to the *Berenice* to check her seaworthiness.

Morgan warned Charlie not to count on his father taking him with him. Montague asked his men for volunteers. Bernard Talbott offered himself and the *Clara*, revising his boss's opinion of him. Ronnie would be his co-pilot. With Montague would sail two workers, Cyril and his mate. Along the coast other men with serviceable craft were volunteering fast. The mood had changed once more, yet no-one knew exactly what would be required of them.

During the next twelve days news arrived from many sources, including the ever-present wireless. Generally it was of the buoyant variety, explaining that the withdrawal of the B.E.F. from France into Belgium was purely strategic, not the retreat that some pessimists imagined.

Boat owners contacted others, telling of the round-up of craft large and small, up and down the length of the south-east coast.

A new kind of activity was gripping Lodford. Military and air force personnel were close to outnumbering inhabitants. Gas masks were not left at home, air raid sirens no longer considered only tests. The newly formed Local Defence Volunteers were inundated with men too old for active service, but prepared to put up road blocks and bear arms again. Strangers were looked on with renewed suspicion. Could they be the forerunners of a full-scale Nazi invasion? The aerodrome was daily filled with the noise of aircraft. On the Gormson Road, traffic set up a regular humming throughout the days and nights. Through the Villa's open windows it reached the ears of those trying to sleep. Preparations for occupancy of the Anderson shelter were concluded.

Morgan's composure was tilted this way and that by clandestine visits from Patch. If he managed to lure her away to the pavilion, drive her to some trackless lane instead of the shops, even steal a few moments at her door, it was sufficient for the time being. She had put aside any reflection on the depth of his feelings. The children were safe in Barmford. Heaven knows where Cathcart was. So, if she was soon to die, and Patch was soon to die, it was better they make the most of the present. Patch had said as much himself.

She remembered the heroine of some picture at the Prittend Gaumont with exactly the same feelings. In aligning herself with film stars Morgan felt safe. She could be sure that she was not in love, only with the idea of it. It saved her from her special interpretation of guilt. For this she was thankful, and slept better than she should in the face of bleak prophesies. Only a pity the star had to die at the finale because, as every picture-goer knew, heroines must always pay for their sins.

A dour, grey-haired man, claiming to be a billeting officer, came to the Villa on 25 May. The Retchen sisters hid in the pantry until Morgan made him swear he truly was looking for billets, and had not come to strangle them. For him the promised identity cards could not come soon enough.

He declared Charlie's childhood bedroom fit for use. When she told him that Rhoda's bedroom was only temporarily vacant, he made a note. Morgan refused to let him make a note of the fourth bedroom, repeating her father's assertion that it was awaiting her maternal grandmother. About the attic he made no comment.

Together he and she toured the house, peering into sitting rooms, dining room, box rooms, kitchen, pantry and larder, even the cellar, as if they might house a few infantrymen. She gave him tea that did nothing to sweeten him. He said the "billetee" would bring a ration card. It might mean extra provisions, depending on classification. His prime advice was to wean the family off biscuits and jam. He made no comment at the sight of crates stacked beside the back door, along with Montague's waterproof clothing, sea boots and kit bag. She told him her father, a hero of the last war, was going on a dangerous mission. Did he know that Belgium was about to surrender?

His parting comment, that the fortunate should aid the needy, meant that the Villa Rouge would not wait long for a newcomer.

The following days flew by in a welter of preparation and alarm. Ack-ack fire rumbled ominously in the distance and had everyone looking skyward for an invisible enemy. The alert sounded more than once, sending them into the shelter, to emerge at the all-clear none the wiser.

Prices in the shops were rising. There had been huge losses of planes in France. A barrage balloon had been seen over the sea at Prittend. There was talk that the wireless factory would be moving to the country.

A Treachery Act was passed in Parliament. Beetle Drives at the Women's Institute had been cancelled. All aids to the enemy, such as signposts, were being removed. The secret installation at Iverdon was housing something called R.D.F., whose rays might be fatal to local health. On the next tide all seaworthy craft would be called to muster. No idea so far of their destination.

Visitors to the Villa were more numerous than usual. It was as if everyone had heard about the departure of the small craft and wanted to come and see for themselves.

A knife grinder arrived early and unasked, pedalling his cumbersome tricycle near to the barbed wire. He and the baker's boy stood together with the milkman. They were gesticulating towards the east, at the sky, at the cruisers riding high on the spring tide. A detail of sappers, who had been out that morning scouring the river with binoculars, moved them away.

Morgan and Charlie were in different moods. Hers, mingled with some excitement, was of resignation that Patch might be absent for an unspecified time. Charlie was angry that Montague would not allow him to join the voyage. That he was being left in charge did nothing for his frustration. He spent little time in the Villa, absenting himself until late, coming home to work in the garden then shutting himself in his room.

It was the evening of 25 May. Montague asked Morgan where Little Josh was. "What have you done with him, eh?" Her father's jocular manner was somehow threatening.

"Charlie's off somewhere, I suppose. I do wish you would not call him by that silly name, Pa." She was watching him covertly, trying to gauge his mood. He had been getting back home very late for the last two days, saying little and looking distracted. She never remembered him so tired.

"I can call him what I like. It is as much my business as it is yours. If not more." He left the room. She could hear him in the lobby still worrying over his needs on the *Berenice*. He then went upstairs.

It occurred to her that she had not studied her father so acutely for years. One looked into one's baby's eyes for signs of discomfort, disharmony. She had learned to look at her husband, but not her father. Until now Pa was what he was. Late in the day she was trying to assess his character in a situation as unsettling as it appeared perilous.

She thought it curious that her father had changed into a suit and lovat tie. After supper she heard a motorcar stopping. Hurriedly he rose to his feet. Then it became clear why he had changed his clothes: Coral Floster's unmistakable voice outside could be heard giving instructions to her husband. Her air of command was at odds with his apologetic demeanour. Following behind was flying officer Parclay, holding a dog rose. He offered it to Morgan, on whose lips was her most important question.

"Patch . . . er, Flight Lieutenant Woodborne, cannot come, I'm afraid. Soon to be airborne. Like most of us." He seemed truly sad for her.

Morgan dropped the rose and prepared to give her guests a drink, wondering whether alcohol was too celebratory for a leave-taking.

Mrs Floster cut through the hospitality by peremptorily asking her husband to go and wait in the car. The group captain did as he was told.

"Flustered Floster!" Parclay whispered in Morgan's ear. His arm was around her shoulder. As was the arm of Montague around Coral Floster's waist.

Morgan's next shock was to see her father and Mrs Floster side by side on the first stair.

"Pa! For heaven's sake, where are you going?" No reply. The pair continued upward. "She is a married wom—" She was muffled by Parclay's hand over her mouth.

For a few seconds there was quiet, save for a blackbird warbling in the twilight. Parclay still held her in a firm grasp. Then he kissed her. She tried to pull away, aware that her father and Mrs Floster had stopped on the landing and were watching them over the banisters. The flying officer kissed her again.

She heard her father call, "Pot calling kettle black, if you ask me!"

Then came Coral Floster's high-pitched laugh, fading as the couple went on towards Montague's bedroom.

A few minutes later Charlie came in via the back door. He had made no sound, and expressed no surprise at seeing people in the hall.

Morgan asked him what was the matter.

"Nothing." She waited. "Piglets. Twelve of them she's had," he muttered, but on his face was the blackest of looks. He was glaring at Parclay.

CHAPTER SIX

Charlie and Morgan were at the foot of the Villa stairs, barred by the first rays of early sunlight.

He had been standing for several minutes before fetching her. "What's he doing up there?"

"Sorting his socks."

"He's never done that before."

"Yes he has. When Mother died he did the same. Pa went into their bedroom and sorted his socks. It means something."

"Perhaps he wants you to darn them," Charlie whispered, in what she thought was a nastier tone than usual. "I've got plenty of holes in mine."

"This is no time to be facetious. Pa is going soon."

"I don't suppose he said when. Nobody tells me anything. I just have to work it out for myself."

"Won't be long now."

Since yesterday, when all visitors had departed, near peace had descended on the Villa. Charlie was still downcast. The Retchen twins had not come as usual, perhaps due to their mother's misplaced notion that, on the day of his departure, the captain should be left with his family. What Morgan really needed was for the twins to put their special order into a house made chaotic by events. She wanted rooms cleaned and beds stripped, especially the double bed in what was once her parents' room, now her father's, to rid it of the lingering presence of Coral Floster.

Saying goodbye to him was being overridden by a desire to disinfect the scene of his betrayal. However irrational this might be, and she knew it was, she could not help it. Her father had betrayed her mother with Coral Floster and that was that.

If Morgan had told Charlie he might have asked, 'What about Rhoda?' But somehow she did not count. This anomaly was not something that Morgan wanted to probe. All that was presently bothering her was how, or whether, to broach the subject of her father cuckolding the group captain.

After a breakfast that decimated the rations and after demanding a mound of sandwiches that used up more, Montague asked his daughter to come into the garden.

She followed him willingly, hoping to hear some explanation for the previous evening's betrayal. He might tell her he had, like her, behaved on a whim, with an unstoppable rush of heat to the loins. She was ready to believe that deprivation might have caused it, although it was distasteful to imagine one's parent indulging in sex.

Charlie at the back door was halted by a wave of Montague's hand. He pulled a face and stayed put. Morgan went out with her father.

"Little Josh has a bone to pick with me!" How could her pa be so lighthearted? "Fine day for sailing," he said. "But not for him." There was a light breeze. He wetted his finger and pointed upward, saying jokingly like a schoolboy, *"Fair stood the wind for France."*

At the corner of the house she blurted out, "How could you, Pa?" But when he asked her how could he what, she had not the nerve to continue. They toured the vegetable garden as if he had all the time in the world. He said that Charlie had better water the runners, for it could be a scorching summer. Soot from the chimneys was best for the asparagus. And salt air. Berenice had liked a nice plate of it with lemon. "No more lemons for a while though."

From her mother's favourite rose bush he picked a bud and tried to stick it into a buttonhole. It fell, and he stepped on it when they crossed the lawn. She had no idea where they were going. His need, she sensed, was for movement of any kind.

At the gate he picked up the fallen bars and laid them aside. "Get this mended," he said. "And . . . get a buck and a doe. I've told Charlie before, he won't catch much with those snares or that gun." Two more steps and another instruction: "Ask Brodir, or that friend of Charlie's, to get you a hutch with sweet hay. No lettuce. Not good for rabbits. Never liked it much myself."

He was leading the way around the fence, past the chickens, across the grassy mound, down to the ponds. Yellow irises were reflecting in the water. A dragonfly, sparkling pink, skimmed over them. There was the plop of a fish or a vole.

For a minute she thought they were going to sit on the grass. But her father stood, gazing in the direction of the piggery. "I've made arrangements." He was speaking slowly. She waited. "The women from the mill cottages –" pointing in their direction – "they will do shift work filling flour bags, so you won't need to take a turn."

She was astonished that her father could even have considered such an occupation for his daughter. "Charlie will be supervised in the office," he continued. "With help from the army, lorries should not be too much of a problem." He was almost talking to himself. "Might have to use horses and wagons if the worst happens." He still was not looking at her. "Bear in mind they are bound to keep it running. Paperwork won't be your concern. Threw's a good man, as land agents go. And he'll be watched by Grouming." It was too much.

"Finance so far is good." For the first time looked squarely at her. "Which brings me to you." This, she knew, was serious. "Go to see Maurice Grouming. He'll know what to do."

"Pa! Why are you talking as if you are not coming back?" Her father's behaviour with Mrs Floster had become secondary.

He continued. "Give it a month or two. I've seen to it you'll have enough to keep you going for a time. The banded box in my drawer . . . Be cautious about showing it. Josh has not quite yet grasped the value of money. And don't tell the boy anything he cannot deal with."

With that he started back to the Villa, asking if she had understood, adding that if they stayed any longer the stink of pigs would cling to them forever.

Morgan helped her father into his seaman's jacket. Charlie fetched his boots, and returned in time to see him pocketing a gun he had never seen before.

"Webley Mark IV. 11.6 calibre, I think. Been with me all through the last war. I would have preferred a captured Luger." The idea made him laugh. Looking enviously at the pistol, Charlie wished he had something better than a puny rifle.

"Josh, I want you to get to the barber's." Charlie was already agreeing, although Morgan could see his hair was recently trimmed. "They'll run the Derby for certain. I want you to put one pound each way on anything ridden by Gordon Richards. Understand?" And to Charlie's question, Montague replied, "The money's in the shell case on my dressing table." He continued, "And if that horse wins, put it on something good in the St Leger. If they run that this year."

"But the St Leger isn't until September." Charlie's comment was not lost on Morgan.

Montague continued packing jumpers, navigation charts, a compass, into his kit bag. It was evident much thought had been given to everything.

A tapping on the back door. Ronnie Talbott had been sent, he said, to help load the *Berenice*. It was time to leave.

"Don't you get up to any mischief while I'm gone, Little Josh," Montague told him. "And I don't want a sending-off party. Just her, Morgan."

"What mischief? What do you mean, Pa?"

"He knows what I mean."

She walked with him from the garden, across the drive to where the wild grass began. In the distance the masts of small boats could be seen, already turning with the tide. On all craft large and small were signs of activity. The sun, shining on Union Flags and ensigns, was adding a festive air. Cruisers were already heading downriver, the noise of their engines fading as they rounded the bend.

Still talking as they approached the river's edge, her father said that Threw would be doing his usual round of farms. Those rents would be left in Grouming's capable hands.

But Morgan must remember that her mother, always thoughtful, had put her house, her family and the business before her own needs. It was a reminder to be conscientious. His mother and sisters could always be relied upon for guidance. As for Granny Dorp, her farewell advice to her son-in-law, he smiled, had been to avoid mermaids.

They had gone beyond gravel onto shingle, then sand. The barbed wire had been separated. They walked along the shore skirting onlookers, mainly women, the tide lapping at their feet.

Her father was walking fast and she had trouble keeping up. She was aware that his demeanour was unusual. His hands were twitching or shaking. She hoped the heavy oilskin might be the cause of his sweating face.

"Code name 'Dynamo'," he muttered. "Sheerness. After that, God knows! But they will likely head to the beaches around Ostend. Or further south to Dunkirk."

At the boathouse men were untying their dinghies. She recognised one or two workers, but nobody acknowledged her. Ronnie Talbott, swamped by a pair of thigh waders impeding his efforts to push a ladder, looked in danger of toppling into the water. His father, already starting the motor, was urging his son to get a move on.

Montague said "You know what your mother's last words to me were?"

"Was it 'Dynamo'?"

"Nonsense, girl! She's been dead these eighteen years. Her words were 'Three, four, seven, five, seven, three'."

She waited, thinking her father's nerves had given way. He put his arm around her and drew her to him. "Our Co-op number," he whispered. "Use it when I'm gone."

There was the smell of petrol, tobacco. Montague climbed in the dinghy and started the outboard. "Don't you go upsetting the boy needlessly," he called. And he was away towards Cyril and his mate, the waiting crew.

Morgan stayed watching the *Berenice* and the *Clara* raising anchors.

Leaving. The sun was bright on waving hands. The boats still in sight and no more waving, she did not linger, abandoning the scene to go back to Charlie.

He spoke very little until mid afternoon. He had eaten his eggs and bread fried in dripping, so she ceased thinking he might be unwell. And that was all there was in the larder. There had been little time for shopping. When she asked if he minded making do with corned beef, he replied that nobody was interested in what he thought.

An unexpected bout of claustrophobia sent her outside with her knitting. Charlie followed. He sat on the grass, his back to her, facing the almost empty river; looking at sparrows squabbling in the hedges, at puffballs of cloud, at anything other than Morgan.

He began a rambling tirade, some of it drowned by the roar of aircraft. Starlings, adding to the din, were preventing her from following his complaint. As its main drift became clearer, she began to pay proper attention.

Charlie was saying he had come home the previous evening just before dark. First it was the car. Then the cigarette smoke. The smoker was standing under the trees. He had shouted "Hey there!" for it might have been a Nazi in disguise, but it was only Group Captain Floster. The group captain was unresponsive and Charlie didn't know what to say anyway. But it was strange seeing him standing there, looking at his feet and smoking like that. Especially so late in the evening.

A May bug landed with a thump on Morgan's knitting. With a shriek she shook it off, making an unnecessary fuss, for Charlie was going to say something unpleasant. "I am going indoors. It's too dangerous out here." With luck he would not follow her. But he did.

She escaped to the large sitting room, thinking the mirrors would make it seem larger. All around were reflections from glass-fronted cabinets whose contents were recasting images from photographs in silver frames, from pictures on the wall reflecting the cabinets, the photographs. It was too much. She was in a shooting gallery of light. Her pa had gone, leaving her as Charlie's target. She quit the room in a hurry.

Charlie found her in the small sitting room, trying to concentrate on a sock.

"I hate knitting. Whoever invented the 'Victory Wonder Sock' ought to be locked up with it. In a room like this."

He picked up the ball of air-force-blue wool. "Who is this for?"

She snatched it back. "No-one in particular. The Women's Institute collects them and sends them off to the armed forces."

But he thought he knew. "I was telling you something out there." Deliberately oafish he thumped down in Montague's armchair.

Silence.

"Are you coming to church this evening?" There was no reply. "Church, Charles?"

He would not be deflected. "That Floster chap was waiting for some-one out there last evening."

"I am not in the least interested in what the group captain was doing. And I asked if you were coming to church."

"No. What good will prayers do where Pa's going? Our army's cut off, Eden says. Our boats won't stand a chance against the Luftwaffe. They will strafe them." He wanted her to notice the word "strafe", recently learned from the postman. He began staring at her like Bela Lugosi, a look that he hoped she would recognise. His childish gurning had amused her, but not now.

"Do stop that silly nonsense. Get on with what you have to say and be done with it."

"I saw something yesterday."

Had he somehow seen her father and Coral Floster going to his bedroom? This would have been impossible, unless Charlie had already been in the house, upstairs perhaps. No, she would have seen him pass her in the hall.

"I was going round to the back door."

"What's unusual about that?" If one's shoes were dirty, one went the long way round to the unlocked back door. If reasonably clean, one opened the front door with a key.

"I looked through that little window."

"So?" Knowing that attack was best, she said, "Great merciful heavens Charles, get on with it!" Adding, "Whatever you thought you saw."

"I saw you kissing flying officer Parclay. Kissing him is what I saw."

With relief she laughed loudly. "Is that all?" Her mind was whirring, wondering what else he might have seen. "I thought at the very least you'd seen a rhinoceros!" She would have liked to ask him if he had gone upstairs. But she knew he had headed for one of the downstairs rooms.

Later she found Charlie huddled in the snug, his ear close to the wireless.

"Why were you kissing that chap?"

So he knew nothing about Montague and Mrs Floster.

"I was not kissing him. He was kissing me." Which was the literal truth. She added, "He was saying goodbye."

Charlie said, "I don't believe you."

"You heard on the wireless what a state things are in. He must go and fight. For you and me. Fly dangerous aircraft. For us. This country!" She was deliberately raising her voice. "He wanted to say goodbye to you too, but you were very rude and barely said a word."

She was uncertain of his reaction, nor why it should matter to her. Was she protecting his innocence, afraid he might think of copying Montague's behaviour? Or protecting herself from any hint of impropriety? Whatever it was, she wanted Charlie unchanged and unsuspicious as he had always been.

"Group Captain Floster was waiting for flying officer Parclay *outside*."

"So what does that suggest to you, Sherlock?"

"There were cigarette butts on the ground. How long had that chap been kissing you?"

She rose defiantly, tapping him on the head. "I did not time it. The subject is closed, Charles. I am going to church and you should come with me."

"No thanks. Better pray for yourself. And him!" was his parting shot.

Her aunts reprimanded her for Charlie's absence. Montague would not have approved. Now that he was gone there should be no malingering. To Morgan's riposte concerning the absent Grandma Perincall, Harriet said her mother had a headache brought on by Monty's departure. Winnie was administering *sal volatile*.

The church was surprisingly empty. No military, no men in the choir and only a small contingent of the British Legion, whose oversized Empire Day flag had to be parked outside the porch. The Reverend Dorby's sermon included many exhortations to prolong this special day of prayer until all loved ones had returned. They sang "Onward Christian Soldiers" before the blessing, to underline the solemnity of this occasion.

Morgan walked home with Mrs Retchen and the twins. The girls babbled on in their usual way, about the Reverend's wonky wig, the disappearance of all the boats from the river, the bad luck magpie crossing their path, what there would be for supper.

The women had known each other long enough to not talk, though the silence was not particularly friendly. For Morgan had long disapproved of Mrs Retchen's familiarity, not only with Montague, but with her mother whom she had called Berenice.

Why Mrs Retchen chose this particular moment to mention Mrs Perincall was clear. She said that in times of peril one missed one's loved ones more than ever. "Your dear mother, God bless her, would be putting all her prayers into them who's gone to sea."

The evening, although still warm, was causing a heaviness in Morgan she had no wish to explore. She was missing Patch. She had not yet had time to miss her father. How Charlie would cope at work without him was problematic. He would have to handle that alone. If some serviceman or woman were foisted on the Villa, there would be more work than ever for her to do. Her thoughts as she walked were centred on how to charm Mrs Retchen, a not-so-easily charmed woman, into working at the Villa again alongside her daughters. When they reached the gates she still had not posed the question, telling herself there would be time later.

*

On 27 May Belgium capitulated, its army surrendered to the Nazis. In France the port of Calais, a few miles across the Channel, had fallen. Danger was getting closer.

Now it was the twenty-eighth. Montague had been gone two days. Reports on the wireless continued as dismal as the atmosphere in the Villa. Nothing but how "our brave forces, fighting a rearguard action" were being evacuated. With the aid of thousands of little ships manned by "ordinary British men from all walks of life". The area between Great Yarmouth and Folkestone had been designated an evacuation zone.

"That includes us," Morgan told Charlie. "Once they're home they will be able to fight another day."

He seemed to have sunk into a kind of dull trance, going to the mill before time, returning for a solid lunch. Coming home in the evening earlier than usual to consume a large supper.

Perhaps she should have shown him Peter Parclay's letter, since it contained an apology for having kissed her. It was the first time she had received such a letter of friendship. It was confusing. There was no clue to Peter's feeling, other than the end where he had signed it "*with all my love*", which Charlie would not have approved of.

Charlie continued in his silence. After tending the garden and feeding the chickens he was absent until dusk. Morgan thought he might be worrying over Montague.

His mood was not her first concern. Her period was unusually late. For many days, racing thoughts about Patch, Cathcart, Charlie, had kept her irrationally in thrall. She was glad of his taciturnity. It gave her space to think what she might have to do. There was not a soul she could turn to. She had been stupid. She was selfish. She had only herself to blame.

When her period arrived at last, the problem was sanitary towels, since the chemist in Lodford had run out. She could not, would not, endure using rags that would have to be washed. That would have been Rhoda's answer. No, she would go into Prittend. And if Charlie could be persuaded to take the afternoon off, with a promise of driving the

Rover and the pictures, she would be saved embarrassment. What Charlie knew about women's personal problems was a question Morgan had no wish to contemplate.

If only she could drive. Her father had refused to teach her before she was twenty-one. By then she had left home. She had even thought of asking Mr Boxley for lessons. For hadn't the milkman boasted of buying an Austin 8 "with nice leather seats and a lovely fascia"? She could see herself at the wheel of Patch's Riley, speeding through a sylvan countryside, to distant places where no-one knew them.

"The Lady Vanishes" was on at the Prittend Gaumont. She sent Charlie to buy the tickets while she made her private purchases.

They thought the film was good. Charlie prefered "Donald's Better Self", although having been deprived of the cinema for so long, any cartoon would have been fine. The newsreel reports were too graphic for Morgan: "*Every kind of boat from all over the southeast is bringing the British Expeditionary Forces home from Dunkirk by some means or another. These brave heroes are risking life and limb in the service of their country at its time of need. Thanks to their heroism thousands of British and French are being saved.*" She closed her eyes when the music swelled over hundreds of men in the sea, holding their guns over their heads, wading shoulder deep towards their saviours. Were her father and his crew on the *Berenice* already there waiting, gunfire cracking above them? Was it possible to rescue so many vulnerable souls? She couldn't hear or smell it, but she knew the reality was a thousand times worse than what was on the screen.

The Pathé News seemed not to have had any effect on Charlie. He had cheered up enough to want to walk along the sea front. She warned him of the changes to Prittend, a town he had always liked. He said they wouldn't bother him. For the first time she was aware of how little externals impinged on him, as long as he had all her attention. Or as long as he got his own way. Was he like her in that respect? Or was it that she was coming to care more for him, and therefore noticing more? "Botheration!" she said to herself.

The sun, lighting the barbed wire coiling for miles along the beach, was still warm enough for a stroll, the sight made less dismal by hundreds of perching seagulls, white and grey on silver. The pier, stretching out through metallic water, was closed to civilians. They saw soldiers, some going back and forth, others leaning over the rails smoking, as if it were just another Wednesday. Now and then the peace was broken by a plane flying past, which Charlie claimed he could identify.

On the esplanade they passed rows of boarding houses, now the billets of soldiers and sailors. Charlie wanted to revisit the fairground. It had been boarded up. Beside a large CLOSED notice had been tacked a poster. "MEN OF ACTION NEED BRYLCREEM". They could still make out the tops of the bowl slide and the helter skelter.

"Let's not go any further. I'm finding it too drab."

Pointing at the grey shape of a tanker out to sea, Charlie said he didn't suppose many of its crew were worrying about hair cream.

They turned back towards higher ground. "The bandstand is still looking good." Morgan said, pointing at the gold work. "Now they will be playing military music."

"I liked Sousa marches," Charlie remarked. "But he's German, isn't he?" She was glad that his pensive mood, unlike hers, had gone.

Never Land was shut. Devoid of her dwarfs, an abandoned Snow White had been wrapped in burlap, grass already growing between her feet. Around her lay dead fairy lights. Pluto had been covered with roped-down tarpaulin. They approached the familiar zigzag path and began their descent. A concrete pillbox, stuck halfway down the slope, halted their progress. It was unmanned, giving off a mouldy, repellent smell. Its concrete walls were pasted with warnings to keep paths and roads clear; to take cover if the alert sounded; to report any unusual persons to the relevant authorities. They slid down between old flower-beds and shrubs to reach the esplanade. It was quieter there. A few passing vehicles, one or two sailors who ogled Morgan, much to Charlie's disgust. But Prittend had become a garrison, not a holiday resort. The sea looked unnaturally calm. Morgan turned her back on it.

Up on the promenade again they leaned over the parapet, reluctant to leave the sun. Their faces were reddening. A woman standing beside them said, "My hubbie's out there." She was wearing a purple hat and lace gloves. She was not pointing at the pier head as they first thought, but out to sea. "They'll be landing them back here soon," she said. "They've got a few thousand off already, Margate way. And gone back for more." It took a second for Morgan to understand her meaning, that servicemen were being brought back from the Belgian beaches. "It's longer to get them to Dover. Especially with minefields out there."

"Minefields?" Morgan shushed Charlie.

"Dropped in the drink. There'll be injured." The woman was shaking her head. "A lot dead."

Morgan elbowed Charlie, eager to escape the woman's mournful presence.

"The *Lady Errant*. Know it?" She did, but made no reply. "It's only a pleasure steamer. What if there's a storm? A battle royal's going on over there. He's not a real sailor, you see. Gets bilious." Charlie stifled a laugh.

Morgan saw genuine anxiety on the woman's face. She knew she should be as concerned about her father. And Cat. They were at that very moment in the middle of their own battles. Yet her mind persisted in somersaulting from Pa to Patch, from Cat to Patch.

The woman was asking her where she and her young man came from. Another laugh from Charlie.

He was hustled away before he could respond. "It is coming to something when strangers accost one."

"We should have reported her," he declared as they walked along the high street. "She was an Unusual Person, like the poster. But then so's Granny Dorp and she's not a spy."

They were about to pass Oban Street when, out of the blue, he said, "Let's visit our aunt."

"Who?" But Morgan knew whom he meant.

When Montague married Berenice Skeffingley, he hadn't bargained on her sister Berengaria marrying beneath her. That was the verdict of his mother. Thereafter Berengaria and her husband, an ironmonger called Nails, were considered as not quite of the same class as the Perincalls. This meant the Nails could be invited only on unimportant occasions, visited rarely, their opinions never sought. That this liaison was deemed acceptable by Mrs Dorp, the mother of Berenice, Berengaria, and their sister Pandora, was of no account.

"We haven't been for ages," Charlie said. "Uncle Herbert and Frank talk about things. And you haven't seen them for years. Their shop's a marvel."

"Yes I have." Trying to remember a single visit to Aunt Berry and Uncle Herbert, Morgan came up with the day of the christening of their youngest. "We stood for hours in that chapel. Horribly draughty floorboards."

"Where was I? How old? Why does nobody like them?" Continuing to talk, Charlie was leading them down Oban Street, trying to locate the shop, with only a memory of wires and boat fixtures in a dim window.

"You were six." She remembered trying to push his resisting arms into his jacket before the christening. Rhoda had said to take a cake, in case the Nails couldn't afford one. It was embarrassing.

CLOSED, said a sign on the shop door. Charlie rang the bell.

"It's Wednesday." Morgan was ready to go, when her uncle peered around the door.

"Closed!" He shut it. Charlie rang the bell again. It reopened slowly.

Herbert was standing in the doorway. "Is it Charlie?" He squinted. "It's little Charlie! Well, not so little now. Berry will be surprised."

They went upstairs to the kitchen where Aunt Berengaria, who bore some resemblance to her late sister Berenice, was removing her curlers. "Hello Charlie. So it's Morgan, is it?" Her tone was even but not unfriendly. "We heard you were back. Afraid of the bombs, were you?" Rhoda's reaction had been similar.

"There aren't any yet." Morgan seated herself without being asked, directing Charlie to do the same. "We thought it would be nice to pay you a visit."

"Very nice! You were wise to leave London, specially with the children." She glanced round, but made no more mention of them. "But I'm not so sure about coming in this direction. There'll be fireworks soon enough."

Her hair to rights, Aunt Berry took out a knife with a worn edge from a drawer. "Early closing. We've been so busy lately. Still like bread and condensed milk, Charlie? Jam's run out." Charlie said yes before Morgan could stop him. "A run on locks and chains at present, haven't we, Herbert? People leaving, you see. And wire. Copper's getting scarce."

She opened the door and called down a dark corridor that Charlie remembered led to the sitting room. "Frank! I'm putting the kettle on. Your cousins are here." There was a faint response. "It's Morgan and Charlie." A pause while she listened. "Charlie!" she was shouting. "You know – the one with the gammy leg!"

Morgan's memories of her cousin were scant, having last seen him ten years ago. She and Frank were roughly the same age. He had never tried to kiss her, even though they had once been left all afternoon at the Villa, listening to Nelson Eddy on the gramophone. His sister had died and the others had gone to the baby's funeral. Montague had once called him a brain box to his face.

They sat in silence, awaiting Frank's arrival. Outside, seagulls were squabbling on the rooftops. Aunt Berengaria fetched a large teapot. Uncle Herbert put the kettle on.

An "Oh!" from Morgan was at the sight of her cousin, an exact replica of his father. The indeterminate moustache, the same lines around his mouth, could have been his father's. The ginger curls that Morgan remembered had been shaved to a patch of reddish straw. His mother smiled at him. "Your cousins have come on a visit, dear." She was dealing cups and saucers, putting the milk bottle on the table.

"How's your father?" Frank asked. His voice, Morgan thought, had the refined tones of his mother, not his father's country accent.

"Gone to Dunkirk with the rest," Charlie replied.

"Good man," Aunt Berengaria murmured. "And what about Rhoda? How's she getting along?"

158

"Joined up, Aunt Berry. The navy." Charlie was eyeing the butter she was scraping onto a slice of bread.

"She would." Uncle Herbert was reaching for it. "Salt of the earth, that woman. Her brother sounds a rum one, it's true, but she's decent enough."

"Frugal too," his wife added. "Of course Monty should have married her. Done the proper thing, even with her background. Too late now though."

Morgan wanted badly to ask about Rhoda's brother, but refrained. She thought it bad taste to be talking about any member of the Villa household, even though Rhoda had deserted them.

Watching her aunt Berry pouring the tea, handing it round, was like watching a ghostly image of her mother. She could see her mother's smile as she served her friends their Earl Grey. Staring hard out of the window stopped a tear.

"Frank's going to be called up."

Everyone looked at Frank, who continued sipping his tea. "The air force, isn't it, dear?" He shook his head.

"I'm joining the Air Defence Cadet Corps," Charlie said loudly. "It's for volunteers who want to be pilots."

His aunt broke the short silence that followed this statement by saying, "They're bound to put Frank into something useful, with his brains."

"In my experience, Berry, they'll likely do the opposite." Herbert was wagging his head. "If it's anything like the last time. This war couldn't be worse than that, in my opinion."

"Spain." Frank was stared at again. "A practice ground for the Nazis. This time they'll come from the air in numbers." His father was nodding at his son, the expert.

"How is your grandmother Perincall, Morgan?"

She could see Aunt Berry was trying to change the subject.

"He's read *Mein Kampf*. In German." Uncle Herbert was looking at Frank. "It proves that Hitler's a warmonger. Has been all along. Fooled Chamberlain."

"Not all of it, Dad."

"You speak it, don't you, Charlie?"

"Morgan speaks French."

"Monty and me, we were the lucky ones. I was back of the lines with the horses and supplies. He was right there in the thick. Lots of horses died."

"Oh, do get on with your tea, Herbert."

"They gave us mules from South America." Seeing that at least Charlie was interested, Herbert continued. "We had to break 'em in. I've never seen an animal what would injure itself just to get rid of you. But they would. They'd up in the air and come down on all four legs at once." He was seeing it again, and so was Charlie. "Enough to break his spine as well as mine!"

Tea was drunk and no more offered. Charlie got a slice of bread with condensed milk. There would be no biscuits until one of the sailors billeted on the front could get hold of some. Charlie asked if that was called the black market. His aunt replied that if he would like to see the shop, Frank would take him downstairs.

"Charlie's still a boy," she remarked when they had gone, "and shouldn't be bothering with black markets." To Morgan she apologised for not going to Granny Dorp. "For what use is it to go when one isn't recognised by one's own mother?"

The visit was short, Morgan pleading that she had to shut up the hens.

At the street door Herbert told them they were lucky to see Prittend before the British army arrived. Some were already at Dover. A sorry sight by all accounts. "It's defeat. So, needless they'll try to call it a tactical withdrawal, Frank says."

On the way back, driving over the Prittend railway bridge in sight of the aerodrome, Charlie slowed the Rover to creeping pace. It was the vantage point for plane-spotting that he and Ronnie had made their own.

Morgan just as eagerly scanned the airfield. Two men in tin hats ran from a pillbox waving their guns. All she could see were a few camouflaged planes, tiny as toys, that Charlie knew were Spitfires. But not as many as before. He said most of them were across the Channel protecting the B.E.F.

"Frank's boss-eyed," he said out of nowhere. "He won't be allowed to fly a plane. Or if he does – " he was laughing – "he'll fly it straight at a Stuka!"

"He seems very clever. I wonder if he *can* get things that are scarce."

As they passed the Queen Catherine on the Prittend Road, Charlie noted the gypsies had gone. "They must know something. Sinking ship and all that."

"Itinerants, Charles. They move all the time."

"Not that lot. The old lady with the split ear lobe has been around for years. Or she was until . . ." His voice was drowned out by the roar of planes leaving the runways.

For tea Charlie asked for a Welsh rarebit. Montague had taken all the cheese, Morgan said, but there must be ways of getting more. They ate bread and honey on the bare kitchen table. She thought of her mother, who had required prayers before meals. She thought of the little ships in the Channel, crossed her fingers and said a prayer for her father and for all pilots. Neither she nor Charlie wanted the wireless.

"What day is it?"

"Wednesday, the twenty-ninth." Morgan could hear flowing water, the Mill's faint hum. "Pa's been gone nearly four days."

"I'd better put his money on that horse before he comes back, or he'll slaughter me."

He headed for Montague's bedroom, Morgan following, trying to explain that the Derby was run in September. He thought she was mistaken.

She watched him tapping money from her father's shell case. He opened one of the drawers. "He's wearing his truss."

"How would you know that?"

"Sometimes when we go out on the *Berenice* he doesn't bother. But he's going to need it now, isn't he?"

"Charles, don't ask stupid questions. And stop looking at personal possessions." Her father's shoes were neatly aligned beneath the bed. "Pa always cleaned my shoes. Mother's too." She looked round the bedroom. "We shouldn't be poking about in here."

"What's this?" Charlie was dangling a brown disc from a piece of string.

"His dog tag from the last war. All soldiers wore them. He kept his Sam Brown belt too. If it's not here, he's probably wearing it.

"PERINCALL. M. 80698 C E. The rest's a bit worn." Charlie was turning the disc over. "It's made of cheap cardboard."

"Lives were just as cheap too." Sadness was overcoming her.

"Wouldn't you think he would wear it? So he could be identified if . . . if he was killed?"

"Don't talk like that, Charlie. Pa went away to war once before. When I was seven. But he came back." The once agreeable room now looked characterless. "I didn't see him go. Mother didn't want to upset me. He just went, like that!" She snapped her fingers. "We were left on our own for four years. I was eleven when he came home. Now he's gone again, heaven knows where." Her arms were folded protectively. "I'm losing my father twice."

Then she recalled Cathcart's departure.

Charlie had hardly been listening. "They've definitely gone to Dunkirk. Look at his map."

After the chickens were fed and shut in, Morgan broached the subject of the air corps. She asked him why he had only mentioned it first at Oban Street. And didn't he know he was not fit for military service? The questions would not stop coming. Didn't he think he might be needed at the mill if Mr Talbott wasn't there to organise things? And didn't he think he would have to be the head of the household if Pa was delayed? What about his responsibility to the grandmothers? The aunts? To her? There was more. She might have cried the word "selfish" to his departing back.

Just before sunset she went for a walk, to rid herself of a nagging mix of anger and anxiety. No sooner was the house under some control, which was like mastering juggling, when along came another crisis to prevent her thinking she had achieved anything.

At her uncle's that afternoon she had insisted that what was happening in Belgium wasn't a retreat. She had heard it on the wireless, which was a lie. Why did they not reassure her that nothing bad was happening? But clever cousin Frank's reply still circled "If it isn't a retreat, why did they bother to say it was not?" It was all too much.

What about Patch? Where was he when she needed comfort? She walked slowly along the gravel towards the river, almost phosphorescent in the fading light, the swish of the waves sounding lethargic. Along the path, grass had already begun to dry. Late grasshoppers leaped from her tread. She climbed easily through the gap in the wire. It was a slow dusk. The air hot, too hot for the end of May. On Saturday it would be June. The chestnut flowers were already turning brown. An invisible bird was singing loudly in the thorns along the edges of the dyke. The sky beyond was streaked purple over a wash of red. She heard, above the rhythm of the water, footsteps on gravel then shingle, coming nearer.

He called her name loudly, "Morgan!" coming closer, apologising for frightening her. "Morgan, I—" Her kiss stopped him. She didn't want to know how or why or what he was doing there. He was there, holding her so fast his buttons were pressing her breast.

She took him down to the river's edge, pulling him across the stones. Oblivious of mud or sea lavender or lapping water she made him jump from salting to salting, until the Villa and the mill were out of sight. The stile across the dyke, ribboned with barbed wire, was now impassable. Instead she took him down to the beach. They walked along it, on one side the river, the dyke wall on the other. Patch was saying he wanted to stop. To kiss her. She continued tugging him along.

They climbed the steep slope of the dyke, hauling each other up over weeds and grass. From there, the barrier left behind, they could have walked the median as far as the sea coast. As far as the real sea. She told him so, keeping from him her fear that her father might not come back from out there.

She chose a place on top of the dyke, certain that not a soul would come. That only a sharp-eyed passing craft might detect them. A bird rose out of nowhere.

The grass was long and bent under their weight as they lay down. He put his jacket under her, its cloth as warm as the grass. His face and arms looked burned against the whiteness of his body. He showed her the packet of French letters. He told her she was thinner, how he had missed her. How she must have been a beautiful baby, all the while removing her clothes.

She lay back, letting him caress her, a feeling of luxurious abandon so strong it was almost like sleep. It was a slower entwining, not so feverish as before. Again he was taking his time, smoothing and soothing, half singing words she couldn't decipher. Like the unseen tide below them, their bodies keeping time with its rhythm. The light was going gradually.

There was no knowing whether his urgency had in it the same fatigue as hers, a fatigue closer to exhaustion. She could almost have slept while he pleasured her. Her desire was strong, but coming from somewhere deeper, as if his abandonment of her in the last weeks had rendered his body more valuable. To the memory of what had happened before between them, a newer dimension was added. He was her lover who knew her in a deep, biblical way. She climaxed with a cry, stifled by his hand over her mouth. Daylight was fading. She hadn't noticed the sunset.

It was nearly dark. Patch was struggling to dress. Now he was sitting up. His silhouette against the purple sky was rigid, more concerned with his own safety than hers. She was suddenly afraid she might love him, the anxiety of it creeping over her like the dusk. Her skin was damp and cold, yet she felt feverish. He was telling her to get up, release his jacket. He had to leave. He was sitting very still, listening.

Her ears were as good as his. She too heard the engines: a boat coming from downriver not yet visible, not yet rounding the river's bend. She said there was time and tried to stroke his arm. He was fearful, unused to the dyke and the place, uncertain how long the boat might take to reach them.

He left her fastening her frock and raking her hair, saying he was expected on duty soon.

She watched his sombre shape slide down the dyke, hearing rather than seeing him land on the beach being attacked by the tide. His voice was strong, urging her to make haste. She could hear the scrape of pebbles, his curse as his shoes got wet. She scrambled to join him.

Along the river's edge they ran back. She was following his stride, calling, "Wait!" for he would need her to show him the way: rotten moorings were disappearing under the swift tide.

Their parting was one of hands briefly gripped, cheeks scarcely touching. She saw, as he walked away in the increasing darkness, how his fingers went up not to wave farewell, but to rearrange his hair. There was a rising moon, thin and vaporous. A blackbird was still singing on as it always did, but to Morgan this was not a bird of good fortune.

She began to walk home, aware of the distant hum of engines becoming louder. Lights were appearing in the Villa windows. She wanted to shout about the blackout, but thought better of it. Charlie might ask where she had been. Her shoes were wet. It would be wiser to steal in undetected.

He intercepted her in the garden, his urgent voice loud as the sounds of approaching craft.

Other voices were coming from close by, but from which direction wasn't clear. Voices getting louder. A boat engine's noise, steadily rising in competition. Charlie was waving a torch, ignoring her reprimand for leaving the Villa open and lit.

He was urging her to hurry. They were coming. She was turning and turning, trying to focus on the moment, to lose the feel of her pilot between her legs. Charlie was pointing all around as if he too were in a spin.

She wanted to go into the Villa, but he was saying, "No, they're coming." His torch sent a flickering beam across the grass. It moved over the fence to the edge of the garden where it steadied. A minute's wait.

Voices approaching. Then out of the darkness came beams from other torches, signalling. The agitated murmur of conversation rose and fell as they drew nearer.

Four torch beams crossed the trellis of the chicken fence, swung over the grassy mound then turned, blinding them for a second. Standing like ghosts before them were four women, their beams steady, now directed modestly at their feet.

Mrs Grace Talbott spoke first, repeating Charlie's words "They're coming." Three women were beside her, all in the same pinafores and headscarves like factory workers. Morgan recognised them, neighbours from the mill cottages living close to their husbands' work. Inexplicably they were carrying bags and boxes, everything reduced to the dull ochre of torchlight. One woman was holding a yellow sheet.

"Have we met?" This spurious politeness was drawn from Morgan by a desire for normality that she sensed was just about to slip away.

A moment's hesitation, then Mrs Talbott answered, in the curiously menacing voice Morgan had last heard in the cricket pavilion, "Don't have time for that sort of thing." And to Charlie, "Did they say how long?"

He didn't know. Not too long. After all, the police knew. He had phoned the fire brigade.

A mill woman said the B.B.C. was asking for any craft to help with the rescue. Another woman told Charlie he'd better go and close the Villa doors. The curtains too, or the wardens would have something else on their minds. There was mild laughter from the others, from which Morgan felt excluded. The usual order of things was being turned on its head. She did not want to stand in the dark with a group of workers' wives pretending they were as one. She wanted a bath.

"Is there hot water?" Mrs Talbott was addressing her, for Charlie had gone as instructed. "We'll need it." When Morgan was silent – "Yes, it may well be a mite pessimistic. But they've been bringing them in by the hundreds beyond Sheerness. Dover's where the big boats are headed." She stepped closer, trying to instil into Morgan the urgency. "We're bound to get some, aren't we?" Her companions were murmuring yes, yes, yes. "It won't be long now."

The phalanx of women began to move in the direction of the river. Morgan stood in the deeper darkness, waiting for Charlie. Waiting for her head to clear. Trying to drag her body back to earth. She stood gazing at the diminishing lights of the women now yards away; at the ebony Villa absorbed by its surrounding trees. Beyond them the river as black as its mud. The sky in which a sliver of moon hung low, untouched by cloud. The blackbird had ceased to sing. She could hear engines coming louder.

"Don't do that!" Charlie had flashed his light in her face. It moved down to her shoulder, to her side. "You're blinding me."

"You've got grass on you." He was aiming the light at her like a gun. "Grass all over your back. Didn't it prick you?" In the darkness his voice had taken on the same menacing tones as Mrs Talbott. "We'd better get going."

He had moved off, trailing his beam for Morgan to see. She followed it through the last of the garden, where plants' shadows lay across the overgrown fences. It occurred to her that it was almost summer. Spring had slipped away.

Their footsteps crunched the gravel, the sound softening as they reached the spongy soil by the water's side. The tide was higher, coming in fast with a beat that had often lulled her to sleep. Now it was sending messages into her brain, telling her wires to stay strung.

It was a peaceful scene, made almost poetical, she thought, by the women. They were ranged along the river's edge very still, each woman front-lit by the tide, the waves undulating their torches' puny light. They might have been statues. If she looked askance she might have missed them in the dark. They were watching the far reach of the river where pinpoints like stars were emerging from the night. At the same moment everyone put out their lamps. The air was damp. Despite the warm night, a chill was coming off the water.

Eyes were fixed now on the outline of a boat slowly entering mid stream, so slow it might have stopped. It was perhaps a cruiser, dimly lit in a flickering haze or mist, with a quality both magical and pathetic. Morgan thought of Odysseus' return, the sights that awaited him. And what adventures he would have to tell.

"Did you definitely phone the police?"

Charlie said yes to Mrs Talbott, and yes about the ambulances.

Morgan began to shiver. As yet she could not discern which craft it was, or who was at the helm. The women were agreeing with Charlie that it was alone. He said for certain it was the *Berenice*, but his certainty diminished the nearer it came.

It took a long time for the cruiser to reach a point where her engines were cut. Somebody said it was the *Clara*. A woman's voice from the dark said, "He's back, Grace."

"So he is." Mrs Talbot's reply was neutral.

The party on shore stood, mostly silent again, watching, some with fascination, some with consternation, the outlines and shadows of men moving on the cruiser.

By the light of lamps and seemingly in slow motion, anchors were lowered, made fast. From the shore it looked at first like a shapeless, enormous cargo, overflowing the cabin and deck. From this mound could clearly be heard groans, cries, voices raised in indecipherable calls over the water.

Along the beach there was new activity. From nowhere other lights were coming. People arriving and running here and there, some along the river's edge towards the boathouse, some towards the Villa drive. Some were swinging their lamps high, anticipating more help from where they had come.

From the boathouse came the sounds of outboard motors and oars in rowlocks. Charlie went out with others to the *Clara*, standing in the dinghy shouting questions at Talbott, his torch a thin searchlight. The dinghy was briefly swallowed up in the dark, and Morgan could hear only his shouts. Once she thought Charlie called to her, but she could not respond. Her teeth were chattering so fiercely there was no space for speech. She began to sob.

An arm went round her. A voice was telling her to take hold of herself. It was Grace Talbott, saying she must do her best, her body odour filling Morgan's nostrils. "The gaffer'll come. He'll come, my dear."

They could see Charlie and the others in dinghies surrounding the *Clara*. There were attempts to climb aboard, but the throng of bodies on her decks was thwarting them. At the prow they could see Talbott shouting instructions at them about his cargo. From one of the smaller craft someone shone a brighter light.

On shore there was a collective gasp at the sight of this mass of men, the wounded and the well, so welded together it resembled, Morgan thought, a graveyard memorial in shifting granite. The mass heaved and moved, rose and writhed with a noise terrible to hear.

Somebody said, "My God!"

CHAPTER SEVEN

The *Clara*, first to arrive, was anchored in midstream. Lodford firemen cut a passage through the barbed wire. The *Sarah* was next, carrying upriver another cargo of soldiers. And through the night, their lights pinpointing the dark, an oyster smack, dinghies, a ketch coming to help disembark the survivors.

Then the police and the army. Ambulance crews, nurses from the cottage hospital, joined them. The bank manager's wife came out of the darkness waving her W.V.S. badge.

Throughout the evening activity grew. Helpers, medical and military, were realising it might take hours to unload the human cargo. Workers with grappling irons and rope ladders improvised anything to speed the evacuation. Group by group, soldiers were ferried to shore by smaller boats, disembarked, taken to safer ground, the process repeated over and over.

Those men who were able, walked. Others were carried across sand and gravel to await aid on the Villa's lawn. With terrain unfamiliar, illumination erratic, tensions were high.

Ashore there were pleas for water for the living, bandages for the injured, morphine for the dying, tarpaulins for the dead. Little time for anything other than rapid instructions from man to man, woman to woman, doctor to nurse. Low voices drowned by cries for help. Or the voice of some soldier who could be heard trying to lighten a comrade's suffering.

For hours the exhausted and the wounded, their numbers swollen by the *Sarah*'s load, lay awaiting their turn. People came, adding to the chaos. News of the retreat from Dunkirk had spread, until onlookers were threatening to outnumber troops. Only those able to prove they could be of use were let through the gates.

Throughout the night Morgan and the mill women tended the wounded, injecting painkillers when some had never handled a syringe before, calming the distressed, the hysterical. Ambulances came and went, their headlights on a scene eclipsing any theatre. Each time they drove away they left the waiting calling for aid in a blackness more profound, their lives minutes more at risk.

In the long hours soldiers exchanged accounts with no beginnings, whose deathly ends were never spoken. Their voices, telling of cannon and machine gun attack, grew quieter when the women were near, as if these stories were not fit for female ears. For Morgan their murmurings seemed to merge into the cadences of the receding tide.

Around midnight Charlie and Ronnie Talbott went to raid the Villa's pantry and the cottages' cupboards. Soldiers said they had not eaten for days, having trekked through gutted villages on roads narrowed by their burned-out equipment. Others told of being near drowned at Dunkirk, of pushing between floating corpses.

The cricket pavilion became a surgery for the less critically injured, collapsed on the canvas chairs like batsmen run out at the crease. And some ran because their legs would still carry them. Some ran for no reason, having lost their senses. Pursued through the night of trees and thickets, most were caught.

During the night Charlie had persisted long in asking about the *Berenice*. Morgan had seen him questioning this or that soldier, barely waiting for the head shake. He found her, to say that Ronnie had seen a soldier in a Villa blanket trying to climb the *Berenice's* ladder. No time for her to find the shot soldier, who had, anyway, long since given up speech.

Later Charlie told her that Ronnie was a liar, who maintained that Nazi planes had gunned down troops in the water because the R.A.F. was nowhere to be seen for four days.

Before dawn she found Ronnie, handing out cigarettes and smoking. He swore he'd seen the *Berenice* somewhere in mid Channel, going or coming. Definitely near the Belgian coast. There were mines. A torpedo boat had gone down. Frenchmen shot dead on rafts. Horrible. Morgan suspected he was feverish.

Soldiers slowly reviving told her how, after hiding in the dunes, they'd tried to run towards rescue boats, enemy shelling forcing them to retreat. Then back to the dunes until the next boat and the next attempt. The craft were full to overflowing. Some said that oily smoke had saved them from dive bombing. Many waited for days, the strafing worsening. Dead all around. And hopelessness.

Like every helper, Morgan was needed as much to listen as to treat the wounded. In the dark a soldier had grabbed her ankle, insisting on an answer. "Where's Jim? Where's Jim?"

"Safe," she'd replied. He wouldn't release her until she kicked him.

The Villa's sheets and towels ran out. Dr Chilling sent her for bandages to an ambulance. Two nurses were tipping a patient onto the drive. They told her the dead must make way for the living – a corporal waiting on a nearby stretcher. Behind the ambulance was a woman uncurling a bandage. Between sobs she said her husband was out there somewhere. Morgan envied her tears.

No body count was attempted until near dawn, when the last man from the *Sarah* had been landed, like a herring on the ground. Most of the men were as wet as fish, soaked to chest height, their uniforms and boots, if they had any, as burdensome as their jettisoned weapons. Some wore only rags of khaki, having struggled to Dunkirk from places whose names they could not pronounce.

During the night, tripping over supine men, she had been sworn at. Once she'd had the crazy notion that Cathcart was among them. It was the tiredness. It was the hours of having to lift and carry to vehicles waiting to drive them anywhere they could be nursed. Everyone suffering, exhausted by effort.

Half-light revealed the numbers still left. Army trucks were ready to remove them. There was no attempt to sort by platoon or company, only rank allowing precedence. Most were chosen randomly for first transport.

No-one knew the extent of it. Was it only one battered section of the British Expeditionary Force? They did not yet know it had been so depleted that not one unit was still intact. It was rumoured that the same was happening all along the coast. Of rescuers on Prittend pier being forced to go back again to the hell of Dunkirk.

The sky in the east was gradually brightening. Another hot day. The birds' chorus had crescendoed into waves of wild sound. It gave some cheer to the scatter of men still waiting.

Now there was time to rest a little. To begin to think.

Morgan came across Talbott, his body denting the chicken wire fence, cigarette lit as if he'd had no part in the rescue. He seemed not to understand about the *Berenice*. Almost inaudible, he said he didn't know where she was. He might have used the word "bloody" but Morgan was too fatigued to be shocked. He fell silent. When she asked again, he shook his head. She wanted to shake him.

She persisted. Why so many wounded? He replied that the *Clara* had been shot at. It was a strange, unrecognisable monotone. None of his usual deference. The man was near collapse, the cigarette burning long between his fingers. Beneath the grime his face was the colour of its ash.

If somebody had told her she would put her arms under Talbott to heave him upright, she would have laughed. Now it was nothing to persuade yet another victim to lean on her, to walk. Slowly they reached the broken gate, where he sank to the ground. She shouted at him to get up. One of his sleeves was charred. She cried out for aid. A few helpers looked up, then went back to their tasks. He was in her arms again, in a stink of petrol and sweat, dragged from the causes of his plight.

It was dark in the plundered kitchen: food cupboards raided, broken crockery underfoot. Relieved to see a glimmer, she stoked the boiler and put on the kettle. On Talbott she forced the last dregs of brandy. But she lit only the oil lamp, sensing the man, with his hunched shoulders and clenched hands, would want to take refuge in gloom.

She gave him black tea, for the milk had curdled. Found a crust of bread. He pulled at it with blunt fingers, stuffing it into his mouth. She saw the grime deeply embedded into hands raised to cracked lips. On his chin the stubble of a rapid beard. How old was he? What sort of man? He had been an employee a long time, yet nobody mentioned anything other than his devotion to the job. Remembering his flag, she wondered whether he had risked his life out of patriotism, or loyalty to her father.

Her father saying "that Talbott's a deep one" was all she had. She had never before been in such close proximity. A new feeling of pity overcame her usual incomprehension of someone inferior in position. So she sat looking at the river light until he was able to raise his head.

Outside a cockerel began its crowing. Amid the noise she thought she could detect the sound of another cruiser. "Hear that?"

He was listening. Shook his head. "Not the *Berenice*. *The Green Lily* more like." He subsided again and was sweating. She removed his waterproof without complaint. He stayed slumped. Finally she was forced to ask what had happened.

Talbott was slow to begin. "We took 'em off from the harbour first. The docks were the first to go. Smoke. Thick. We got 'em off the Mole. We ferried 'em to a destroyer back and forth." He seemed to be dragging a memory so recent from some deeper place.

Leaning as close as she could bear, she kept nodding encouragement.

"Fog cleared. Weather good," he managed at last. "But we were strafed. A long time to get men on board. Danger of capsize because of the numbers. All hanging on one side, you see." For the first time he looked directly at her and motioned with his hand. "One trawler went over, men, equipment, the lot. Nearly alongside us." He ran a hand across his face, wiping the picture.

"Was it the *Berenice*?"

He was shaking his head again. "We had to get away from the beaches."

"Where is my father, Mr Talbott? Did you see the *Berenice*?"

"I don't remember. Back and forth got too dangerous. Couldn't see for smoke. Pulled back from they beaches. Bodies floating . . . every run worser. We couldn't keep it up. Had to leave. Some." He was trembling. "Sunset . . . blood."

Morgan found Mrs Talbott on the lawn. Ronnie had just left her side, her arms were outstretched as if she had failed to embrace her son. Near her was Dr Chilling, bent over a soldier who was volubly resisting being dressed. The man was probably Flemish, he said, and asked if she could translate. Two other soldiers had thanked him in what might be that tongue. This one, after an injection for a broken collarbone, was refusing to join them. Could she get this obstreperous foreigner into the ambulance?

Morgan told Mrs Talbott she was needed to take her husband home. She replied bitterly, "He told me he was all I was ever going to need. How right he was. I should have been warned." She walked off to the Villa at a slow pace, leaving Morgan sorry that a sensitive man like Bernard Talbott could be tied to such a woman.

Later she wondered if he'd seen action in Flanders. Or was his experience at Dunkirk the more affecting for being new? Her father had recounted only bland memories of his months on the front line. She had never questioned him, nor paid much attention. What had a young person's life to do with old suffering?

The cruiser now anchored mid stream alongside the *Sarah* proved to be *The Green Lily*, a jagged hole in her cabin roof. Only her owner Thady Green had disembarked, so Ronnie Talbott reported. Morgan thought both Talbotts, son and father, seemed to have aged overnight.

Ronnie, although exhausted, still loitered on the lawn with Charlie. At 8 a.m. when she asked why he wasn't going home, he replied that he'd rather let them at the cottage get on with things for a while.

Someone last night had told him there were boats delivering troops aplenty, even as far as Ramsgate. "The *Berenice* may have sailed north to avoid the mines, miss. There were mines in the shipping lanes, see."

Thinking Ronnie looked famished, Morgan told Charlie to take him to the boot room to wash, the upstairs bathroom being out of bounds to a filthy mill boy. Amid the kitchen debris he came to sit down, looking around with curiosity. He had probably never been inside the house before, and was certainly surprised at the chaos. Too tired to explain, she began to prepare breakfast.

All three ate eggs with stale bread fried in lard, agreeing that nothing had ever tasted so good. Nobody spoke until plates were clean. Ronnie admitted to being dog-tired. Morgan begged him to tell her about Dunkirk.

"There were black smoke, miss. The second day I think. The town glowing sort of. Dimmed the sun. I saw a ship torpedoed." On Charlie's face was a kind of envy. "I think it were French." He passed his hand across his forehead exactly as his father had done. "It was all going on all around. No sense to it. They were on a raft. Biggish raft. Stukas got some of em. We were too far away to do anything."

Charlie tried to interrupt, but Morgan stopped him. "Bodies in the water, miss. But not like later on. Thick with them it was then, when we went back. I couldn't see any sense to it all." He tried to rise, but Charlie pushed him down saying, "Go on, Ronnie!"

"Some of ours got sunk. Lots, I think. The *Alice* for sure. There was a German sub lurking."

"He means a submarine," Charlie said.

"I thought *The Green Lily* got it. Dad said not."

"And the *Berenice*, Ronnie?"

"The soldiers were up to their waists. Some went back. Lines of 'em. Ants on the beaches they looked. They told us they was bombed every morn. We were gunned by planes most of the time."

Charlie asked what sort of planes.

"Messerschmitts. I dunno. Bullets flying. The sea was red."

There was a moment's silence. Ronnie rose slowly to his feet.

"It was all going on here too," Charlie told him proudly. "I'll be in uniform soon."

Ronnie left without commenting or saying goodbye.

"It's not fair," Charlie told Morgan. "I should have gone. Pa should've let me."

She told him to get some sleep. He said he had managed a bit in the pavilion last night and would go to the office to give instructions.

In the small sitting room Morgan sank into an armchair. Everything as tired as she felt. Finger marks on the piano. As she drifted into sleep she could hear her mother's voice reaching for the high notes of "The Flight of Ages".

At nine Mrs Retchen arrived with the girls. She was shocked, she said, at the terrible mess outside, not to mention the kitchen. Morgan listened to her as patiently as she could, the comings and goings all night, police sirens and such, had been bad enough. It was all over the place the boats had come back. She wasn't going to let her girls in for piteous sights they wouldn't forget in a hurry. Her road was like Piccadilly Circus hours after. "Dufrene says they're going to put lumps of concrete at the end of Morn Avenue. How are they soldiers going to get out of the school if they're boxed in like that?" She then bounced from the lack of street lighting to the merits of hair curlers over turbans.

Morgan paid more attention when she said there was a clutter of cars at the Villa gates.

"No doubt the Royal Air Force'll soon to be upon us, asking for beverages."

Patch! Morgan ran into the garden to see two vehicles approaching, the R.A.F. truck with its roundels and Patch's Riley, his passenger Coral Floster.

Mrs Floster was the last person Morgan wanted to see emerging from his car. Her husband, clambering from the truck, acknowledged Morgan briefly, more concerned with keeping his eyes on his own alighting passenger.

Morgan wished she had washed more than her face, that she was not so depleted. Wished she were not wearing last night's filthy pinafore. Coral Floster was her usual immaculate self in yet another hat.

The party stopped where the Dunkirk survivors had been lying. Already patches of grass were browning, as rising heat began to dry the blood. Looking around more carefully they would have seen the shreds and rags of dressings, towels and bandages festooning the shrubs. By the collapsed gate they stood staring at the ground, the river, at Morgan, with some bewilderment.

Patch had turned his gaze on her. He seemed to be relying on his group captain to explain why they were there with a stranger. He was a soldier, hatless, in a curiously mottled uniform, standing expressionless, shoulders drooping. Morgan supposed he must be a batman. The group captain took her aside, leaving his wife and the flight lieutenant arranged like bookends on either side of the private.

They wanted, he said, to consult her father on a tricky subject. Driving towards Lodford, he and Coral, they had come across Flight Lieutenant Woodborne quite by chance *en route*. He had also been driving towards Lodford, and at Great Gormson had nearly overtaken them. Morgan, suspicious of her lover's activities, said nothing. She could see how uncomfortable this visit was for him, but nothing could compete with the stress of her night. The heat was increasing the necessity for sleep.

The trio decided, Floster said, to stop for a refresher at the Shepherd and Crook, which of course was in the other direction. They never got to the pub. He kept looking over at his wife and Woodborne, both pressed close to the soldier, who was swaying.

The problem was the private, whom they had seen "almost sleep walking" along the upper reaches of the Gormson Road. He was carrying his jacket bundled up in his arms. The soldier stopped them and asked for a lift to Blytham.

"We all thought this is a queer bird. He was hiding something in that jacket. Thought at first it might be small arms. You never know." The group captain's declaration was one of apologetic appeal, as if there had been an argument between the three of them. "Turned out to be a puppy, that's all." His face contorted. "Ran off, it did."

"But he didn't." Morgan nodded towards the wilting soldier.

"He might have! I've had training in unarmed combat. Claimed he was from St Oswyths at Blytham. Know it? Says the verger's his uncle."

"So what is he doing here?" At this point Mrs Floster, approaching, called out that if Flossie didn't get a move on, they'd all melt.

"Where's Monty? He'll know what to do. I told him, 'Monty will know what to do'."

"About what?" Morgan's patience was evaporating.

"Our spy, of course!" She was looking from Morgan to her husband. "Didn't he tell you he thinks we may have a spy on our hands?"

"Of course Patch questioned him as best he could, but Flossie still thinks he just might be a spy, don't you?" Was there sarcasm in her voice? "So I said we must bring him to Monty, to grill him." Cheerful enough, she was looking hopefully towards the Villa.

"My father isn't here." Morgan felt an unusual pang of pity.

Mrs Floster interrupted her reply: "What on earth has happened to you, Mrs Brodick? She looks completely ghastly, doesn't she?"

"So does your prisoner!" At Woodborne's side, the soldier was buckling at the knees.

She was forced to take them into the confusion of the kitchen, where they persuaded the soldier to drink some water.

Mrs Retchen, after one look at him, confirmed she had seen the man with his uncle, who often passed her place. "He looks as done in as Miss Morgan."

Conversations then followed: between the soldier and Mrs Retchen, that he was an escapee from the scene of the Dunkirk rescue; between Morgan and the Flosters, that the *Berenice*, skippered by Montague and two mill lads, had not yet returned. And between Morgan and the flight lieutenant.

Their particular exchange was more one-sided, consisting of his murmuring "Brave darling" into her ear. His breath sent shivers down her neck. To her simple question of where he had been, the reply was, "Squadron stuff." He made no further mention of the previous night, or the bloody evidence outside.

Mrs Retchen gave the soldier dry biscuits from the pantry and cheese from her shopping bag. The men were amazed to see her try to dry Mrs Floster's tears. She was rebuffed.

Morgan wondered how it was possible for Coral Floster to have feelings for Montague after so little acquaintance. How often had they met? Was it possible she loved him? How many times had they had sex? Did it matter how many? Her thoughts went spinning with fatigue. Did she herself really love Patch? Looking at him, sitting unconcerned beside an exhausted soldier and a husband he had cuckolded, there was only one certainty, they would make love again.

And Cathcart? Her reasons for ever having loved him were becoming warped. Was there something wrong with her that physical desire held her in such grip? Was she sure of her love for her children? She had let them go out of love for them. Or had she sent them in panic? By going with them would she have been a more caring mother? About her own dear, protective mother she would try not to think.

Coral Floster raised her brimming eyes at sounds of movement coming from upstairs. "Monty?"

"It's Charlie," Mrs Retchen replied. "Dog-tired too. Let him rest. He deserves it, same as she does."

Three people turned to Morgan with the unspoken question: why was she allowing a servant to speak for her?

"We were in open fields. Exposed like." The soldier began to talk. He was sitting erect. "Tanks were coming at us. We ran. Me and Blackie hid in a cornfield. There was a canal. I'm a bloody good swimmer, thank Christ!"

"I say, watch the words!" Floster muttered.

"They were coming at us from all sides. We got into some woods. Automatics got the sergeant major. The rest of us ran. They told us to, see? Blood pouring out of his neck."

Woodborne said, "Ladies present, old chap."

"Who were you with, love?" Mrs Retchen was patting his shoulder.

"Fourth Infantry. Shot to bits we were."

"My sister hubby's with your lot. I'll have to get in touch. Ivy will be needing me." With that she hurried from the kitchen.

The soldier again began to tell how he and some comrades had escaped. How he had come across another infantry unit, and together they'd made their way, night and day, along roads he said were filled with the remains of the French and Belgian armies. Mrs Retchen could be heard shouting instructions to her daughters outside.

"They were shooting their horses. It were raining." The soldier paused, raised his head to ask for a cigarette.

In silence the others watched him smoke. They could hear the wind banging an outhouse door. An aircraft passing left in its wake a low rumbling sound. Patch was saying something about wooden propellers.

"I've got to go home," the soldier was pleading. The others looked at Morgan.

"Take him there," she said, "and give him to his uncle."

It was mid-morning before a semblance of normality returned. The firemen, having rerolled their hoses on the drive, had eventually left. So had Morgan's other visitors.

She could hear the fire bell still ringing as she went upstairs. She lay down to the sounds of Thelma and Myrtle thumping rugs, their mother clearing up the kitchen, the roar of aircraft flying low, the wind in the chimneys. But nothing could interrupt sleep.

When she woke, the sun was already casting shadows over the floorboards. She had forgotten to wind her watch. And it was Friday. Outside familiar noises with a new appeal: birdsong, the churn of sluice gates, a plane's sharp sound diminishing as it flew out to sea. From the window she watched the flow of the river, dinghies and rowboats bouncing on the tide, as if yesterday had not happened. She felt as connected to it all as she had before her mother had died. No longer apprehensive, she felt as buoyant as the shadows on her ceiling. She was alive.

Charlie downstairs was eating bacon that Mrs Retchen had bought and cooked. The chickens had stopped moulting, he said. Rhoda used to put the extra eggs into isinglass. The *Clara* needed repairs. *The Green Lily* had run out of fuel, but would be going back to Dunkirk on the next tide. The *Sarah* had already gone. Story was that they were still bringing them back in thousands. With Belgium gone, he didn't hold out much hope for the *Berenice*. Morgan told him to shush. There had been nothing but broadcasts about the evacuation, Charlie continued, as if it Dunkirk was some sort of victory. He said mill work had been halted to rearrange shifts. Someone would be bringing towels. He was going to visit Granny Dorp. His father would have wanted it. Morgan should go to see Grandma Perincall.

Wondering at this new, positive Charlie, Morgan replied that she wasn't ready to talk to her yet.

She stood watching him go down the slope and through the turnstile, waiting until he was out of sight. He had liked her to wave when he was little. The tendency to tears that was overcoming her she put down to the previous night.

Mrs Retchen came to say that Villa work would have to wait. A visit to Ivy was essential. There was food enough for two days and beyond. More careful planning wouldn't come amiss. If Lord Woolton had his way, they'd all have to tighten their belts. She'd be grateful for the coupons and money she'd laid out, because she had three fares to pay to get them to Maldon.

Morgan wandered from room to room. Should she try concocting menus? Think how to replace lost sheets? Write to the children? They must not know of Dunkirk. Work out finances if Pa didn't come back. What to do about a missing father? Should he be reported? How long should one wait? Keep it all from the children. There was so much to think about it was immobilising.

There had been perfunctory tidying of the kitchen, the downstairs rooms, but the house felt tired, invaded; the invaders had left behind an alien aura. She would open windows and doors, let in air, sunlight, let in the noise from outside. Sounds that would drown out faint scrapings that had bothered her since waking. She hoped there weren't rats.

The bathroom upstairs was awash, for which she blamed all men, who seemed always to flood it. Footprints on the hall boards had left marks. No sign of them on Charlie's bedroom floor. By then his feet must have dried. Strange that the footprints seemed to lead to Rhoda's old room.

Rhoda's floor felt gritty. There was a distinct smell, not the usual mothballs, of damp sacks or abandoned sea boot socks.

Struggling with the window catch, she heard the scraping louder. She glimpsed a human foot. Out of the corner of her eye she could see it. Someone was under Rhoda's bed.

She stood rigid. There were breadcrumbs on the floor. The bed coverlet had shifted. It was spotted with what looked like blood. If the bed had been double, the foot might have stayed unseen for days.

Rhoda's hand mirror was the only weapon within reach. Morgan sidled around the wall to the door, then banged it, shouting, "Come out! Come out!" and "Help!", which was all she could think of.

The man beneath the bed came slowly sliding into view. He stayed low, hands raised in submission. No weapon.

He was a soldier, but not a Tommy. His uniform looked damp. Brief dismay that he might be a Nazi changed to recognition that here was a foreigner, perhaps Dr Chilling's truculent Flem. But this man's face was deeply pockmarked. He had a scruffy beard. His right cheek was twitching. His hands seemed clean. Saying something in what she thought sounded like French, he dived back under the bed. No help from downstairs. Morgan prepared to defend herself with the mirror, but he emerged donning a tin hat.

After staring at one another for a minute, each came to the conclusion that the other meant no harm. She allowed him to put on his socks.

He allowed her to herd him downstairs to the kitchen. No sign of Charlie or anyone else. She thought she heard a lorry approaching, but it went on towards the river. What to do?

The Frenchman settled it by sitting at the table. On the stove was simmering a pot of peelings for the chickens, that he was looking at hopefully. Instead she gave him a crust of bread. He seemed nervous, but inclined to believe she was a friend. On his hand was a jagged wound with dried blood that he let her examine. He said in French it was not a problem. Newly skilled, she cleaned and bandaged it with the last of the table napkins.

Dredging up her school French, she began trying questions. Something Cathcart had said about Name, Rank and Number. All she could produce was, "*Votre nom?*"

His eyes brightened at the sound of his own language. Stephane, he told her. He said "*Le Francport*", which meant nothing to her until he added "*Compiègne?*" and she remembered Pa saying the armistice had been signed there.

The soldier pulled a face about her tea. It was difficult to assess his mood, his temper. Why didn't he take off the tin helmet? Why were his hands shaking, the side of his face rippling as if moved by a breeze? Was he demented?

Lodford had its share of crazy people. In her youth an old man would roll a barrel up to Whitley's petrol pump for a fill-up, believing it to be a motorcar. There was the gypsy woman who shouted obscenities at all and sundry. And stiff-legged Gideon Jensen who was still calling, "Hoy".

The soldier was asking insistent questions that she struggled to understand. Tapping his chest, raising three fingers saying, "*Trente trois*". He was thirty-three. She said she was "*trente,*" taking three years off her age for no reason. Her name? He wanted to know it. M-O-R-G-A-N, spelled out, bewildered him.

It was unnerving not knowing what to do. So she poked the stove, shifted saucepans, ran a cloth over surfaces, trying to think.

He was talking on and on. He was telling her names: Paris, Cecile, Blanche, St. Ven-something. Cecile was his sister, she was sure she understood that. But who were the others? And where was Charlie?

The soldier was speaking so rapidly, all she knew was that he was reliving his escape. No language was needed for her to understand he was seeing the horror.

They both heard the aircraft coming. It flew so low she ducked. The Frenchman stood up shouting, and collapsed.

184

Wondering if it was her lot to heft sick men, she dragged him to the small sitting room, a safe distance from possible tradesmen. There she locked him in.

For the next hour, during her housework, she checked on him from time to time. But he stayed on the sofa, cheek twitching, tin hat on his chest, in what looked like normal sleep.

Charlie came back at last from Granny Dorp's, saying he would be going to give Talbott instructions. He sounded pleased with himself. Noticing the two teacups he said, "You want to watch that Arpent. Don't let him in the house while I'm not here."

"Don't be so bossy, Charles," her mind on the hidden Frenchman. "How's Granny Dorp?"

"She's been cutting nettles. The moon's in Sagittarius."

"She used to give me nettle tea."

"What for?"

"My skin."

"There you are, then." His reply made little sense. "Granny says to take red sage when you want to stop it. What does she mean? And watch the moon's phases when you wash my hair. Friday's for cutting toenails." His admiration was evident. "She has a recipe for flannel tongue. She can charm warts."

"She's loony – you said so yourself."

Morgan once loved Granny Dorp. Now the disloyalty she felt manifested itself in unkind words. She couldn't help being thankful that her grandmother had lost her reason, so nobody now would listen to her secrets. It wasn't fair to feel such guilt, just as it wasn't fair that her beloved mother had died instead of her mother's mother.

Before Charlie's birth, before her mother's death, everything had been simple. A childhood no child might experience again if this war worsened. Belgium gone, Dunkirk in flames, fear of invasion. The house invaded by a Frenchman asleep in the sitting room. The only consolation was that her mother had died in 1922. She could never have borne this.

All Morgan wanted was to get the intruder out. Make him somebody else's problem. She needed Patch, needed someone older than Charlie to take responsibility.

For Charlie's likely reaction to her dilemma was making her hesitant. She was coming to see how complicated he really was. How his perception of certain situations was not always the happiest. He did not stamp his foot like Cathcart, or browbeat her like her father. But recently he had lapsed into sullen silence, lasting more than a day, over some action or other of hers. He had always been protective of her, even as a child. Now she was seeing this protection might become despotic. She did not need Charlie venting his anger on an unfortunate soldier because she had been alone with him.

It was no use. She had to tell him. As precisely as she could, she said there was a soldier, French, possibly deranged, sleeping on the sofa in the other room. His name was Stephane. Not violent she insisted, only in need of an escort to get him to safekeeping.

Charlie entered the room cautiously. For some minutes he peered closely at the soldier, still soundly asleep, his helmet on the floor.

"Leave him be!" Morgan pulled him away by the back of his jacket.

Outside the door, she locked it.

"He doesn't look very mad to me," he said when they were back in the kitchen.

"You must do something, Charlie. Go to the mill. Phone the base at Iverdon. Locate the group captain and Flight Lieutenant Woodborne. They'll know what to do. And flying officer Parclay," she added as an afterthought.

Charlie shook his head. The air force had better things to do than rescue stray Froggies. He did not say he suspected all she wanted was to contact Parclay.

"We shall call the police on the office telephone. I'll have to ask Mr Talbott first though. You'll have to come too."

Morgan refrained from asking why, since Charlie had so recently claimed he was now running things.

They left the Villa noiselessly, Morgan fearful that the Frenchman, finding himself in a locked room, might run amok.

The chickens were peaceful as they crept past, the ducks on the ponds busy with young, the pigs wallowing. Charlie showed Morgan the baby Saddlebacks. They would make fine bacon.

Away from the river's cooling breeze, the heat seemed to have gathered in Mill Lane. The Union Jack on the Talbott's flagpole stirred now and then into feeble life. The front garden looked orderly with its clipped hedge. Pruning of dead vegetation had taken place.

Morgan's hand on the doorknocker was arrested by a sudden yell of pain coming from upstairs.

"What's that?" Another yell.

"It's Mr Talbott chastising Mrs Talbott," Charlie sounded matter-of-fact.

"What for?"

"Probably nothing, Ronnie says. I've heard it before."

"You have heard him before and said nothing?" Morgan was whispering. "If anyone did that to me, I'd kill them."

"I'd kill them for you," Charlie replied.

They stood outside the cottage until the yelling stopped. Then a continuous and rhythmic thumping sound. They waited until it subsided, waited longer then rapped on the door.

It took several minutes before Talbott came downstairs. He was in his shirtsleeves, and mortified to discover who his visitors were. His face, no longer grey but flushed, took on a deeper red as he flattened his hair and reset his braces. Grabbing his jacket he apologised for keeping them waiting. His shirt was not adequately tucked into his trousers.

"Yes, miss? What can I do for you?" Behind him was his wife, descending the lower stair. She nodded at Morgan without speaking. As her husband moved aside to speak to her, she backed from him into the kitchen.

"It was nothing really." Morgan was thinking rapidly. "We were wondering if . . . you'd had any more news . . . of my father. And the *Berenice*."

She didn't want to stay looking at this man, nor ask him anything at all.

He was sorry but no, patently wishing them gone.

She hustled Charlie down the path, knowing the manager was watching them. Back past the sties and through the turnstile she hastened them, only slowing down at the grassy mound. To Charlie's repeated suggestion that they could have gone on to the office to telephone, she gave no reply.

"And why didn't we tell him about the Frenchie?" he asked.

She had to look calm. "He was not buttoned up."

The chickens clucked as they passed.

The Villa was undisturbed. No sound from the sitting room. In the kitchen she lingered, trying to gather strength.

"Has the Frog gone, do you think?" Charlie asked.

"No such luck."

"Did Mrs Talbott walk into something in the dark the other night?" he asked.

"No such luck!"

"Mr Talbott said last night she may have got away."

"Who, Charlie?" She was whispering.

"The *Berenice*. She could have gone round to Prittend. Or Dover. Anywhere along the coast. Mr Talbott never saw the going of her. Ronnie told me there are three routes home, two of them mined." He was pointing at the map. "I love that boat. He may have chosen any of these routes."

"Who?"

They sat in silence, Charlie biting his nails, Morgan chewing her lip, listening for the soldier, hearing from outside a sound less ordinary, the clip-clop of horse's hoofs on the drive. They waited, neither knowing what for.

The front door knocker boomed. Charlie went to answer it.

Morgan rushed to unlock the sitting-room door. Stephane was up and rubbing his eyes. He smiled at her and fetched his boots, side by side under her mother's *escritoire*.

She led him into the hall. Charlie at the front door was addressing someone: "You should have come round the back."

The man on the step, touching his cap, ignored Charlie and began talking to Morgan in an accent she recognised as Irish. He told them his vehicle, which they might peruse on the approach to her residence, was designed for light work. As was the horse. Therefore what was inscribed upon the side of his conveyance – LIGHT WORK DONE WITH HORSE AND VAN – was the truth of it. That just about summed it up.

Charlie was saying there was no work light or heavy, when Morgan interrupted. She asked the Irishman how much he would charge to take someone away. A man, in fact. The Irishman peered into the hall, his eyes alighting on the smiling and twitching Stephane.

"He looks damp," he said. "What's up with him? Been in ditches? A fugitive from justice is he?"

"No! He is," Morgan said grandly, "one of our brave allies who has recently escaped certain death in France. He is dried out. He needs to be taken to Lodford police station. He must report that he is alive and well and ready for duty. Do you know where that is?"

The reply was unexpected. "Ever seen a barrage balloon, madam? Great big things they are, with wings. But they can't fly because they're tethered, see? Somebody's gone and tied them down. Like me!" They waited, sensing he must not be hurried. "So . . . like them I have certain things of a tethering nature – wife, children, four to be exact, of the female persuasion. Household expenses, so to speak."

He again peered at the soldier. "He doesn't look all that well to me, madam." Stephane acknowledged him with a mock salute. "I've seen that sort of yellow skin in Cork people."

"He's French," Charlie replied. "The French are yellower than us."

To stop any more discussion, Morgan offered the man half a crown. His eyes lit up, but his head shook.

It took some haggling, but the move was finally settled at four shillings. To Stephane the explanation of his destination took longer. Morgan's linguistic skill, admired by Charlie and the Irishman, resulted in a torrent of incomprehensible French that she assured them was of no account.

Her words to the van man were terse. She would be at Lodford police station on Saturday early, to check if her guest was there and properly transported.

Before climbing up beside the driver, Stephane took a chain from around his neck. He closed her fingers over it. *"Le Saint Odo – protecteur de dames extraordinaires."*

That evening a message came from Thady Green that the swell off the Dunkirk beaches meant it was impossible to take off more soldiers. The fleet had had to sail home part empty. Storms were brewing.

On her way to bed, Morgan heard someone moving in her father's bedroom. It was Charlie. "You shouldn't be in here." She closed the blackout curtains.

In his hands he was holding Montague's cut-throat razor. She said to put it back. Her father's room was already taking on a museum look. It was cleaned by the twins who made the bed each day. She did not know how they dusted, for every surface was covered by something. So unlike Rhoda's clinical bedroom.

Tentatively she opened a leather box. Inside a worn red booklet entitled *Active Service Soldier's Pay book*. From it dropped a printed letter. It was from Field-Marshal Kitchener exhorting the serving soldier to show himself *"in the true character of the British soldier"*. Charlie, over her shoulder, read with amusement, *"In this new experience you may find temptations both in wine and women. You must entirely resist both temptations, and while treating all women with perfect courtesy, you should avoid any intimacy!"*

"That's enough, Charles." But she was unable to stop him delving further.

He was holding two official forms, brown with age. "PROTECTION CERTIFICATE AND CERTIFICATE OF IDENTITY (SOLDIER NOT REMAINING WITH THE COLOURS) and SOLDIER'S DEMOBILISATION ACCOUNT. This one's filled in with indelible pencil. Once they'd finished with him they didn't bother to use a pen."

It was true. Having fought for his country, what did her father have to show for it except these pieces of paper? A list of EARNINGS AND STOPPAGES AND SAVINGS. And on demobilisation, only this rubber-stamped register to show for his efforts: NO. 1 DISPERSAL UNIT PURFLEET. If her father didn't come back from Dunkirk, she wondered what kind of communication she would be looking at then.

"Here are his medals." Charlie was stroking the coppery figure. "Who's this?"

"Victory, of course. She has wings. See?"

He turned it over: "*THE GREAT WAR FOR CIVILISATION 1914–1919. Supposed to end all wars.*"

"We mustn't rummage about like this," Trying to hide her curiosity. A smaller box revealed a single engraved cufflink, a packet of Beechams Powders, a betting slip, a packet of condoms that she hastily hid. And a set of brass buttons in a nest of dust.

Charlie remembered his father saying his horse had liked to rub his head along his uniform buttons, making them greasy.

Another piece of paper. "No guesses what these are! *SQUAREHEAD MASTER (mid season semi-erect) straw 40 ins. semi–flinty. RED STANDARD RED RIVETS (bearded).*"

From a corner of the box, Morgan removed a twist of tissue paper. In it was a wedding ring, *Berenice* engraved inside. She had worn it herself when she had gone to stay with Aunt Pandora.

"Look!" In Charlie's hands was a photograph. "The *Eugenie Fair*, our old cruiser." He would have pocketed it had she let him.

"Why did Pa call her that?"

Charlie said she was probably called after his second name, Eugene.

Tired, yet fascinated by her father's room, Morgan delved into another drawer and found a crumpled paper bag. In it a collection of old postcards, each one a view of a different French village. "Pa must have been to these places." The writing on the back of one had been entirely scribbled over. There came to mind her mother saying something about not expecting any man to be too faithful.

"Who's she?" Charlie had a sepia photograph of a young woman smiling in a doorway, her arm in a sling. "Wounded peasant?"

"Funny that he kept it all this time."

Now he was holding up a Light Ale bottle. "Rhoda's favourite."

She said. "He won't like us poking about."

But his attention had turned to a tiny marble bust on a plinth. "This was Rhoda's. It's Queen Victoria."

"She's very white."

"She's dead!" Their laughter was conspiratorial.

They should have opened a window, Morgan told Charlie later. The smell of tobacco and flour seemed to have penetrated everything. But somehow to cleanse her father's room was too finite, as if she would have been relegating him to the ranks of the fallen.

Charlie that evening asked about money. She told him finances could wait a while. Next week perhaps. "Pa will be back by then, for certain."

Montague did not return on Saturday. Boat owners came with sympathy or optimism, telling their own stories of how they had evacuated the troops. Already these experiences were taking on mythical form: thousands of Davids had smitten the Nazi Goliath so thoroughly that the war was a small thing and soon over. Few felt like mentioning the losses of men, equipment, vehicles, artillery, abandoned on the other shore.

Charlie worked in the garden until lunch, bringing in sufficient vegetables to make the small topside into a meal. In the afternoon he went off "to check up on things".

Morgan sat within sight of the river, but turned away from the scenes of rescue. She read the children's and Cathcart's letters. Cat's, already out of date, told her little other than that he was well. Nothing about going into action. Billy's letter proved equally disappointing, all his literary effort put into describing a dog, not even the Timmbold's, a stray that had wandered in and gone again. Of his sister Terry he wrote nothing. Morgan fell asleep to the sound of the lulling tide, the letters fluttering across the wounded grass.

Charlie's loud voice woke her. He sounded cross. Flight Lieutenant Woodborne had telephoned the office with a message for her. She tried not to show interest. "He says to tell you that the R.A.F. engaged with the enemy. When I asked if he meant Dunkirk, he said, 'Tell her that's where I was.'" His voice had risen. "What if a spy had been listening?" He was glaring at her. "Why would he want to send you a message? About that!" He was almost shouting.

Rising, Morgan kicked over the garden chair. "Great merciful heavens, Charles, can't you see the man was . . ." she was hesitating, ". . . defending Pa and the rest of them? I had asked this officer why he wasn't doing his duty!"

It was the best she could think of on the spot, but Charlie went to bed that night still in a thoughtful mood.

On Sunday at church they sang "Eternal Father" with the rest of a fervent congregation, including Charlie, Grandma Perincall and two of the aunts. Afterwards they went to the Perincall tomb, which Morgan thought vulgar with its Corinthian columns and forlorn statue. Nevertheless, from her handbag she produced one of her mother's roses that she laid, saying nothing, at the angel's feet. Charlie did not know what to make of this emotional gesture he could not understand.

CHAPTER EIGHT

After the surrender of the French on 22 June, 1940, Dunkirk still raw, there was a rising sense of pessimism. Distant losses that had once been mere numbers now were taking on more personal meaning.

It was alright for Mr Churchill to claim that the R.A.F. had won a victory at Dunkirk. What kind of victory was it, Dufrene asked Charlie, if France was left in the hands of the Nazis? Had he heard that Paris had been bombed near to extinction? That no more troops could be brought off those vile beaches because of the Messerschmitts? He'd seen the survivors. And he wasn't half sorry about Captain Perincall. In June there'd been air raids up north. Had Mr Charlie heard? He had been right in May about the Maginot Line.

Charlie was looking at the official envelope, hoping it would regularise his position at work. His father absent, he had little authority and no power. His relationship with Talbott, who was behaving peculiarly, could hardly be called close. Neither discussed anything other than business, apart from the extraordinary night of the *Clara*'s return. Memory could not rescue the noise, the hysteria of that night. Least of all could it assist in estimating Talbott's response to changes.

Never before had Charlie bothered to assess anyone's character. Morgan's objection to what the man did in his own home had set him thinking. Talbott knew more about milling than he. It was no good wishing he had paid more attention, instead of scurrying off with Ronnie or Jerky to somewhere more fun.

From the start he hadn't liked the menial jobs. Climbing through the woodwork, breathing flour to get at a broken chain or an out-of-kilter spindle, had never been his idea of employment. They made his muscles ache, his injured leg sore, and made him cough, Secretly he had always thought the buildings fouled the landscape. The floodgates had definitely fouled his leg and that was something he would never forgive.

Rhoda had told him to be thankful the business was keeping a roof over their heads. And where was Rhoda now, who would know what to do in this situation, with no shilly-shallying? Unlike Morgan, who just wanted to wait and wait.

He gave her the letters. One she tucked away unopened. An official one said that someone from the Women's Land Army would be billeted on them. She complained that she hadn't the faintest idea what to do, least of all about a Land Girl clomping about in muddy boots.

How was she going to cope, with rationing getting tighter and no idea what do about money? The responsibility was giving her a dreadful headache. There were the grandmothers to consider. The aunts. Not to mention Uncle Herbert, Aunt Berry and Cousin Frank in Prittend that was turning into a military stronghold. She was failing all of them – Charlie, her absent father. The purpose of this dramatic performance was to divert attention from Patch's letter in her pocket.

Her outpouring alleviated a genuine worry: war had truly come. Now anyone close to her, especially Flight Lieutenant Woodborne, was in peril.

To see his sister like this affected Charlie. He told her she must not worry. They would do what Pa had said and make an appointment to see the bank manager. Very soon.

When he had gone she opened Patch's letter.

Ever My Darling,

Things are hotting up here. Thank "G" I volunteered early and got to know the pitfalls. Easy to get caught out. We lost a lot of chaps over France but keep it under your hat. Plenty of action there & more to come this side. So far, cross your fingers, I being one of the lucky ones. I am missing you most horribly and thinking of you a lot while I catch my breath for the next onslaught.

New recruits coming in soon. Like us they will have to <u>learn</u> on the job. They are <u>more than</u> welcome! but I won't let them get any ideas about you my sweet. Can't help thinking about your . . . ! They can't take that away from me Ha! Ha!

P xx

p.s. We <u>Shall Never Surrender</u>!! (W Churchill)

She was uncertain about the distracted tone of the letter. But of course, for the past month Spitfires and Hurricanes had been flying over in numbers. Lately, from the bus, she had seen on the aerodrome signs of more construction, preparations for something imminent.

She had stopped staring skyward, ceasing to wonder whether Patch was piloting one of the Spitfires. It was too nerve-wracking. There were rumours that Britain's Air Force was not as prepared as the nine o'clock news claimed. She wasn't foolish, and agreed with her father's assertion that when politicians began to talk in grandiose terms, calling on God's aid, there was genuine trouble in the offing.

Arpent, with a stranger from Ironside wearing official A.R.P. armbands, came in earnest to insist on stirrup pumps and buckets of sand. In a big house like the Villa Rouge, they warned there would have to be vigilance, especially about the roof space.

Bombs had already dropped in the north of the county, the stranger said. The estuary's turn would come next. As if to underline this, there was a loud bang followed by two more. "Invasion is what we all have to expect, madam," the warden's voice was chilly. She hated being called madam. The shopkeepers did it in Tufnell Park. The barrow boys called her "love", to Cat's annoyance.

"Don't worry, Morgan. They're testing a new gun over the river." Arpent was all sympathy. "This side's the ack-ack battery, see? Twin defences."

His companion was looking around. "We are putting air raid posts into private houses, so that wardens are collectively on the job, so to speak."

Here Arpent interrupted. The Villa might be too far for wardens. He personally would be available in case of fire. Morgan gave him a grateful nod.

"We have river enough on our doorstep," she said. "And Simon here to call on. The Land Army is arriving soon."

"One needs sand, not water to extinguish incendiaries," the stranger told her. "You do realise, madam, that this house is very vulnerable." He was searching in his satchel. "If the enemy comes by sea or by air, this river will be one of their main entry points. If our boats can get across the Channel to Dunkirk and back then, I can assure you madam, theirs can do exactly the same." He handed her a pamphlet: *IF THE INVADER COMES – what to do & how to do it. STAY PUT.*

"We do have the army on our doorstep." Arpent was agreeing with her.

"My colleague will have many more crises to deal with, should the worst come to the worst." The man was looking as if he had decided to stay. "The activity around here pleases me," he said. "Do you know they are constructing two anti-tank cubes per day here?" She did not. "Have you seen the pillboxes along the coast?" She had. "They will form a system whereby, via a series of iron posts through which barbed wire will be threaded in a spiral, a complete defence network will be in place." The man was a living textbook.

"They will definitely not get through, Morgan. We will fight them on the beaches, eh?"

Simon's reassurances meant little, for his colleague was hinting that the army might be laying mines along the Lodbrook. Seeing Morgan's look of alarm, the man softened his tone. "Only if necessary."

"How will we get to the boats? Next, our river will be full of them!" Images of mines exploding where the Dunkirk wounded had lain, mines holing boats at anchor, shrapnel bringing down birds, forced from her an unexpected cry.

Simon was grabbing his notes, saying they would leave.

"Yes, you should!" It was no use beating about the bush. Her nerves, already stretched, could not stand it. Now other vehicles were approaching.

Mr Boxley's milk float was impeding two army lorries rolling into view. Behind them a motorbike and sidecar. Boxley was grappling with his horse.

"Great merciful heavens, we are already invaded! This place is like a Michaelmas market."

The lorries, to Morgan's surprise, drove past the Villa towards the river. She went to watch. They stopped, turned with some difficulty and went back again, halting under the chestnuts out of sight. There was shouting. Boxley's float came into view, the Retchen girls trotting to meet it, curious about any visitor. Beside the fence, the horse began to eat sweet grass, while its owner went rattling his way to the Villa's back door.

Morgan watched Coral Floster climb from the sidecar of a B.S.A. ridden by her husband. In his leather helmet he looked like a baby in a bonnet.

Shaking Morgan's hand he said that he, or rather his lady wife, had come to inquire after Captain Perincall. Intelligence had it that he was still missing. Mrs Floster's voluminous scarf had become entwined with her goggles. She was trying to involve her disinterested husband in its management. On her face irritation was mingling with grief. "It's weeks since Monty's gone!"

Again Morgan wondered at the depth of her feelings. Their affair had been such a well-kept secret it had hardly seemed an affair at all. She did not seem the sort of woman her father would find interesting – neurotic, self-centred, in need of attention. Not at all playful.

A picture came to her: another hot day, of sitting on the riverbank with her parents. The water had made Morgan's woollen swimming costume sag. He had joked about it. Her mother tapped him on the shoulder and his panama flew off. They watched it curling along the beach, over the waves, tumbling from view beyond the dinghies. She was twelve. That day they had laughed a lot and Morgan had stuck cleavers in his hair.

Not that she knew much about him. During her teens their relationship had been fraught, his attention diverted from his daughter's problems by his wife's increasingly invalid state. During her thirteen married years Morgan had seen him infrequently. By his own admission he disliked travel. Nor did he put pen to letter easily, preferring the brevity of postcards.

She had supposed it was the war taking his energy. Perhaps the fragile Mrs Floster had contributed to its depletion. Did her father need a dependent partner? One who more resembled his late wife? Was he seeking the counter to his mother or efficient Rhoda?

Coral Floster was settling into tearful mode. Morgan, at a loss what to do, suggested they go together to look at the river. After a glance at her impatient husband, she agreed.

It occurred to Morgan that her choice of direction could have been more sensitive. But as usual she could not make up her mind whether she wanted to be nice to this woman. Was she a rival, or naturally manipulative?

Unseen soldiers beneath the trees whistled at them.

"What on earth is the army doing here?"

"Nobody asked them to come," Morgan replied. "Every person is turning into a petty official."

"Which regiment are they? I am sure they must have a purpose." Mrs Floster, holding down her skirt, was talking in a high, nervous voice. "Are they the Auxiliary Military Pioneer Corps? I hear they are doing much construction in the area, fortifications and such. They are certainly not King Edward's Horse!" The joke was lost on Morgan. "Which battalion do they come from?"

Feeling inadequate, Morgan deliberately led them through mud churned up by the debarkation. "Artillery probably. From the barracks."

They stood watching the receding tide. The breeze was having little effect on the heat. Mrs Floster's face had flushed, as if she weren't used to sunlight. She was pointing at *The Green Lily*. Its cabin roof was a patchwork of repair. "Monty's was nicer than that one. Or that – " pointing at the *Sarah*. "We used to sail round to Blytham for oysters at the Wherry." With a scrap of handkerchief from the bracelet around her upper arm, she dabbed her eyes. "I loved its little wooden wheel." Her heels were sinking into the ooze.

Morgan stared through the haze at flimmering scrubland across the river. "Are you talking about my father's cruiser, the *Berenice*?"

"What else?"

"That boat was named after my mother."

Mrs Floster gave a dismissive shrug. "So he told me. I truly cared for Monty. A wonderful companion. Considerate. Understanding." Her tears had stopped.

Morgan was finding this candour unsettling. "Does already being married cause you any problems?"

Mrs Floster paused before replying. "Neither of us seems to have any difficulties about that, do we?"

"And does the group captain have any problems?"

The group captain's wife was extricating her heels from the mire. "Only his own." She sounded too casual. "My husband's in love with the air force."

Following her towards the house, Morgan was wondering exactly how to broach the subject closest to her. "I hope he is not in love with Flight Lieutenant Woodborne!" This feeble riposte was the best she could manage.

To her bewilderment, Mrs Floster stopped wiping her shoes on the grass to say, "Dear me! How perspicacious of you!"

Boxley, with his crate of empties, was waiting by his horse. Beside him stood the group captain, swinging his helmet. The milkman was trying to make himself heard above the clatter under the trees. He was calling something to Morgan about children and Gloucestershire. She did not want Mrs Floster to hear anything private, so she told him they would speak soon.

The group captain, sweating beside the float, seemed relieved to see his wife. Morgan thought he bore a resemblance to Mr Boxley, who was fond of drink. She apologised for leaving him outside with the horse, but could not bring herself to ask them indoors. He exclaimed that time was precious – "The enemy is at the gates" – and they must away.

Lunch that day of kidneys and bacon, potatoes and spring greens Charlie ate heartily, lauding his vegetables. He seemed in high spirits. He joked that the rhubarb was his work, but not the custard! She should appreciate how difficult gardening was for one man. Morgan asked what had become of their old gardener.

Since Mr Phledge had retired Rhoda hadn't wanted another one, Charlie said. " It was throwing money away." He began to intone a child-hood rhyme. "*I went into the garden and found a silver farthing. I gave it to my mother to buy a baby brother. The brother was so cross—*"

She stopped him. "It wasn't up to Rhoda to decide something like that."

But Charlie, intent on avoiding any Rhoda discussion, said the Retchen sisters were skipping on the drive. "Soldiers turning the ropes, Myrtle and Thelma leaping up and down like mad things. Singing at the same time, fit to bust!" Did Morgan remember, "Kymanary kilterkary kymanary kymo", from when she had taught him to skip? "*Kymanary kilterkary kymanary kymo!*" He was pleased at how much he was irritating her. She had to beg him to stop.

"You'd think soldiers would have better things to do. You too."

"Like shovelling horse shit for the garden?" Charlie knew such crudity would annoy. Morgan collected the plates and turned her back.

"I've phoned the bank manager who says he can see us on Thurs-day," Charlie called. "Eleven o'clock sharp."

She began to wonder if he, since the Dunkirk night, was becoming too assertive. She reminded him Thursday was market day, and he should have asked her first.

Markets had become smaller than before the war, for which she was grateful. She had rarely enjoyed them like Charlie. There was no joy in watching frightened cattle herded into pens, ignominiously labelled by a man with a dripping glue pot. She had hated the rattle of their hoofs on the cobbles; detested the sight of Jeremiah Jorden beating them with his stick. There he was, fourteen years later, still wielding it.

She and Charlie wandered around the square together, he stopping to prod a pig and air his knowledge. "Not enough meat yet. Too young." Or, "Only good for breeding."

Hating the cries of distress and the stink, Morgan wanted to leave immediately. Only when she had accompanied her father to a horse sale had she been thrilled by the Shires, manes and tails plaited, hoofs shiny with oil.

For a moment her attention was riveted by a Percheron, its penis dangling like a rubber hose. Before she'd had a chance to distract Charlie's gaze, Cedric Brodir had whacked its cock and the erection had retracted. "This is no place for us, Charlie."

But he had noticed her Sunday frock and hat, even her earrings that she had not worn recently. "You shouldn't have come in that get-up. It's too dirty here."

"You're right. I think we should go." The Women's Institute clock was striking eleven. "Charlie, why don't you go to the market in Long Alley and buy a rabbit, as Pa said." Before he had time to demur, she had pressed two shillings on him. "I'll pop in to Mr Grouming on my own, so that he doesn't get confused. And meet you in the Harlem tearoom afterwards." Leaving, she was telling him to keep the change.

Charlie between the pens, disconcerted at the speed of her escape, narrowly avoided some sheep hobbling past.

The bank manager, a stooping man with an oatmeal complexion, greeted her with the words, "My goodness!" before escorting her upstairs to his sitting room. He introduced his wife, whom she had last seen in the light of torches, dispensing tea to wounded soldiers. Mrs Grouming cast her a probing glance and left them.

The room was full of dark, oriental-looking furniture. Seeing her interest, Grouming began talking about the British Empire and its implications for the war. He couldn't help looking to the Far East, for that was where his father had been, in the diplomatic service in Kuala Lumpur. He had travelled extensively in China and the Japanese islands. During this monologue, to which Morgan felt entirely unable to contribute, she sat gazing at some intricately carved figures on a bureau.

The bank manager spent a long time musing over Japan's history of bellicosity, its desire for *Lebensraum*, wondering where it would lead if the conflict widened. She sat wondering how to turn his attention to clarification of her position and Charlie's.

The clock on the wall chimed the half hour before she decided on action. Producing her handkerchief, prepared with her precious *chypre*, she began to sob.

The rest of the interview was plain sailing. Having been comforted by Grouming, whose hand she let rest on her shoulder, she accepted his assurances that finances would be forthcoming. And listened to a written statement he had prepared in advance:

The prosperity of the Perincall Tidal Mill in the ownership of Captain Montague Barling Perincall, has given rise to much optimism on the part of the bank. Investments have not been misdirected. The mill – as we understand it, owned and run for many centuries by previous members of the same family – has continued with increasing good fortune even in this time of uncertainty. The Villa Rouge, properties and acreage, is the fulcrum of a monetary plan which is being nursed to fruition within the stewardship of the bank – the managers of the family finances – and with the assistance of Mr Portland Threw, land agent. Rest assured we, and he, will do our best in the absence of Captain Perin-call to fulfil the enterprise allotted.

Before departure, Morgan forced down a cup of perfumed tea from Mrs Grouming, who seemed to have caught her husband's disease of verbosity. Held in her keen gaze, Morgan could do little but listen to the lady's view that following Norway's surrender, then Italy's defection to the Nazis, only misery could be predicted for Europe. There was a strong indication that once Canada had declared war, as was imminent, South Africa, Australia and New Zealand would ultimately join her. It would become a world war. What were Mrs Brodick's views?

Standing on the pavement, Mrs Brodick wondered if everyone knew more than she. Above her head, from the curlicues of the Women's Institute clock there drooped the afterthought of a Union Jack. Could it ever be replaced by a swastika? She wished that she had had the wit to ask for a copy of Grouming's statement, for its opacity had disturbed her.

Over tea at the Harlem cafe she told Charlie the interview had been simple. She had little idea how to begin discussing their predicament. It was not fair to expect him, hardly out of short trousers, to grasp its implications. From now on she would have to buck up her ideas (as her father had often told her) and try to foresee how events might affect them. It was not a question of confronting problems when they arose – this had always been her way. Now there was a need for more thoughtful planning. At this she had not had much practice.

She did her best to distract Charlie. What was in the box at his feet?

"A rabbit. Ernie Shottle's going to deliver the hutch."

"Who's he?"

"Missing fingers?" She didn't know him. "That's why he's not in the army, but he's got a bayonet under the bed. The blighter asked me how my bobby-dazzler of a sister was. I told him to mind his own business."

"So perhaps this Ernie won't be so quick to deliver a hutch."

"Oh, yes he will! He says he wants to get another look at you." A pause while Charlie appraised her. Again he asked why she had worn her best frock.

"Tell Ernie that if he's coming to get a look at me, he must bring hay."

"I've already done it." Charlie hesitated. "Well, not in so many words."

On the bus home he told her the chicks he had hoped to buy were croupish. Not worth the money, especially now they might be poorer.

Morgan assured him that Grouming was releasing contingency funds for them, until the whereabouts of Captain Perincall was known. "All it needs is my signature now and then, so you won't have to bother. Grouming will be handling Threw's farm rents as usual. It was a long discussion."

This last was meant to allay Charlie's suspicion that she had been anywhere else. How guilty he was making her feel. On the corner of West Street she had bumped into flying officer Parclay. He was with a neat-looking Waaf whom he did not introduce.

Enthusiastic as always, he asked Morgan if she would be coming to the dance at the Women's Institute. "Our own R.A.F. band." Of course she said yes. He told her that Patch warned him she would rather be left alone. "After the loss of your dear father, that is. No news, I suppose?" She shook her head. They separated, Morgan reassured by this proof of her lover's jealousy. Parclay's parting words were, "See you on Saturday, God and the Luftwaffe willing!"

It was necessary to tell Charlie about the dance, but not how she had found out. Nor how much she liked the flying officer.

The evening was not the success Morgan envisaged. The R.A.F. band, four musicians attempting to keep time, played to a hall full of soldiers and airmen, thumping the floor like thunder. There was no sign of Patch. She had to be content with Parclay, who left a cluster of local girls and remained as close as Charlie would allow.

His aim was to prevent anyone from dancing with his sister. One or two bolder soldiers had tried approaching her, but had given up.

Parclay, ignoring Charlie's attitude, danced with Morgan more than once. She, who had always loved to dance, was as pleased with this man's facility on the floor as she was to be on the floor at all. He said with her anything was easy.

For the first part of the evening Morgan stayed in the arms of Parclay, her attention more on the hall door, through which she was willing another pilot to come. Charlie sat watching his sister through the fumes, checking reactions, proximity, smiles. His view was hampered by the crowd filling a space smaller than the senior school. Everyone seemed to be having a better time than he.

In the middle of the Gay Gordons he intervened. Snatching his sister's hand from Parclay's, he pulled her away from the line. If she later complained about his boorish behaviour, he would say that he had been defending her against malicious gossip.

So he was obliged to dance with her himself, the wounded leg giving his movements a jerky quality. In the quickstep he turned her clockwise and clockwise until her head was spinning. His foxtrot put them in conflict with better dancers. When they collided with Agnes Humer and her lance corporal, Charlie went so far as to blame them. Caught in the middle, Morgan elected to stay calm, ignoring his remark about girls throwing themselves at servicemen. He did not see how she watched the door.

The tango was interrupted by an announcement that air force personnel were required for duty. This cleared the floor and lessened the crush. Parclay, apologetic, held Morgan's fingers for longer than Charlie thought necessary. At the pilot's departure he muttered, "Good riddance."

After the interval Vela Kymmerly asked him to waltz, but he said he was whacked. Morgan also refused Vela's offer, so had to let Vela sit with them. It was turning out to be a trying evening.

Amid the din, Morgan missed much of what Vela was saying, about how a postmistress was always one of the first to know what was going on, that her mother would have been proud of the victory at Dunkirk. Then Vela said Archie's name, and Morgan bent closer to prevent her shouting.

Her brother Archie had actually telephoned from up north. If he had known of their mother's death he would have come home sooner. Archie said he was going to fight. Morgan wanted to ask if he would be coming to say farewell to his sister. Charlie was trying to catch the conversation.

She decided to hide in the lavatories for as long as she could, hoping that Vela would tire of Charlie. There was no sign of Flight Lieutenant Woodborne. She continued to watch the door until 11 p.m. when the party broke up.

A kind of gloom settled over the Villa, despite the glorious weather. The lack of news of the *Berenice* continued to cast a shadow. The daily arrival of Mrs Retchen, who had reluctantly agreed to recommence her Villa duties, brought with it disaster-ridden stories that tested Morgan's resolve to face up to reality. She said the rationing of tea was as sure an omen as the downfall of the Channel Islands, or the installing of machine guns along the Prittend seafront. Miss Morgan had better watch the pennies, now that income tax was going up. As for refugees, "We're going to be overrun with them. And we won't know the difference between them and the Nazis. They're all foreigners."

She was in full flow, pointing toward the cricket ground. "What's a drainpipe doing lying there, bang on the cricket pitch?" She had asked a lorry driver, who told her it was an anti-tank device. Yes, Morgan had seen the monstrosity. "Probably ordered by a high-up with shares in a concrete factory. With that stuck there, they Local Defence Volunteers will have no trouble fending off a lot of desperadoes!"

Released from the silence of her home, Mrs Retchen unleashed on Morgan much of what she was hearing on the wireless: the new government had clapped Mosley in prison, which was where they were putting all fascists; margarine and bacon would soon be things of the past; Nazi U-boats were sinking a lot of our ships.

Morgan struggled to feel the loss of an aircraft carrier or a couple of destroyers. She thought the Dunkirk disaster might have desensitised her. But the disappearance of bacon and that her favourite Prittend cinema was to be turned over to manufacturing army overcoats, were harder to bear.

They visited Grandma Perincall, Charlie's true objective the Iverdon R.D.F. station. The idea of consoling his grandmother on the disappearance of Montague had never entered his head. Morgan knew she would find it impossible to console a woman whose feelings were under such control. It occurred to neither that their grandmother, having lost two sons in the last war, might have lost the ability to display grief.

Aunt Harriet said that Monty should never have gone to Dunkirk, leaving four vulnerable women at risk. Aunt Maud preferred to think he had died a hero. Aunt Winnie's floods of tears at mention of him were difficult to cope with. She too seemed to take it personally. "He let us down. He went and died, just like the rest." Morgan and Charlie spent most of that afternoon receiving unwanted advice on how to manage a decapitated household.

Morgan told him he should be glad his inheritance might come early. This said to make him feel better, for she was unsure how he really felt about the loss of Montague.

"What do we actually know about wheat and flour and stuff? I tell you, Morgan, it's going to be difficult without him."

They had been watching a vermilion sunset from a spot on the riverside not overcome by barbed wire. The evening air was still warm, as it had been for weeks, everything drying up. On the dyke, grass turned to hay, heat haze still misting the far shore. Morgan wanted rain to wash away the signs of disaster. Charlie wanted it for the garden and the cricket pitch that, despite the concrete impediment, he hoped might be used for at least one more match.

"Pa was selfish," Morgan said. "He should have let you go to grammar school, like me. You were clever enough. But he wanted you at work."

Charlie did not respond to this test of his feelings.

"You know what he told Mama when you were born? 'I always wanted someone to help with the business.' That's the sort of man he was."

"Much good did grammar school do you!" Charlie replied.

"What do you mean?"

He felt less afraid of her now, as if he had been pushed into adulthood. He had been thinking about the Air Defence Corps. One day he would wear a uniform, with the badge he coveted. With that he could enter any official facility he wished. It didn't matter that Ronnie Talbott, who used to be his one and only friend, apart from Jerky Tag, had declared himself a pacifist.

As he dozed, Charlie was relishing the thrill of becoming part of that brotherhood of airmen for whom killing was heroic. Parclay, who had wormed his way into Morgan's affections, would be excluded. Of late Charlie had also had some misgivings about Woodborne, for whom she had evidenced some partiality. Sometimes she just made his head spin.

It was a week before Morgan told Charlie exactly what the bank manager had said: "We shall have to wait seven years for Pa to be declared dead officially. After a court hearing, that is."

All Charlie could say was, "I'll be twenty-five then."

"And I? I shall be at least forty." Her fingers went up to her throat. "Do you think this awful war could go on that long?"

"I hope so," Charlie replied.

More air raids in the north of the county gave rise to warnings of invasion. So many that people became inured to them. Some kept a lookout for spies, carried their gas masks and checked their shelters. Sandbags multiplied around municipal offices. Notices went up about walls having ears, and keeping a watch for the enemy. But by July apprehension had yielded to routine. Pathé News told of minor victories against Nazi U-boats. Yet threats of further rationing, due to continuing losses of cargo at sea, began to lower spirits.

Group Captain Floster's proposal of a cricket match brought cheer to the Villa, and a plethora of willing airmen. Given the current calm, weather and events permitting, he suggested Sunday. It would be between any military personnel who could be mustered, and those locals able to "make contact with a ball". It was, he knew, extraordinary under the circumstances, but he was positive that Captain Perincall would have approved.

On Friday before the event two aircraftmen were sent with cricket gear. The pavilion floor, still bloody from its Dunkirk occupants, was scrubbed.

Sunday was bright and hot and much of the male population of Lodford turned up for the match. Older men came to do their bit, replacement for absent sons. Their daughters flocked in numbers, with memories of encounters at the last match. The arrival of a squad of soldiers, aircraftmen, officers and a group of lively Waafs, put Morgan in mind more of a county fair than a ball game.

Flying Officer Parclay and Flight Lieutenant Woodborne got there early. Charlie's greeting was less than enthusiastic. He intended to keep them both under surveillance.

He saw how Morgan stayed close to Woodborne, chatting eagerly as they retreated into the shadow of the trees. Parclay murmured to Charlie, "Got to forgive, old chap." But his look was not a happy one. "Battle excitement and all that makes chaps do funny things." He patted Charlie's shoulder. "Not much time left before the balloon goes up."

The concrete pipe was rolled off the pitch. It took twenty minutes and the strength of both teams, leaving behind a patch of barren earth. One wicket was cracked. The scoreboard, last used to lay out the dead, was repositioned. The sight boards were left where they were in a barn near the church.

It was daringly suggested by a flight sergeant that women at the crease would better balance the opposition – the R.A.F. considered superior cricketers. Talbott, disapproving of this novelty, said his wife would be making the tea as agreed.

But what tea? A quartermaster sergeant of the Artillery, a useful all-rounder, suggested he fetch a few packets from the barracks' stores. For that he would need a woman's advice. A nod from Talbott sent his wife climbing into the lorry beside the sergeant. They drove off.

With the best bowler gone, preliminaries were lengthy. Morgan and two Waafs were given batting tuition. If she feigned less knowledge than she actually possessed, it was because of the fun of being hemmed in by the flying officer and the flight lieutenant, vying to correct her stance, confirm her grip. Both were whispering instructions in her ears, that she was not trying to make sense of.

Mrs Floster, who had no intention of helping, had gone to sit on a cushion under her sunshade. Having given up several attempts to attract her husband's attention, she reverted to scrutinising him. He watched his pilots. Charlie watched Morgan and primed the scoreboard. Two girls from his school hung around hopefully, until the Retchen girls sent them packing.

Someone shouted, "Let's get on with it before dark!" Others seemed happy to wait.

The sun through the trees dappled the grass, the women's frocks, their parasols. The steady hum of traffic along the Gormson Road was blurred by the voices of people pretending, for a short time, there was no war. For Morgan the scene had an aura of melancholy, as if many knew this might be their last match.

The alert sounding caused little stir. Eden Dufrene said that tests employed the all-clear, but no-one paid him attention.

It was agreed to postpone the game until the return of the quarter-master sergeant, a first-class bowler of googlies. The players, like the crowd, settled into somnolence. Already some of the fielders were lolling under the flowering chestnuts.

Morgan was seated on the pavilion steps, her two pilots sprawled on either side. They were joking in a desultory way, while she closed her eyes and let them admire her as they wished. She suspected their talk of impending dogfights, two-minute stand-bys and dangerous dives was meant to impress her. It was not a day for separating bravado from fact, or for thinking about the future. She would have liked to sleep.

The army lorry arrived at last. Mrs Talbott, helped from the cab by the sergeant, was holding the tea. From the other side there emerged with difficulty another soldier, an army officer carrying a kitbag.

Charlie saw at once it was Cathcart, his brother-in-law. Two lance corporals in the outfield saluted. Group Captain Floster came hurrying over.

The sergeant said that he and Mrs Talbott had given the officer a lift. He had been trying to get to Mill Lane via the pea field, but the ack-ack battery was blocking his route. After checking him in case he was a spy in disguise – at this Mrs Talbott actually laughed – they had brought him along. Watched by her husband she hurried towards the pavilion, refusing the sergeant's help.

Morgan, eyes closed, had not yet noticed her husband. Charlie went to greet Cathcart, who was looking around.

"What's going on?" Cathcart had sighted his wife, bookended by her pilots. "Who are those fellows?"

"The Royal Air Force."

"I can see that. What are they doing with my wife?"

"Teaching her to play cricket."

"Aren't you supposed to have a ball for that? Hit it with something called a bat? Used to in my day." Cathcart was surveying the field of khaki and blue. "Since when did our women play cricket? She isn't." He pointed at Coral Floster in the distance.

Charlie wasn't sure whether he wanted to defend Morgan or join in the criticism. There was an underlying bitterness in Cat's tone that too closely resembled his own present emotions.

"Why are they playing games at this time?" No reply. "Don't you know," Cathcart sounded angry, "our shipping has been attacked in the Straits of Dover?"

"Cat, darling!" Morgan had leaped to her feet, sending Parclay sideways.

Her embrace, hampered by her husband's kitbag, was brief. She held him at arm's length, appraising him. He smelled strange. His face she hardly remembered, lined like a miner's, ingrained with coal dust. "You should have told us you were coming." She kissed him firmly on his dry lips.

Someone clapped. She acknowledged them. "My husband," she called, "back from the war!"

They stood side by side, apart. She began to talk too fast, saying cricket was an attempt at normality after the chaos of the *Clara*'s home-coming.

He was making no effort to listen. "This isn't my kitbag," he told her.

With a wave at Woodborne she indicated that the match must begin without her. Still talking, she was leading Cathcart towards the Villa.

The teams were reconvened, opening batsmen summoned and everyone's attention drawn back to the game.

At the Villa Morgan let Cathcart wash while she prepared what he was willing to eat. He refused the precious cheese. She gave him buttered bread with a few strawberries from the garden. He ate in a disinterested way, staring around the dining room.

She took refuge in questions. Why was he carrying someone's kit-bag? Because he had lost everything at Dunkirk and had been kitted out with what was available. Had she said that the *Clara* had been there? His interest was marginal. Where had he come from? Dover, picked up by a pleasure boat out of Clacton, like a hundred others. The pleasure boat got hit. A minesweeper had rescued some of them. He then sank into silence. She knew that for the time being she had lost the husband who had been so eager to leave her and the children in '39.

"Have you been back to the house?" He might have read her thoughts. "I'll need underclothes and such." A shout from the cricket field startled him.

"It's just high spirits. So pleasant. A lovely game in a green space between ancient trees." She was sounding like Coral Floster.

He was sitting still, not looking at her.

"The children are well." She was pre-empting the question. "I'll show you their letters. Terry writes now. They're quite grown-up."

"I sometimes wonder what kind of mother you really are," he said, getting up suddenly, his limbs moving in a strangely disjointed fashion.

213

She thought he was coming to kiss her, but instead he gripped her by the elbow and steered her towards the door. "Let's go and find your father."

"Pa's not here." She was pulled down the front step. Still in his grasp she stumbled beside him through the garden. He was almost dragging her across the grassy mound. "I wrote! Cat, I wrote."

They reached the edge of the cricket ground before he released her, nearly falling over Coral Floster. In the clearing the cricket was seriously under way.

"Well, well," Mrs Floster said, making no attempt to rise. "And who is this importunate officer?" Cathcart stood, eyes fixed on the players in the circle of sunlight.

Morgan's brief introduction, followed by as brief a description of Montague's disappearance as she could manage, brought back Cathcart's gaze. And tears to Coral Floster's eyes. "We," she told him, pointing towards her husband, "were deeply fond of Monty."

"A good man," Cathcart murmured. His attention was on the two pilots waiting to bat. "Come."

Charlie watched the meeting between Cathcart, Morgan and the airmen. Watched them approach the pavilion. He decided that his fielding duties were extraneous and closed in to get a better view. The sergeant, ready to bowl, reprimanded him.

Charlie's brother-in-law had been a cheerful fellow as he recalled, so he was not surprised to see him smile as he shook the pilots' hands. At the pavilion steps Cathcart ordered Morgan to go and help "that woman" with the teas.

She went without protest, finding Mrs Talbott setting out crockery with plates of sandwiches. She was surprised that the mill manager's wife was hatless. Not so surprised at the bruise on her arm. With a brief nod Mrs Talbott continued working. There were strange odours in the warm room, blood and musk that Morgan determined were human.

With this woman she felt a new kind of companionship. With her, after all, she had spent the most harrowing night of her life. In silence they carried on preparing the tea, her concentration more on what she could hear on the veranda.

"I'd be grateful," Mrs Talbott was addressing her; she'd said it twice, "if you'd stop Charlie going on at my Ronald." She was looking at Morgan in a not unfriendly way, her voice firmer than normal. "He doesn't want the killing, you see. It's his nerves has affected my boy. He's gone off it."

After a moment Morgan replied, "Yes, that was a terrible night. He suffered. It affected us all."

"Ronald doesn't want to join that air defence thing. But Charlie's deaf to it. Won't listen."

"I will tell him," Morgan said. "Don't worry. We both know there must not be any more violence, must there? It must be stopped."

With this exchange she thought they had reached enough of an understanding for her to add, "We women must stand up and do something about it. We are not as weak as we imagine, are we?" Mrs Talbott with bent head said nothing more, leaving Morgan to turn her attention to the outside.

There was Coral Floster's high-pitched agreement – "so wonderfully British" – with her husband's opinion of cricket. He seemed fixed more on what Patch was saying about a pilot's need for speed. She began jokingly berating Flossie for deserting his role as umpire. Sounds of clapping masked her reproach, in which Morgan had detected insecurity.

Then Cathcart's voice questioning someone. Patch replying about the billets at Iverdon. About aircrews soon having to live on the aerodrome. Next he was telling Cathcart how long the R.A.F. had been stationed in the area. It was reassuring to hear how cheerful her husband sounded.

Mid afternoon. During tea the players divided themselves into army and air force as if prearranged. The civilians sat on the grass close to Mrs Talbott and the sandwiches. Only Lieutenant Brodick stayed talking to the pilots. Morgan, handing out tea, began to watch him more closely, puzzled. There was an underlying incivility about him at odds with his overt friendliness. His letters were the same, the calm sentences hinting at deeper darkness.

Resumption of the game had lost its urgency, as if interest was dissipating in the enervating air. Charlie was bothering less and less with it. He wished the banter between Cat and the pilots would turn to the subject of aircraft.

He had been slow to realise that his brother-in-law was more intent on questioning them about their billets, their spare time, than anything to do with the conflict. Cat was visibly irritated at their insouciance. It was the first time Charlie could see the difference between a man scarred by war and those who could look on it as sport. This was not the brother-in-law who, long ago, had tried to win him over with conjuring tricks.

Women had clustered around the returning hero. One asked him if it was true that Jerry had got into the British side of the line.

"There was no bloody line!" The word sent her recoiling. In the silence Cathcart mumbled about no tanks and having to run. "No reserves to back us up. Shot at near the river."

Charlie was looking at his sister. She might not have heard Cat, for her gaze was on Woodborne. How much happier she was when she looked his way. Then he began to see that Cathcart had noticed this too. Cat's attention, fixing less and less on Parclay, had in it a sort of warning that Morgan was unaware of. Cathcart's true attitude, like Charlie's, was of resentment.

Talbott suggested they should finish the cricket before nightfall. There was another flurry of activity while his wife collected the crockery. Before Morgan could follow her, Cathcart was beckoning. They were going back to the house.

Wishing the pilots a good innings, he led her from the field, saying over his shoulder, "Survivors need all the comfort they can get." In a mock salute Woodborne raised his hand and stayed watching them pass from light to shade.

Cathcart called from under the trees, "Why weren't you R.A.F. chaps there when we needed you?"

Then Charlie understood that, for all the bonhomie, his brother-in-law did not like the flight lieutenant. The puzzle was that Parclay had missed out entirely on Cat's wrath.

Morgan and Cathcart went upstairs to her bedroom. "My old room," she told him.

"Better than sleeping in barns. Beware of dogs behind barns. And shells."

She had half expected him to rush her into bed, but he stood looking around.

"What's this?" he was pointing at the medal hanging from her mirror.

"That's St. Odo."

"And who's he when he's at home?"

"He's a French saint."

"And where did you get it?"

"A French soldier gave it to me." At the sight of her husband's face she quickly added, "The night they brought them back from Dunkirk." He was looking at her without expression. "The injured. Dead." She was speaking urgently. "On the *Clara*, the manager's boat. I told you out there." The evening sun was turning his hair grey. "It was terrible, Cat. They were lying all over there." She was waving a hand. "Wet through they were. So dark we used torches, flares. Anything."

"Don't talk to me about wet through!" He had taken off his shirt and she saw the slash on his back, from shoulder almost to hip. The skin had puckered in the process of healing, along it patches of raw flesh, blackened by iodine.

"Oh Cat, whatever happened to you?"

"Shrapnel. Better than in the neck." The medal was in his hand. He threw it onto the dressing table. "So what have you been up to while I've been away?"

"What do you mean?"

"'Hanky panky', I think they used to call it."

She was looking at him in astonishment. "What about you?"

His expression was cold. "What do you mean?"

"What's sauce for the goose is sauce for the gander."

"Not in your case it isn't." His face was grimmer.

"And why not?"

"You're my wife's why not." He was facing her directly now.

"And you're my husband."

"Who have you been talking to?" He was picking up things – her hairbrush, powder puff. Reading the label on her bottle of scent. He was staring at the floor. "They warned me about you. They told me you were a flirt, but I didn't believe them."

"Thank you very much!" She said it sarcastically. The noise from the cricket match had become suddenly louder. She went to the window in time to see Charlie coming across the grass. She closed it. "This is all a bit late, isn't it, Cat? If you don't know who I am by now—"

"The mother of my children, that's who you are. And what I get up to is none of your business."

She tried to think of the last time they had quarrelled. But it was too long ago. "I found a postcard among Pa's things." Trying to distract him. "A French postcard."

"I suppose you're going to say it was a naughty one."

"No. A view of a village. The writing on the back was scribbled out."

"So what is your point?"

"Nothing at all." She was suddenly tired.

He came towards her. There was an oily stink from him. "I want my children to look like me," he said.

"Wherever you father them?" It was out before she could stop it.

His hand came up and slapped her hard on the cheek. It was exactly like her father slapping her, as he had on that one and only occasion.

On the stairs she nearly toppled Charlie. He saw her burning cheek, furious eyes, parted lips. Heard the door bang as she rushed into the garden.

Charlie asked Cathcart, still standing in the bedroom, what had happened. "Family matters" was the reply.

Then Charlie too saw the wound. "Where'd you get that?"

"Shrapnel." Cathcart's voice was almost inaudible. "I got up the ladder. That was the worst bit when they hauled me in." He paused then went on louder. "What is she doing to me? Gave me a jab and I went out. Where has she gone? All the way over I kept asking for a doctor. Needed another jab. The pain, see?" He was gazing at the garden below, where Morgan had emerged near an apple tree, her shadow wavering over the dry lawn. At her feet was the rabbit in its temporary cage.

Cathcart put an arm around Charlie's shoulder. "This isn't my fault. She's changed." With a sudden movement he pushed Charlie aside, ran downstairs and into the garden.

Charlie stayed at the window watching them. He saw how his sister backed away from her husband, not in fear, but as if preparing for confrontation. Their conversation lasted several minutes. He noticed how stiffly Cat held his arms to his sides, and how Morgan waved hers in the air.

He saw their attention claimed by something happening on the cricket ground. He opened the window. Lorries and motorbikes were starting up. There was shouting. He caught a glimpse of two women in moth-like dresses hurrying towards the gates. Cars were leaving. People coming back from the river path were asking what was going on.

He saw Cat quit the garden. Saw Woodborne and Parclay, pads under their arms, approaching from the cricket ground. Charlie called to his sister, but her attention was on the meeting of the three men. After the briefest of conversations they shook hands, then the two airmen hurried off in the direction of the drive.

No alert had sounded yet the ground, in what seemed like minutes, had cleared of everyone save for a few stragglers who, seeing the abandoned pitch, hurriedly left.

That evening Cathcart said he knew all along it was bound to happen. France going to the enemy with no resistance. Our forces badly weakened, the next step was invasion. Morgan and Charlie were dismayed.

He said he'd had a look around, and there wasn't much they could do if the enemy came by sea. With sufficient warning they might activate the Rover. The air force chaps had implied that the early warning system at Iverdon, one of a chain, was tracking a lot of German aircraft activity. So, in his opinion, the most likely invasion would be by air. Soon.

"A Heinkel crash-landed this year. One was shot down over the estuary last November. And a Dornier before that." Charlie didn't know why he was feeling so edgy. "We're ready, aren't we? The Spitfire's an incredible machine." Morgan sat looking apprehensive. There was no visible sign that Cat had hit her.

"The Spitfire's got its drawbacks." Cathcart sounded positive. "In winter they ice up."

"It's summer now," she said. "There are other planes at the airfield."

"Probably Hurricanes. They left us without cover on the beaches."

Eager to forget their earlier encounter, Morgan pressed her husband's hand, saying, "*We shall never surrender!*"

At Cathcart's bidding the discussion ended. Soon afterwards they went upstairs, leaving Charlie sitting staring at the nail marks his clenched fingers had made on his palms.

CHAPTER NINE

It was no surprise when Cathcart slumped into bed, leaving his clothes in a trail. Immediately he turned away from her and went to sleep. Before putting out the light she kissed his cheek, knowing that exhaustion and pain were to blame for his recent behaviour.

She lay long in the dark listening to his breathing, trying to work out what had changed in their years together. Why she still had the same sexual needs, found the same thrill in his touch. Why he did not. Why he had left her for a life of physical denial. Had he become as bored with her body as with suburban life? Had she too unthinkingly accepted it as inevitable and been forced into action by circumstance? Were they bound only by Billy and Teresa? She could see their suburban nest's little life as finite. She touched his shoulder. Why did she still long for the comfort of his body?

An owl hooted loudly. Cathcart mumbled something and groaned. She would have to wait. But the thought again came creeping that perhaps it wasn't him in particular whom she loved to make love to, but any man offering physical fulfilment. There had been few chances during their marriage to do other than wonder about sex with another man, and for that she had her cinematic heroes. She was the same passionate woman she had always been. Wasn't that why Cat had married her? Their wedding night had been a wild one.

Again an owl. She could hear the faint rush of water through the floodgates, the drone of a plane taking off.

She knew too well that most men were not much interested in pleasuring women beyond their own needs. Even Archie had been too speedy, and he was one of the loving ones. Comparisons would not leave her. She lay looking at those remembered faces, feeling their hard exploratory hands, hearing the softness of their words.

In the night Cat had not exactly made love to her. Rather it had been a falling on her, a grinding which she bore as best she could, telling herself that this stranger would change again to the cheerful person she had known. The effort exhausted him, yet he sought her hand and clasped it for so long she had trouble extricating it. His body was still giving off yesterday's aroma, harsh and foreign, as if his experiences had sunk deep into him.

At 3 a.m. she woke to find him nearly under the bed, asleep. Barely waking he scrambled up beside her, where they both spent the rest of the night disturbed by his bad dreams.

Sparrows squabbling in the apple tree woke her. Cat beside her still sleeping. His breathing, as heavy as the weight of his arm, was a sensation she had almost forgotten. She would have to get used to waking with a man beside her.

Six o'clock. No Charlie getting up. Her doll with the bleached eyes was looking at her blankly. It was disconcerting. She leaped from the bed and pushed the creature over. Cathcart stirred but didn't waken. He looked older, the youth in him, energy she had loved, not visible. She went to wake a surprised Charlie with a cup of tea.

They sat at breakfast in the kitchen, the sounds of aircraft louder now.

"Alice Dance has offered me a job in the butcher's. She thought the shop would suit me. Or the abattoir, if I like." Charlie sounded matter-of-fact. Morgan wondered if this was a test. "Don't fancy cutting up dead bodies though."

The abattoir, one of the memories she most wished to erase: seven years old then. In Long Alley with her father. They had stopped under a high window. He told her that cows were killed in there. Ever curious, she asked to look and he had lifted her up. Through the bars, at that instant, she saw a man hammer a metal rod into the side of a cow's head. The animal fell and so did she, weeping into her father's arms.

She went to feed the chickens, watching the grains multiply through her tears. It was everything she was crying over, the murdered cow, Charlie, Cat's behaviour, her father's fate, her children liable to forget her. All came swimming in.

A motorcar, seeming to flow between the trees, coming closer. It was long and low, cream coloured with a black roof that glittered. A woman was driving, another woman beside her.

Charlie came running. The older woman, so tall she seemed to take minutes unwinding from her seat, was so thin her emerging shadow barely crossed his path. She stood surveying, first Morgan and Charlie, then the house, the sweep of the garden, the river. She was dressed in brown, with a squashed hat.

The younger woman jumped out, extending a chubby hand. She was colour from hat to hem and looked about to burst from her frock. The contrast between the women was startling.

Hands were shaken. The tall woman was addressing Morgan. "I am Mrs Minnery. This is my daughter, Florence." Morgan shook off the image of a huge baby stuck between the legs of this skeletal creature. "You are undoubtedly Mrs Morgan Brodick?" They might have arrived sooner, but for the search for petrol.

Charlie whispered to Morgan that the car was an Armstrong Siddeley.

It took the unloading of three leather suitcases for her to grasp that this was the new lodger, the Land Girl.

Mrs Minnery requested an inspection of the house, saying that at first glance it seemed suitable enough. She was bone thin, so emaciated that Morgan was reminded of a story about a cadaver that haunted children's bedrooms.

The women were taken from dining room to sitting rooms, to Montague's study, through the snug and the lobby, into the boot room and conservatory. There were no comments. They paused beneath the stained-glass window in the hall. Neither remarked on its magical light.

Then upstairs, peering into cupboards and one bedroom after another. There seemed no way of deterring Mrs Minnery from opening all doors, ignoring her daughter's mild protestations. Morgan noticed how briefly the mother scanned each room, while Florence's scrutiny was keener.

They stopped at the intended bedroom, that Mrs Retchen had gone to some effort to make pleasant, with a quilt and refreshed curtains.

"This won't do at all. Too small by half. Our girl will explode in here." Morgan was inclined to agree, imagining her bursting out of the window.

Florence followed along the landing, peering around her mother's thin frame. It was Rhoda's room. Mrs Minnery declared with finality, "This will do. Those will have to go." She was pointing at the ruched lampshades, the Singer. "Florence does not sew. Other than that, this is acceptable." Turning to her daughter, "Fetch your suitcases yourself, dear. The boy downstairs has an impediment. You will have to learn to be self-sufficient. It will do her no harm." This last addressed to Morgan, shadowing her as she headed below.

Again they looked at the sitting rooms, Morgan studying the furniture with the fresh eyes of her visitors and generally liking what she saw. She could not dispose of anything of her mother's. Yes, Florence would have access to both wirelesses. Yes, her laundry would be taken care of unless, here Morgan paused, unless her clothes required special attention. And yes, Florence would have breakfast every morning, dinner at night.

"A good breakfast, mind. I have seen the poultry. She will give you her ration book." Mrs Minnery bent to speak low. "I believe that the Land Army, which she would choose despite our best efforts, work their volunteers." Her cheeks were rouged. "The other toilers will not be housed here? That would not do."

Morgan saw, that behind her mother's back, Florence was pulling faces. "Mama likes to be thorough," she whispered as they entered the kitchen.

"Oh!" The cry was at the sight of Cathcart, hunched over a plate of fried eggs, fork poised in surprise at the intrusion. Across the back of his shirt was a long pink stain. His attempt to rise was hampered by a pistol's lanyard beside his plate.

Mrs Minnery opened the oven door and peered in. They watched in silence. "Excellent. This will do nicely." And, indicating Cathcart, "He does his work well."

He went back to his breakfast as if they had never been there.

Mrs Minnery said other houses had been either unsavoury or their owners unsuitable. Of course, she told Morgan, she would have preferred a lodging nearer Iverdon. Mr Brodir the farmer had suggested Florence might live in the farmhouse. But that did not appeal. At this, Florence made a thumbs-down sign and bit her lip. Morgan tried not to smile.

"And who is this young man exactly?"

Charlie had rushed in, saying the car was a twelve horsepower. He shook hands.

"It is a four-cylinder, twelve-horsepower saloon, purchased by my husband in 1938. That is the sum of my knowledge. It could have brought us here in record time if there had been adequate signposting. Could it not, Florence?"

"It certainly could, Mama." Florence of the smiling face added, "She drives like a demon! Would you like a spin?"

Morgan was feeling control slipping. "Excuse me, Mrs Minnery, but how did you obtain the fuel for that enormous motor?" Florence was grinning again.

"I am glad you asked that, my dear. Perspicacious." Mrs Minnery looked strangely pleased. "I am a magistrate." And that was that. Her daughter kept grinning. "May I suggest we have lunch?"

Food had entirely slipped Morgan's mind. For five people, not counting the Retchens, lunch might have to consist of slivers of bacon, if Cat had left any, bread and dripping, cold cabbage, spoonfuls of shepherd's pie. Or dried beans and boiled wheat. With eggs of course, served on the best china. Now she was thinking crazily.

Her visitors had gone to the car and returned with a hamper and a cloth-covered basket. A grateful Morgan prepared the dining table with the best cutlery and the cut-glass cruet, on her mother's embroidered tablecloth. She set a place for Cathcart. He might have gone out somewhere, for a door had banged.

There was a loaf with a crust, cheese and butter, ham on the bone, young lettuce from the Minnery greenhouses. The hardboiled eggs, Mrs Minnery commented, were indubitably Coals to Newcastle. Morgan and Charlie looked with wonder at pickled walnuts. The dish their hostess called *tête de veau* both knew was really brawn. She produced fruit that had been grown, she said, in the family's hothouse. "I want you," she told Charlie, "to take two peaches and give them to those poor girls beating carpets."

"Their mother is there too." Charlie was encouraged by the looks the daughter was giving him.

"In that case, take three." He went out with them.

The meal over, Mrs Minnery offered cigarettes from a black box. Morgan remembered with a jolt that Aunt Pandora had smoked Balkan Sobranie. Even now she could smell the scent. In the evening they would sit in her back garden in Hackney, watching the sun set beyond the railway line.

An ever-increasing level of aircraft activity was interfering with conversation. Morgan asked if her visitor had plans to stay: it was clear that something unusual was going on in the sky. The alert began its crescendo and they went outside to look.

Overhead, plane after plane was rising into the distance of a cloudless sky.

"I shall go directly back to York," Mrs Minnery was addressing her daughter. "It is unsafe for me here."

"We have an Anderson shelter in the garden," Morgan replied, wondering why it was not unsafe for Florence too.

"No thank you, my dear Mrs Brodick. I have never skulked underground in my life and I do not intend to do so now."

"Neither do I." Morgan's reply was echoed by her new lodger.

"One last question . . ." Mrs Minnery was pulling on her gloves. "Do you have stables? No? Pity. Florence has a good seat. Mr Brodir will be impressed with her equine knowledge." She had a foot on the running board. "See that she swims, will you?"

"I love swimming," Florence said.

"Get off some of that *avoirdupois.*"

They watched Mrs Minnery start the Armstrong Siddeley, her head almost touching its roof. Then Morgan understood why her hat was crushed.

She drove away at speed, watched from the gate by the others.

"Mama likes to be seen as a daredevil." Florence was following her landlady into the house. "She fancies she's at *Le Mans*. She liked you. It's people who fawn over her she loathes. That oven business was her way of testing you."

"Did I pass?"

"Flying colours. If you hadn't, I would have stayed anyway. We are going to get on like a house on fire." Florence was pulling a face. "That's the first banana I've eaten since last year. Mama is given lots, but Rolly and I – he's my brother – have to go round the back-to-backs handing them out to unfortunates. It's not fair. You'd think she was the brigadier, not Daddy."

Rolling thunder diverted their attention. Two tiny planes were circling one another, leaving behind thin whorls of smoke. Charlie said one was a Stuka. They were fighting.

After the all-clear Mrs Retchen took her girls home, saying her nerves had gone. There was no sign of Cathcart. Charlie went back to the mill.

Morgan and Florence spent an hour clearing Rhoda's cupboards and packing her suitcase for the attic. Morgan could not explain why her father's ex-housekeeper should possess two exotic evening frocks.

Florence was an interesting talker and Morgan, deprived of welcome female company, willingly listened. She said she felt guilty at not obeying her father by joining the army, or even the navy. She showed Morgan her Land Girl's outfit, not at all embarrassed to drop her clothes where she stood. Her naked body was as round and dimpled as her face, and so without blemish she might have been an infant. Morgan rushed to shut Rhoda's bedroom door. The cord breeches, shirt, socks and shoes, all in shades of fawn, turned Florence into a replica of her mother through a distorting mirror. The felt hat, sitting on her curls, sent them both into mild hysterics.

Florence was curious about Rhoda. Her background.

Morgan once asked her father where Rhoda had come from. The reply was, "Over Wolverhampton way." Charlie once said Rhoda had only one holiday away from the Villa before his accident, when he was eight. She had gone with a suitcase so big it took two to lift it onto the lorry. Was away an age. She had missed his birthday, which was why he remembered. The suitcase came back light as a feather. He didn't ask why.

"Who's he?" Florence was holding a leather frame. They peered at the photograph of a man in an artificial pose. "It's been touched up. Lipstick, see? They used to do that to me. Gave me Marlene Dietrich eyebrows. How old is he, do you think? Don't fancy him. Do you?"

Morgan did not. He was not Ramon Novarro or Tyrone. She was wondering whether Rhoda's sequinned frock might be cut short to fit her. Patch would certainly love her in that.

Neither woman took any notice of another alert, or the constant sounds of aircraft. In one of Florence's suitcases was a box of chocolates that she seemed unable to resist.

By five, Cathcart had returned carrying binoculars. Introductions were terse. But to Morgan's relief her husband seemed to like the Land Girl, listening to talk of her horses as if he were genuinely interested. He didn't notice her look of dismay when he accepted a chocolate.

He had been, he said, to the barracks, to arrange protection of the mill. In exchange he had agreed to let them use the cricket pitch as a practice ground. Practice for what? There would be no more games of cricket. Or any other games for that matter. Didn't Morgan know there was a war on?

Florence deftly averted the evident hostility by asking for a lift to the farm at Iverdon, for she was curious about her duties. Morgan thought it would be an opportunity to visit Grandma Perincall on the way.

Ignoring Charlie's objections to taking a gift, a trug of vegetables joined her and Florence on the back seat. It was only the second time that the Rover had been out of the garage without Montague. Cathcart put on his uniform, saying the police wouldn't intercept an army officer.

He stopped at the house only to set his wife down, driving on with Florence to the farm. He would be returning within the hour, he said as they left.

Morgan was greeted at the door by a subdued Aunt Winifred. Harriet and Maud had been evacuated with the Little Gormson infant school. She begged her niece not to upset her grandmother, who was feeling the loss.

To Morgan's eyes Grandma Perincall looked her usual self. "How is the mill?" was an unusual greeting. "Was that a motor car we heard?"

"Yes. Cathcart brought me here. He will visit you soon."

"I see. And the boy, is he doing his work properly?" Morgan thought so. "Why no word of your father?"

A police inspector had come to the Villa to tell Morgan that "a source, which, for security reasons, he wasn't free to disclose", had seen the *Berenice* with a hole in her bow. Near the French coast. And she wasn't to make too much of this. All Grandma Perincall said was "Hmm."

They sat in the garden, Aunt Winnie's Plymouth Rocks pecking round them. "My son is not to be killed off that easily. Look at your husband – he came back. In one piece, I hope?" And with a swift change of subject, "Why no stockings, child?" She had noticed Morgan's bare legs.

"I am saving a pair for best. The others are more darns than lisle."

"You are turning into a didicoy. There were looks on Sunday."

"Oh, Grandma, what do I care about looks? Have you seen my nails?" They were held out for inspection.

"Get those Wretched girls to do more."

"Retchen. They do enough. If I'm not careful, their mother will take them away."

"Did Charles tell you my girls have been evacuated?"

"Er . . . No." Inwardly Morgan was questioning when Charlie might have found the time to visit Grandma Perincall. And why.

"Well, they have. To Nottinghamshire, lock, stock and barrel." She looked stern. "Winifred and I were expecting someone to call and enquire if we were managing. Winnie does what she can at her age, poor soul."

Morgan wondered how old her nearest relatives were. Could her aunts still be classified as girls? How old was Aunt Maud when she had fallen in love with the soldier killed in the Great War? From his photograph on the kitchen mantelpiece beside the coronation mug he could not have been any older than Charlie. The soldier, posed rigidly in perfect puttees, had a face and hands so impossibly smooth that retouching must have gone on there too. His frame, with its corners like wooden crosses, gave him a religious significance. She had wanted to ask Aunt Winnie if she too had been in love like her sisters, but did not want to frighten her.

"How is your other grandmother faring?"

"Fine, I think, Grandma."

"I ask myself, Morgan, if it is fitting that your late mother's mother should be cared for by people who run a public house."

Morgan sighed. "They look after her at the Three Tuns very well."

"Perhaps. But I ask myself whether, for instance, they take proper cognisance of her hygiene."

"I think they must do."

"There you are! Such personal affairs should not be attended to by people like that, even if your grandmother has lost her reason." She was pausing, but only for breath. "She came down in the world when she married that cabinet-maker Dorp. In my opinion he was the undoing of her."

"Sorry Grandma, I'm not clear—"

"She may have been driven mad by his excesses."

"What excesses, exactly?"

"Nothing to occupy your mind."

"She is only touched some of the time. The rest she's fine, if a bit—"

"That is exactly my point. When she comes to, what does Mrs Skeff-ingley . . . Dorp make of this publican handling, for example, such items as her *directoires*?"

Rising in her chair, Morgan sent chickens scattering. "Great merci-ful heavens, Grandma! Shouldn't we be grateful to the Corys? Some-times I wonder what century you're living in!"

Her grandmother's cheeks flushed. "I hoped you had learned to control yourself better by now."

Morgan subsided with a mumbled apology.

They sat in silence, until her grandmother suggested magnani-mously they go in for tea. Winnie was called to make it.

In a corner a pile of comics caught Morgan's attention. They seemed so out of place.

"You may take those for Charlie." Her grandmother was waving a disparaging hand. "If Pip, Squeak and Wilfred are not beyond him."

Morgan, knowing she would be forever held responsible for Charlie's lack of education, asked where on earth the comics had come from.

"They came with the young private. He was here for a few days, wasn't he, Winnie?"

Aunt Winifred was agreeing. "Very polite he was, Morgan. He was here while they searched for his . . . unit, I think they called it."

"A nice enough boy. Filled the oil lamps and so on. He started a plot for us for the potatoes. One can't have enough potatoes." Grandma Perincall stared out of the window at the invisible plot. "Yes, Maud and Harriet will be back soon enough. All this fighting will blow over." Her words were more reassuring to her than to her listeners.

"I will be able to finish digging the rest," Winifred said. "The ground is still moist there. But Harry didn't think potatoes would do well in the wet."

Her mother intervened. "Nonsense, of course they will! His name was Harold."

"I bandaged his arm," Winifred whispered.

Morgan didn't ask if Harry's digging had caused his injury, guessing that it had not.

At last Cathcart arrived with Florence, thus delaying Morgan's longed-for departure. Her grandmother seemed less than pleased. Morgan guessed she disapproved of a married man driving about with a strange spinster.

"You are fortunate," Grandma Perincall observed to Cathcart, "to have come back from those very same grounds where my boys still lie. But they were in the thick of it."

Everyone looked towards Cathcart, whose expression had darkened. "Yes, I don't suppose a railway siding in Dieppe could be called 'the thick of it'. They were looting the trains, you see. Our job was to stop it. We were forced back. There was heavy fighting on the roads." He straightened and winced. "We moved across country, but we didn't know where we were. It was raining."

The room was suddenly so tense that Morgan could hear a fly buzzing. Florence's eyes had widened. "Bombers overhead. Shells. I left what was left of my men back at a farmhouse. Two of them so badly hurt they couldn't go on." Cathcart paused. "He wanted me to shoot him." No-one in the room asked who or whether. "Roads almost impassable. Dead animals. Burning vehicles."

Grandma Perincall, shifting in her seat, made to rise.

"When we got there we hid in the dunes. Queues of them down the beaches to the ships. But they kept sinking them, see?" Now he was unstoppable. "Three days . . . they took us out to the big carrier . . . Messerschmitts strafing us from first light. Boats around us sunk. Smoke everywhere. The water red . . . The smell. Corpses floating—"

"Corpses are not a suitable subject for conversation!" Grandma Perincall was marching to the door. Winifred had her hands to her face.

"Three days' wait to be rescued." Cathcart's voice had risen. "No food. Nine out of twelve sunk was why we were sent back. Some of us waited for *three days*. My men lined up in water to their shoulders. Machine-gunned!" He was shouting. "Back to the dunes again to wait. Shelling! At dawn they bombed us, so we were . . ." But he was talking to the closing door. "Eight hundred men lost on just one torpedo boat." His voice was fading. On either side Morgan and Florence were grabbing at his flailing arms. Winifred, collapsed on the pile of comics, was sobbing.

The evening was quiet. Morgan and Cathcart sat in the garden with Florence, watching the high smoke trails dissipate, the sunset blood red and fading. Grandma Perincall was not mentioned, nor wireless reports of dogfights over the North Sea or British casualties. Morgan saw how Cat's face had resumed a more normal look, as if the afternoon's outburst had drained him. She appreciated Florence's attempt to lighten the atmosphere:

"Twenty-two shillings and sixpence, not much for what Brodir expects of us girls. And some of that for bed and board." She thought she might manage the ploughing, if she could hang on, with two Shires dragging her through the furrows. At home her horses were more the jumping variety.

Her habit of chatting about inconsequential things was, Morgan saw later, accompanied by keen observation. To cheer up Charlie, Florence told him such a good joke about a talking horse that he asked her to repeat it. When Cathcart was tiring of her chatter, she ceased. They were sorry when she went to her room, saying the lorry was picking her up early.

Cat made love to Morgan that night silently, fast and in a black bedroom still warm from the day. He did not ejaculate inside her, saying he didn't want to bring any more children into such a world. When she inadvertently touched the wound on his back, he gasped.

She dreamed of being trapped in a box, irritated by a tapping on the flap. Awake, she told herself it was the wisteria, not gunfire. It was Charlie tap tapping on the door, to say that the new girl was crying in her room.

At half past three, they found Florence fully dressed and in tears. She was wearing the regulation felt hat. On her feet she had a pair of gumboots just visible under a long oilskin smelling of disinfectant. Morgan's first instinct was to laugh. Charlie could not stop. Florence said she didn't care what time it was.

How could she go to work looking like a cesspit cleaner? Nobody would talk to her, least of all some nice man. Only men wore long khaki shirts. On the coverlet lay her overalls, that Morgan could see were sizes too small.

She persuaded Florence into her nightdress, gave her hot milk and tucked her in like a child, with the promise that Brodir would be spoken to soon.

In a matter of days Florence had changed her mind. The other Land Girls looked a lot worse. And some, not accustomed to rising at six, were already complaining of exhaustion. She told Morgan in Charlie's hearing that Cedric Brodir was a randy old dog, sniffing round all the girls. "I swear if it weren't for these britches, he'd have had me at least once already." This spoken with an insouciance that Morgan envied. Florence's tendency to leave the bathroom door unlocked, or actually open, sufficiently dismayed her to remind her lodger there were men in the house.

Cat's attitude to his wife seemed daily to switch between comradeship and watchfulness. It distanced them and exhausted her. The wound on his back, that he allowed no-one to touch, was still troubling him.

"We're going to Granny Dorp," he told her a few days later.

"What if she's not there?"

"She lives there." He had not understood her meaning. "We'll take Charlie. She liked him."

"She is frightened of him." Morgan had never before expressed this thought. At times even she felt Charlie was . . . threatening? . . . inflexible? Charlie was . . . too difficult to pin down.

*

Cathcart once told Morgan he had a soft spot for Granny Dorp. She reminded him of his late mother, woolly minded, but sharp at the same time.

They found her sitting on a stool by the brook outside her back door. She smiled when she saw them, went indoors and came out with a bowl of strawberries.

"Hello, Monty." She was looking at Cathcart. "How's life in the trenches? Let you home for Christmas, have they?"

Hoarse laughter from the kitchen. A man in shirtsleeves emerged. He was Cory, the landlord of the Three Tuns. "She takes the biscuit, don't she?" Morgan liked his good humour. "The wife says she keeps us all going." He looked hard at Cathcart, who was wearing one of Montague's jackets. "Army, were you?"

He fetched chairs. "I was in the Dragoons last time," he said. "Seconded from the Territorials out there." He was urging Granny Dorp to come and sit down again. "Blood and guts," to Morgan, "excusing the language." He made a lunge at Granny Dorp throwing a strawberry into the air. He watched it squelch at her feet. "Waste not, want not."

He pushed the old lady onto her stool. She said loudly, "Where's my Berenice?"

Unhesitatingly the landlord replied, "Out for a drive, Mrs Dorp. Out for a nice spin."

They sat hearing the water racing in the brook. Martins were flying low over it. Finches were in the may blossom, whose scent was perfuming the air. Ringdoves calling. "Seems like a lull in the fighting, don't it?" Cory said. "Over at the airfield they were on two-minute stand-by, so they say." He sounded knowledgeable. "Sleeping in their kit, so to speak. They've lost a kite or two. Came into the pub last evening, a few of them. First time since Jerry hotted things up."

He lapsed into silence, rerolling his shirtsleeves, looking from one to the other for conversation. "So there must be a lull," he added.

Cathcart stood up. Granny Dorp watched with interest as he took off his shirt. The landlord's "Dear, dear!" chorused her sighs.

235

Morgan saw her husband wince when her grandmother touched the wound. It had bloodied her father's shirt.

She told Florence there had been no questions from Granny Dorp. She put cabbage leaves on Cat's wound to draw out the pus, and some herb mixed with oil. In her tiny kitchen were many jars of dried herbs, some labelled. Charlie said he knew elder and marigold. When he was tiny she had put mouldy cheese on his cut finger. She had treated his bad leg with self heal, singing to drown out his cries. As soon as Rhoda's back was turned, he had torn off the dressing. So his grandmother gave up. Florence asked if he were sorry now, but he didn't understand what she meant. Charlie said she should see Granny Dorp's pretend-to-eat trick: empty fork to open mouth. It might be the reason she was shrinking.

During the afternoon a child of about seven appeared, uncombed and silent. Looking entirely at home, she munched a crust from a plate in the sink. Morgan told Florence the cottage could have been built for a child, everything in miniature.

The landlord's wife, much younger than her husband, came to collect her daughter and watched Granny Dorp wind Cat in a tight bandage. They stayed until five, sharing his bitter-tasting tea.

Cory and his wife insisted on taking Morgan and Cathcart back to the pub, where they sat in a bare room behind the saloon. Morgan's chief wish was to leave, until she glimpsed Patch Woodborne in the bar, leaning against a pillar. He was in his flying jacket, white scarf wound around its collar. It was not a woman he was talking to so animatedly, but a fellow pilot. The man moved into view, revealing a bandaged head. Her heart turned over. Now there was real warfare. Men were being injured in the skies, just as Cat had been on the ground.

Cathcart said, when Mr Churchill told them they must be prepared, he wasn't wasting breath. If the dogfights of the previous days had subsided, it was only for the Hun to remuster. Then the Stukas and Heinkels her brother was always so pleased to praise would come back threefold. And after that?

*

236

"I hope you paid them at the Three Tuns," Charlie said on Saturday. "They'll expect extra for the bandage." He was watching Morgan trying to iron Cathcart's shirt. The letter Eden had brought was still lying unopened.

"One of the girls should be doing this while their mother's away, not I." She was overheating.

"The twins can't do ironing. Rhoda always did it before. They tried, but they can't manage the twiddly bits."

"Sometimes, Charles, the way you express yourself leaves much to be desired." He enjoyed her speaking to him like this.

Cathcart came in. "Leave the boy alone." In his hands was the revolver he seemed to carry everywhere. "He's a grown man now." Charlie looked at him gratefully. "All this talk of ironing when we should be talking of war. What did our leader say: 'If we fail, we'll sink into a new Dark Age'? Doing our duty doesn't mean doing the ironing."

"Well, Cat, will you enjoy wearing your shirt like this?"

Charlie, filled with sudden anxiety, looked from one to the other.

"I need my electric iron."

"Go home and get it."

"Can't you? I have so much to do here. Mrs Retchen is at her sister's again. Florence is extra work. She's always dirty."

"Easy to get an iron here," Charlie interrupted. "I'll ask Jerky to get one."

"Who's Jerky?" Morgan and Cathcart asked in unison.

"My pal. Lives over at Ironside. Next to the railway line."

"Not in one of those shacks with a tin roof! Old tyres and such all around? Their children came to school with shaved heads."

"That's Jerky." Charlie sounded pleased. "He can get most things. Lucky too. Won on the Derby, Pont . . . something'. But they say the horse racing's going to be cancelled now." He thought for a moment. "Morgan, Gordon Richards lost."

She knew he was meaning Montague's bet, its loss a bad omen.

She spat on the iron, which gave a loud crack.

Charlie had retrieved a tea towel. "Rhoda always irons them."

"If you mention that woman again, I will strike you with this." The flat iron was put near his cheek. He found the threat strangely exciting. Cathcart said nothing.

Charlie pushed the letter to her. "Looks like her writing."

She put it on the mantelpiece and changed the iron for the hotter one.

Cathcart said to Charlie, "Isn't she going to open it?" To Morgan, "Open it. Your father hasn't got a forwarding address."

"How can you be so unfeeling?" She slammed the flat-iron on the stove. "Neither of you will be satisfied until you know what Rhoda says."

She began to read the letter aloud:

> *Darling Monty*
>
> *No news so far from you. Its been two months. Are you alright? I do worry. Hard at work here book keeping & doing the wages. We had a hockey match against HMS . . . can't say what! Life here not bad but wish you wld write. Give love to Charlie.*
>
> *Ever yrs Rody xxxx*

Charlies snatched it. "She's still there. H.M.S. *Boskall.* 'From 3rd. Officer R. Swell'. She hasn't been promoted."

"She might be, sooner than she thinks," Cathcart replied. "With each sinking, everyone left alive gets a leg-up."

'How cynical," Morgan remarked.

"I've seen a barrage balloon." Charlie was changing the subject. "Big silver thing. Like a pig!"

"Talking of pigs," Morgan said, "what is the name of the pig man?"

"Who?" Charlie knew how she hated unnecessary questions.

"You know him very well." She was pointing towards Mill Lane. "The one in the frayed blue jumper, rain or shine. Always raises his cap." Ignoring both men's questioning looks, she took the ironing to the airing cupboard.

Charlie followed. "Cat says I've got to ask why you want to know the pig man."

"I don't want to *know* him, Charles. Not in the biblical sense! Just his surname." He hated it when he couldn't fathom what she was up to. "He might be willing to provide us with a little extra bacon, that's all."

"Oh. You don't need him. I'll ask Jerky. On second thoughts, I don't think he knows Asher . . . !" The surname on his lips, he stopped. Before Morgan could do more than grin, he had run downstairs, angry with himself for disclosing what she wanted to know.

Cathcart, cleaning his shoes, told Morgan that Charlie had gone to the corn exchange with Talbott. "Message is he'll be late for his tea, so not to wait."

"What do you think he's up to?" she asked.

"I do not know and I don't care. You mollycoddle that boy. You're not his mother."

Morgan silently watched her husband through lowered lids. He was ignoring the alert that had just sounded. He took the binoculars and went outside. She followed.

Nothing to see in the cloudless sky. Nothing to hear but the wind sighing. There was the sudden noise of a Spitfire, cracking the eardrums as it roared towards the estuary. Then another. And another. And another.

The sound of heavy lorries starting up. "The army," Cat said.

A voice began shouting orders.

"I gave them permission," Cathcart was indicating the cricket pitch. "Ack-ack crew called back to duty."

She ran ahead of him. Under the trees she was obstructed by the concrete drain. "What have they done to the pitch?" Sunlight was exposing divots displaced almost to the outfield. In front of the pavilion were five wooden gibbets. From each dangled a sack.

"Bayonet practice." There were trickles of sand beneath them. He was gesturing with an imaginary bayonet: "'Stick it in! Twist! Withdraw!' 'Twist' is the important bit." He was smiling. "Now ask me why."

"Why?"

"Otherwise the blade gets stuck, doesn't it?" She saw how alert he had become.

Alert, too, to something happening towards the river. "Hear that?" It was the scream of an aircraft out of control.

They ran into the open. Far away, an airplane tiny as a beetle was spiralling downward, leaving behind a straight sky trail. And way above, high in the very blue, were puffs and smoke trails in figures of eight. The wounded plane dropped headlong out of sight, beyond the trees on the other side of the river. They waited, Morgan near tears, Cathcart exhilarated. "That was interesting. I suspect I'm going to be recalled soon."

He turned away from the scene as if it hadn't happened. "My stuff needs to be ready, such as it is. You'd better get on with it."

It was the harsh tone, Cat sounding less like a husband and more like the officer he was, directing lower ranks. She watched him walking away, the wound sufficiently healed to allow more freedom. Yet his gait, stiff and erect, was as inflexible as his attitude.

She made her way back, looking skyward, seeing only vapour trails. At the lost gate, a burst of gunfire from the senior school. She waited. Silence. A robin began its high trill. And through it came an equally familiar sound of sobbing.

It was muffled and coming, she thought, from the Villa garden. The river and the sobbing seemed to flow together in one long mournful undulation. She passed her mother's roses, pygmied by the drought. The robin's song continued. She crossed the lawn to where the tumulus of the Anderson shelter was blocking her way. The shelter's door was out of place. The sobs had grown louder. She peered into the interior, knowing to whom they belonged.

"Myrtle?" The crying subsided.

The shelter smelled musty. Morgan located the candle and matches. Sitting deep inside was the hunched form of Myrtle Retchen. She must have been there for some time. Her shoulders were shaking, her hair in a wild stook. The frock was torn, her feet and legs caught up in the muddy remnants of her knickers.

Morgan hugged her, which she would never have done before the Dunkirk night. She rubbed her arms and hands, dried the tears, until Myrtle could speak.

Her story was garbled so that Morgan, to make sense of it, had to rearrange the retelling. To some of her questions there were answers. To others there was a shaking of the head, more tears and bursts of quick anger.

Sitting beside her, Morgan repeated the story back to Myrtle for clarity, waiting until there was agreement that what she was recounting was the truth of it:

"You were in the garden with Thelma." Yes. "Thelma went home because your mother wasn't there to get lunch for you." Yes. "You walked with your sister along the drive, because that is what you always do." Yes. "A soldier saw you." Yes. "He was standing watching soldiers sticking swords into sacks." Some of them, yes. "He took you back here, stopped at the old gate and asked if you liked chocolate. You said yes." Yes. "Nobody else saw you." No. "You showed him the rabbit in the hutch because you thought he might find it a bigger one." Yes. It's too small. "He said he'd find one and give you chocolate, but down in this shelter." Yes. "You came in here with him. He put his hands on you and you liked it." Yes. "But when he tried to take off your clothes you didn't like it."

At this point Myrtle began to sob again. Morgan held her until she calmed. "He pulled you onto the floor and you couldn't stop him. He hurt you underneath." Underneath. He wouldn't stop. "Then he stopped and left you lying here. How long ago?" Myrtle didn't know how long. All she knew was that he was a soldier, and he had done something nasty to her.

Morgan finally got the girl to her feet, un-amazed by the sight of blood on the bench and on her clothes.

There was nothing to do but take her into the Villa for a bath, put her into one of her own frocks and give her an aspirin before taking her home to Thelma.

Cathcart was of the opinion that Myrtle was exaggerating. Or didn't know truth from fiction. Morgan held her tongue to prevent Charlie, who had finally come back for supper, from hearing unsuitable things.

Cat's last words before bed that night were no surprise. "That Retchen girl probably led him on." For him the incident was irrelevant.

He refused to go to church, saying no God would have allowed the carnage he had witnessed.

Grandma Perincall and Aunt Winifred were there, deprived of their customary Perincall pew by army officers overseeing other ranks. Threw, the land agent, touched his forehead to Morgan. She looked for the R.A.F. in vain. Thelma and Myrtle were huddled together at the back of the church, still without their mother.

Charlie, whispering, hoped Mrs Retchen would be back soon because Thelma had proposed to him. Morgan's loud 'What?' raised heads from their prayers. "It's a leap year, 1940. Women can propose." They sank to their knees.

Morgan did much thinking during "Fight the Good Fight", gazing at the twins. Ever creatures of habit, they were following the service, Myrtle showing no signs of her ordeal.

The Reverend Dorby's sermon had, for Morgan this Sunday, a particular resonance: "*God brought him forth out of Egypt; he hath as it were the strength of an unicorn: he shall eat up the nations his enemies, and shall break their bones, and pierce them with his arrows . . .*"

The bellicose quality of his address was understandable. She saw heads nodding at his exhortation to take heed of the Old Testament, Smite the Ungodly and listen to the Prime Minister.

The service over, she insisted that Myrtle and Thelma wait with her in the churchyard, until the rest of the congregation had emerged.

At first Myrtle refused, saying she didn't want to see any man, but with Morgan's prodding she began to look in earnest at each emerging soldier. Once outside, the lieutenant formed his squad into marching order.

"Is he there?" Morgan whispered. No. "Is that him?" No. "Him?"

At last Myrtle pointed at a young soldier in the front row. His instant reaction to her recognition, the lift of his head, told Morgan he was the guilty one.

She confronted his officer, explaining as calmly as she could what the soldier had done to Myrtle. A knot of curious parishioners came closer. Charlie, as embarrassed as the lieutenant, kept trying to attract his sister's attention, to tell her that Grandma Perincall was distressed. The officer, red-faced, listened to Morgan impatiently, begging her to lower her voice. She raised it, forcing him to confront the accused soldier. She and the rapt congregation waited.

"My man refuses all knowledge of any assault. Says he has never met the girl. Does she have witnesses?"

"Of course there are no witnesses. He took her alone into our shelter!" Morgan was furious. "You allow your men to behave like beasts?"

"Perhaps madam, if something did happen, and this private here says it did not, perhaps the girl –" nodding towards Myrtle – "led him on." Thelma had started to weep.

Myrtle's attacker who was grinning, backed away when he saw Morgan advancing, pulling Myrtle by the wrist. Charlie had never seen his sister like this. He put out a restraining hand.

Rejecting this, and her grandmother's command not to make a scene, Morgan grabbed the girl's shoulder and swung her round. "Look at her!" she was shouting.

Silence in the churchyard, except tut-tutting from the Reverend Dorby's wife. People edged nearer. Morgan was pushing Myrtle at the soldier. "Look at her!" Showing the bruise on her wrist. "Look what you've done! And worse. Much worse. How could you? She's a child."

The lieutenant kept his distance. "There is nothing to be done, madam. I sincerely advise you to take yourself and this young lady off

home. We have a war to fight. There is no time for storms in teacups."
He was looking at the crowd for agreement, but most stayed quiet.

Morgan had lifted her Bible. In one quick move she banged the soldier on the side of his head. In the same instant with raised knee she hit him squarely in the groin. He doubled up, his groan echoed by some. She heard a faint, feminine cheer.

Morgan dragged Myrtle from the churchyard at speed, the congregation making way for her as if for the bride at a wedding. Charlie followed with a tearful Thelma, at whose questions he could only grin.

The four of them walked rapidly along the Gormson Road, Morgan, hat set in place, saying nothing, Charlie and Thelma trying to keep up. And Myrtle lagging behind, seemingly her normal self.

Pedestrians were passing in both directions, some of whom said good day and raised their hats. Barely acknowledging them, Morgan kept walking. Myrtle behind her had started repeating, "She whacked him!" to whoever was in earshot.

Two army lorries sped past. Charlie caught a glimpse of soldiers laughing.

At the Villa gates, Morgan said she alone would take the twins home. He gladly left, eager to tell Cathcart and Florence what his sister had done.

Mrs Retchen was back home at last. "Miss Morgan whacked him one!" was the first thing Myrtle told her mother. "She whacked him one, Mum! She whacked him!" This she kept reciting during Morgan's attempt to recount what had actually taken place.

They went into the garden, a space dwarfed by the hump of the Anderson shelter. Morgan supplied enlightenment as best she could, ending with the episode in the churchyard.

"I think you should keep a better eye on your girls," she said at last.

"I don't take too kindly to that sort of advice."

After what she considered had been her most courageous act, Morgan was deflated. "I just mean they are growing up in the middle of some danger. They need protection."

Their mother wasn't pacified. "What do you think I've been doing all their young years? Trying to keep them out of the trouble you got into!"

The words were out. The women looked at one another, conscious that at long last the cat was out of the bag, Morgan now certain that Mrs Retchen had known the truth all along.

CHAPTER TEN

It was true that in the main the Perincalls were content to let things happen, usually waiting until action was forced upon them. Berenice, born a Skeffingley, put her beauty to good use in 1907 by marrying Montague, the least inert of the clan. After marriage she too acquired inaction as a way of life, finally succumbing to an illness that she and everyone in the family took for granted was incurable. Except her mother who, in her saner years, was constantly, if randomly, pursuing cures on her behalf. Running through Montague's veins was a practical streak that made him dismissive of his mother-in-law's decoctions.

In Morgan, perhaps through Granny Dorp, ran a more febrile searching strain. It now occurred to her that she might have chosen to marry Cathcart and not someone more like herself, in order to find some balance.

But had her father's blessing been the deciding factor after all? And had he given it purely because Cathcart happened to be there when needed? Had she chosen him freely? Perhaps she was a true Perincall, only pushed into action by circumstance. She was now admitting that he had never been her main focus.

Then there was Charlie. Living with him since September 1939, she could see that his were complications equal to hers. But she could never decide which were the most bothersome, his uncertain temper or his increasing alienation. Looking at her previous life, it seemed she had been existing in hazy expectation that nothing much would ever change.

It was the unpredictability of the times, exposing sensitivities long buried. It was Cat, constantly putting before them the most disheartening prophecies.

Trying to disagree, Morgan might claim that things were not

completely bad; only half of France was in Nazi hands. There was no gainsaying that the other half was governed from Vichy by a puppet regime. Cathcart derided the Americans' offer of aid to the Allies. The Yanks, he said, could have stopped the conflict spreading by declaring war themselves.

One evening, before bed, Florence told Morgan her husband was one of the glummest men she'd ever met. Was it because he was to be recalled to a new regiment? Cathcart had confided only to Flo that he was probably headed for calamity, just like Monty. The news that morning had been of the loss of hundreds of British fighter planes. Cat, looking triumphant, prophesied immediate invasion and put his pistol under his pillow.

Morgan suspected his tales of pilots and aircraft lost in action were meant to quell her hopes for a certain flying officer. Instead they brought him frequently to mind. One afternoon she glimpsed Patch in an R.A.F. vehicle in the square. He looked more like his own careworn twin. With Cat beside her, she was unable to attract his attention, suspecting her husband had noticed him.

It was not exactly displeasing when the coalman told her she looked like Hedy Lamarr. Cathcart remained suspicious of any man's attentions. When he did not query the remark, she knew something was amiss.

A few days later while she was pulling onions, Cat stood watching Florence taking in her washing. "She's wearing your pinafore."

"I lent it to her. Encouragement to help in the house. She's dreadfully untidy."

"Fat lot of good that'll do. She's too careless for that."

"Fancy you noticing."

"Don't lend her things or she'll start taking liberties." Florence grinned at them and thrust out a hip. "I've seen her type before." He sniffed. "She says a bomb dropped near her farm." With this he went indoors.

Morgan went to look at her favourite hen, whose speckled feathers were causing her admiration and guilt. With luck that same bird would arrive naked and roasted on their Christmas table. Did she mind if Cathcart looked at Florence like a prize hen, while pretending to criticise her? Was she herself about to behave like a true Perincall and let things happen anyway?

She could smell rain. Florence had gone indoors. Morgan wandered to her seat overlooking the river. Like the cricket pitch, her river had been invaded. The water was the colour of Cat's uniform, no shimmering current. Few boats, the *Berenice* still missing. A barge was swinging against the tide – one of the stackies with a load of something from London? Where did the bargees eat, sleep, when they landed? Why were her nights so restless? Patch changed? Cat so strange? Charlie enigmatic?

Splashes of rain. She ran from the lawn, afraid that her precious crêpe dress would shrink. The French windows were already sparkling with raindrops. She saw Cathcart enter the sitting room and stop. The flash of his cigarette lighter made his face a gargoyle. The flame was held out to someone in the room. She saw the bent head of Florence, cigarette in hand. Their bodies fragmented into streaks of rain. The downpour stopped as promptly as the scene she had happened upon.

Fine weather, occasionally showery, held right to the end of July. Air raids continued. Bombs dropping on the other side of the estuary towards London were less distressing than stories of fighter pilots wounded or lost.

Florence said the promised good harvest meant more work. Brodir was still reclaiming land. Charlie said that, thanks to Cat's intervention, there was help at work from the army. Women from the cottages were doing overtime filling sacks. So he would have breathing space.

It pleased him to let slip that Cathcart was not always working at the mill. He had seen him, more than once, with Floster, his wife, and Woodborne outside the Shepherd and Crook. What Charlie was doing at Little Gormson was another question. And there was, he told Morgan, another attraction at a certain farm, a chubby Land Girl who could handle a team of horses three times her size.

Morgan had seen Cat one evening idling outside the bathroom, Florence smiling sweetly as she passed. Morgan instinctively hid. She saw her husband closing in on her from behind. And Flo waited, letting him cup her breasts with both hands.

Had Cathcart ever been unfaithful? She worried that she had never considered this critical. And curious that she had never thought of other men. That is excluding Ronald Kermalode, with whom she exchanged fervent kisses in the dark at the office party in '36. Sweet sherry had a part in that. Or, dreaming of dallying with Errol Flynn, could she be accused of phantom infidelity? She could acknowledge with honesty that women locked into domesticity were less likely to stray. How could she blame Cat for what she was now putting into action?

Was he merely possessive? Only when they were with others did he watch her. But how could she equate that with loss of love? After all, he had been near death and was needing to feel alive.

Cathcart often cycled with her into Lodford, on Montague's bicycle with the carbide lamp. He showed no interest in her library books or purchases, only in the people she met. "Who was that? . . . How do you know him? . . . Whose husband is he?"

They were sitting on the British Legion wall one morning, taking a breather, when she asked him why he spent so long at the mill. It was not a test, more a need to know if he was trying to escape. "The telephone's there," was the terse reply. "My regiment's having to re-form."

She had never asked when, afraid he might think she wanted him gone. He admonished her for removing her shoes in public. She had made a fool of herself in St Margaret's churchyard. She should behave. As if his recent encounter with Flo wouldn't have shocked the denizens of Lodford had they witnessed it. Not that she said this to his face. She told Charlie, in a moment of weakness, her husband fancied their lodger. Charlie had looked thrilled.

True, Cathcart was distancing himself. He announced one evening that a soldier could not afford sentiment. Yet he fretted over the children. When was Morgan going to see them? She had shown him their letters which he searched for grievances. He homed in on their clothes. Billy and Terry must have grown. She must take them new ones. He said Boxley had agreed to take Morgan with him when he went to Barmford. His boys were "shooting up like runner beans". Cathcart did not know how unreliable the milkman was.

One Saturday, when over their heads battle after battle was raging, Mr Boxley's horse-drawn float arrived. The horse, minus its driver, was oblivious of the pounding of nearby guns. Charlie said, "Boxley's in the Redwood. He'll come, sooner or later. He always does."

The horse cropped the meagre grass, the Retchen sisters hopping around it. Finally Boxley arrived, saying he had gone back for a crate. He had a habit of sucking on his few remaining teeth. Mrs Brodick should watch out for thunder, the top of the milk had a tendency to turn. She used to love to hear thunder bouncing around the clouds. Now it was hard to tell the difference between it and distant guns.

Boxley spent longer than usual sorting empties before approaching Morgan. She was expecting some secret, but all he said was, "You and your hubby settle with me, missus, about what he mentioned, and I'll gladly do the trip." Then she knew she would be going to Barmford. It was strange how her longing to see her children was dimming her desire for Patch.

Meanwhile she must concentrate entirely on Villa matters. Charlie and Cathcart out of the way, she went looking for Asher the pig man.

She hung about in Mill Lane, the roar of machinery loud. Beyond the fields and hedgerows, through the poplars was the Gormson Road. Along it the usual traffic. Cycling towards her was the bank manager's wife. Recognising Morgan, Mrs Grouming dismounted. In her regulation W.V.S. uniform and feathered hat she looked overheated.

She stood undecided, until her eyes alighted on the pigs. Were they not interesting creatures? She was leading Morgan to them, oblivious of the aroma. Standing by the pens, she began telling of her pig-rearing days, of departure for the Far East and of exotic swine.

"See the beige snout?" Her finger poked at one. "The line can be traced through the female. Unlike us, they say!" Her smile revealed intractable dentistry. Saddlebacks were of little interest to Morgan, until she heard the word "tasty".

They walked back onto the lane. "So what are you doing in these parts, Mrs Brodick?" echoing Morgan's thought.

"I live over there." She was pointing towards the Villa's cloak of trees, theatrical in the sharp light. The sky pure blue.

"Of course you do." The eyes of Mrs Grouming were the same blue. "How can we forget that night?" Under her gaze Morgan was uneasy. There was something on the woman's mind. "I want to ask you a personal question." Morgan's mother had considered them bad manners.

"Mrs Talbott – do you think she would she consider doing voluntary work?" She was pointing at the Union Flag. "I am, as it were, getting a second opinion."

"She is a very helpful kind of woman,' Morgan answered carefully.

"She was a brick. We are starting a N.A.A.F.I. club for the services – 'Navy and Army, Air Force Institute'. In the old infant school. Teas and such for our boys off duty. We have a dartboard from St George's vicarage. There will be billiards."

A flight of Hurricanes erupting over their heads cropped Morgan's reply. "Mr Talbott might not like his wife going out in the evening. But I could help, if you need a volunteer." The thought of escaping the Villa, if only for an evening, was exhilarating.

Mrs Grouming shook Morgan's hand. The canteen plans would soon be finalised. "Our boys in blue will have prevailed by then, will they not?" She was looking skyward. "Our son is a pilot, a special breed. Like the pigs! But young men are foolish. If he should come out of a dive too fast he could black out. Or crash to earth because the fuel stops flowing through." Morgan backed away from her oscillating feathers, wondering whether plumes were part of the W.V.S. outfit and when she would stop talking.

"The fuel tank is dangerously close to the pilot. On the other hand," her voice had risen, "there is hardly any storage space in the Spitfire."

Morgan's imagination leaped to sandwich tins.

"Those Browning machine guns use up ammunition so fast the pilots have to rearm at base. And refuel. So Heinkels are not shooting at him there!" Mrs Grouming was tucking her skirt away from the spoke strings. "Don't worry about Mr Talbott. He'll come round. I have had dealings with a few recalcitrant husbands in my time."

A woman carrying two buckets was approaching. She had helped on the night of the *Clara*'s return. Phoebe Asher's hands then had been bloody.

She refused Mrs Grouming's N.A.A.F.I. request on account of the pigs and Asher needing help. Mrs Grouming said so be it and cycled off.

Phoebe asked Morgan if the Gaffer had come back. She and Asher were worried sick about Cyril and his mate who were on the *Berenice*. Not a sign since.

Morgan listened patiently, when all she wanted to know was whether she could acquire a decent quantity of bacon.

At last, when sympathy and hints had run their course, she put the question of pig procurement as bluntly as she could.

It was a matter of money. Phoebe's eldest daughter, volunteering in the Food Office sorting ration books, was given cash "only now and again". So "Pay for a pig, you gets a pig."

The deal was done by the sties, whose stink had become just another country odour.

Before they parted, Phoebe mentioned Rhoda Swell. She, Dora Talbott and Rhoda had often gone to the pictures together. "Dora's loving the Wrens," adding, "but who wouldn't, after the goings-on in that house?" The day was turning out to be a curious one.

Mrs Retchen met Morgan on the Villa steps, complaining that the house was a thoroughfare. People nowadays treated other people's halls as if they owned them. Coral Floster was standing at the foot of the stairs, having got into the house unnoticed.

Morgan was suspicious of her over-friendly chatter. Mrs Floster began to tell how she and Flossie had been rescued from near death by the Home Guard. "A huge bomb, two days ago! Roof tiles off, windows shattered. Door blown open." She was enjoying it. "Naturally we are a prime target." She was as immaculate as ever in the same frock, although hatless. "The Nazis know about the R.D.F. Chain Home Low is on their agenda." She gasped. "Pretend I haven't said that! Top Secret."

"Mrs Floster, what are you doing here?"

"We have been, or rather *I* have, been made homeless, Morgan . . . may I call you that?"

Mrs Retchen watched, frowning. "Our home is overrun with people in tin hats. Flossie's beside himself, says security is being breached. Keeps talking about Fifth Columnists." She sank onto a stair. "They cut off the electricity in the house for one whole hour.

"Flossie says it's no place for a woman. He's staying at the camp." Fingertips to forehead she stood up. "And I cannot lodge with any old body. I am the regional commander's wife after all," which was not strictly true. Morgan and Mrs Retchen exchanged looks. "Flossie says this is the best possible place for me. So I must throw myself on your mercy." Seeing Morgan's hesitation she added, "For the sake of your dear father."

"What does Mrs Retchen say?" Morgan had turned to her.

"Really? These are unusual times." Mrs Floster's eyebrows were raised. "Were those her daughters I saw in there –" pointing – "in your drawing room, shelling peas?"

Morgan had no wish to explain that Myrtle, and Thelma in sympathy, refused to enter the Anderson shelter. Their mother claimed that nonetheless the Villa was a safer place than her home during a raid. And they were on hand to continue working.

"I shall bring rations," Coral Floster added. Mrs Retchen nodded grudging assent.

"You will be in the smaller guest room." Morgan was imagining the extent of Coral Floster's wardrobe. "Not much space for clothes. A Land

Girl has one of the other bedrooms. Did you meet her when you met my husband? Recently?"

If she hoped to learn more of Cathcart's meetings with Patch and the Flosters, she was disappointed. The yes she received at least confirmed that Charlie had been telling the truth.

"We shall need a rota." Morgan could foresee another Florence who did little apart from wash her undies. Mrs Retchen frequently complained about her discarded brassieres and cami knickers. Morgan mentioned cooking, hoping that Mrs Floster might have second thoughts.

"Oh, I love to keep busy." Her visitor sounded enthusiastic. "I'll go and tell Patch to bring in my things."

The shock of seeing Patch Woodborne limping into the house carrying suitcases rendered Morgan speechless.

His behaviour was as circumspect as if they had barely met. She took refuge in action, chivvying the twins to prepare lunch with the usual eggs and Charlie's salad.

Charlie and Cathcart came in to eat. Cat in a more pleasant mood than Morgan had seen him for some time. He conversed with Mrs Floster and was friendly to the flight lieutenant. Patch told Morgan quietly that Peter Parclay was lying in a Canterbury hospital, after a Messerschmitt 109 attack over Kent. He had "pranged his kite". Sadness rose in her. She would have liked to know if someone, a woman perhaps, cared enough to visit him.

Patch spoke of the seriousness of the situation. How few replacement planes and pilots there were. How they were borrowing them from the Fleet Air Arm. Even training foreigners. Some planes were being pulled back out of enemy range. Cathcart again asked why there had been no air cover during the exit from Belgium. Patch explained they had been inland intercepting the enemy. Cat told him a pleasure boat had rescued him. It was as if he and the flight lieutenant had suddenly become brothers in arms. Morgan was astonished to hear them agreeing to exchange visits between the aerodrome and the R.D.F. camp.

After lunch Mrs Floster pleaded with Patch to entertain them. She shepherded everyone into the sitting room, ordered him to the piano, as if the Villa were hers. It was indeed a curious day.

From the first notes, it was clear the flight lieutenant was relishing the chance to perform. His voice was light. When he had first sung to Morgan in the church porch it had reminded her of Fred Astaire.

He started "Once In a While" theatrically, dragging it out until he reached "yesterday's memories", when his gaze turned to her. Charlie and Cathcart were already looking unimpressed. "Deep Purple" had them discernibly shifting on their seats. Morgan was thankful her husband did not understand the significance of "You'd Be So Easy to Love", even though the words were suggesting only a temporary liaison. So, at its end, she smiled and clapped along with Mrs Floster, who was calling for more.

With little urging Patch rendered "They Can't Take That Away From Me". And, through diminished applause, "It's a Hap Hap Happy Day". Between the songs the cockerel had begun to crow. Coral Floster, the only listener patently enjoying it, sang along with the relentless repertoire.

"Would you like to hear one of my own compositions?" Patch said.

"Hang On or You May Get Lost in the Shuffle" received Mrs Floster's spirited applause that disguised the others' lacklustre responses. "Paul is going to be a great success professionally."

Morgan remembered how impressed she had been by Patch's talk of the authenticity of lyrics, and how Art mattered more than money. Yet even then she had questioned his lack of interest in her love of poetry.

Seeing his fingers ready to play again, she said, "Would everyone like a cup of tea?"

Charlie wanted "Roll Out the Barrel". Morgan thought the song was common. Cathcart said he preferred some air.

He walked out of the room, followed by his brother-in-law.

"Unsatisfactory" was Morgan's later summation of the concert. Florence laughed and asked if the budding composer was handsome. This gave

255

Morgan the opportunity to ask her outright if she had already met Patch. Florence said yes, and how tired she was of men trying to get into her drawers.

"Wouldn't it be nice to forget about married men and, some day soon, go out, just girls together?" Morgan said she had too much to do.

Coral Floster asked Morgan why she couldn't have Monty's bedroom. They were making her bed together. She pointed out that the strafing of Channel shipping was getting worse, implying that his chances of returning were becoming more slight. Her eyes were slightly moist. Morgan, adamant that his room remain empty, was fixed more on what Florence had implied about Patch and his private life than on her father.

"Won't you miss your husband?" Morgan said at last.

"Gracious, no! All that talk of victory rolls. 'Chocks away'! How crass." Staring out of the window, shoulders hunched, she sounded deflated. "Nice view. Better than pylons and pillboxes and . . .", she paused " . . . pilots who are other women's legal property."

"To which pilots do you refer?"

"My dear Mrs Brodick, do we have need to give our songbird a name? Isn't it sufficient that he is already caged?"

This, their entire conversation concerning Woodborne's marital status, set their relationship on a better course. It also solved for Morgan the mystery of why Mrs Floster was happy to be so far from his new quarters at the camp.

She learned too that Patch was wounded, and more seriously than he would have them know. Strangely, Coral Floster confided she was glad that Flossie's flying days were over. This switch from lover to husband, this distancing from them both, had Morgan baffled. There was no Peter to ask what he thought was going on.

On the Saturday that Third Officer Rhoda Swell arrived at the Villa, Cathcart's exasperation increased. Here was another female, in a Wren uniform, come to take up room. He had no time to do more than realise it was Rhoda Swell, in horn-rimmed spectacles, before she had marched into the hall and up the stairs.

It was no coincidence that Morgan chose that afternoon to accept Florence's invitation for a bicycle ride. They were to head for the Brodir farm at Iverdon. Flo wanted to impress, showing her the fields she was helping reclaim for wheat and sugar beet.

They reached the Hectoring Mason before giving in to fatigue and thirst. Morgan had to point out to a reluctant landlord he had no right to refuse a Land Girl a drink. He let them sit outside with their barley wine, begging them to be inconspicuous and leave if the alert sounded.

Soon they had agreed to put off cycling and enjoy the sun.

Morgan decided to overcome her suspicion of Florence's reliability as a confidante, for she felt no animosity towards her about Patch or Cat. Only in the security of the bicycle sheds at school had she ever talked about sex before. But with whom else could she broach what was on her mind? Flo's casual approach to the delicate subject had given her courage. Was hers normal upper-class behaviour?

Could she herself be considered normal, with sex so frequently on her mind? "I think about sex a lot," she said.

"Men think about nothing else." Florence readily confessed to having known men intimately. She had once been engaged to an Honourable in the Guards. "He wore a corset." Two cyclists were dismounting nearby. "What put me off," she said in a voice as resonant as her mother's, "was that he was so very much a virgin." The cyclists remounted and moved off in haste.

Morgan felt reassured that perhaps only in the small world she customarily inhabited was she a rarity.

She told Flo how she had lost her virginity to her science teacher. She couldn't believe his satisfaction at the pain he had caused. Washing her underwear, without Mrs Retchen's mother discovering them, had been a problem. Laughing, Florence begged her to omit the gory details. Morgan said she later discovered that Mr Maes was keeping other sixth-formers after school.

"How unsurprising!" Florence cried. "You were lucky not to become pregnant."

Soon after that Morgan first saw Archie Kymmerly. This she did not tell Florence. He was cycling along the Villa drive, bringing her mother a telegram from the specialist in London. Hands off the handlebars, he was whistling into the spring air. Unlike her, he was carefree. And beautiful.

Instead she said, "I liked men for their looks," naming Tyrone Power. Cathcart. Patch.

"Looks and breeding," Florence declared. "Brodir has neither. And a wife from the same stock."

"Flo, you're a snob." What would she have thought of Archie?

Archie. She could see him now cycling along the Villa drive, buttoned jacket, pillbox hat strapped under his chin, dark hair, blue eyes, sweet breath.

"Old Brodir lets us girls watch the bull servicing the cows." Florence was amused. "I've seen more stallions at it than he's had hot dinners. Still, he keeps me away from killing rats. Charlie's awfully good at it. I wish he'd come to the farm more often, but he's always hanging around the R.D.F. station."

Morgan wanted to apologise for his thoughtlessness. But Florence was wanting to talk about diminishing social distinction among Land Girls, airmen. Particularly aircrews. Poles and Czechs were being recruited as pilots. And heaven knew from where they had originally sprung.

Morgan knew the war was bringing about change. Because of it she'd met Flo. And Peter, and Patch. Because of it she had lost her home and possibly her husband. Her children were distant, her father missing, his house disrupted. The future might consist of just tomorrow.

They sat outside the pub for an hour, until the landlord came to ask if they were there to put him out of business.

At the Villa, Cathcart was in a bad mood, caught between Rhoda installing herself in Montague's bedroom and Coral Floster voicing a prior right to it. Charlie told Morgan he had bet on Rhoda and won.

On the way home from the railway station, Rhoda had complained to Charlie that she was not missed, least of all by his father. He had to tell her that Montague and the *Berenice* had not been seen since 29 May, along with Cyril and his mate. That the cricket pitch had been ruined. He had a rabbit. And there were two lodgers at the Villa, one of whom was in Rhoda's old room. He said it had taken the wind out of her sails.

Morgan thought Rhoda looked fatter, or the uniform was a good disguise. The spectacles suited her. Gone was the bad permanent wave. Now her hair was rolled over a scarf. "You're looking well, Rhoda."

"He's not." Rhoda was staring at Charlie. "No meat on him at all," adding, "But still good enough to eat!" as she hugged him.

She accepted Monty's room grudgingly, for Florence was a paying guest.

From the outset her attitude to Coral Floster was hostile. When they had met before at the Villa there had been some rivalry.

At meal times Charlie enjoyed their sparring over Montague. Rhoda, torn between telling Mrs Floster too much about him and wanting to be seen as his intimate, spoke of his generosity. Mrs Floster retaliated with tales of jaunts on the *Berenice*.

Florence took refuge with Morgan, refusing to have her rare free days spoiled by two women fighting over a – possibly dead – man. She said Rhoda was lucky to be in an office making up sailors' wages. If she had to cut and coppice for a pittance, she might brag less.

Morgan found herself more in Rhoda's company. With Charlie at the mill or elsewhere, and Cathcart avoiding them, the women renewed sharing the Villa's management. Morgan could see how Rhoda's ability to organise was more help than hindrance. Rhoda had become less critical, engaging in topics that she would once have avoided. One now held her tongue and the other her counsel.

Morgan told her about the night of the Dunkirk rescue. Rhoda admitted that Montague was at the heart of her decision to enlist. In the Anderson shelter's intimacy, guns booming, Rhoda confessed that she couldn't have expected Monty to marry her. In the same breath she was declaring that she would never consider going out with ratings, only officers. Plenty were always coming in for their pay, inviting the Wrens to their mess, to dances, country jaunts, hockey matches, Wrens versus Sailors. It was hard for Morgan to feel anything but envy.

Rhoda told her that some unhappy girls had been sent home from Southport. She loved the life in Weymouth, where there were lots of compensations for being billeted in an old school.

"We thought you were on a ship."

"Might as well be. Have to do your face balancing the mirror on the top bunk!"

Morgan had already noticed that Rhoda's previously bare face was a curious orange. She had plucked her eyebrows and was wearing lipstick.

It was not long before Rhoda's enthusiasm, seemingly unmarred by Montague's absence, began to irritate: on H.M.S. *Boskall* the fodder was excellent, the servings huge; she had seen a grapefruit for the first time. Mrs Retchen told her not to put ideas into her girls' heads.

She complained to Morgan that Rhoda and Mrs Floster were discussing unsuitable subjects in front of the girls: goings-on at the R.D.F. camp, a peeping Tom outside Rhoda's dormitory. Myrtle had been hustled out of the kitchen. Morgan was beginning to find Rhoda's naval tales dispiriting, particularly when Charlie chose to repeat them. It couldn't all be fun. Weymouth had been bombed. Did he know that Wrens had to do fire-watching duty?

Charlie had missed Rhoda's lilting voice. "What were it I told you before I left, Charlie?" He couldn't remember. "I said, 'Make sure the girls riddle the ashes.' You can get a deal from cinders. Now, have they done just that? No! Come winter . . . Oh, why should I care?"

He found her one morning sitting on the back step, eating pickled onions. Why had she not come home in February? She'd had "things to do", but wouldn't be drawn on what. She whispered in his ear that she'd been seeing the captain of a minesweeper. "I'll get over him yet." He was at a loss to understand. Nor did he want to understand why she had chosen to desert him.

Coral Floster kept out of her way, generally managing to avoid any tasks. With rationing monthly more stringent, the daily needs of eight people were taxing. Now there was serious talk of a points scheme. Charlie claimed he wouldn't mind living on fish and chips or offal. Cathcart, too, insisted he wasn't fussy as long as something was on his plate. In any case, he would soon be with his unit, leaving the women to their wrangling. He'd tell his batman how lucky he was not to scrub floors, wash windows, beat carpets, polish brass, feed chickens and clean out the hutch!

The rabbit, at last properly housed, had to be found anything still green among hedgerows and fields withering in the exceptional heat. Charlie claimed it wasn't all his job. Winning the war was by far the most important business.

Morgan was in the kitchen one Sunday morning, attacking a cabbage. Mrs Floster, Florence and Cathcart were still in bed. Rhoda had gone to see Granny Dorp, not a person for normal hours, who might be up and in a present frame of mind.

"Jerky and me, we've been out shooting." Charlie dropped the bird in front of her.

"Jerky and I," she corrected him automatically.

"They're easier to pluck when they're warm."

"Nobody eats seagulls, Charlie. Not even in wartime. Rooks will be bad enough, if it comes to it. Although Pa says rook pie isn't all that bad." She turned from the sight of the bird's glazed eye. "Take that thing away." Grabbing it by the legs, he swung it close to her face before stamping off.

"Go shoot a rabbit!" she shouted after him. "Especially that one in the hutch." Then she said, "Damn!" out loud.

The thought of Barmford was increasingly appealing. She would see her children and get some rest, from Rhoda's encomiums of naval existence, from Coral Floster's bewailings, from Florence's often unsettling presence and Cat's war prophesies. She wanted distance from Patch.

Cathcart said he could not visit the children, duty called. For this she was glad.

It was settled that Mr Boxley, having been paid for the petrol, should drive Mrs Brodick alone to Gloucestershire. Mrs Boxley, left to run the dairy, was said to agree with Cathcart that the children must be brought home if at all unhappy. Morgan concurred.

The exchange of letters between the Brodicks and the Timmbolds took a week.

On a fine Saturday at the beginning of August, during a lull in air raids, Morgan and Boxley set off early for Barmford. In the boot of his Austin 8 with the masked headlights were clothes, toys for the children, eggs and vegetables. What Morgan did not know was that in one box was the driver's emergency supply of beer. He said they should get to Gloucestershire before nightfall. He had taken the precaution of studying the map.

She had foreseen a journey given over to finding suitable subjects, so she was grateful that the milkman was happy to concentrate on his driving. He seemed a prudent driver, not taking too many risks and keeping his expletives about other motorists too low for her to decipher.

The roads mainly consisted of military convoys going in the opposite direction. With the car windows open, she had no problems with his smoking. She was enjoying the sight of meadows and woods, familiar yet fresh enough for this to be an adventure.

They were making good time approaching the outskirts of London, when Boxley drew into the forecourt of a public house on the arterial road. No, she had not heard the alert. Yes, she would wait in the car while he dealt with some important business. He trotted round the back of the pub, which looked closed.

She sat feeling vulnerable. It was over an hour before he returned, talking about colleagues.

He pushed into her hands a bottle of stout. "Wouldn't do to let them see a lady drinking in public, now, would it?" He was pleased with this sign of sensitivity. At her refusal, he said he might drink it himself. He smelled of alcohol.

From his pocket he handed her a sheaf of photographs. Making no attempt to start the engine, he drank her stout while she scanned them. It was wearisome finding something agreeable to say about a row of beach huts, a seaplane landed on choppy water, a rangy dog, three people in overcoats seated on a beached hull. Explanations from him were meagre.

She could see he needed time to rest, for he had begun to flop sideways when he closed his eyes. When his watch, dangling from a waistcoat pocket, hit her on the hand she knew something was amiss. He was fast asleep. It was already past eleven o'clock, but she could not shake him awake. They might have stayed longer had not two Home Guards tapped on the window asking for identity cards. Offering his, Boxley explained, unasked, that his dicky heart had caused his deferment. "It could go at any moment." He started the engine and they roared off.

They drove past factories and through urban areas, taken at what Morgan thought was excessive speed. She began to notice her driver was occasionally swigging from an unlabelled bottle. They had circuited London before she plucked up the courage to ask him how ill he really was. This was greeted with laughter, but no real reply. "I'll need a breather soon, missus. All this driving takes it out of you."

Twenty minutes later he wheeled into a side road, coming to a halt outside another public house. "Afternoon's turning a bit thirsty." He was already opening her door. "We'll get you into the snug."

Not wanting to be the target of strangers, she refused. Boxley went in the pub alone.

During the next three-quarters of an hour many people entered. Few seemed to leave. Morgan's chauffeur was not among them. She took her sandwiches from the boot and sat eating them, more and more disturbed by the missing Boxley.

It was four o'clock when he wandered from the Battered Duck. He sat down heavily in the driving seat, proffering another bottle of stout. "Closing time." He clutched the wheel like a lifebuoy, then slowly slumped over it.

"Merciful heavens, Mr Boxley! What next!"

People were leaving the pub, making their way to cars and bicycles, trudging off on foot. One man, an ordinary seaman, was hesitating. Morgan correctly guessed he was uncertain what to do. He first approached a lorry, then changed his mind, then began to move in her direction. She watched closely. He looked quite sober.

She called out, "Excuse me, sir!" The sailor's head went up. He gave her a long stare before approaching. "May I ask you something?"

The stranger leaned in at her window. He did not smell of drink. His eyes had lighted on the sleeping Boxley. "Yes ma'am?"

"Can you drive?"

"Depends which way you want to go."

"First to Gloucestershire. Then across to Barmford, to be precise."

"Can't do much about the last bit. I can get you as far as Stroud way." His accent was reassuringly rural.

"That will do nicely," Morgan replied, not knowing at all where Stroud was. And not caring. This was an emergency, which the stranger by some miracle might resolve. "Please help me with . . . him, if you would be so kind."

They lifted the sleeping milkman onto the back seat, where he curled up and continued sleeping.

"Your husband's got a right skinful."

The sailor drove off carefully, seeming at home with the Austin. When asked to go faster he obliged, agreeing she would be hard pressed to get to Gloucestershire before nightfall. She told him she had been hoping for a detour via Tufnell Park, but could now see the impossibility. The sailor, who introduced himself as George, said he was not aiming to be seen in that direction. London was dangerous in more ways than one. His mother, who lived in Swindon, had seen bomb damage. Morgan had noticed demolished houses along their route, others untouched. For the first time she began to worry about the safety of number twenty-eight.

They were well into Oxfordshire without delays when an air raid warden tried to stop them at a country crossroads. The sailor drove around him without slowing down, explaining to Morgan it was best to get a move on.

Conversation was sparse. Morgan asked where his ship was berthed. "That's another story. Let's say I should have stayed with sheep." She asked no more personal questions, letting him drive in silence. Glancing at him now and then, she was reassured by his calm profile.

During the late afternoon they stopped at a roadside cafe. She offered to buy tea. Boxley was still sleeping.

In the cafe they talked about boats, his father's a narrow boat, her's a cruiser. She liked his quiet way, his open expression, finding he bore some resemblance to Peter Parclay. Then on to talk of books, for which she discovered they shared an interest. She thought it modern of him to let her pay for the tea.

Having trusted the sailor this far, she decided she could tell him what was on her mind. "But only if you feel up to it."

George listened carefully, then said he'd "give it a go".

So they changed places. With trepidation and an anxious glance at Boxley she took the driving seat.

The going at first was slow, but the sailor proved an excellent instructor, not getting cross like Cathcart when she clashed the Austin's gears. Nor did he laugh at her double declutch. Several stuttering miles later she began to enjoy the new experience. George, sharing her pride, said she was a natural driver.

There was no chance to question the advisability of crossing England with a stranger. The concentration she needed to cover the miles took her mind from other stress.

Somewhere near Cirencester she filled the petrol tank unaided from the can in the boot, proving her independence.

The Gloucester turn-off approaching, George said he would have to leave her soon. It had been a real distraction. Could she handle her husband?

They stopped beside a river, where the breeze cooled her trepidation. George wished her good luck. She pushed a ten-shilling note on him, telling him not to talk to strangers!

She waited for him to walk away. The sailor turned and raised his arms in the air. Then she observed that he was carrying no kitbag, nothing. And that she would never see him again.

During the next part of the journey there were frequent stops to ask directions. It proved useful to say she needed to get a sick man to Barmford in a hurry. Each person directing her peered in at the milkman and gave directions sympathetically.

Barmford within reach, Boxley revived and took over the wheel, unabashed and unsurprised, saying they had better get a move on. There was no mention of the lost miles.

His comment, which Morgan found unfathomable was, "My wife will be vexed if the boys have lost their Portuguese."

"Your children speak Portuguese?"

"It's best to marry a foreigner, missus. Takes longer to find out what they're really like."

Barmford looked a pleasant place in the half-light. They drove through chestnut trees like those around the cricket ground. She liked the stone houses and walled gardens with their fruit trees.

Mr Boxley found the Timmbolds' cottage, after touring the village twice in deepening dark. He would return to pick her up on Monday because of the milk round. There was a scent of wood smoke in the air.

The Timmbolds liked Morgan, once they had got over her beauty. They had kept the children from bed, and left her alone with them until her emotions had settled.

Billy and Terry, monstrously grown, had acquired Gloucestershire accents. She made a mental note not to tell Cathcart. Neither child asked after their father, so she told them how brave a soldier he was.

The children at the outset were wary, then clung to her, but soon were content to take Rex the dog upstairs. Morgan could understand how they looked to Mrs Timmbold for instructions and found this reassuring, telling herself that her children had found a proxy aunt.

At first she couldn't understand what the Timmbolds were saying. After an hour her ears became accustomed to their cadences. "Billy had a stone in his nose but it fell out eventually." She did not question how long "eventually" was. "Terry is eating her crusts."

Mr Timmbold, a man of even fewer words than his wife, was a surface miner working in the local colliery. It was evident that he and his wife loved the children deeply.

Supper being neither offered nor requested, Morgan was glad to sleep early. She had heard the children's prayers and put them to bed. Hers was in the attic among sacks of withered apples, the scent permeating the room. The apple she ate, core and all, was delicious.

The children woke her early from a satisfying sleep. Outside the noise of sheep roaming the green, geese calling near the pond. Billy warned her to avoid their beaks. Rex had been pecked twice.

After breakfast her children took her into the forest to show her, they said, their secret places. Teresa's was the reservoir, where newts like dragons swam in the weeds, where they dangled their fingers in the crystal water. The dog dashed among trees that they said were chestnuts good to eat. Morgan's trepidation at such a wild playground diminished as they wandered from one sunlit clearing to another. The forest was as familiar as any park to them. She must love it too. They ate apples sitting in a shaft of sun, the children telling her of things they and Rex had seen and done.

They were at the edge of a chasm staring down into a fissure many feet deep. This was Billy's favourite place. "Look, Mummy, at the sheep." Through saplings sprouting from its walls she could see the canyon floor. Among rusty tins and detritus lay the corpses of animals. He said that Mr Timmbold told him it had been an ammunition dump after the war. Neither child was fearful. She pulled them back, forbidding them ever to go near the edge again.

She was realising her children had a taste for danger. At lunch they told her of a stone quarry, where they sometimes played after school. Mrs Timmbold suggested that Morgan go with them, to reassure herself they would come to no harm.

The quarry, Morgan decided, was wide enough to station two Spitfires. She feigned an admiration she wasn't feeling. In the heat of late afternoon, standing above walls sliced like cheese, she felt almost faint. Quantities of rock had collapsed and tumbled to the floor below.

Billy said they must go to the bottom to throw stones at tins. She began to wonder from which parent her children had inherited such courage. She could only agree to follow. He descended with the ease of a goat, telling her where to place her feet, urging her on. Teresa, too, was negotiating the descent at speed. In minutes the pair were on the quarry floor shouting, their echoes bouncing around Morgan's head as she searched for footholds. The dog had found his own way down.

"Come on! . . . Come on!" Morgan was pleased at their admiration. A graze on her leg reminded her of Charlie's love of climbing before his accident.

There was a dinner in her honour of faggots, peas and potatoes. A steamed pudding with raspberry jam. She knew there was comfort in the cottage, but felt bound to mention her children's love of adventure.

"We keep a good eye on them. We shan't let them come to no harm." Strangely she believed the Timmbolds. But a disused quarry full of boulders was not, she said, her idea of a suitable playground. "It don't do to keep the little ones too safe. Specially with what they might have to face in the next year or two."

Her children were growing up, Terry six, sun-freckled now and not so thin. Billy, ten and wiry, hair like Charlie's over his eyes. How free their lives had become. In London there had been no chance to roam and climb. They were discovering the excitement of challenge, something as a country child she had taken for granted.

That evening when they were asleep Mr Timmbold showed her a

photograph of the children holding hands with Prudence. All three were smiling. "Taken on a special occasion, which were their coming here." He stowed it away, saying, "Grown a bit since then they have, the pair of them."

Mrs Timmbold displayed the children's schoolbooks, proud of Terry's handwriting and Billy's spelling. "They are taken to Sunday school and church, if time allows." There had been no mention of church that Sunday, for which Morgan was thankful. "They are no trouble at all, bless them."

From the many glances exchanged between the Timmbolds, Morgan knew they had something important on their minds. Not until the mantelpiece clock had struck half past eight did Mr Timmbold say what it was.

If Mrs Brodick had come to take the children away, would she please reconsider her decision, their being so settled, and that included Rex? There were tears in Mrs Timmbold's eyes as she declared that Morgan would be welcome to visit them at any time day or night, at any season, if only they could keep the little ones.

Morgan said she had no intention of taking the children away. The Timmbolds' affection for them would make missing them easier to bear. All she asked was that Billy and Teresa should be supervised more closely around dangerous locations. And that Teresa's best hat should not be squashed under a miner's coat.

Monday afternoon came too soon. Trying not to show her sorrow, Morgan let her tears drop on their heads as she hugged them. She told them to be good to one another, to look after the Timmbolds and be kind to Rex.

Mr Boxley arrived, crimson-faced but sober. His two boys, close in age at possibly twelve years, were sitting in the rear of the Austin. "They're coming back with us." Mrs Timmbold's gift of sandwiches and cider went into the boot beside his crate.

On the journey he complained that his children had not been billeted with somebody posh, because they were working class. They should have gone to the major, where they'd have had a good life, instead of being stuck in a cottage half the size of their own. Morgan replied that her children were living in a cottage and were very happy.

"If your nippers were sent out in the morning with a slice of bread and marg and told not to come back until dark, you wouldn't like it."

There were murmurs from the back seat that sometimes they'd had jam. And cake. Their father admitted they could tell a few whoppers. Nonetheless he was bringing them home.

Afraid that Boxley was casting longing eyes on each pub they passed, Morgan offered to drive.

It was no job for a woman and might lead to deaths. Norb Humer the undertaker had been testing mass-produced coffins. "By government orders." Why? "Because coffins might get scarce if this war gets worse. And if women gets to be drivers." How the coffin testing was done, the milkman did not reveal and she didn't ask.

On the journey he seemed in a pensive mood, rarely reprimanding his arguing offspring when they rattled the back of his seat. An occasional shout quelled them for a few miles. With Morgan he was more talkative, distracting her from thoughts of her children. His topics were mainly fixed on mortality. Each time he spoke of death he slowed down, as if afraid his life might end at its very mention. There were many silences. At one point he told her he wanted his wooden leg interred with him. She wondered but refrained from asking how he was managing to drive with a wooden leg.

Her mood began to be affected by his, changing like the colours of the passing landscape, from bright afternoon to grey evening. She shut her ears to the squabbles on the back seat, thinking of her children's absent father. Of Charlie.

It was a pub near Watford that Boxley found impossible to resist. His boys were asleep uncomfortably entwined, giving off a smell of unwashed bodies. "Look at 'em," he said, "Babes in the bleedin' Wood!"

This time Morgan went into the pub and ordered ginger beer. That she soon became the centre of attraction to a bar full of servicemen went unnoticed by Boxley. He had acquired his own audience, whom he was regaling with tales of a milkman's gruelling existence.

With perseverance she persuaded him to continue the journey. Twice she was refused a detour to Tufnell Park. "I have better things to do, missus, than quibble with you." She guessed he had in mind other known pubs *en route*.

In fact they stopped twice, at Morgan's insistence by the roadside, the diminishing light barely sufficient to locate his box in the boot.

The boys woke up just before Struttleigh, their re-energised tussles stilled by the sounds of air raid sirens, the darkening sky suddenly alive with searchlights. Boxley dropped Morgan at the Villa gates, stopping barely long enough for her to claim her luggage. The cider, a gift to her husband, had gone.

She walked along the drive in the light of a half moon lying on its back. Ahead falling flares were changing the river from silver to gold. Now and then their brightness eclipsed the moon. For a few seconds a nearby flash lit up the cricket pitch. She was passing the pavilion. On its porch she could see two seated figures, their shadows as huge as the dangling sacks of sand. At the sound of her footsteps the couple quickly separated from a close embrace.

The woman, she knew, was Mrs Grace Talbott. And she could have sworn that the man adhered to her was the quartermaster sergeant, last seen at the final cricket match.

CHAPTER ELEVEN

When Morgan got home that night she found Simon Arpent and his A.R.P. companion in the kitchen, with buckets of sand and a stirrup pump. The Villa was now a temporary air raid wardens' post, which they would vacate when all signs of danger had passed.

She asked Charlie for a cup of tea. He said he wasn't sure how. When she said it was time he learned, Arpent laughed. Charlie said Cat was in bed, so was Flo. Coral Floster had gone off with her husband, Rhoda into Lodford, ignoring the alert.

Despite Charlie's hostility, the visitors did not leave until a messenger brought news of enemy activity near Struttleigh. Morgan sent the trio into the night. She thought Cat might be feigning sleep, but was too tired to care.

She would not have mentioned the stone quarry had not Billy written about it to his father. There were questions and more questions, until she agreed that Cat should complain to the Timmbolds. Grudgingly he acknowledged that Gloucestershire was safer than an estuary strafed by fighter planes or bombed by an enemy unable to unload on its intended targets. He said that Junkers had fuel for only ten minutes flying time over London. She dare not ask the source of this information.

Charlie told her that Iverdon parish hall had been set on fire by incendiaries. He and Flo had gone for a walk. Mrs Floster's praise of her husband was boring them stiff. He was holding a piece of curled metal. "Found it Sunday, along the lane behind St Margaret's. Flo got stung. I told her Granny Dorp eats nettles."

"We'll all be eating them soon."

"We went into that barn behind the church. Where we put the sight-screens."

She was imagining Florence trying to lure Charlie under cover.

"Guess what it is." He was picking at the flaking metal. "At first we thought it was a Dornier, or a Junkers, but it isn't." Pausing for effect. "We think it's an Avro 504 from the last war." Morgan smiled at the idea of Florence having any knowledge of aircraft. "Jerky says he can sell it and share the swag."

"Please don't use slang. It's common. Who does it belong to, this . . . chunk?"

"Nobody. Barn's overgrown. Swallows' nests and old straw. Flo swears she saw a polecat."

A few days later Charlie had more news. Granny Dorp had been to the Villa over the weekend and gone home again. Cathcart had not mentioned her visit. Yet it was he who had fetched the old lady during a raid, having seen flares over the Lodbrook. He thought a building alight near the Prittend Road might be her cottage, or the pub.

According to Coral Floster, Granny Dorp was not having a good evening. Mrs Cory told Cathcart she had given up trying to persuade her charge to come to them for safety. Cathcart told Florence, who told Morgan, that he led Granny Dorp to the Villa under the wire in Hatts Lane, over the floodgates, past the mill houses and the piggery. The sight of the pigs in the searchlights' glare stopped her forward movement.

"She was either frightened of guns or loves pigs. She stood for fifteen minutes admiring the animals, while hell was breaking loose around them!"

Charlie told how they had tried to get her into the shelter. "She just stood like a statue." In the Villa she decided to wander around downstairs. Then upstairs into bedrooms, until Rhoda got cross.

"I finally had to lock her in."

"Lock her where, Charlie?" Morgan already knew. She had seen the disordered jars that had been Rhoda's pride. The opened bags of dried fruit saved for Christmas. Flour between the flagstones.

"In the pantry."

"Did you not think she would eat everything in sight in there?"

"She did a bit," Charlie agreed. "She wanted to make a cake. You could see that." He was interested in watching the old lady forget what the ingredients were for. When she went for the poker to lever open the stove, he intervened. "That was when I shut her in."

Florence took up the rest: "When the all-clear sounded, we came out of the shelter for tea. Rhoda found your grandmama in the pantry." She was enjoying the memory. "I saw a bare foot, then a leg, then the other leg, but no slippers!" These theatrical statements exasperated Morgan. Granny Dorp was lying among what remained of the cheese ration. Some jam was in evidence.

"She was asleep," Coral Floster added unnecessarily. When things had settled, Cathcart persuaded the old lady to look at his wound. She waved a hand over it. And that was that.

Morgan could see Cat's good humour was due more to his imminent recall than to her grandmother. What his interest was in Florence mattered less than she would have imagined. Her distant children stayed in her mind. Were they missing her? Would they forget her and their father?

Feelings all around were altering. She and Rhoda were working almost as a team. Her view of Coral Floster was changing. The more she saw of the group captain's wife, the more she detected a sadness that she had mistaken for pride. Perhaps it was pride forcing the woman to disguise whatever she was enduring. Morgan still did not actually like her, but admitted to herself that jealousy was playing a part. As for Florence, there was little to dislike about someone so cheerful, who could lighten any atmosphere.

It was she who dissuaded the Nails, arriving unannounced saying their lives were in danger in Prittend, from lodging at the Villa. Flo acted mercilessly. She showed Aunt Berry her bedroom, where she was to sleep with a Land Girl who got up at five thirty. On a mat beside the bed she had scattered some soil. Her dirty overalls were lying on sheets as grey as Berengaria's hair. Uncle Herbert was shown the bath where he would be sleeping, to be vacated at five thirty so the Land Girl could wash. Frank would have to sleep beside his cousin Charlie, in a bed not quite made for two. Charlie's cousin refused the offer.

Rhoda was contemptuous of Mrs Nails. In the summer of 1928 she had been snubbed by her at a family dinner. Berengaria had come near to calling her a servant. Rhoda said that Monty had stood up for her, offered her a seat beside him. For all that the conversation, according to Rhoda, had been "right boring".

It was Cathcart who suggested the Nails should contact the police at Plumberow or Struttleigh who were handling refugees. If they wished he would accompany them there himself. For this Morgan was grateful, feeling guilty that Florence and Charlie were treating their plight as a joke.

Charlie told them later that cousin Frank had not been called up, but nobody knew why. He looked pleased.

Mrs Retchen wasn't pleased at the number of people at the Villa. She hinted that if the Nails had stayed, she would not. And if Granny Dorp had taken up residence, Thelma and Myrtle, who were frightened of her, would have made themselves scarce. Irritated by this threat, Morgan found herself appealing to Rhoda, something she would never have done in the past. But relationships now were as fluid as the river.

Rhoda visited Mrs Retchen at home, getting her to agree to an appraisal of the work with a view to streamlining it. Morgan should tell Charlie and Mr Cat, as diplomatically as possible, to keep out of the way. Rhoda said privately that little was needed to improve the Villa's organisation.

Cat dismissed it all as argy-bargy. His concentration was on how soon he might leave, and that his kit would be ready. Now that his wife was a hardened traveller, he said with some irony, she might finally rescue their missing things from Tufnell Park.

Charlie was worried. He told Morgan if she went to London she would hate the crowded trains. "They say the suburbs are being hit."

Finding her in the kitchen instead of the shelter, he reiterated his warnings.

"I left a lot of things there, Charlie. My books. A bolt of Macclesfield silk. Cotton to match. Bias binding. Needle case. Thimbles."

"Scissors?"

"Yes! My electric iron. And there's the sewing machine."

"What's wrong with mother's old treadle in Mrs Floster's room. Rhoda always used it."

It was the wrong thing to say. She turned on him. "You wouldn't understand. One wants one's own possessions. I left lots of valuable things behind. My fur tippet. *Sentimental Education*." She was tugging aside the blackout curtain to look at a sky scudding east west. "Two lovely lipsticks," she was saying. "A bottle of *Evening In Paris*. It's criminal really."

"Those things sound easy enough to find." Charlie tried to keep his voice casual. "I could, if I went."

"Charles, you can find nothing in the cupboards here."

"That's because there's nothing there!" But this time he hadn't made her laugh.

"Oh, I don't know . . ." She wandered into the scullery, with him close behind. The ack-ack had ceased. A sheet from Florence's bed was soaking in the sink, billowing like a parachute. "Help me with this," lifting it with tongs. "This is so awful." The sheet draped across the draining board. "I'm soaked." The tongs clutched in one red hand, with the other she was holding out her skirt. Her wedding ring was missing, the green ring still there. "London can't be worse than this, can it?"

"What about the children? You can't take them back there."

She offered him the end of the sheet. He twisted it violently. Faint sounds of the all-clear came through the window.

"And there's their rocking horse." She was staring into space again.

"How on earth would you carry a rocking horse? What about trains and such? It would take you days."

"Not if I drove."

"You can't drive, Morgan. What's more, it isn't allowed."

They stood facing one another, tugging the wet sheet between them, she telling him to avoid the floor. He did his best, keeping his eyes on her, trying to ascertain exactly how far her thinking had gone.

"I don't mind the train journey." He didn't mind any hazard as long as she was prevented from going home. How could he bear it if she decided to stay?

One week into August, Cathcart went away to his regiment. Morgan and Charlie saw him off at the station, where another train crammed with soldiers was waiting in the sidings. Farewells were brief, although Cathcart, like his fellows, hung out of the carriage window waving until they had passed from sight.

"Cat called me 'Little Josh'." They were walking along West Street. The Lodford fire engine passed, bell clanging, volunteers on top struggling into their uniforms. Simultaneously the air raid warning started to wail.

"There goes our chance to buy meat for tomorrow." She knew there would be nobody to cut it until Mr Dance got back to the shop. "Tell Alice to learn butchery. You're a friend of hers."

"No, I'm not!" If he was given a few sausages on the quiet, that was Alice's concern. Charlie didn't want his name linked with any woman. All he knew was that Morgan filled most of his conscious thoughts.

Rhoda was always telling him to buck up and forget about his sister's desertion. She had no family, except a brother near Birmingham, who ignored her pleas for help all those years ago. Her brother was never grateful for the items she could now afford to buy him.

Charlie had heard Rhoda's story too often, for she hung on to grievances. He was lucky having two grandmothers, Rhoda insisted. Granny Dorp could hardly be considered, he said. Rhoda countered that he should be worrying about Grandma Perincall, so close to the receiving and transmission site she might as well be living in one of its bunkers. It was only a matter of time before it and she went up in smoke.

Charlie, on his trips to the site, often called on her, really to consult Aunt Winnie on the raising of carrots. About this subject she knew more than he, and could be persuaded to talk.

On a previous visit there, his grandmother with raised eyebrows had shown him a cutting from the *Prittend Standard*, guessing it might interest him:

HUMAN REMAINS DISCOVERED
NEAR THE VILLAGE OF IVERDON

The gruesome discovery was made by Miss Winifred Perincall who was gardening beside a ditch alongside the family property. The remains were in a fairly good state of preservation. The legs & arms were little touched by the passing of time but the skull crumbled when handled. There is some evidence of a legendary nature that the remains could be those of a local smuggler.

She told him that Montague, when not yet free of his Fauntleroy suit and ringlets, would have enjoyed the discovery. Winifred had not.

Charlie intended to keep the skeleton story to himself, aware that if he told Morgan or Rhoda they would know his actual goal was the R.D.F. station.

He could not contain himself for long. On the walk from the station he told his sister. Morgan's attitude was predictable. She accused him of using Grandma Perincall as a cover for something unspecified, but illicit.

She did not speak to him any more until the library, where they encountered Mrs Grouming, with books and a box of cigarettes she said was for the N.A.A.F.I. On which evenings could she expect Mrs Brodick to help, as promised?

"You're like a dog at a bone." Charlie had questioned Morgan once on their walk home, twice during teatime. And again while she was trying to listen to *I.T.M.A.*, not her favourite programme, but better than listening to him. She could only reply that she did not know whether the

R.A.F. was allowed into the N.A.A.F.I. She was going to do her bit for the war effort, whatever his suspicions about a certain flight lieutenant.

Coral Floster was making matters worse: "Did you know that Patch Woodborne has been called back to duty?" She said they were flying sorties day and night. Sleeping in their flying gear. "Flossie's worried stiff about casualties." Morgan avoided looking at Charlie. "Flossie might be called to make up the pilot numbers. He has his wings, you see."

Morgan asked Florence why she thought Mrs Floster was so concerned for a husband she apparently despised. Florence's reply, that Mrs Floster was in love with her husband, was laughed at. "You'll say next that Flossie loves her!"

"Sadly, no," Flo replied.

The weather was more her concern. "August will be crucial." They might have to work day and night for the harvest. If it rained the wheat stems would become elastic and moist and couldn't be cut by machine. "Kibbled wheat is wheat harvested too late and already sprouting. When it starts to grow, it's only suitable for animal feed. The nation will go hungry."

"Since when did you start talking about The Nation?" Florence was sounding too much like Cathcart. "I thought you were only interested in bloodstock."

Rhoda's leave had ended. Morgan surprised them both by telling her she would be missed. Rhoda thought that Wrens would be needed to keep the wheels turning down south. "Mr Cat says the Luftwaffe has thirty minutes flying time over the south coast." The navy was suffering bad losses. There was hope that food and guns might be coming from America by something called Lend Lease. A man on the wireless had said to watch coal supplies. Come winter things might get serious.

"And keep the Rover going," Rhoda said. "The battery's fine, Jerky thinks." Morgan was wondering how Rhoda knew Jerky, when Jerky had looked at the Rover and whether Rhoda had found out she had driven Boxley's Austin.

"I've said my goodbyes to Charlie." Rhoda had her handkerchief out. "Look after him, won't you?" Morgan was nodding. "In the Hope of the World tin you'll find his favourite sponge."

"Alright. But if he says once more '*This* is my favourite cake', I shall throw it at him!"

"Charlie hasn't got much. Now Monty's gone there's only you." Rhoda as always was defending him. "Talk to him nice, like. And find him some work that's above board."

"He's working at the mill."

"Not much. Mr Cat and Talbott have got the army in. The women's bagging the flour. Come harvest it might be different." Rhoda was looking hard at Morgan. "Charlie doesn't know which way up things are. That's his problem, see?"

For a moment Morgan had felt the familiar stone in the stomach. But Rhoda, having blown her nose, had changed the subject.

Florence went with Rhoda to the station at six o'clock in the morning, while Charlie was still asleep: one of the Brodir drivers had made an early-morning detour. The Wren was seen off on a packed train by a group of Land Girls, who waved at her and the men in all the carriages.

Charlie was morose for several days, refusing to go to church with the women.

In Grandma Perincall's opinion he needed the Reverend Dorby's guidance. Before the start of the service she admonished Morgan for laxity. Charlie was showing signs of moral turpitude. Winifred had found him stringing up blackbirds. His explanation, that dead rooks were hung up to scare the live ones off the crops, was insufficient. It had done nothing for Winnie's nerves. Morgan whispered that Charlie was trying to be helpful, and he was missing Rhoda. With difficulty she dissuaded her grandmother from asking the Reverend to pay Charlie a pastoral visit.

To the question of why Aunt Winnie was not in church, her grandmother replied that Winifred was not well enough. Harriet and Maud, still evacuated with the schools, would be back soon. That all one needed in these difficult times was backbone.

The church as usual was full with locals and servicemen and women giving loud voice to the Reverend's choice of patriotic hymns.

After church Grandma Perincall detained Morgan. "What sort is that young woman?" Florence was waiting with the other Land Girls. "They drive about in open lorries for all to see, male and female together, good families picking up bad habits from the others. Does she behave herself?"

"Flo's always very cheerful, Grandma."

Grandma Perincall nodded a greeting to the Talbotts. For such an ancient woman, all of seventy Morgan decided, her grandmother was still good-looking. An ivory comb holding her hair gave her a Spanish air, a style she had kept forever.

"They work them hard at Brodir's. She mucks out. Carts it. She cut her thumb on a billhook."

Her grandmother's attention was fixed again on the Talbotts, shaking hands with the Reverend. "How rude of that person to be staring like that."

Following Grace Talbott's gaze, Morgan saw a couple on the other side of the churchyard. The man was a fishermen from Blytham who supplied them with shellfish. The woman, she decided, must be his wife. What had certainly caught Grace Talbott's attention was the way the couple were standing, shoulders touching, hands interlocked. She thought for a moment they might commit the impropriety of a public kiss. This must be his last Sunday before joining the armed forces. She thought she saw Grace Talbott sigh as she walked off. Grandma Perincall had already turned away.

Morgan was surprised when Florence, joining her for the walk home, mentioned Mrs Talbott. Like Grandma Perincall she called her "that person", saying the veil on her hat was unsuitable for a working-class woman. "Of course," Florence added, "one can see the need for it if one has a black eye."

Morgan began to serve at the N.A.A.F.I. Like everyone, she was becoming inured to the sirens, the firework skies. The infants' schoolroom, whose floorboards had spiked her tender knees, had been transformed. At one end was a billiards table, at the other a dartboard. There were notices about walls having ears, keeping the blackout shut and refraining from spitting. Streamers had been looped overhead. The tea urn had come from the Lodford golf club, cups and saucers from the Harlem cafe. No improvements could be done to the lavatories, from which servicemen always returned laughing at the miniature nature of the toilet bowls.

The canteen's atmosphere, the music, were to Morgan's liking. Not so the absence of the R.A.F. The army was there in numbers, a few sailors on furlough. Mrs Grouming in a pinafore seemed less intimidating. She mentioned "fraternisation" only once to her volunteers, taking it for granted that working-class women would wash and clean, middle-class women would see to the refreshments. But she was invariably kind to all her helpers, particularly those from the Dunkirk rescue.

At home Charlie was complaining about the lateness of his tea, the washing of his clothes, anything implying neglect. Mrs Floster, who attempted to take him under her wing, was rudely rebuffed.

She and Flo tried to distract him during Morgan's evening absences. But playing Newmarket or whist in the damp shelter, they said, did not lead to cheerfulness. Charlie stayed morose.

Mrs Floster told him she would volunteer at the N.A.A.F.I. While keeping an eye on her husband, she could watch over Morgan. Mrs Grouming accepted her offer gratefully.

"There'll only be Flo and me left here alone," Charlie complained to Morgan one morning. He was picking wool from between his toes.

"What on earth are you doing?"

"It's the fluff from under my bed working its way upward."

"What am I supposed to do?"

"Collect it for a bird's nest?"

Morgan laughed. "In that cupboard is a thing called a broom. Do you know what it is for?"

"Why don't you demonstrate?" There was no laughter. He sounded bitter.

In his hearing one evening Morgan mentioned how much she was missing her marocain outfit. Mrs Floster, knitting an air force balaclava, asked what colour.

"Wavy brown silk."

"Where is it?" Charlie was already interested.

"In the wardrobe in the big bedroom."

"I can get it for you."

"You'd forget to close it against the moth."

They had noticed his eagerness. "I could fetch Terry's doll. The one with a funny name?"

"Oh, children! They didn't even want me to interrupt their story." Morgan was pulling a face. "Mrs Timmbold reads to them every night. I used to read Epaminondas to Terry." She saw his frown and added, "Didn't I read it to you?"

"Rhoda read me Superman! She had comics like the ones at Grandma Perincall's. Her brother gave them to her."

"When ever did Rhoda talk about a brother?"

Charlie was defensive. "Everybody can have a brother. Even you!"

To his surprise Morgan turned pink. Coral Floster looked at her with interest. There was a pause. "Oh, I remember now, there was mention of him at Aunt Berry's."

Trying to make amends for whatever the offence, he said, "I definitely could go to London. Much more easily than you. At any time." He waited.

"Possibly." Morgan was trying to decide whether a moody Charlie would be reliable left at home if she drove to Tufnell Park. The problem was petrol. And Charlie's missing friend, Jerky.

She had tried and failed to bewitch the mechanic in Whitley's garage, who was wary of the handwritten document she tendered, ostensibly from the mill office. All he needed, he said, were petrol

283

coupons. For those she would need Jerky, and to get to him she needed a compliant Charlie.

It was Charlie's bad moods and Jerky's absence that finally prompted Morgan to ask him to go to London. At 9 p.m. he was in his room, wrestling a bullet base with pliers. His wireless was playing music she didn't recognise.

She said she had decided to let him go to Tufnell Park, her grazed leg being a hindrance. Hiding his jubilation he asked if she was certain. She was, on condition that he leave number twenty-eight with curtains closed and all doors locked.

"I'll bring the rocking horse if you like."

"Do what you want." She was smiling. He knew he had won. "You will need the keys. You can bring the doll too. Pammy's black, of course. He will only fit in the biggest suitcase." She looked down at his leg. "No, don't bother. Just take mine."

On leaving she said, "My favourite books are beside the fireplace." And, pausing at the door, "Why don't you bring your friend Jerky here soon? Then we'll have somebody, while you are gone, to give us advice and so on. In case we need any." It sounded lame.

Charlie could see how Jerky might be useful in keeping an eye on his sister and reporting back. His only worry was Jerky's preoccupation with sex. His friend had lent him a sexual manual in a brown-paper cover. The section that made him laugh was *"How to Obtain an Erection"*, since it should have been how not to obtain one. On his return he didn't want to hear from Morgan about inappropriate behaviour from Jerky, but did not mention it to him in case it gave him ideas.

Florence liked Jerky who called her "sister" at their first meeting and gave her a toffee. Mrs Floster showed no interest in him whatever. The group captain's wife was spending more time at her Iverdon house, or in the snug of the Queen Catherine close to the aerodrome. When she came to the Villa it was often only to use up the soap flakes on her hair. She had attempted again to appropriate Monty's bedroom. Morgan again refused. Nobody should take her mother's place.

"Don't let Jerky take liberties" was Charlie's intriguing introduction to someone whose crumpled face and corresponding clothing made him look beggarly.

Morgan tried not to prejudge Jerky Tag, on whom she was expected to keep a weather eye, without being given reasons. He looked not much older than Charlie.

Morgan wondered if he had been to the Villa in her absence, for he seemed very much at home. His air of familiarity was general. His sharp intelligence evident. After one meeting, Morgan felt safe enough to ask him if he might find her some sugar.

He arrived next morning with three bags of it. Charlie had gone to work.

"How much do I owe you?"

"Five shillings, miss. Five shillings."

"What? That's steep."

"Alright, alright, two and six. And give us a kiss, kiss."

Morgan backed away. "How can you say such things, Mr Tag? How old are you?"

"Sixteen and three-quarters come Tuesday. In September, I'll be seventeen, teen."

"Do you realise I am old enough to be your mother?"

A grinning Jerky held out his hand. She handed over the money, saying, "We shall not mention this. Especially not to Charlie." Jerky's eyes lit up. He began to walk around the kitchen picking things up, examining them.

"Shouldn't you be doing your proper job?"

"What's that miss? What's that?"

"Florence tells me you're a hedger and ditcher."

"Seasonal, miss, seasonal."

"What did you do before the war?"

"This and that that. Here and there."

"You seem to know a great many people, Charlie tells me."

He was looking at the cookery book, open at the steak and kidney pudding recipe. She did not want anyone to touch it, for it had been her mother's. She saw herself at three, on a chair in this same kitchen, ready to cut her first carrot. She could feel her mother's fingers, hear her voice calming Montague's horrified remonstrations.

"I seen the skellington." Jerky had startled her. "Charlie showed me the paper."

"Not the actual skeleton!"

He laughed. "He says his aunt's scared of 'em. Scared." He was looking carefully at Morgan. "I took her a bit of butter, like, butter. Make her feel better."

"That was good of you." She was returning his gaze. "So you . . . know people?"

"Yes. Generally, yes."

"From whom one can obtain things?" He was looking at her quizzically. "Would it cost a lot for . . . certain items?"

"In general, no, no. I could get you a couple of sheep for that there lawn, haw!"

Their conversation continued in this vein, until consensus was reached on how many petrol coupons Jerky might supply, relative to her budget. There was a tacit agreement that for Charlie's ears their discussions had been confined to obtaining food.

Nobody saw Charlie off from Lodford station. He didn't want it. He loitered on the platform where he and Morgan had waved farewell to Cathcart, and the Land Girls had seen off Rhoda. The train, as usual, was delayed.

He stood looking over the railings towards St George's church with its alley of beeches. Surrounding it the golf course, now invaded by cement obstacles like theirs on the cricket pitch. Beyond that the aerodrome, alive with the noise of departing planes. On the far side he could see the old hall where a certain Queen Catherine – history not being his strongest subject – was supposed to have slept.

He wandered back over the bridge and glimpsed, on the Lodford side of the line, the old infant school where Morgan served in the N.A.A.F.I. He noted that this was a good observation point.

It was exciting to be going on a rail journey. That is if the train ever came. None of his rare visits to see Morgan and Cat in London had been rewarding. If he waited for an invitation she berated him for not coming. Turning up unasked, as he and Montague had done once, her welcome had been cool.

The train took forever, stopping at stations and in between. The heat from packed bodies, soot and cigarette smoke made the compartment disagreeable. The travails of wartime travel loosened tongues, and Charlie found himself forced into conversation. A woman in a snood told him she made aircraft parts in an Alperton factory. Her daughter offered him a corned beef sandwich and showed him her split arm, caused by flying glass. Afraid he might be mistaken for a conscientious objector Charlie, for the first time in his life, emphasised his disability, saying it was a war wound. Soldiers and sailors, sitting on their kitbags in the corridor, outnumbered civilians. He wished he were in uniform, forgetting that at nineteen he would not yet have been called up.

At Stratford, the sirens delayed the train for some half an hour. Passengers waited in tense expectation for the approach of enemy planes. A few said they could hear the faint thud of bombs unloading on "some poor wretches".

A couple of Londoners were going back home: he and his wife were homesick. The man told Charlie the enemy was using air bases from the coast of Norway right to the south of France. England could easily be invaded. A vicar with a bundle of leaflets assured an amazed carriage that no Nazi planes would fly as far as London. Passengers began to cite reports of more civilian casualties. Handing out his leaflets, he said the all-clear was God's protection.

Charlie read his while queuing for a bus: *Psalm 25/21: I sought the Lord and he answered me, he delivered me from all my fears. Those who look to him are radiant; their faces are never covered in shame.* It went into his pocket because paper was scarce.

Morgan had instructed him to use only buses. She could not endure the thought of him trapped underground in an air raid, although she had breathed nothing of this to him.

Cathcart had warned that London might be changed, bombs falling, potential chaos. From the bus Charlie could see only the usual queues. The sight of houses and shops looking intact cheered him, for the journey had already taken too long. Throughout five hours or more he had eaten his sandwiches and drunk the ginger beer the twins had forced on him.

As his goal became nearer, he thought of Morgan's anxiety for his welfare, Cathcart's pessimism, the runner beans not being watered. To his left and right only scrappy gardens, no visible birds. Here and there a ruined building or two, still smoking.

The bus driver set him down some distance from Morgan's road, saying there had been a bad raid. Charlie walked towards the smell of burning. By the Three Graces pub, people in groups were staring at smoke drifting across the chimney pots. He had heard no siren, yet men in tin hats were running about. An ambulance bell was clanging. He remembered that Morgan's road ran between the pub and a railway junction. He crossed over to look.

The rail tracks were clearly visible through a parapet with a hole in it the size of the Rover. No barrier to prevent a fall below. Engines and carriages were toppled and jackknifed into craters. Rails protruding like spillikins were being levered into place.

He eventually located Morgan's street and wandered along it, seeking number twenty-eight. On his left some houses were totally intact, others had windows devoid of panes. He saw a woman shaking a teddy bear out of one of them. The shrubs in her tiny garden were rimed with glass. A tree next door had a lopsided look, half charred, green and leafy on the other side. In the clouded sky silver barrage balloons looked like a Granny Dorp vision.

He picked his way along the street, through masonry and tile, following the course of fire fighters' hoses. The fire engine was parked at the end in a pool of water, its occupants sitting on the running board, smoking. They looked exhausted.

The bomb must have hit the terrace a while ago. In the air a lingering smell of gas and sewage. The sound of water trickling. An A.R.P. warden and a policeman were clambering over the debris, kicking aside rubble, ropes, clothes, and staves, raising dust fumes. They pushed at the loose bricks of a wall papered with roses.

Did Morgan have wallpaper with roses? Which was her house? Charlie could not count how many houses had been destroyed. They had conjoined into one indistinguishable ruin.

Among the wreckage embers were flickering between walls still standing in isolation. He could see other houses in other roads untouched, intact. In one a man was leaning from a window chatting to someone below.

From somewhere nearby heat was rising. He could feel it on his face. The smell of sewage was stronger. His foot hit a chunk of stone. He felt glass through his sole.

He told a policeman he was looking for number twenty-eight, his sister's house, empty since September '39. He remembered only the stained-glass birds on the front door and SEA VIEW in gold letters. It was one of Cathcart's jokes. The policeman told him to enquire at the A.R.P. post. The dead and injured had been taken to hospital.

It was, possibly, three o'clock. Shadows small, the sun still hot, made hotter by the smouldering debris. Charlie, stumbling along, tried to count each terraced house and its plot. He was, he thought, near the end of the street where rivulets of water were gathering into pools. And where the fumes were faintest.

Someone sitting on a slab of pavement was blocking his way. He could have sworn she swore at him.

He picked up her sketchbook. It was an effort. He was suddenly tired, a weight like the wreckage around pressing him down. Noticing his difficulty, the girl took Morgan's suitcase from him and, putting it down, forced him to sit on it.

"You're very white." She was looking him over. "That pullover's a mistake." He allowed her to take off his jacket as if he were her child. She threw it on the ground. Her copious hair brushed his face, hiding hers. She removed his cap and his Fair Isle, pushed him off the suitcase, opened it and put them in it. She had a strange scent, not exactly earthy, more animal, like the dirt he was sitting in.

Head bent, he heard the sketchbook drop. Heard her leave. He thought she had gone for good. With his foot he tipped open her sketchbook and stared at a page: the wall with the rose wallpaper, drawn tower-like on a wiry tumulus crowded with objects – a shoe, china flowers, bicycle handlebars, false teeth. Granny Dorp came to mind.

The girl came back at last carrying a cup. "Water. Nothing else around." He drank and felt better. She was probably his age. Her clothes, like her accent, were extraordinary. She tossed his cup across the bombsite, the water arcing silver as it fell. She was breathing loudly. When he risked a glance, she was staring boldly back at him. Her face had an olive tinge.

"This isn't going to last." The alert sounded close by. "Come on!" She had grabbed his jacket.

Charlie allowed himself to be pulled along the road, her goal a spired church not far away. Morgan had never mentioned a church. Other people were hurrying from all directions, blocking the gate, weaving between the gravestones.

The crypt was cool. She pushed his jacket at him. A booming had begun, followed by the response of guns. Someone shut the crypt door with a bang.

The girl sat beside Charlie on a stone seat, hemmed in closer as people continued pouring in for shelter. Again and again the door thudded from opened to closed, light to dark.

Someone lit a hurricane lamp, illuminating women in frocks and headscarves. Men were calling instructions that wove into the crying of children, the boom, boom of guns.

The scratch of the girl's pencil. Oblivious of everything, she was drawing the women opposite, transmogrifying them into creatures not quite human. He waited for tails to start sprouting. In minutes the entire page was obliterated by her strange marks. He closed his eyes.

"I am Maya." He felt the tip of her pencil on the back of his hand. At first she had reminded him of the gypsy woman behind the Queen Catherine. Now her voice, sounding reassuringly educated, had in it a sort of northern lilt. But his knowledge of geography was sparse. She did not sound like Rhoda.

"I am Charles Eugene Perincall."

On the far side of the crypt, the drone of conversation was pierced by a baby's harsh squall. A woman shouted, "Shut it up! The din outside's bad enough!" The crying continued rising, falling and rising again, until its mother pushed it onto her breast. Cigarette smoke was swirling, threatening to engulf everyone. A quavering voice began to sing "There'll Always Be an England", others joining in.

"Can't stand this! We've got to get out!" Maya grabbed Charlie's suitcase. She was heading for the exit, falling over feet and bundles, leaving behind a chorus shouting that it was dangerous outside.

The sun was still shining, the heat as intense. In the street an occasional official in a tin hat, a cyclist, a dog foraging. The sound of guns had receded. Maya said enemy aircraft had moved to the docks. Charlie was content to follow, already satisfied she would keep him from harm.

She led him through empty streets before stopping at a terraced house, intact, stucco white with high steps. "I live here." She fished around her neck for the key.

Somehow he knew this sort of girl would live in this sort of place. Her clothes were not ordinary. Or, if they were, she, by the act of wearing them, was making them extraordinary. Her voluminous frock was ruffled, ribboned and patched. The hall they entered had that same cluttered look, the walls covered with pictures, photographs, cuttings torn from magazines. Granny Dorp's secret room.

The house was as quiet as the street. The volume of artillery had receded. Their footsteps on the bare stairs echoed all the way to the third landing. Maya said the all-clear would sound. It did.

The ancient wallpaper in her room had been painted over with birds and insects. The kitchen lino was blotched with green paint. On the stove she put a kettle to boil. He collapsed into a rocking chair bound with red rope. The blackout curtains were looped with Christmas tinsel. He stared at a door on which was painted, life sized, an armoured soldier. One half of the soldier's face was blanked out with vermilion. He closed his eyes on memories of the *Clara*'s human cargo.

Downstairs the front door was opening and closing, footsteps telling that other inhabitants were returning. The sounds of banging doors becoming fainter, and fading. A man shouting further and further away. A voice trailing off. A kettle rattling. Silence. Dark.

Charlie woke up as sunlight crossed his face. Maya was sitting opposite, two cups on a tray at her feet.

He rose, pretending he had not fallen asleep. "Who's this?" On the mantelpiece a photograph of a woman, her tam o'shanter and upturned nose giving her a clownish look. In her hands she offered two long paintbrushes.

"My mother."

"Is she Scottish?" he asked for want of something to say. No reply. He suspected Maya had been orphaned. Looking at the sparsely furnished room, the inadequate gas fire, he said, "Is she dead?"

"Might as well be." Why she laughed was not clear.

"*Is* she dead?"

"No, 'fraid not. My dear mother is trying to hang on to me, but I keep escaping."

"You should keep in touch." He was tentative. "My mother died when I was a baby. It's something I think about."

"My mother wasn't any great shakes in the maternal department." She sounded casual. "Lots of em aren't."

With unusual insight Charlie replied, "There must be a reason you keep her photo."

"She used to be a governess, out east. Rajahs and all that nonsense."

It puzzled him that as she was making the tea she was unwinding her necklace. "Tinned milk alright?" The kettle was still boiling. The wall over the cooker was a steamy blue.

A painted line of the same blue ran from the kitchen, across the door jamb, into the room where he was standing. Along the line were spots and dabs of other colours.

"Go and look if you like," she called. "And turn off that kettle." Teapot in hand, she was watching him.

He saw that along the blue line was drawn a procession of creatures some human, some animal, some coloured, some monochrome. "It's what you call a frieze, isn't it?" He was peering closer. "This is a pig's head. I know about pigs."

Maya was pleased. "It's my *menagerie*." She sounded French. "My work will be in the Royal Academy one day." She made the tea and found four biscuits.

"How do you become an artist?" The question was naive, but her gaze was discomforting, her eyes disguised by the profusion of her hair. The flickering sun on her was due, he thought, to the haphazard latticing of the windowpanes.

"Either you are or you aren't." She seemed disinterested.

Wanting to impress, he said he was a miller. Milling was dangerous. It was noisy. There was the danger of explosions. Sparks were a constant threat.

"Just like now!"

He embarked on a description of a tidal mill worked by water-power through sluice gates. She let him talk, now reaching for a pencil and her sketchbook. No audience had seemed so interested in pit wheels, gear wheels, runners and wallowers. By the time he had arrived at why the stone nut could be disconnected, allowing the main shaft to drive the sieve, she had outlined his face and darkened his hair. "The sacks of grain are hoisted to the top, emptied into bins, then through a hopper—"

"Keep still," she commanded. "I want your mouth."

"The Saturday corn exchange is where we have to bid. You bite on a grain—"

"Keep quiet. The light's going."

He wished she would offer him something more substantial than a biscuit.

"I'm called after a variety of wheat."

"Charlie's a funny name for wheat."

"Pa calls me Little Josh. 'Early to mid-season', see? Good thing he didn't call me Red Standard or Rivets. Or Squarehead Master!" It was doubtful she knew what he was talking about.

She was staring into space. Wanting to hold her interest, he told her his mother had died giving birth to him, although Morgan had said it wasn't true. "Her name was Berenice." Maya's attention was on a few puffs of smoke or cloud passing across the window. "I have a sister called Morgan." He waited for some reaction, but there was none.

Next he tried something dramatic. "We found a French soldier under a bed. He had escaped from Dunkirk."

"I shall escape," Maya declared, "to France." It sounded unlikely. "I had a French pen-friend before the war. For the moment she's not in contact."

"My sister can speak French."

"So can I!" She sounded aggrieved. ""That's why I've got her."

"France is occupied. Not all of it, I think." Cat had told him something about Marshal Pétain.

"She's *in Provençe*. Mountains and lavender and *absinthe . . .*" Maya had moved to the other side of the room, where she was kneeling by the window.

"Absent?"

She was searching in a carpetbag. "I learned French at school. Where is your sister's school?"

Charlie laughed. "My sister's thirty-three! Her name is Morgan."

"What a lovely name – Morgan le Fay."

"You know about her?"

"King Arthur's enchantress. She wore her hair in a hoop of gold."

"She wasn't actually called after Morgan le Fay – Rhoda told me."

"Who's Rhoda?"

"Used to be our housekeeper. Joined the Wrens. Pa was furious, leaving us. Like Morgan." He shrugged. "No, Morgan didn't leave us. Well, she did in a way. No." He was rubbing his forehead, his eyes.

"Rhoda told me that Pa told her he agreed to the name Morgan, because the Morgan was his favourite motor car. I daren't tell my sister that!" Maya watched him laughing to himself.

"She might have been called Annabelle. Rhoda told me my father told her that my mother wanted Morgan, after Morgan le Fay. So Pa agreed."

Maya was suddenly enthusiastic. "Anna the beautiful!"

Although this girl's powers of concentration were limited, Charlie decided she was intriguing enough.

From the carpetbag she had taken a drawstring sack, then replaced it. The sun had moved, putting the room into shadow. He shuddered, wondering what he was doing with this stranger, how he would get home, explain things to Morgan. Where he would be sleeping.

"I've got to go and eat," he blurted out.

Searching in a cupboard, Maya found the largest piece of cheese he had seen since before the war. She slapped a chunk between two slices of bread and handed it to him. He ate it without speaking. It was delicious.

Neither of them heeded the alert, its scream slowly dying, while downstairs people were hurrying from the house. Somewhere the thin notes of a clock chimed.

Maya made more tea. She put it with their cups and evaporated milk on a tray. "Sugar's all gone." She was carrying the tray into the room with the knight on its door. "Come on!"

He knew it was her bedroom. Again she called, "Come on, then." And he came.

It was the tone. Rhoda's commanding voice. Or Morgan's. Perhaps that was why this new person reminded him of his sister. They bore no resemblance, apart from good looks. Nor would they like each other. There would be a war fought over him. But who would win?

She was still calling him to come. The food had strengthened him. He stood in the doorway of her bedroom watching her disrobe. For want of something to say, he asked where she had got the lump of cheese.

"Never you mind." She stood exposed, as if nakedness were normal. "Look here pretty boy, do come on!" She had climbed into the bed. He could see her breasts. "But close the curtains. The wardens will be by later."

He didn't know how much later she meant.

CHAPTER TWELVE

Maya was looking at him appreciatively. "Oh, Charlie, you've got a nice one there!"

"Have I?" He had certainly obtained a satisfactory erection. The writer of Jerky's sex manual would have been proud. It didn't seem so bad having Maya stare at him, although the sight of her naked was daunting. When he saw the dark triangle between her thighs, only ever clandestinely glimpsed in other girls, a feeling of relief nearly overcame him. Maya, plainly experienced, told him he must take things slower. So Charlie knew she knew he had never been with a woman, that it didn't matter and that all would go well.

Another intimation was his injured leg. She had said nothing about the cicatrice being pretty big and ugly, Cat's first comment. Scars were special was her only remark, as her finger traced the break line. He had muttered about a shrapnel wound, uncertain of her reaction to untruths. As she pulled him onto her, she looked impressed enough.

Through the night the thud, thud of gunfire was the accompaniment to Charlie's initiation, the room the theatre of his best dreams, where he was giving the performance of his life. Maya was insatiable, rousing him from sleep to force yet another condom on him that he was hardly able to retain. When the last one was littering the floor, she told him she didn't care.

She had spoken little during their copulations, indicating he should do this or this, but mostly content to let him do what his body urged.

In the small hours Charlie had suddenly remembered a chapter in Jerky's book, then happily rejected it. Unlike the manual there had been no preliminary words of love, nothing the book called "foreplay", none during sex and none afterwards. Once or twice Maya had told him not to be so rough. But they were both intent on fulfilling her primal needs. Her gasping climaxes were proof that he kept on doing that.

Daylight was creeping around the curtains by the time they drew normal breath, lying apart, still bathed in sweat. She had not succumbed to the fatigue that was drawing him into sleep. She had risen and taken the drawstring bag with her into the lavatory. When she returned Charlie, somnolently curious, had asked what was in it. "Never you mind."

Having made tea she climbed back into bed, balancing the tray on her bare knees. "You can sleep when we've had this." She was poking him. "I want the tea leaves for a dye. Comes up like sepia on Whatman. Oh, do wake up!" She pushed a biscuit into his mouth that he ate, before turning over and going back to sleep.

There was no clock in Maya's apartment. He knew it must be late because they had undressed, made love, dressed, undressed, made love for an age until they had dressed properly and finally. It had been dark, now it was light. In the night there had been three alerts, the intermittent sound of bombing far away to the south, and two all-clears.

What he couldn't understand was how safe he felt. "What time is it?"

She didn't believe in Time. "Look here pretty boy, I'm an eccentric." She was gripping his chin. Were her eyes hazel? "I am an artist. You'll have to get used to me."

Charlie was bewildered. Was this an intimation there were to be other encounters? If so, how were they to be arranged? Did she seem the sort of person who planned things?

"What's an 'eccentric'?" he asked. "Does it mean you run around in circles?"

She tapped his shoulder. "There's more to you than meets the eye."

"I have a grandmother who runs around in circles."

"There you are! I shall be like her when I'm old. I shall smoke very good cigars."

"Do you have grandmothers?" He asked the question casually, testing how much of his life he could confide.

"Did have." Maya was in the tiny kitchen cutting bread, searching for the cheese. She could have sworn she had plenty. Charlie had long passed the ravenous stage.

"I stole my grandmother's scissors," she said. "Got them so gummed up I threw them in the river." She was waving a knife. "I blamed it on my brother."

"You have a brother." The idea was pleasing. "Is he like me?" Charlie crammed the proffered crust of bread into his mouth.

"No, he's stupid." She sounded indifferent. "You're more . . . dangerous." Adding, "I hated my gran."

"I am dangerous." Charlie was wanting her attention. "I do things. On purpose."

"Oh, yes." Maya had found the cheese.

"I once did something to my sister's husband." He hoped she was listening. "I put salt in his semolina. I was twelve."

"You must have hated him." She was putting cheese into a sandwich.

He was glad she wasn't judging him. "I did a number one in his beer, as well."

"Lucky it wasn't a number two!"

"I don't mind Cat these days."

The noises of war outside had long since ceased. There were people returning, entering the house.

"Cat? What cat?" She had raised her head, listening. "You'd better go. I have things . . ." It was indistinct. She was wrapping the sandwich in newspaper and saying again he must leave.

He was shaken. It was so quick. He wanted to stay. Tell her more of what he had told nobody. Things he should have been able to tell Morgan had she been there when he wanted her.

He had to find a way to stop Maya pushing him out.

"Our headmaster was Mr Portmas." He saw her aiming for his jacket. "Beat the living daylights out of me." She was holding his suitcase. "A cane, a ruler, anything. You lined up and got called in." He felt rising anger. "Listen!"

She stopped and waited for him to continue.

"I had these welts all over me. My leg too." He was staring anxiously round the room, at the creatures along the blue line. "First I thought of a knife, see. Better not to get your hands dirty, isn't it?" He was fixing on the soldier.

"You should have seen them lying on our lawn. It was red with it." He knew he had her attention. "They needed my grandmother's herbs. She gave some to Cat to drink. Some on his wound. My friend Jerky said she was famous as far as Hingdon."

Another door slammed. There were voices downstairs. "Charlie, you *must* go now!" He tried to evade his jacket she was holding out. Something fell from a pocket.

"Mr Portmas diced with death, he did." He was gabbling while Maya was forcing his arms into his sleeves. "A razor blade in his pocket, see?" She had shoved the suitcase at him. He was being pushed towards the door. "Blood. Blood. He looked like the Canterville Ghost. Nobody found out."

It was all so fast. He was on the landing, Maya standing in her doorway. He thought he heard, "Give my love to Avalon." So fast. He heard her say she was finished. And "Go!" before her door closed.

On the stairs he squeezed past two men ascending, who eyed him with suspicion. They smelled of booze.

He swam into bright daylight, so bemused he did not know in which direction to head. Why had Maya pushed him out so peremptorily? Should he go back? Ask her full name? Check her address. Slowly he wandered on, trying to think.

Street names were in short supply. He stopped a man pushing a coal cart. The man looked suspicious when Charlie asked the name of the road. Further on, a woman in overalls pointed him towards a bus queue.

In the middle of his disquiet he had the feeling he was being followed. Thinking it was Maya proved wishful. At a third look he saw a dog staring back at him with orange eyes. He stopped, the dog stopped. Walking, he could hear the pat, pat of the animal close behind. It had a brown matted coat.

By the time he reached the bus stop he was sweating and still perturbed. The dog sat beside him as patient as any passenger. When the bus arrived it leaped on behind him. He couldn't shake off the creature. However much he shouted, kicked out, it persisted in staying as if joined to him by an invisible leash.

At the main station it waited beside him, licking up his sandwich crumbs, trying to lean against his leg.

On the train people asked the dog's name, its breed even. He wished the war wasn't making everyone so nosy. In the carriage two girls were discussing "Gone with the Wind" showing, he heard, at a Leicester Square cinema. Charlie looked at them covertly, wishing they would talk more about the much bruited fire scenes, and less about Scarlett O'Hara's curtains. Only once did he feel a mild sexual urge, at the sight of white thighs and suspenders as he helped one of the girls with her suitcase. The dog growled.

For the rest of the journey it sat quietly at his feet. Charlie, entirely forgetting about it, drifted into troubled sleep.

Morgan was sitting staring into space when Coral Floster came in. It was eleven in the morning. The breakfast dishes were still lying on the table, beside a parcel tied with waxed string.

There were no loaded questions from Morgan, trying to ascertain whether Mrs Floster's absences had involved a certain pilot. The evasive replies would normally have frustrated her.

But she sat silent, her hand limp on the parcel in front of her.

"What's the matter? Are you unwell?" The group captain's wife was removing a diaphanous scarf from hair so tightly permed it gave her the look of a circuit judge. "What is it, a bomb?"

"It's for Flo," Morgan replied. "From her mama."

"Oh! Let's hope it's not like the last one – wintergreen and camphor!" Mrs Floster went up to her room.

Morgan sat where she was, the soft river light filtering over her hands and arms. She put her fingers to her face, feeling its imaginary ripples. She wanted to think, but couldn't find a way.

It was Archie's fault. His fault for coming back. That was all. Archie Kymmerly had come to the Villa instead of Eden, to deliver Flo's parcel.

The shock of seeing him on the doorstep. No warning. No bicycle bell, no postal van. There he was, the same Archie of the bright smile, his beautiful face now shadowed by a trilby.

Then he had worn his pillbox hat sideways, his telegram delivery uniform making him look like a playful child. Now his face was wrinkled like one of her mother's overwintered apples. She knew it was the real Archie underneath.

"Hello, Morgan." There was the heartleap of joy, exactly as it was every time they had ever met.

They had stood facing one another, engaging in a "what brings you here?" kind of conversation. It was the unfamiliar Scottish inflection interfering with absorption. Yes, Vela had said he had been living up north for the longest time. He wanted to see his sister before joining up. Looking intensely at Morgan, he suddenly put his hand on her shoulder. Another shock. If she had touched him first, would he have felt the same thrill?

She knew he didn't want to leave. She couldn't let him. Nobody else but the twins around, banging about in one of the bedrooms while Coral Floster was trying to rest.

He already knew the way to the kitchen. They sat opposite each other, elbows on the table among the crockery. He was to have his medical examination in Prittend, the Black Watch his preference. There was nothing about his having missed her all those years. But Vela must have told him that she was at the Villa. About her present status Morgan mentioned nothing, certain he already knew. And that it didn't matter.

He told her he had done carpentry, and stroked the table edge. Breadcrumbs stuck to his hand. His fingers were rough when he grasped hers. He was talking about having survived, or both being survivors. She couldn't quite follow. Her mind, her body were whirling. This had been rehearsed only in dreams. In reality she was being downed by a force against which there was no resistance.

302

Archie's query about her father brought her back. No doom-laden tone, but she knew the strength of his question. She could not say her pa was dead, simply that he had not yet come back from Dunkirk.

"Any loss is hard to bear." He pointed at the Straits of Dover on Montague's map, saying he'd read that many had gone down there. He wasn't keen on dying too soon, though more afraid of pain than death.

She felt these feelings were for her alone. Had they not confessed them exclusively to one another? There would be no need to tell him he was her missing half, for he had always known it. It would not take long to discover that neither had changed. She already knew why he had come back after eighteen years. It was not to see his sister.

Time did not enter the equation, nor any other hindrances. She was sorry for any man who might have thought he was the love of her life. Cathcart she would gladly have sacrificed had Archie been within reach. Patch? Now could she see his transient appeal. The truth of it was that it had only ever been Archie.

He said he was sorry about her mother, saw her tears and patted her hand, proving to Morgan he must have kept track of Villa events since their separation. She said he was taller. He hoped so, the kilt swung better on a tall man.

Was he married, did he have children had not mattered at that meeting. She had been fixed solely on the moment.

When he had gone feelings of guilt flooded in. Grandma Perincall's voice emerged: *"You were never anything but a trollop! Eighteen years of the chance to atone, thrown away in an instant."*

On the table were Morgan's letters to Billy and Teresa. She had failed to finish one to Cathcart. Belatedly she was wondering whether he had received all those others so assiduously composed. During her affair with Patch she had struggled to write anything to him. Now, after Archie's appearance, she must find enough mundane topics to fill pages. They would be compensation for him who might not be sharing her future.

Mrs Floster came downstairs wearing such an odd outfit that Morgan almost commented on it. Her grey dress and laced shoes looked more suitable for a nun. The hat, like a beached seabird, was perched on her waves. She was carrying her handbag.

She sat down. "I'm expecting Flight Lieutenant Woodborne." She sounded dispirited. "He's giving me a lift back to that dreadful house." Morgan kept silent and neutral. "Don't let that silly episode in the churchyard bother you. People always talk. Although," Coral added, brightening a little, "it was rather dramatic."

"Why should it bother me?"

"I was secretly on your side. If any man had done that to me, I don't know how I would have behaved."

With amazement Morgan saw that people might have thought it was she who had been attacked by the soldier.

"Would Flossie have come to my rescue?" Mrs Floster was screwing and unscrewing Morgan's bottle of ink. Her demeanour, like her clothes, was unfamiliar. "It hasn't worked, you see."

Her mind full of Archie, Morgan said nothing. She wanted no confessions, especially from this woman who had always caused such varying emotions.

"I might as well be one of those war effort saucepans." Coral Floster was dabbing an eye. "He doesn't want me. Never has, really. So it's no use staying away, is it?" Was she talking about Patch? "There are people better at it. But his shirts I have boiled in that horrible copper! Can you believe it? Starched his collars. Darned his socks. What more can I do? In bed he—"

Morgan stopped her. She wanted no tales of bed, whoever was in it. "His mind might be on winning the war."

"Flossie . . ." Coral Floster continued, "Flossie has interests I must go and do battle with. You see . . ." A loud banging on the front door. "Oh! Patch is here. I have to go."

Morgan accompanied her into the hall. "Absence does not make the heart grow fonder, believe me. His batman will come for the rest of my things."

Woodborne said the weather was getting worse. And he wished to talk a bit. He too seemed subdued. An injured man facing two lovers at once, Morgan thought, might account for this. She felt slight relief.

He led the two women into the sitting room. Fears of another concert began to rise. Morgan hoped the twins, noisy on the stairs, might break up this unwanted trio. But they left for home. Patch seated himself in Montague's chair.

He said he was going on leave. Worsening weather meant there was a lull in air battles. They had nearly got Jerry licked. He was talking at speed, but did not mention his wounds.

He was speaking about how danger made men do stupid things. The women listened, more concerned with their own existence than his, their sympathy superficial. To Morgan, the revelation that someone was waiting for him was a mere statement of fact. His wife wanted reassurance, he said, that her unborn child's father was still in one piece. All Morgan could think of was that day in 1922 when she had said goodbye to Archie.

Patch headed for the piano, but only to tap a key and close the lid. Morgan sighed with relief as he made for the door.

With barely a wave he marched through the hall and out of the front door. Coral Floster was still in the sitting room looking for her handbag.

The alert sounded. Through its last wail they could hear Patch's Riley revving up. As the two women stepped outside, he was driving off in a blast of exhaust.

Coral Floster looked in amazement. "There's gallantry for you!" She was tearful. "Nobody wants me." She sighed deeply. "I really must try to pull myself together. Think of our brave boys and all that. Curses on them!" She wiped her nose. "How am I going to get home?"

Not having the faintest idea what she was talking about, Morgan surprised herself by saying, "I can drive you to Iverdon."

Coral Floster said she was amazed that Morgan could, and that she would drive a car during an air raid without official permission. Was there sufficient petrol?

The Rover, proving more of a warhorse than Boxley's Austin, collected a scrape from the garage door. Coral Floster said the upholstery was beginning to feel sticky. Morgan begged her to speak as little as possible of her father, or anyone else, until she had got the hang of the beast.

They drove at a sedate pace along the Gormson Road, aware that above them plane after rising plane was headed towards the mouth of the river. Already hard gunfire, emanating from the senior school, was assailing their ears. Nervous at the wheel, Morgan tried to block it out.

The sound of artillery was reverberating, it seemed, all along the river. Above it and the engine's roar were Coral Floster's high-pitched cries. Morgan drove on, trying to think only of Archie. Was he safe indoors, or looking up at battles like those overhead? Perhaps he had never seen Messerschmitts and Hurricanes circling and swooping, looking like harmless toys. Archie had never been concerned for safety. He and she had cycled along this very road, so often and carefree, during a summer as hot as this.

Coral Floster screamed. Morgan tightened her grip on the steering wheel, her wandering thoughts grounded. She struck the brake hard. She and Archie had been making love in the field behind St Wynfrith's. The Rover slewed into a weedy bank and stopped close to a ditch. Her passenger, gasping for air, was gabbling unintelligibly. Morgan unwound her window, letting in a cacophony of guns, planes, birdsong, trees. They were close to St Margaret's, where she had first resisted Patch.

"The bombers are coming! We'll never get there!" Coral Floster had found words. Grabbing at the door handle, she left the car. In a crouch she made her way round to the other side. Only her proximity to the ditch prevented her from opening Morgan's door to drag her out. "We'll die!"

Faced with this hysteria, Morgan felt unnaturally composed. She grasped Coral's hands, telling her she was not in danger.

They stood in the road, the running engine louder than the noises of war above them. High up they saw the familiar vapour trails, heard the drone of fighting planes. The quick bursts of fire sounding from so far below like ripples over stones.

Mrs Floster's trembling had ceased. "Flossie assured me there will not be bombing." Her voice quavering but calm. "He says we are winning in the air."

Morgan was still looking skyward. "Doesn't look like it from here." A plane, black against the sun, had dark smoke pouring from its fuselage. Around it another plane was circling.

"Croydon airport's been hit." Coral Floster had ceased looking. "All he's worried about are his beloved airmen. What does it matter to him if they drop bombs up north?"

Gunfire had grown louder, was coming nearer. Morgan said, "Get back in the car." It was a command. "We must find cover, try to get back to the Villa."

"No! I *must* go to Iverdon." Mrs Floster was already getting into her seat. "You promised."

Morgan manoeuvred the Rover onto the road again. As her passenger demanded, she drove on through Little Gormson towards Iverdon. Thoughts of Archie flickered. Was she, in pleasing Coral Floster, risking death? The noise around them had not abated. Were they to be a target for a low-flying Nazi plane? Was Archie somewhere safe? She drove on, torn between speed and abandoning the vehicle.

Almost to Great Gormson, she glimpsed low trees on the right of the road. A familiar lane. At its far end refuge, a barn in which she and Archie had first coupled. She swung the Rover round.

Coral Floster had been deep into repetition of her husband's opinions. "No!" she shouted when she saw what was happening. She went for the wheel.

Morgan hit her fingers. "We're taking cover. Can't you hear it? We're a moving target."

Low branches rattled the car roof. She drove along to the lane's end. The barn, still there beside a wheat field, looked smaller than in the summer of '22.

She and Archie had climbed to its loft. The straw had cracked and rustled under them. The first time, with Archie so close over her she couldn't breathe, she had begged for a moment's air. All that extraordinary afternoon they had made love.

Mrs Floster said, "What safety is there here?"

They had looked from the barn's window across acres of gold stubble. Seagulls were keeping up a clamour like babies. The river was a thin shimmer of blue.

Each stolen time they met, the same magic. Whatever they shared became golden like the field of wheat. Those times, all their meetings, still held a place in her memory that could never be surpassed.

Her memories were not marred by the fact that she would quickly become pregnant. Archie said they had made something that would bind them together like the wheat sheaves.

"Look!" Coral Floster was pointing, not skyward but closer. The burning plane had vanished. Swirls and white trails were still embroidering the sky, but below them, someone on a parachute was slowly descending.

"He's going into the river!"

Morgan was the first to leap into the wheat field, followed by Coral Floster shouting as the stubble scored her ankles, "Don't leave me!"

She knew this field of her father's. Knew that towards the river lay another field. Beyond that, the sea wall, protecting Villa land from tidal attack. She headed for an opening in the far hedgerow, keeping her eyes on the descending parachutist, feeling the scratch of thistles. Behind her she could hear Coral Floster's complaints, a swear word as she too was scratched. It occurred to her that Coral was less blue ribbon and more energetic than she seemed.

"He's going into the water!" They halted, panting. The parachute looked larger in its descent. As it swung and billowed, the figure beneath it disappeared.

In the next field, potato ridges proved less hostile. They hopped between the rows, kicking up earth. On the other side of the dyke the top of the parachute was billowing in the breeze.

"He must be over there."

Mrs Floster pulled Morgan across a dry ditch. Gasping with the effort, they climbed up the side of the dyke. They were on top of the sea wall, beyond the barricaded stile and the last pillbox. The Villa out of sight a few miles away.

"There he is!"

Below them, rusted barbed wire had coiled on the side of the dyke. Lower down, a narrow beach left by a receding tide. They saw the parachute caught in the wire, languidly moving as the breeze ballooned it. No sign of the pilot, or of anyone. The air battle overhead had moved further out to sea, the guns' booming ricocheting off the water. Birds were flying low through a heat haze obscuring the far bank.

The women walked carefully towards the parachute. A skylark rose suddenly. Coral Floster screamed. Another scream as she too saw what Morgan was staring at. On the slope of the dyke in the barbed wire, entangled and trapped in his harness, the pilot was lying. The breeze in the parachute's folds was lifting one of his shoulders.

They slid down sideways, grasshoppers leaping, onto the strip of sand.

The man seemed to be unconscious. His face, hands were bloody. There was blood on his forehead, running from under his helmet. His leg was twisted awkwardly in the wire. A boot was missing.

"He must be one of ours."

"No!" Morgan, like Coral Floster, was whispering. "He's wearing jodhpurs."

"He could be ours." Coral Floster was bending low. "See if his top button is undone." She was trying to get a better look. "All our pilots do that."

"Stop talking nonsense, Coral. You can see he's a Nazi." He looked very young. She thought of the Dunkirk survivors, equally bloody, equally young. "We'll have to get him out of there."

"If he's a Nazi, why not leave him?"

"He may be alive. His arm is moving."

"It's the wind."

Morgan thought she had seen his fingers twitch. She said the first thing was to get him out of the harness. Parachute cords caught in the barbs of wire were causing the entanglement.

She was about to unfasten the strap around his leg when his body jerked violently. By pulling at a shoulder strap she released one arm. His eyes opened wide. The arm snapped upward, hitting her on the forehead. She staggered back and her hat flew away. Coral Floster, grappling with swathes of torn parachute, screamed. The pilot, as if in reply, screamed as loudly, his freed arm flailing in a futile circle.

Now he was howling, his body writhing as Morgan again tugged at the ropes. Foreign words came streaming from him, sentences unrecognisable. She knew she was hearing the same invective, the same agonised pleading she had heard all night long on 29 May. He went on screaming while she struggled with intransigent buckles.

The parachute was bunched in Coral Floster's hands. Pushing the pilot's head against the barbs, she stuffed the silk into his gaping mouth shrieking, "Shut up! Shut up!"

The sounds of the all-clear came faintly through the air.

For an age they struggled to extricate the man, whose struggling was slowly diminishing. Their calls for help blew away on the breeze and no-one came. At some point he lost consciousness.

It was while they were dragging him free that the pilot revived, cursing them through his gag. His eyes were wide with pain as inch by inch they shifted him. His noises, unlike Coral Floster's, were losing strength. The last of the wire they prised off his bloody foot with a driftwood spar. Shreds of his trousers stayed impaled on the barbs. They had released him.

Morgan pulled the silk from his mouth, but the airman had sunk back into unconsciousness. All their strength was needed to stop his rolling body taking them with it as it gained momentum on its drop to the beach. A rising wind still billowed parts of the parachute not caught in the wire.

At their feet the pilot lay, seemingly dead, the sand red under him. They stared hard at this first proper sight of the enemy.

"Have we killed him?" Morgan said. The tide was already coming in at speed, drawing away his blood, returning it diluted.

"What do you suggest we do next?" Mrs Floster's shrill voice had a sarcastic edge.

"We must get help."

There was little hope that some soldier with binoculars had sighted them from a pillbox. Nothing but an aeroplane returning to base; a homing bird; the waves. Faint anonymous humming sounds; the deep boom of a solitary gun.

Morgan thought it would soon be evening. Coral Floster again began to pull at the shredded parachute, gathering it, tugging its cords. The man lying at her feet groaned. His eyes and mouth wide open, he moved sideways. His fingers began slowly to claw at the pocket of his flying jacket.

It happened fast. Morgan saw the handle of a knife in his bloody hand. A flash of memory. She kicked him. Coral Floster, with a shriek, grabbed the knife from him. Morgan watched her raise it and watched her stab him in the chest.

They stood, seeing the blood turn his fleece crimson.

They knew he must be dead, but neither could touch him. The incoming tide, washing over their feet and his, was turning his grey sock black. The ripped parachute puffed above their heads.

On the slope of the dyke they collapsed. Morgan looked anywhere but at the man below. Wisps of cloud were forming. Every sound – the waves rolling pebbles, the breeze rattling grass, the whirring of insects – entered her hearing as loud as a tuning orchestra.

Neither woman spoke. A new fear was being born. At last Morgan said, "Someone must go back and tell what has happened."

At Lodford station the stationmaster, called from retirement, told Charlie he'd have a time of it feeding the dog. It followed him down the slope and bounded into the brook narrowed by drought. Charlie was relieved to see it wading under the Plumberow Road tunnel. He hoped it would go as far as Ironside Lane and get lost in some field beyond.

The town was noisy, army lorries everywhere. Crowds walking on the shady side of West Street were jostling for pavement space. In the square two shire horses were drinking, their bridles held by a Land Girl who wasn't Flo. There was a queue at the butchers, where Mr Dance in a bloody apron lifted a saw. The image of him with it raised stayed fixed in Charlie's mind as if it were a waxwork.

Only a few people queuing at the Co-op. The smell of frying next door irresistible. He joined the line waiting for fish and chips. He felt he hadn't eaten for days.

"Hello, Charlie." It was Vela Kymmerly sounding cheerful. Charlie muttered a reply, wondering who was managing her counter.

"My brother's come home," she said. "Archie's looking after the office." She and the fish lady agreed how wonderful it was that Archie was back from Berwick-on-Tweed, come to cheer them all up. Charlie felt nothing but irritation. In the past he had avoided Vela's tales.

"Nice dog!" The animal had appeared from nowhere, sitting beside Charlie as if it had never left him. It shook its wet coat over Vela. She fed it a chip, that it gobbled down and asked for more. "He needs a bit of a comb!"

"You can have him." Charlie was serious. Vela laughed and went back to work.

Not caring, Charlie ate the fish and chips from the newspaper on the way home. The day was still hot. Food and thoughts of Maya occupied him throughout the trek home. How dare she throw him out! Unreasonable. Unjustified. He was almost hating her.

The dog followed him, gobbling up a fallen chip and scraps of batter. The all-clear went as Charlie approached Morn Avenue. He would have to go the long way round, because the avenue was blocked. The dog growled at him for aiming a kick but stayed almost to heel all along the Gormson Road.

People were walking slowly. One or two acknowledged him. But the town was overrun with strangers. At least they didn't want to know his business. He was glad that foreigners were being interned on the Isle of Man. His one regret was the absence of the Italians who ran the ice cream parlour on Prittend sea-front.

At the Villa gates the dog bounded ahead. Charlie saw it racing around the cricket pitch, marking the pavilion steps, the gibbets, the concrete drain and tree trunks. He wouldn't let it follow him into the house. It sat outside the front door whining until he locked it in the garage.

The Villa was deserted. Nobody in the shelter. No sign of the Retchens. He called for Morgan, but his voice had a hollow-house echo. Upstairs her bedroom was reassuringly unchanged with no signs of packing. Mrs Floster's room seemed unusually empty for one so in love with clothes. In Flo's room the usual chaos except the bed, neatly turned down by Myrtle or Thelma. He grinned at the thought of Maya's unruly one.

The sitting rooms smelled stale. In the smaller one, the faint aroma of cigarettes. The piano lid was shut.

The kitchen looked odd. On the table were dirty cups, a few plates, some cutlery. And an unopened parcel addressed to Flo.

Slowly it began to dawn on Charlie that he should be concerned. What if something had happened to Morgan? There had been an air raid. Where would she have gone? Had there been incendiaries? Who would have looked after her?

He was considering going to Jerky for advice when someone entered the house. It was Mrs Floster, but not the immaculate woman Charlie knew. Her dress, clinging and damp, was distinctly dirty. Her hair was dishevelled. Her shoes were gouted with mud, her stockings torn, her arms scratched.

She was trying to gather what at first he thought was a counterpane. "Parachute." It flopped to the floor. "Charlie, you must come. Now! She's with him . . . Morgan . . . waiting." Mrs Floster was pointing downriver.

At the sound of Morgan's name Charlie asked no questions. He simply followed Coral Floster out of the house.

They went through the coiled barrier, along the beach and up the side of the dyke beyond the stile. Hurrying behind her, he thought he heard "pilot" and "trapped . . . situation". Speed and the wind were carrying her words away. Birds had risen in panic from the blackthorns. He was panting and tripping on tufted grass, trying to keep up with her. She ran on and on. He had never seen such energy.

Then the thin silhouette of Morgan, waving from the top of the dyke. He could see how distressed she was. Closer, how pale. She drew him to her and kissed his cheeks. Pleasure flooded through him.

"You're in a defence zone." He wanted her out of it.

"Look, Charlie. Look!"

He saw the ragged remnants of silk fluttering from barbed wire; down on the diminishing beach, the body. It was lying partially out of the water, one arm akimbo, feet and legs moving with the incoming tide. He knew he was looking at a corpse.

They told Charlie they had found the pilot like that. Kept repeating they didn't know what to do. He could not cope with hysterics. But Morgan was asking him for answers, agitating his arm, asking what to do. It troubled him that he hadn't come to her sooner.

He could not tell how long the body had been dead. Nor why they had taken off its harness. Perhaps they thought it would be useful. The war made everybody think about waste.

He said, "This should be reported."

"No!" Morgan was adamant. "Why? Too far for the police. They couldn't get him over the barriers."

"He is the enemy. They could throw him into the flood gates," Coral Floster suggested.

"He might float." Morgan was nervously looking around.

The discussion went on until at last she admitted that the pilot had been alive when they found him. Charlie couldn't understand her panic. She kept repeating that he would have died anyway; one look at his injuries was enough.

They scrambled down to the body. Charlie examined its pockets and withdrew a deckled photograph of an old woman with a child. He sniffed the air. "He's been burned. Smells like Saturday roast." Flies were settling on the dead man's face. The jacket had fallen open revealing a shirt, bloodstained. An empty sheath dropped onto the sand. Charlie saw the knife, still lying where Coral Floster had dropped it, and picked it up. "See! He was armed. We could tell the police that."

The women continued watching him pull the body to and fro, as if it were meat. At any moment he would see the stab wound.

Morgan said, "He was stabbed." She had seen Coral Floster's pleading expression. "By me, actually. Self-defence."

"You murdered him!" Charlie was all admiration. He had the knife between finger and thumb, the blade visibly bloody.

"You must fetch the police." Coral Floster was steadying. "Nobody will worry twice about a dead Nazi. See on his jacket, the eagle? Morgan will say he attacked her. Will you not? I shall back her up."

"What if there's a trial?" Charlie had directed the question at Morgan. "I mean, there might be an inquest."

Coral Floster aimed a foot at the pilot's shoulder. Flies buzzed. "He's probably wearing identity discs. That will positively prove he's the enemy."

Charlie thought an inquest wouldn't be so bad. "We would all be heroes for capturing him."

With rising vehemence Morgan again said no. She had already taken one foreigner, the Frenchman, to the police station. Or sent him there with a dubious Irish person who might not have been so neutral. "I am not going to risk giving them another, especially a dead one. We must get rid of him."

"What Frenchman?" Coral Floster was now composed. "We cannot stay here all afternoon. We may be spotted."

They concluded they must give the pilot burial at sea. In Charlie's words "dump him".

He pocketed the identity discs, the knife, its sheath and the photograph. Telling them to bind the dead man with his harness, he left, saying he had an idea.

It was risky to commandeer the *Clara*, but Charlie felt invincible. Now he was a man. Now his sister, her house in ruins, would need his protection. What to do about the R.A.F. around her like cockroaches was for another day. First he must free her of a dead Nazi.

The tide almost high, he rowed out to the *Clara* moored mid stream, unfastened her tarpaulins. There was fuel on board and the engines turned over nicely. No-one watching.

He steered her into mid channel and went full throttle towards the east. He passed a pillbox built into the sea wall, seemingly deserted. There was relief when the mill disappeared from sight. He was making good time. On either bank there was nothing unusual. No small craft or fishermen, upstream or down.

Then, at a bend in the river, he saw Morgan on the top of the dyke frantically gesticulating.

Getting the dead man from beach to rowboat, rowboat to cruiser, tested the strength of all three. The body left a pink trail on the sand, fading into a muddy slick left by the wash of the tide. There was argument about the blood.

Another argument on the *Clara*. Coral Floster was all for pushing the body overboard fast. But Charlie, listening only to Morgan, took them further downriver. Morgan and Coral Floster crouched beside him on the bloodstained deck, fearing they would be seen. But only a solitary soldier, manning another pillbox, turned his binoculars on them. Charlie waved in a friendly fashion. There was no shout to heave to. With his sister at his feet, he knew everything would be alright.

They were approaching more open water, yet the engines' reverberation sounded louder than he ever remembered. He told her they would have to stop soon. The Blytham boat yards were coming into view.

He decided to drop anchor at a bend, where the east-west view was the most restricted, wide sky, sea wall winding, blanketing trees, estuary clear.

One of the *Clara*'s anchors they attached to the binding harness. The body, heavy to roll, was handled most adeptly by Coral Floster. Morgan begged her to cover his face.

Her suggestion they give him, a combatant, at least the semblance of a burial service, was overridden. There was real urgency. All aware of the turning tide, the time it was taking, of their luck running out. Or the possibility that Mr Talbott might need the *Clara* himself. Charlie said no. Lately there were signs that Talbott was on the sauce.

As they tipped the dead airman overboard and watched each final bubble, Coral Floster remarked, "Won't someone miss that anchor?"

"We can't do anything about it." Charlie was already turning the wheel.

"What if he floats up again?" She was phlegmatic. "They'll know he's been murdered." Morgan did not acknowledge her look.

Charlie, pleased with his part, headed the *Clara* upstream. He wondered why his sister said so little on the journey.

That evening he presented her with a trophy, a piece of parachute cord the colour of seawater, cut off with the pilot's own knife.

Morgan hid it in the family Bible. On occasion she examined it for signs of blood, but there were none.

Charlie did not understand why she and Mrs Floster told no-one, not even Flo, about the killing. He had tried telling Morgan of his admiration for her having finished off a Nazi, but she repeatedly stopped him.

The way she had taken the loss of her house pleased him too. His hope that she would live forever with him might be fulfilled. Morgan had mourned for her books and the Macclesfield silk. About bricks and mortar she felt less. The gloomy London house could never contend with the Villa Rouge. That Cathcart was to be posted abroad might delay the problem of telling him.

Her worries revolved around whether Archie was really the lover to whom anything could be confided? What would be his attitude to her complicity in a murder? And what about Charlie, home for only a few hours yet more . . . grown up? She had involved him in a crime that, on the face of it, he had handled with equanimity.

There was something else difficult to pinpoint. At supper she had covertly watched Florence's coy reaction to him. When she had ruffled his hair Charlie had smiled oddly, instead of rebuffing her.

There was talk of the harvest and grain for milling. Flo was telling him about sugars. She said rain might spoil the wheat if they couldn't get it quickly off the fields. Charlie said it would be the best harvest they'd had for years. It was as if the pilot's horrible death had never happened. Or that he could brush it off like a bothersome gnat.

Morgan had wondered whether Flo's presence was the reason for normality. Yet Coral Floster was eating calmly. Manifestly her only concern was that she should be driven to Iverdon the next day.

Before supper there had been some tension between Morgan and Mrs Retchen who, on finding a deserted Villa, had waited behind. She had not commented on the weary trio coming from the river. She prepared the supper table, asking no questions about a patently unusual situation, her silence implying that normality was paramount.

All Morgan wanted was to eat, then get to bed. She questioned the presence of the tablecloth, napkins, milk jug, the jam pot.

"You dear mother would turn in her grave. Who makes jam can say what it's put in. And Miss Florence was brought up proper."

There was something else Mrs Retchen had to say, but that could wait. She and the girls departed in time for Mr Churchill's evening broadcast.

Coral Floster persuaded Morgan and Charlie to stay up for the Prime Minister's speech. Too exhausted, they could not react to the rousing words. *"Never in the field of human conflict was so much owed by so many to so few."* Mrs Floster cried a little.

Morgan gave vent to irritation about the dog. Locked in the garage, it had been barking throughout the broadcast. Charlie should never have brought it home. "A brown and white spaniel once scratched me." When he said he'd give it to Granny Dorp for protection, he was joking. As he was when he added that she was an eccentric.

"Eccentric! She's not some sort of specimen." This tougher Charlie worried her. Yet she too was toughening up because of this horrible war, and now she had a hand in a murder.

She decided she would think about Charlie in the morning. As she would about her future relationship with Archie. She could not be the same impulsive person of last September. She was not about to rush into another meaningless liaison like that with Patch. This was different. She and Archie were always meant for each other.

Hearing Charlie coming upstairs, she struggled from bed to waylay him. He was to swear not to breathe a word about the Nazi pilot. She whispered that Flo might have strong views on killing. Charlie shrugged and murmured, "Fox-hunting?"

Florence was in the bathroom singing "Night and Day" above the gush of water. Coral Floster came out of her bedroom, clutching a kimono. She said she couldn't sleep until she knew how they intended getting her to Iverdon. Had Morgan forgotten about the motorcar, still sitting outside a barn in a lane? Neither replied to Charlie's question about who had been driving the car.

He had the answer: if Mrs Floster would ride on the crossbar of his bicycle, he would get her as far as the Rover. He would drive her home then bring the car back where it belonged.

Morgan could see he was distracted. It was no use asking him why he wanted to get to Iverdon. She knew the R.D.F. station was an obsession. She let him go to bed, but waited for Flo, afraid that fatigue would arrive first.

It seemed an age before Florence emerged in a surge of steam. Morgan made a note to check the coal supply. She said they must be prepared for difficulties. Florence in her nightdress stood patiently, her bare arms glistening as pink as ever.

"Flo, I must tell you, and everyone, that the bathroom's going to be out of order for a while. Plumbing problems. In fact it will be unusable from tomorrow. For a day or two."

"Seemed fine to me." Florence said. "Water lovely and hot."

"In summer one can wash elsewhere." It was better to get it over before she found herself asleep on her feet. "You can use the sink downstairs."

"Where the vegetables are scrubbed? The boots!"

"Or . . ." Morgan hesitated, ". . . you could bathe in the river. Just for a day or two."

"But the Lodbrook is salty."

"Not very. Especially nearer the boathouse. Private too. And very refreshing. You're a good swimmer."

Surprisingly Florence, after some consideration, acceded. It might be good fun. The girls could join her after work. Morgan agreed. That night she would have agreed if Flo had suggested bringing the whole work force, including Mr Cedric Brodir and his plebeian wife, in their bathing suits.

She slept deeply, troubled only by a dream of an airman's missing boot. It disturbed her for several nights.

When she woke, Charlie and Mrs Floster had set off by bike to the Rover as planned. Myrtle and Thelma were sorting laundry, but their mother was waiting to talk to Miss Morgan.

Morgan said she was already late for an appointment. She left, making for the Redwood pub opposite the Villa gates. Jerky would not wait very long, having said he was needed elsewhere. And Morgan needed Jerky.

He was still waiting for her. She was glad she did not have the bicycle, for Jerky was at the wheel of a battered Austin. Was he old enough to drive?

He had brought newspaper and sacks. She commended him for his forethought and apologised for being tardy. He told her he knew where Mill Lane was without any help.

Morgan began to wonder what Mrs Retchen had wanted to talk

about. Upsetting her, she told Jerky, was to be avoided at all costs. He said not to worry. When everything was in place, the lady would be well pleased.

At first Mrs Retchen wasn't pleased at all. Her mood changed when she knew the reason for the bathroom's closure. She and the girls would do their to best to help. What couldn't wait was what she had tried tell Miss Morgan since the morning:

The previous evening when she'd come to collect her girls, about half past five or nearing six, a stranger, a man, had come to the Villa asking for Miss Rhoda Swell.

For a split second Morgan imagined it was her father, his mind deranged by his travails.

"He said he was Miss Rhoda's brother. I told him she wasn't here." Mrs Retchen paused. "He was a bit put out. But so was I, seeing this place was like the grave and the girls on their own for I don't know how long."

"Where is this brother now?"

Mrs Retchen was still in a state of annoyance. "Tall fellow. Not like Rhoda, that's for certain. Well, in some ways he bears a resemblance. You'll see."

"Where is he now, Mrs Retchen?"

In an unusually dramatic gesture Mrs Retchen waved an arm. "At my house. Been there since last evening. Well, I couldn't leave him here. He might *not* have been her brother, if you get my meaning. How could I ask? People's circumstances are private. I had to give him our liver and bacon. He ate the lot!"

"Great merciful heavens, not another visitor!" It was too much. "I suppose he ought to come here."

"Told him an hour since, so I don't know what's keeping him. Not like Rhoda at all."

"What is his name?"

"Says it's Elm something or other. Couldn't make that out neither."

They went into the hall, where Mrs Retchen swiped the banister rails with her duster. Morgan sat on the stairs, irresolute. One visitor gone, another arriving. It wasn't fair. Were people always going to come between her and Archie?

A double knock on the front door. Mrs Retchen recognised her daughters' laughter.

Thelma and Myrtle were standing on either side of Rhoda's brother, as close as if they were related. All three were smiling.

CHAPTER THIRTEEN

In the garage the dog was barking furiously. Morgan took a few neck bones from the stew. Rhoda's brother asked what she was going to do with them.

What was she was going to do with him? He was confounding all her knowledge of what men were like. Yes, he was wearing an ordinary jacket and trousers, carrying a homburg. But there was a strangeness about him, his demeanour. His face had the soft quality of a woman's. His voice, although deep and with Rhoda's accent, brought to mind some comedian on the wireless, who made incomprehensible jokes. She had no idea how old he was.

He told her his name was Elmo, then Elmer. She asked directly if he had made it up.

"Oh yes. St Elmo. Him and Erasmus, patron saints of sailors and stomach ache." He was gazing hard at her. "Can you believe this belly ache has turned sailor?" She couldn't make him out.

His irritation at Rhoda's absence was tempered by amusement that she had joined the same service. "My stuff's at the station." A good indication, Morgan hoped, that he would leave soon.

He was in the kitchen, extraordinarily hungry, eating another breakfast. She felt freer to be generous with food since her relationship with Jerky. And after winning a skirmish with the bank manager.

"I am Patroclus. That's what night school does for you."

She felt bold with him. "I don't believe you. You're probably Fred. Or Eustace."

"Useless? But not in all departments. I'm a dab hand with an oily rag." His hands were tanned, with blackened fingernails. "I never could handle a needle, though."

He was looking appreciatively at the egg on his plate. Morgan watched him cut off the top with a knife, thus failing one of her mother's tests of refinement. She would have expected no more of a brother of Rhoda.

"Very acceptable." He grabbed a slice of bread. "No time for sewing sails. We're U-boat fodder, we are." And without pausing he added, "Rhoda told me about you, once."

"Only once?"

"You don't know which way is up, she said. She said for someone with very fixed ideas, you have a lot to learn. Have you? Do you?"

"War unfixes a lot of ideas." He had Rhoda's watchful eyes, a little like the dog's. "We didn't know you existed. Oh, Charlie might have."

"My sister keeps things to herself, does she? That doesn't surprise me."

"When she came back on leave she was Third Officer Swell, full of adventures!"

He was more interested in buttering his bread. "*Change and decay in all around I see*," he intoned. "I tell you something strange –" He was pointing the knife at her and she could smell him. It was a real scent – "dogs have disappeared. Yours is a rarity."

"Perhaps they've all been eaten."

He laughed. "Killed and eaten. Have you had a lot of people killed here? The looks I got. I feared for my life. If I was a spy come down by parachute, wouldn't I make a bit more effort to blend in?"

She thought he would have trouble blending in anywhere. Changing the subject from parachutists, she said, "A brown and white spaniel scratched someone a long time ago." He showed no interest at all.

"Your name isn't really Patrocle, is it?"

"Patroclus. Why not? I took a while choosing it."

"But why?"

He studied her for a moment. "Some other time. You're still a trifle young for the grown-up world!" He was laughing again.

"Now you sound like Rhoda."

"My sister thought you were more a full-grown manipulator. Sound like you?" His hard gaze implied he wanted a response.

She said she was more the manipulated. Always at someone's beck and call, when all she wanted was a little corner to herself. It was curious she could tell this stranger a private feeling. "Rhoda must have done a lot of talking about me."

Elmer went on eating. When Morgan asked about a ration book, he said he was due soon at Chatham, but would appreciate a bed.

He could have Charlie's old room if Mrs Floster, another lodger, didn't come back to sleep, He did not ask to take over Rhoda's.

She left him starting on the jam while she went to the garage, where the dog was whining. It ate the bones ravenously. It had urinated on the Rover's running board.

They were standing in Mrs Floster's vacated bedroom.

"Nice view." Elmer was gazing towards the gleam of the river. "Now I see why Rhoda was so defensive." She did not comprehend. "'Time and chance'," he said.

"Shall I call you Patrick? It's easier than Patro-whatever and sounds better than Elmo."

"Elmer will do nicely." Together they made the bed. "*A little slumber, a little folding of the hands to sleep!*" Morgan hoped he wasn't another Reverend Dorby.

"Pity about the garden. Pedestrian. Rhoda and the young master did it, apparently." He was looking around. "This room's horribly *jejune.* Where is the adorable boy, whose photo she wouldn't even show me?" He asked this casually, but she knew he was interested.

"This was a group captain's wife's room." But she was talking to his bent back. He had pulled from under the bed Coral Floster's hatbox. From it he took a scrap of a hat that he perched on his head, adjusting the veil in the dressing table mirror. "Suits me, don't you think?"

He seemed unoffended by her laughter. Morgan told him Rhoda's things, the ones not in Weymouth, were in the attic.

It was somehow in character, she thought, for him to keep the hat on while they climbed the stairs.

All the previous days' heat had gathered up there. Pigeons were scratching on the roof. Mrs Retchen could be heard below, calling and calling for Myrtle.

Behind Rhoda's suitcase was the portrait of Morgan's mother, looking as fresh as if the young camper had just painted it. Its presence was disturbing.

"She was my mother."

"Very artistic. That's why it's up here, I imagine! Consigned to oblivion in the Gods."

His shadow, curling across the furniture and boxes, brought to mind the cockerel.

"Your sister came here because my mother died. But you knew that?"

"To be honest with you . . ." The sentence unfinished, he was dragging out Rhoda's suitcase.

She doubted his sincerity, and felt some pity for his sister. From the suitcase he had taken a frock that sent blue sparks across the boards. It was the one Morgan had longed for. He stood holding it against him, his veiled forehead close to the rafters. It was definitely not Rhoda's. Another was in his hands, the peacock thing she had also packed. An ultramarine feather went rocking to the floor in a shaft of light.

"Are you a film actor?" she asked with sudden enlightenment. "There was one about a leopard called Baby."

He said lightly, "I'm quaking to find out more!"

She hesitated, wondering whether he would like being allied with Cary Grant in a *peignoir*.

"Has she?" He was tut-tutting loudly. He had discovered the broken zip. "No, she hasn't." He shoved both frocks into the suitcase and shut it. "I won't be needing these for a while anywise. Club closed for the duration. Which, in the opinion of Yours Truly, is a big mistake." He flapped a hand. "Let's get out of this haunted place."

He followed Morgan down to the landing. "Sorry, but I must up the hill to Scarborough. Where is it?" She was mystified. "The Queen of Watering Places, dear?"

She pointed to the lavatory. "The bathroom is out of use at the moment. You may wash downstairs. Or have a basin in your room."

A few minutes later Elmer came downstairs grinning. "Do you know there's a pig in your bath? I hope it's dead."

"It must be – it's only half a pig." She wished the sight of the body, albeit a pig's, floating in a pink pool was not so forceful a reminder of another.

Mrs Retchen came to complain that Elmer, upstairs napping, was using up her precious Lifebuoy. He had already purloined the captain's shaving tackle. Thelma had told him he could take the Vaseline. Claimed it was for his hair. "Those girls seem to have taken a fancy to him. The Lord knows why."

"He hasn't got much hair."

More concerned with the pig in the bath, Mrs Retchen needed a source of saltpetre.

Morgan's mind wandered from this as she cooked and finished wiping up. It was too quiet. No sirens, no aircraft, nothing but a few clouds patterning the blue coming in on an easterly breeze. Earlier she had walked as far as the Gormson Road, unusually deserted, only the wind in the elms and rooks calling. There was the scent of hay, mingling with that of broad beans her mother could detect from a mile away.

She had wanted to drive somewhere, anywhere, although she knew it would be towards Archie. But he must come to her. And soon.

Drifting through the Villa rooms, pushing cushions, righting chairs, she stopped in the small sitting room. The silence was disturbing. Charlie at work, or claiming to be, Elmer asleep upstairs, Mrs Retchen and the girls somewhere.

She would have to confront her problems. To decide what she really wanted, what her actions might unleash. The war had brought her from one kind of confinement to another. Had Archie come to save her? Or only to complicate? Did she want him to be more than the same lover he was? She was beginning to see that desire and gratification did not necessarily mean commitment.

The Villa Rouge was now her home, but not the home of her children or Cathcart. He would expect to pick up the old ways, if he ever came back. And that was in doubt.

Within all the insecurities lay an emerging excitement. She wondered how many women were having to adjust to new lives, to make decisions based on longings that might be fleeting. Simple happiness had always been elusive. Had she now forfeited any right to it by being complicit in a murder?

She had not heard the car, or the Villa door. Hadn't heard him come into the room. At first she thought she was seeing Archie's distorted reflection. When he kissed her neck she knew it was Peter Parclay, although his boldness surprised her.

He said he was one of the lucky ones, one burned arm and leg. Nearly ready for action. "Pranged over the southern counties, Jerry above me. Lucky I wasn't in a bomber. Last week one made it home, rear gunner alive. Missed the latrines by a hair! They hosed another gunner out of a Wellington over at—"

"How can you talk about it so lightly?"

"Morgan, any one of us might be killed." He leaned his head on her shoulder. "I'm angling for sympathy." His proximity was lessening her tumbling thoughts. It pained her to think of him in pain.

"You have seen Patch? He has told you?" he said.

"That the flight lieutenant is married? The suspicion was always there. But so am I, married."

He took her hand. "I really don't care. You see, I am not. And I want to be." He was stroking the green ring. "I know now there isn't much time any more."

For a moment she felt closer to him than to any man with whom she had never slept. Then thoughts of Archie intervened. "Wouldn't you like to take me on as your sister?"

"Never." He was shaking his head. "Never!"

To escape such potent intimacy, she took him into the kitchen for tea. She asked how he would manage. She could see how uncomfortably he sat, trying to ease his body as he talked.

Radar was the name of the game, he said. Without it they'd be fighting blind. He would be working at the Iverdon station. He was a grounded boffin.

Uncomprehending, she nodded.

Did she know there was a chain of radar stations around the coast? "Bawdsey was hit in May, but it's operational again. They tell us when to be on stand-by. The frequencies are adjustable. Peak power of two hundred kilowatts. The pulse generator's locked, you see, to the British grid to synchronise the Ch transmitters. The transmitting antennae – they're on different levels."

She suspected that talking was an attempt to overcome his pain.

"They've improved the receiving antennae, but work's to be done. Jerry's clever at coming in under the radar. That's where chaps like me are needed."

"Should you be telling me all this?" But she was content that he was treating her as an equal.

"And frankly, Morgan –" he leaned closer – "it was touch and go. They were tying our planes up with string to get them back up." He looked older than she recalled. "The action's moving south now." He drank his tea. "They're calling it the Battle of Britain, saying we've saved the day!" Relieved to hear him on a subject other than their relationship, she let him talk on.

Charlie was confronted with the sight of the flying officer and his sister. He sat down between them. He suspected they had been discussing subjects other than magnetrons and microwaves. It pleased him to learn that Parclay would be fully occupied on the R.D.F. site.

Morgan said, "So there'll be lots of Waafs for you to play with, Peter."

"There isn't time for such talk any more, Morgan."

"I have had a letter from my husband." This she said hastily to deflect him from any intimacy, then regretted it.

Cathcart, having discovered that Teresa should not have been evacuated without a parent, was asking why, how this had happened. She could not voice this. Guilt was beginning to weight on her.

Long after she had sent Parclay away, Charlie continued to sulk. And Morgan continued to maintain that she and Peter were just friends.

"No man can be just a friend to someone like you."

When she asked where he had spent the night in London, he did not reply.

Mrs Retchen was complaining that Rhoda's brother was using up all the hot water. "No thought for anybody but themselves, those people."

Florence came in late, declaring that stooking sheaves was ruining her back. Discovering the half pig in the bath, she screamed unnecessarily loudly. Sent to the boot room, where there was no lock on the door, she stripped to her cami knickers, saying she was too tired for the river.

At supper it was plain what she thought of Elmer, for she refused to pass him the Worcester sauce. Everyone seemed tetchy. The wireless news of losses to U-boats in the Atlantic added to the air of disquiet.

The Timmbolds wrote that Billy and Teresa had been inoculated against diphtheria. This note Morgan sent to Cat, glad to have something to tell. She wrote of Elmer's visit, but not of Flo.

To fill space she told him Aunt Winnie had cut off all her hair and was hiding in her room. This from Charlie, en route to Group Captain Floster, who had promised to get him a civilian job at the radar station.

On Saturday morning Jerky came early, bringing saltpetre. He watched it go into the pickling solution with his illicit sugar and salt. And stayed while it boiled and cooled, handing out unwanted advice. Mrs Retchen told him she well knew how to slice up a pig's head and pickle trotters.

Jerky's intention was to warn Morgan privately about Charlie. In the hall he said that her brother was buying and selling contraband. He put an imaginary cigarette to his lips. If she needed anything, like more salt and sugar, she had better come to him, rather than put Charlie in a situation. "I don't want my pitch queered. He hasn't got my balance, my balance, see?"

Mrs Retchen said she'd known Jerky since he was a toddler. His ear was the result of being swiped at by his mother's crutch. Myrtle refused to scald the pig's ear because it looked like Jerky's. At school, she said, he was always whacked for doing naughty things that had to do with cigarette cards and marbles.

They spent all morning jointing the half pig, Morgan wishing she had never instigated the whole business. Occasionally one of the twins would leave without consent, coming back only to dissolve into fresh tears over the dismemberment.

Granny Dorp's unwanted foray in the pantry meant a search for the cloves and whole spice. The hams were immersed in the spiced liquid and put into crocks weighted down with stones. Thelma was sent in search of bay leaves for the brawn. Every bristle was burned off the half head.

Elmer stood, arms crossed, watching the process with distaste. He covered his eyes at the sight of the pig's eye impaled on Mrs Retchen's knife. "I must fetch my kit from the station."

Thelma asked if she could go with him, and to Morgan's surprise her mother agreed.

"You let him go alone with your girl?"

"Yes, of course. No problem there."

The question was how to preserve good bacon for keeping. They agreed the Anderson shelter was the coldest place. An excess of pork belly, curing in salt and sugar, was another matter.

Mrs Retchen said, "Give some to Mrs Perincall." But Morgan had no wish to reveal how she had acquired so much pork. She thought the bank manager's wife, a woman she was coming to admire, should have a few rashers.

"No. They get enough from here already, Grouming and his crony, that land agent. They say Threw's building a nice pile at Blytham for his daughter and new son-in-law. That one's due for call-up, but he's been deferred. Takes the biscuit." Mrs Retchen raised a wrinkled finger. "Normal like, I don't talk out of turn."

The siren sounded while they were scrubbing down with ammonia. Boxley joined them in the shelter, oblivious of the narrowed space. He said his boys were holding the horse, skittish with the air raid. Myrtle Retchen was out there too, refusing point blank to come into the shelter. The dull sound of bombs dropping far away kept the others taking cover until the all-clear.

Charlie came home at six, ready to grumble about everything. He said it was woman's work to rid the bath of bloody scum. No, he was not coming to church the next day, he had better things to do. Too tired to argue, Morgan gave him an early supper and went to bed.

Grandma Perincall was not in church. Neither was Winifred. Nor Flo, who had pleaded harvest exhaustion. From the Reverend Dorby came the announcement that the service would be curtailed. Many of the brave servicemen present were due for recall to battle the foe in foreign fields.

Morgan noticed Threw in leather gaiters and quality corduroys. The girl beside him, doubtless his daughter, was equally smartly dressed. After the service he raised his hat and hurried her to a young man, waiting with a horse and gig.

Morgan felt obliged to cycle on to Iverdon, to find out what was wrong with her grandma. She had left Flo instructions on how to coincide the vegetables and gravy with the roast pork.

Pleased at her grandmother's offer of lunch, her spirits fell at the sight of ham. The two ate together. There was no sign of Aunt Winifred.

"She is upstairs." Grandma Perincall was visibly irritated. "Winifred is a melancholic. The first of the Perincalls to give way to pessimism. Apart from your father's great-uncle. Not a real Perincall. He threw himself under a hay wagon. That may not be true. He may have put it about himself for personal reasons."

Morgan could only assume that this great-uncle survived the hay cart incident, at least long enough to relate it. Sensing that her grand-mother's vexation encompassed more than Winifred, she decided to hold her tongue.

With all her attention on a cherry pie with custard, she was taken aback at being addressed in a condemnatory tone:

"You bit your Aunt Winifred. I put it down as the start of her decline."

Thinking her grandmother was joking, Morgan laughed.

"Baby teeth can be quite sharp."

There was no solution but to stay longer in order to mollify her, even to holding her wool skeins for winding. The atmosphere did not improve.

Aunt Winifred had long been behaving strangely. "Twist, twist! Twisting her hair all day. It put one's nerves on edge. I told her about it, and what did she do?" Morgan waited. "She cut it all off! What nonsense!" Her grandmother sighed. "You should see the condition of the green-house."

The shuffling upstairs sounded like Aunt Winnie. Morgan wondered how her father would have reacted to this state of affairs. But to bring up his name now was out of the question.

"Harriet and Maud are doing their best in Nottinghamshire. Against heavy odds, it seems. Evacuees, from Birmingham *and* London –" here she nodded at Morgan – "have head lice. Some are illiterate. Some not house trained!" She lapsed into brief silence. "I must warn you, child, that the privy caught an incendiary bomb."

This was news indeed but, had Morgan said this, she might have been criticised for not having heard it already.

"The fire was doused by passing airmen. The privy must be rebuilt quickly. It isn't seemly for two women to have to crouch behind a tarpau-lin. The carpenter cannot start work because of Threw's new house." Here she raised her eyebrows at her granddaughter.

"New house?"

"Yes. This agent has a perfectly good house already, yet he can afford to build another. There is, after all, a war on." She was raising a knitting needle. "It may be for that daughter of his, who looks as if she has hookworm. It might be judicious to make a few enquiries." Her grandmother's eyes were wide. "Nothing hot-headed. In fact," and this an afterthought, "look towards that bank manager – Crooning, is it?"

With a glance at the door, as if Winifred might be lurking outside, Grandma Perincall whispered, "Go *yourself*, Morgan. Do not take Charlie. Or that Land Army person. From what I have observed, she is showing some fondness for the boy." Putting away her knitting basket, she said Morgan should go home, for she needed a nap.

At the door she said, "Does the girl know that Charles is to inherit? I sincerely hope you can keep control. Threw is a good agent, but greedy. Always first with his knees under Monty and Berenice's table. Not like his father."

With relief Morgan bade goodbye to her grandmother, who as usual had more to add on the doorstep. "I hear they've been dropping bombs on a Sunday. What is the world coming to?"

The brief lull in aerial attacks came to an end with the return of brilliant weather. And the news that the East End had been bombed. Retaliation was fast. Berlin was bombed, setting off attacks on both sides. Stories of destruction across Merseyside filled the newsreels and papers. No more was the Villa quiet. Over its rooftops Nazi bombers were passing on their way to London's docklands.

Elmer said he should have joined the R.A.F. Morgan thought him lazy, hanging around her, his chatter as distracting as it was fascinating. "'Join the navy and see the world', they told me. You can guarantee all I'll ever see, at least in mixed company, is the inside of an engine room. And the sea washing over me, more than like."

Nevertheless he was optimistic. "War is wonderful," he told Morgan one morning, while they were huddled among the pickling crocks. "It lets us be what we really are."

"Some men don't want to fight at all. Our manager's son objects to war on principle. My husband, though, says it's his duty."

"Oh, save us from the noble ones! I've had to fight for my survival, I can tell you. This war for me is a godsend. I can't wait to get back to my shipmates. And they can't wait for me!" Elmer was waving his Woodbine. She wished he wouldn't smoke. And wished, too, that she understood more of what he seemed to be divulging, for his company was curiously beguiling.

The Retchen sisters found him irresistible, hanging around in the hopes of persuading him to join their singing. Their allegiance had shifted from Charlie, who avoided Elmer and spent less and less time at home. His reason the arrival of quantities of grain needing processing.

Florence, home late and exhausted, limited her conversation to yields and targets. Nobody wanted to discuss losses in the Atlantic, Russian advances in eastern Europe, the fighting in North Africa, where Cathcart had probably been sent. Charlie's talk was of what they would do if the Nazis arrived.

Only Eden Dufrene and his compatriot, wearing their A.R.P. badges, came to the Villa. They declared it was now an air raid post, "Nerve centre of this area."

They drank Morgan's tea, consumed their sandwiches and sat for hours chatting. Elmer they eyed cautiously. Morgan had a suspicion that Eden was as much taken with the sight of her and Flo in their night-dresses as he was with his official duties.

But his prompt dousing of an incendiary bomb in the attic saved many things, not least her mother's portrait. Charlie and Morgan handed the stirrup pumps and sand while Elmer, in Coral Floster's kimono, did little but agitate about his frocks.

After that night, Eden's partner never came back. The postman told Morgan it was the sight of Elmer in kimono and calamine lotion.

The baker's report was of bombs on the other side of the Lodbrook. From Prittend were stories of the pier on fire, of soldiers evacuated from an hotel on the sea-front. Mrs Retchen had it from P.C. Callum that the Nails family had found cushy lodgings with a retired colonel in Plumberow.

The sounds of take-offs and landings at the aerodrome had long since been ignored. The rare sight of an autogyro had so enthused Charlie, he told Flo about it. She warned him that if he skulked around the airfield perimeter, or watched, whatsoever, from the railway bridge, he would be arrested. When he told her planes had been destroyed on the ground, she accused him of spreading pessimism. He decided she was an ugly person.

His sister meanwhile was blossoming. She was eating more and looking better, thanks to Jerky. Not that he told her this. Instead he said that Jerky was fed up because she was too demanding. She had wanted a tarpaulin to cover the illicit coal supply.

"Your sister wants the earth," Jerky said.

"She certainly does!" was Charlie's admiring reply.

What Morgan wanted most of all was Archie. At the post office, from Vela behind the counter, she learned that missing paperwork was causing delays in his call-up. With a patiently waiting queue behind her, Morgan had to hear the rest of Vela's tale. It was not, as she hoped, about Archie, but about Mr Talbott who, Vela whispered, had dropped to the ground outside the Three Tuns in an advanced state of inebriation.

Morgan took to lingering in the square. Or, seated by the window in the Harlem cafe, she would scan passers-by, looking for Archie. Then she would rush home, thinking she might have missed him there.

She went to the post office on a market day, convinced that Archie would be helping with the Thursday crowds. There he was, charming a customer. Morgan managed to achieve his counter, where she passed her note under the grille. He took it with barely a glance and handed her the stamps without a word.

At the N.A.A.F.I. she served her weekly turn, hoping against hope that Archie, newly uniformed perhaps, would turn up. The clientele were mainly soldiers, prepared to be shipped off to places even warmer than Lodford. They seemed cheerful enough, but flirting for Morgan had lost its charm and she struggled to match their bonhomie.

Not a man took any notice of alerts. They carried on playing billiards. Or went outside to watch tracers outshooting stars. The knowledgeable ones knew by the engines' sounds whether the enemy was overhead, how far away the bombs were likely to drop.

One evening the quartermaster sergeant told Morgan that the enemy was unloading bombs on the estuary. She had gone outside for cooling air. He said there was a bomber's moon, but it would be unlucky indeed if one hit her Mill. She guessed the cause of his confiding manner might be her silence. She had made no mention to anyone of the night she had seen him with Mrs Talbott. Unlike other ranks, the sergeant was spending entire evenings at the N.A.A.F.I. That those particular evenings coincided with Grace Talbott's was no surprise to her.

With days of increasing cloud came some relief from attacks. The canteen again filled with service personnel from the aerodrome. One evening it was Group Captain Floster who came into the N.A.A.F.I. leading a group of aircraftmen. Clearly he had been drinking. Beside him limped Patch Woodborne, who waved at Morgan, beside the tea urn with Mrs Talbott.

The crowd that night was particularly excitable. Arguments kept erupting around the billiard table, yells and cries at every missed pot. There were complaints that the darts players were obstructing the dance floor. The R.A.F. had taken it over, as if every gramophone record would be the last. Patch shrugged, as if to say that boisterousness was only to be expected. Mrs Talbott said something about grown men, but she was smiling.

Group Captain Floster, gyrating alone to "Flat Foot Floogie", was obviously out of control. Morgan saw how he tried to wrap his arms around any airman within reach. And how Patch recoiled from his advances.

It was always the group captain who called for the next dance, and attempted to wind the gramophone. His behaviour was inciting the younger ground crew to louder laughter, wilder approaches to the women. Morgan was surprised that the Waafs were as disapproving of the men's antics as those serving them. At nine o'clock a leading aircraftman had to be stopped from urinating into a bucket of sand.

Mrs Grouming called for the music to be turned off, the tea urn shut, the dartboard closed. Within half an hour the evening was over.

At the gate Morgan heard Patch behind her. "Let me give you a last lift home, sweetie. I'll soon be on my way to Basingstoke."

She declined. Cycling was fine on such a warm night. Behind them emerged a knot of airmen, still in high spirits. At its centre Group Captain Floster. Ricocheting between them, he was still attempting to embrace whoever was closest. Amid laughter and swearing an untidy pavement scuffle started. It might have become serious, Patch said, had not their camp commander been the instigator.

He fell against Morgan with an apology. In the moonlight she saw him wince with pain. He reached for her hand and put it to his lips. "Farewell, lovely one."

"Farewell, lovely one!" The group captain had emerged from the *mêlée*, intent on embracing Patch, but buckling into the arms of a corporal.

"He's been drinking all day. We can't take him home or to the squadron like this."

"Go to the Villa," Morgan said. "Charlie's there and Florence. They'll see he sobers up." She thought it wiser not to mention Elmer.

The group captain, attempting to say individual farewells, was hauled towards the flight lieutenant's Riley.

Patch kissed Morgan's cheek. "Be good to Peter. Don't let him bore you to pieces!" He followed the unruly group to his car.

Outside Whitley's garage she was waylaid by Charlie, hiding behind an advertisement. She berated him for giving her a shock.

"Where have you been at this time of night?"

"To Jerky's."

"You haven't. Jerky is fetching dabs from somewhere on the Brod."

No response. They walked a few paces, the sound of the brook noisy in the silence. Morgan could see Charlie's hunched shoulders. "Where is your bike?" She stopped. "You haven't driven the Rover!"

Driving the car without her permission was more than he would dare. He had left his bicycle leaning against Willams', before going to his lookout on the railway bridge. He had been watching the infant school since early evening.

"You didn't want Flight Lieutenant Woodborne to drive you home?" he said at last.

So she knew he'd been observing her. She was leading the way across the street. There was the swish of an unlit bicycle passing too close.

"I can manage without anyone's help. Including yours, Charles." They had reached the grocery shop. Below it the brook shimmered. "Let us get home, at least before midnight." She waited while he collected his bike.

"Where is he going now?"

"Who would *he* be?" She was trying some levity. Of late Charlie had become more likely to retort bitterly to anything spoken in jest. Flo had noticed it, and offered the opinion that what Charlie needed was a girl. "The flight lieutenant is going back to base soon, I imagine." It wasn't the moment to mention that Patch was probably already at the Villa with the inebriated group captain. "Were you thinking of asking for a lift too, Charles? You know how much you love to hang around the Iverdon camp."

"Not as much as you love to hang around pilots!"

They had pushed their bicycles as far as Droopers, on the corner of North Street. In the square a few rowdy soldiers were splashing water from the trough.

She thought that at any moment Charlie might mention the Nazi pilot, say something about her involvement, even threaten to tell the police. Was he capable of claiming he'd had no part in it? He was not trustworthy any more, exactly like Coral Floster. This could be upsetting. Or she could tell herself that Charlie irritated her most when she felt he had a reason.

She cycled home, leaving him to follow. She should never have let him go to Tufnell Park. Heaven knows what he had seen. Dead bodies perhaps? Perhaps the sight of the parachutist had turned a mind already affected.

Had Granny Dorp's wits begun to erode because of some dire event? Insanity might run in the family. Morgan had lately dreamed of a pig's trotter that twitched. In one dream Archie was approaching with a knife. These thoughts occupied her all the way to the Gormson Road, where she discovered that Charlie was riding alongside and had probably been doing so for some time.

That evening he made not one comment at the sight of Group Captain Floster, mouth agape, asleep on a sofa.

While searching for chicken feed early the next morning, Morgan inadvertently let the dog out of the garage. She watched it rush off towards the cricket pitch, marking tree trunks as it went. At the sound of an approaching car it barked furiously and raced towards Patch's Riley.

Coral Floster was the passenger. She refused to alight until Patch had seized the dog. Morgan told Charlie he should stop it barking, for people were still sleeping. She ordered him to feed it. Still in sullen mood he dragged it back to the garage, muttering inaudibly.

The noise had woken Elmer, at the front door wearing the kimono. At the sight of her garment Mrs Floster yelled, "How dare you! How dare you!" Elmer retreated upstairs.

It was going to be a difficult day. Mrs Floster had reverted to her normal flimsy frock with matching headgear. Her curls had unclenched. There were no signs of the ordeal they had recently gone through. But should one expect, Morgan asked herself, Coral Floster to have blood on her hands?

She showed her into the sitting room, where her husband was still slumped on the sofa, his shirt as crumpled as his face. On his chin a day's stubble. He flinched at his wife's kiss, begged her to leave him alone or bring him the hair of the dog. She retreated to the kitchen, where she sat upright with a triumphant expression, while Morgan made tea for everyone, including the flight lieutenant.

Patch sounded maudlin. He was being transferred to ground duty. His wounds were taking too long to heal. He might never see them again. He talked about his wife. How the threat of death rendered all pilots crazy, prone to do stupid things. Morgan thought this might be an oblique apology to both his listeners.

He began to hum some tune. From the outset his breaking into song had irritated more than pleased her. So had his past tendency to require nothing more than his head on her bare breast. True, he had been dog-tired after hours in the air, but why then did he seek her out? She knew they had little in common, had made love only three or four times. He, like her, had evidently been living only in the present. In sympathy Morgan reached for his hand. Coral Floster sat smiling on them like a duenna.

At that moment Charlie came into the kitchen. Then, because of Maya, he knew they were lovers and walked out again in anger.

The visitors stayed only long enough to drink tea, wrestle the group captain into his uniform and settle him in Patch's car.

Coral Floster lingered long enough to tell Morgan she had at last found "a real man". "The trick is to keep him away from Flossie," she said, before joining her husband in the Riley.

Patch drove off at speed, narrowly avoiding a farm lorry coming in the opposite direction.

Elmer was beside Morgan in the Villa doorway. Behind him Flo, now dressed in her working clothes, waiting for what she called her "Iverdon Taxi". Hoots and whistles from the Land Girls on the lorry were aimed at Elmer.

"Rude hussies! Rude!" He was wearing a close-fitting sailor's uniform. Flo's co-workers hauled her up onto the lorry.

"Those breeches are far too small for one so fat," Morgan remarked.

"Extreme constraint," Elmer whispered. "You can't beat it." She didn't know if it was a joke.

They retreated to the kitchen where he began, without asking, to fry breakfast. Yes, she would have some. No, Charlie apparently did not want any. She felt suddenly deflated.

"Posh, isn't she?" Elmer was pointing with a spatula. "Used to getting her way that Florence, by the look of her." Lard ran from the pan as he was sliding an egg onto a plate. "A handful. So is that lovely brother of yours." Keeping his eyes on Morgan, he dropped the bacon beside the egg. "But not a match, if I may make so bold. His lordship's sights are set in another direction." He held a seat for her as if he were a waiter. She took the proffered cutlery and kept silent.

"I wish I could hang around to see how you handle it." Whatever he was trying to say, she didn't want to hear it. She wanted everyone to leave her alone. Leave her and Archie to take up where they had left off.

Elmer was offering her a slice of bread on the point of the knife. "R.A.F. show-offs the lot of them, with their white scarves."

"The group captain told Charlie silk stops their collars chafing." Patch had told her how a pilot had to swivel in the cockpit.

"Florence may fancy your Charlie –" Elmer paused dramatically – "but so does that bold group captain." If he had expected some reaction, he was disappointed. Morgan yet again had not understood.

Pushing her plate away she got up, leaving Elmer, smiling to himself, to finish his breakfast alone.

She discovered Charlie sitting on his unmade bed. She told him the girls would be in soon to tidy up. "Your room's a disgrace. You haven't got anything dangerous in here, have you?"

"Only a few live bullets!" It was true. Charlie had been searching for ammunition in surrounding fields. So far nothing large. Somebody at Struttleigh said they'd seen a land mine coming down by parachute, that Jerky claimed there was a market for. The best fun was to open a live bullet, take out the cordite and make a satisfactory explosion.

He and Ronnie Talbott used to shoot at targets behind the pavilion. Ronnie, even then, hadn't seemed keen on the whole exercise. Dunkirk had ruined their friendship.

"Go and eat your breakfast, then go to work. What are you doing in here anyway?" Morgan stood looking at the pictures of aircraft on his walls. At her engagement portrait, taken when she was twenty. At a suspiciously large box of Capstan cigarettes. She waited.

Charlie, with bent head, suddenly exclaimed in a loud, anguished voice, "Why do you love him and not me?" The cry was so intense it was almost animal.

It startled her so, all she could do was turn on him. "You're doing too much thinking, Charles. Too much running off." Struggling to think of something else. "The aunts are teaching children with lice." At the door she added, "Stop selling things. Wash your neck, it's grimy."

Mrs Retchen, arriving with the girls, said the weather was bad for washday drying.

Charlie had finally left, walking to work past the piggery, so he had no idea that Archie Kymmerly had cycled up the Villa drive.

Doffing his trilby, Archie handed Morgan four letters, one with the usual army postmark, that she hid, out of habit, in her pocket.

Standing almost to attention, her lover looked uncomfortable in his tweed jacket. There was no mention of her surreptitious note to him.

Was he the same Archie? He had the same blue eyes, but they were looking at her with an expression she did not recognise. First he was saying sorry, he was in a hurry. Then that the gate needed repairing. She should have thought of this. She invited him to appraise it.

Deliberately she led him through Charlie's garden. Drought had stunted the marrows; there would be hundreds of tomatoes, he could have some; the early potatoes were small; the onions not too bad. Nervousness was causing the babble. It had never happened before.

Had he already joined up? Regretfully, his papers weren't yet in order. This wasn't the talkative Archie of old. She suspected he was wary of being seen. She said her father was still not back.

She wished he would look at her, tell her intimate things. She was tingling with the need to touch him. He removed his jacket. The sight of wiry hairs, sprouting through the buttonholes of his shirt, dismayed her a little. It came to her in a rush that he and Cathcart were thirty-eight, the same age. How horrible time was.

Archie was saying oak was best for the gate. She would be needing a new latch. Again the strange, unanticipated Scottish burr.

An air raid warning. Aircraft were already arriving overhead, almost at the siren's dying notes; one so low it sent Archie flat. There was a rush of wind followed by the rattle of bullets across the garden and on. The raspberry canes fluttered. The sound of enemy planes went rolling and roaring under low cloud. Morgan stood immobile, astonished to see Archie on the ground. Then understanding he had probably never been so close to war.

He was dusting his knees. "I can hear a dog."

"I don't like dogs," she said. "One scratched me once." If Archie remembered how the dog jumped at her in the lane in 1922, he did not respond.

"Vela will be wanting me."

She offered to drive him to Lodford. She would hold onto him for as long as possible.

He found the Rover impressive. Told her he'd learned to drive but never had a car. She remembered their bicycle rides.

A glimpse of a face at an upstairs window. It might be Mrs Retchen, alerted by the engine, but she didn't care. The old recklessness was taking hold. She drove off fast. Outside the Villa gates, Archie made no protest as she headed towards open countryside. That was where she and he had always gone.

He spoke little until she had negotiated the crossroads. "It's better to signal before you turn, so people know which way you're intending." Had he recognised her grandmother's house as they sped past?

Blytham was Morgan's destination, that special village where he and she had spent their untroubled days, breathing the tarry saltiness of beached boats and oyster beds. There had been Saturday evenings in the village hall, dancing around a stove to music from a gramophone. They were never recognised. It was a village where everyone minded

344

their own business and let lovers mind theirs. The landlord at the Smugglers turned a blind eye to their youth and served them alcohol. They conjured stories about him, an illicit love life the reason he smiled on them.

When the tides were low, they had picked their way across the salt marshes, finding sea holly and lavender, mementoes to take back to their separate homes. Sometimes they made love in the barn that hadn't been so derelict then. Sometimes they crossed the fields and rolled together in the long dry grass near the dyke, disturbing nothing but beetles and curlews. A body contorted in a leather harness now tainted that memory. Once or twice she had secreted Archie into her bedroom.

She dared not mention those times. Archie was as remote as if he were any passenger out for a spin.

They had reached the fork, one way to Blytham church, the other to East Blytham proper. Nothing to see but hedgerows dividing the flattest of landscapes, here and there a hawthorn bent westward by prevailing winds. He was still silent, and she was thinking and thinking what to say, what next.

She swerved the car. This decision, instantaneous, nearly tipped them into a ditch. Archie swore. She swung the cumbersome Rover around, to head back the way they had come.

"So you're still a mad thing, then?" He had found his voice. She relaxed, squealing the tyres a little on the bend past her grandmother's house, making again for Little Gormson.

It was a spur of the moment decision to go down the lane behind St Margaret's. It led only to lonely fields of harvested wheat. The Rover's wheels were sending up dust clouds.

She stopped the car and turned off the engine before a barred gate. Beyond it acres of golden stubble, where rooks by the score were foraging. To the east the thud of distant gunfire, interspersed by the long notes of a ship's siren.

Morgan sat very still.

"It was after your ma died you were a mad thing." Archie wasn't

345

looking at her. "Vela wrote you had this reputation for gallivanting. That's partly why I stayed away."

She waited in trepidation for him to ask why she had driven them here. "Partly?"

"He gave me money to keep away."

It was too demeaning to ask how much her father had given Archie. She hoped she was worth hundreds.

"Is it hot in here?" She felt her face.

"Yes, angel."

He shouldn't have used the old name. He would not have said it if he hadn't wanted her to kiss him. Or he would have pushed her away. He would not have returned her kiss so passionately, run his hard hands over her breasts.

They would not have wrenched open the Rover's doors to get to the back seat, or pulled off each other's clothes while they were still kissing. Loudly she cursed suspender belts, and petticoats, and shirts, and ties. She heard his laughter as a growl. Remembered, as if it were yesterday, how his fingers explored her, his lips licked and bit. How he would always murmur the name. His breathing was rasping in her ears. She could smell tobacco. The leather seat was sticky on her bare back. He penetrated her quickly. She called out his name. He was gasping and didn't respond.

So it was over faster than before. Faster than she ever remembered it, her head pinioned, Archie on top of her, still gasping like a landed fish.

To sit up was a wrestle. He was so close she begged him to open the window. Seagulls, low flying over the fields, sounded like babies.

They dressed quickly and went to sit in the front seats as if nothing had happened. His face was scarlet. He did not demand they go back immediately. Like her he sat silent, staring out at the golden field dotted with black birds, at the grey sky alive with white ones.

"I did want to marry you," he said finally.

How strange, she thought, that marriage had never entered her head.

346

"Your father said you were too young and feckless. Perhaps you still are!" His smile was meant to take the sting out of what he was saying.

She said, "So were you. We both were," knowing that what she had just allowed, had wanted to happen, was exactly what had occurred in the summer of 1922.

"I'm sorry the bairn was lost."

It was a second before she understood his meaning.

He said her father sent him the news of the stillbirth. And more money. To keep away. "Enid suffered the same loss with one of ours." He paused. "I respected his wishes, didn't I? You cannot say I did not."

Then Morgan realised two things: that Archie did not know she was delivered of a healthy child in 1922; that he was married and had another child, or children.

She looked at this new Archie with a clearer gaze. What had happened to change her soulmate into this? Strange how closely he resembled her husband.

In silence they watched sea-birds fighting over a dead creature. When Archie grinned, she thought it was about them. He was asking if she thought her pa would cough up more money to see the back of him again. It was a horrible thing to say.

He was only joking, because her father was dead. Things had changed, maybe for the better.

His mind was always easy to read. "If Pa is dead I don't inherit anything." She had to be understood. "My brother Charlie is the heir, but he will have to wait seven years for it." She started the engine and backed fast down the lane, wanting to end this unsavoury conversation.

At the Villa Archie recovered his bicycle, under the gaze of the twins and their mother. But before letting him go, Morgan had one more bothersome question. Why were his call-up papers not in order?

He was leaning over his saddle, averting his gaze. "There's a tribunal. It has to be sorted, see? I was in jail for a wee while. They rummelled me, see?" She got the drift of it. "Had to. Nothing left in the pot." He stood erect and she could see humiliation. "We'd spent it all, hadn't we?"

Of course he had. In that he was the Archie of old, with no thought for tomorrow. Just like her. It was at that moment she began to feel she might have lost him a long time ago. And that, given time, she might not mind so much after all.

Of the letters Archie had delivered, one was from the children, one from Cathcart and one from Rhoda The fourth, an official looking one, was addressed to Charlie. Morgan left it on his bed.

The few sentences of Billy's letter did not mention the enclosed snapshot of them, holding Mrs Timmbold's hands and smiling. Nor why both her feet were bandaged. The children were growing so fast. Billy's main interest was the big bangs they'd heard. Terry's contribution was that "*a lady give me a sammon dress I likd it*". Suspicious of charity, Morgan decided to send them clothes. She wondered if Cat would receive the photograph if she sent it.

Rhoda's sparse information was that the grub was good. And that she was engaged to a midshipman called Nigel, currently refitting at Portland.

Cathcart's pencilled note said "*A dip in the sea but could have done without flies*". The next line had been scribbled out by the censor. Their relationship was becoming even more fragile. In newsreels Morgan had seen soldiers fighting in the Libyan desert. If Cathcart, like her father, should not return, how would she feel? At least, she decided, she would not have the problem of Cat knowing about Archie and the child. The thought brought on guilt.

CHAPTER FOURTEEN

At the post office Morgan casually asked after Archie.

"Getting him behind this counter is a struggle." Taking her parcel, Vela led Morgan to one side. "Friend to friend, our Archie's been in worse trouble than he's letting on. Why would he join up?" His wife. "He married her when she was in the family way." She poked Morgan's arm. "Who knows by who, if you follow?" There was a whiff of scent. "It died. By then the knot was tied."

She whispered, "If it weren't for her, he wouldn't have got caught up with trouble." She stamped 24 August in Morgan's army pay book and counted the allowance. "Our mother always warned him about the easy life."

Morgan wandered in the square. Was it possible that Archie was escaping from his wife, like Cathcart? She spent precious coupons on a tin of apricots. In Droopers haberdashery she vacillated over a hat, a replacement for the one lost when Coral Floster stabbed the Nazi. Neither he nor his boot had entered her dreams again.

If only Archie would invade them. There was no denying the hold he still had on her. Her throat constricted at thoughts of him. She would try to get him deferred. Make him her official carpenter. Ask Jerky for petrol coupons, new sheets, shoes for the children, a lipstick. Making decisions gave one strength.

She caught Mr Grouming, in Home Guard uniform, emerging from his bank. He agreed to the appointment she was not looking forward to. Charlie had refused to help. She must ask for money to repair the house, ever under attack from salt-erosion, and now from the enemy. No father at hand. No Cat who had wanted to organise everything.

Would women, after the war, so willingly relinquish power? Look at

Flo and friends, doing men's work on the farm. And Rhoda, quitting housework to become a Wren. W.A.A.F.s and A.T.s were going about their business as self-assured as any man. She would ask Peter about a job at the aerodrome or radar station. She could be a sailor, like her father.

She was late. The dinner was dry and Charlie's temper frayed. She told him he ought to help Elmer with the washing-up. "If you're not careful, I shall go and join up, like Rhoda." Charlie's expression had changed. "Or run off with someone who'll appreciate me more!" She shouldn't have said it. His chair crashed as he ran from the room, leaving his pudding uneaten.

Elmer shrugged. "Somebody's got the hump."

That night, from their separate beds, they heard the steady drone of aircraft. In the small hours of Sunday morning they were forced again into the shelter. They sat among the pickling pork, the flimsy door rattled by the noise of guns and tracers.

All were late for Sunday breakfast, the chickens not fed. That central London and the East End had been bombed did nothing for Charlie's gloomy mood. He wondered if Maya had survived. She didn't deserve to.

Elmer, in naval uniform, was bemoaning the disappearance of the kimono. He pushed a finger into the milk and licked it, asking if it were fresh. Florence let out a cry of disgust.

"We're too late for church," Morgan said. "Grandma will be cross."

"Has she got some hold on you?"

No reply. "Why aren't you at work?"

"Threshing's done." Florence said she was due six days' paid holiday and a rail warrant. She was giving Elmer a meaningful stare. "I may go home to see if Mama's lined up any real men."

He poked his fork into the fat of her arm. "So what will Sugar Plum be up to there?"

"Oh, Charlie, do tell him to stop it."

Charlie kept his head down, to avoid the sight of Flo's dimpled flesh. It was too hot to stay indoors. Morgan was pleased that he had fed the hens, but his runner beans needed the hose. The cold frame was closed, so they could say farewell to the salad. In the garage the dog began to bark. It swallowed the leftovers from lunch in two mouthfuls. Feeling sorry for it she let it out. It followed her docilely from the garden.

A cooling breeze was bringing the low drone of departing planes. Elmer had wandered outside somewhere. No sign of Charlie or Flo. She examined the gate, that Archie must take a long time to fix. The Villa's burnt rafters would present him with a challenge. Then the cricket pavilion. Like Penelope, she could creep out each night to undo his day's work.

She wandered shoeless on the grass, the dog loping at her heels. She saw Elmer approaching from the ponds. He was leading Granny Dorp by the hand.

He had found the old lady throwing sticks at the ducks, "because they were eating the spawn".

"Tadpoles are frogs now. This is Mrs Norma Dorp, my maternal grandmother." Morgan backed away as her grandmother dived to kiss her. The dog growled.

"She's harmless." Elmer sounded as if they were old friends.

"Harmless, Monty?" Granny Dorp echoed. "Venus on the half-shell. Windy day!" She was tapping his arm, tugging him round to face her.

Obediently he bent down, content to let her pull his collar, unknot the lanyard, examine his Adam's apple. He was allowing her fingers to creep over his chin, his cheek.

Morgan watched her grandmother's forefinger hovering near Elmer's eye. "What on earth is she doing?"

"She has disengaged a little eye jelly, that's all." Elmer straightened up. He put a hand to his chest. "Don't get much tender care. Never have."

Morgan remembered Granny Dorp's words about her widowed father: "Lonely people tend to love too easily".

"What can we do with her?" Her grandmother's last calamitous visit came to mind.

"We shall all dance a little bit." Elmer grabbed Granny Dorp's hand and reached out for Morgan's. She backed away. The dog growled. Dealing with not one but two crazy people, plus an unpredictable dog, was too much. She blamed the heat.

Elmer began to hum a tune, urging Granny Dorp to move. Down the slope she went with him like a child, trying to emulate his steps. If Archie were there he would laugh at the sight. Morgan felt a pang of pity for her grandmother, tripping on the grass.

A shout from the turnstile. Waving his arms was Cory, the landlord of the Three Tuns. She wondered how long before he had noticed her grandmother's absence. He scuttled crabwise past the dancers towards Morgan and the dog.

His fingers were making damp marks on his cap. He had come to fetch the old lady, who had slipped away like an eel when his back was turned.

"For an old 'un she has a right turn of speed."

"As you can see!"

Cory stood undecided. "I might as well give you the message some-one give me about an anchor."

Morgan shivered. One of Mr Bernard Talbott's anchors was missing. Might she have seen any unusual activity on the river? She shook her head. Her granny's laughter came faintly on the breeze. Cory was apologetic. She said she had seen a barge, adding for exactitude it had red sails and was low in the water.

She realised that Talbott must be one of the regulars at the Three Tuns. She said he should come in person. And would Mr Cory take her grandmother back to safety, without damaging her clothes on the barbed wire.

They walked down to the ponds, where Elmer had been waiting with Granny Dorp. She jumped up smiling and closed in on Cory, who took avoiding action as she tried to sniff him.

"She's squiffy." Elmer's remark caused some tension in the other man.

"A drop now and then keeps her content. Mrs Brodick –" Cory was addressing her granddaughter – "may I mention the matter of remuneration, if you get my meaning?"

Morgan said she would see to it.

Keeping a firm hold on her grandmother, the landlord steered her away, calling over his shoulder, "And please remember, I did mention that there anchor."

Granny Dorp went uncomplainingly with her guardian. The dog followed them at a distance until they had gone from sight.

Elmer seemed amused. "Who was that chap?"

"Landlord of the Three Tuns. Paid to look after Granny. She's trouble."

"Aren't we all?" He still sat on the turf, hugging his knees. "Whose anchor was that then?".

"Our mill manager's. Always losing things." To distract him, she repeated something her father had said about Talbott, "'There are no more children. He ploughs too much of himself into the business.'"

Elmer laughed loudly.

"He has a wife called Grace Talbott." It was still a mystery that she could tell this stranger almost anything, despite his sharp gaze.

"Name sounds about right for the wife of a Mr Talbott."

"I work at the N.A.A.F.I. on some evenings."

"So I believe." He was studying a dragonfly.

"I've seen Mrs Talbott with an army sergeant. In our pavilion." She sat down. "It was . . . intimate." She knew he knew she was waiting for his opinion.

"I'm not one to pass judgement."

"I have always had problems with right and wrong. Getting carried away, if you see what I mean. This war's mixing them up."

"But we have to hang on to good old good and bad old bad, don't we?" Elmer coiled sideways, his bell-bottoms collecting grass. "At least, after we get what we want!"

All of a sudden it was too late to tell him about Archie.

On her feet again, she looked down at him stretched out, arms above his head. "Lunch soon. Cold pork, as if you couldn't guess."

"Grub is grub." Elmer stayed where he was, not bothering to sweep the insects away.

He spent Tuesday morning packing. Mrs Retchen put the blankets out to air. Florence swam in the river long past high tide. Thelma and Myrtle went to watch her through the barricade, as if she were some exotic fish. Charlie had again refused to go with Morgan to the bank.

Her request for details of rents owing and financial transactions was hijacked by the presence of Mrs Grouming. Her defence of her husband proved daunting: he was the essence of probity. "What you are impugning to him, Mrs Brodick, attaches to my good name too. We are as one."

The meeting was cut short by the appearance of Dora, the Talbotts' daughter, in Wren uniform. No explanations were given, other than that Dora was spending her leave with the Groumings.

At his door, Grouming promised Morgan that receipts would be forthcoming, however onerous his Home Guard duties. She stood on the pavement, wondering why an innocent man would need his wife to defend him.

Elmer was less than sympathetic. "Don't get het up about it. Did you expect him to roll over and tell you he was a thief?" She should have demanded there and then to see the books, before he could cook them. "Times haven't changed because there's a war. Liars and cheats still exist. Us excluded!"

Florence remarked that people used not to share private matters with strangers. This was aimed at Morgan, who knew this would be her parents' attitude too.

Elmer had no advice to give. Morgan suspected he didn't care. Neither it seemed did Flo. Both barely listened to her complaint that she might need a man to go to the bank with her next time. Peter Parclay would have tried to help. "I wish Pa were here," she said.

Next morning Elmer announced he was leaving.

Charlie might have muttered "good riddance".

"Are you a proper sailor? There's no ship's name on your hatband."

"Censorship, my dear." Elmer touched Morgan's cheek. "I'd better get going, lovely one. 'Following seas' and all that. Do try to grow up a bit more. Just keep at it and you'll get there."

Passing his kitbag in the hall, Charlie kicked it as he left for work.

Mr Boxley was to give Elmer a lift to the station. Morgan waved goodbye on the step. She was as sad to see him go as Myrtle and Thelma, to whom he had given each a sherbet fountain.

Jerky came later with a bag of oranges. "I were fishing. Funny what comes up on the end of a line line."

Mrs Retchen graciously accepted three oranges, then sat down to listen, as if she'd been asked.

Jerky said a Nazi had been shot down not far from Struttleigh Common. He was locked up in Lodford police station, until they could find someone who admitted to speaking his language.

Mrs Retchen said Councillor Cramweir offered to have a go at translation, but only in the presence of witnesses. The Nazi had cheekily been demanding food nobody had heard of. Sergeant Callum's wife felt sorry for him and gave him a bully beef sandwich.

Jerky left both women talking. But he had whispered to Morgan that Charlie, "without going into details", might have been involved somehow with the capture of the airman. Morgan kept wondering if Jerky had misunderstood to which Nazi Charlie had referred.

Charlie had definitely altered since the day of the killing. Were his illegal dealings spreading? Alice Dance was giving him chops free of coupons. When Florence had queried it, he had virtually told her to mind her own business. If she went on leave they would all have some peace. Flo had gone off in a huff. Charlie announced that his letter was, almost, an authorisation to join the Air Defence Corps. Soon, he said, he would be in uniform.

In the following days Morgan continued looking for Archie. Outside the library she had been confronted by Dora Talbott with a message: Mrs Grouming would be obliged if Mrs Brodick would serve at the N.A.A.F.I. as promised, not just when she felt like it.

Morgan could not ask Dora why she was staying with the Groumings. Nor why she had inked seam lines down the backs of her legs. Dora seemed pleased to talk about the Wrens. How joining it had saved her.

"Rhoda Swell is engaged to an officer."

"I'd like to see all men drowned."

"How is your mother?" Morgan replied.

"Mum's acting queer." Dora lowered her voice, exactly like Vela. "Dad's standing off, she says. He don't know what to make of her, thank heaven. Keep an eye on her, will you? I'm never going back there." Her eyes were filling with tears. "Our Ronnie's off to be a stretcher-bearer, of all things. Daft, isn't he?" She hesitated. "Is she going to disgrace us all?" Not waiting for a response she walked off.

Morgan watched her striding past the Congregation Chapel as if their conversation had been small talk. Coming in the opposite direction was Archie.

She felt exposed, facing her lover in the middle of North Street. He looked less careworn, more the self-assured Archie of old. Heat had suddenly concentrated between her legs. He told her how pretty she was, and she knew she was done for.

He said he would go and fetch his bike from over the road, if she'd wait a bit. The post office clock told her there wasn't much time before preparing supper.

There was no consultation. They cycled along West Street to avoid the square, past Willams, alongside the brook, past Station Hill. Then beneath the trees, following the course of the narrowing stream, until it went out sight under the Plumberow tunnel. Neither needed to voice why this choice of direction. They had always been of one mind. Since time was precious, Ironside Lane was their goal.

It had been their least favourite destination, resonating too closely with more sombre thoughts. The lane had the same dank atmosphere, despite a late sun dappling the brambles. Warmth was still filtering through the beeches. Wild garlic, old man's beard, damp vegetation were familiar scents. In the brook beside them the water ran clear as ever, minnows in it outpacing them. Sheep's parsley, more profuse now, impeded their wheels as they made for a certain bend. From there they knew they would not be seen.

Their bikes, one on top of the other, lay among the weeds. They crawled through the same gap in the fence that Charlie and Ronnie had gone through for rabbits. The field was bathed in such revealing sunlight it sent them towards the security of a tree.

She lay down. He put his jacket under her, then methodically unbuttoned her frock, his trousers.

There was nothing in his kisses for complaint. He kissed and kissed. But without warning came thoughts of Patch and of Cathcart, whose ardent attacks had lacked this same something, whatever it was. She put her mind to blank, returning Archie's kisses with passion. It would be alright, she was telling herself. She was folding him in as tightly as she knew how. It was bound to go well this time, if only he didn't stop.

But in minutes Archie was pushing her away, pulling at his jacket pocket for a packet of condoms, exactly as Patch had done.

He put one on. She heard, "Better safe than sorry," as he grabbed her shoulders and pushed her under him again. "A stitch in time, eh?" The kissing resumed.

Then he was done with kissing. And what had at first felt like attack became the same feverish conjoining it had always been.

He was moving fast to his climax, all the while staring skyward over her head, in a way that had nothing to do with adoration. She could have been any woman.

As she watched the man rearing over her, her enjoyment began to fade. Only at his final cry did she experience the ghost of a thrill. It was over quickly, like the last time. Unlike the last time, she was left with an ache in her solar plexus, not coupled with fear of discovery. He lay depleted and separate. She felt like sobbing.

In an effort at calm, she forced to the fore another meadow long ago: she and her parents, walking across the fields. She was ten again, conjuring clover, buttercups, the hum of insects. Meadow cool, sun hot. Lying looking up through seeded grasses for an endless moment, at pimpernel, speedwell, bee orchid, the flowers she pressed for Granny Dorp's wildflower book. In the hedgerows birds were kicking up their summer din. It was imperative she lie there forever, holding on to that feeling of being uniquely alive. One day she would tell Peter. Her mother's voice: "Morgan. Grandma is waiting. Morgan!"

"Morgan!" Archie had sat up, his focus already shifted to thoughts of leaving.

"You can't leave me like this."

"I'm not up to it any more." She thought of those times they had made love within what seemed, in retrospect, like minutes. Had her memory been deceiving her for nineteen years?

He brought out a watch, not her gift to him at their final goodbye. She still wore his ring with the dubious stone. "Time flies," he said with the old Archie smile. "Vela will be wondering."

She thought they would abandon the field. But he had something on his mind.

There was hesitation. "Angel, that mill manager of yours is getting a reputation, I hear." She waited, suspicious. "All that grain coming in. It seems to me – an outsider, mind you – what you need there is a more responsible person."

Here was the old Archie, an open book. "Like you, for instance?" Strange that a few hours earlier she would have handed him Talbott's job on a plate.

"And why not? I've experience." He ignored her smile. "Your brother's too young to run that enterprise. Everyone says so."

"And who is 'everyone'?"

"Vela." He paused, looking the other way. "And Enid." The pause was longer. "My wife. She wants us to prosper." On his face was an expression Morgan didn't recognise. "Bad times up there. We had to sell her piano."

So that was it. If Archie couldn't have the mill, he would have the next best thing, a job running it.

"And where would you two live?" How distant she sounded.

"Och, we'll find a place, with all these frightened people deserting their homes." He was looking around, as if he might spot a house among the tussocks. "She'll like the climate here."

"The sun's going in," Morgan replied.

He was dusting his sleeves, smoothing the beautiful hair whose colour was dimmed, not by sunlight, but by age. "That Talbott's not to be trusted."

"That's rich coming from you!"

Suddenly Archie kicked at a tuft of grass. "You are not understanding me, woman! You know fine well what I mean."

They crawled through the fence to their bicycles, Archie talking to her back, his voice revealing desperation. And she knew it was for the sake of this importunate Enid he had found steel.

His last words were, "You see, angel, I love her. She's under my skin."

At the entrance to the lane they went their separate ways.

Cycling home, Morgan felt a relief parallel with the hurt. For in future Archie and Charlie need never have close contact.

Her aunt Berengaria Nails stopped her as she was passing the Co-op. Morgan dismounted. Her aunt was pleased with the Plumberow colonel, whose little fads she could tolerate. As for Frank, they had taken him off to somewhere secret and mathematical. "It's what comes with brains."

Eager to leave, Morgan let her aunt chide her. "Your father, God rest him, would never have turned away kith and kin in favour of strangers. He and my dear sister always kept open house."

It was true. There were times when the Villa was crowded. Relatives on the lawn, lounging in rooms, dining noisily. Uncle Herbert laughing fit to cry at one of her father's jokes. The isolating factor must have been her mother's illness.

She cycled home, trying to think cheerful thoughts. All that would come to mind was some sadistic aunt, button-hooking her into gaiters;

Charlie, on her wedding morning, screaming while his hair was combed; her mother's wasted hands on hers. Was the secret of coping never to recall anything? Never resurrect the loved? Or the unloved? What would Peter say?

The weather stayed warm. Nazi bombers continued to fly towards London each day. Only in the early hours did anyone take the alert's warning seriously and shelter. Her father had been right, the bombers, guided by the river, were more likely to release unwanted loads on their return.

One washday Mrs Retchen told Morgan she would not let her girls have permanent waves, on account of the raids. Mr Dringley had left her friend Mavis fastened to the electric machine. All her locks had been singed off. "I'm getting their hair out of rags. Now it will look like yours, Miss Morgan, nice and straight." Morgan did not find this agreeable.

Mrs Retchen was in a talkative mood. "My mother said to me, 'Gladys, we may not have what that family has, but don't envy them. Their troubles are to come.'" Morgan could not imagine why Mrs Retchen had chosen this subject. She fed a sheet through the mangle.

"Miss Morgan, an apology is in order. The other Sunday I was a bit hasty. Thinking about my Myrtle now, I can see you thought you were doing your best."

"Thank you, Mrs Retchen." Morgan had heard the back door open, and wondered if it was Charlie. "Let us forget it, shall we?" She folded the sheet into the tin bath.

"You went a lot too far at St Margaret's, it's true."

"That soldier got less than he deserved for doing what he did to Myrtle."

Mrs Retchen was staring at Morgan. "Lucky my Myrtle isn't in the family way."

"And what if she were?"

"She has her mother to look after her. Just like yours." A faint sound coming from the kitchen alerted both women. "Some things are best left to take their course. That's what your dear mother told your father, didn't she?"

"Is that you, Charlie?" Morgan called. No reply. She waited warily. Only the hum of traffic filtering through the open windows. "And you think my mother's advice to your Myrtle would be the same now?"

"You had as much sense then as my Myrtle has now, if you ask me. What's the difference?"

Morgan could feel anger rising.

Mrs Retchen's colour had heightened. "Your mother took hold of the situation her way. My mother told her to do different. She was wrong."

"This situation *was* different, Mrs Retchen. A man didn't force me. I wanted to have the child." As she spoke, Morgan knew this was not the truth.

"And your dear mother saw to it that you did, God bless her." Mrs Retchen was shaking her head. "It weared her out."

"And what would my mother say if she were here now and your daughter was . . . expecting? Which Myrtle could have been?" Never had a conversation been so explicit. It was a kind of relief.

"She wasn't a believer in killing. And it wasn't for want of means. Her own mother, your grandmother Dorp, helped at plenty, I can tell you. It wasn't a question of pushing gin down their throats and hoping. She was very good." She paused. "So they say." Another pause. "You didn't do any good for *her* nerves."

"So I was the cause of Granny Dorp losing her mind?"

"I'm not travelling that road. But without her, my dear, you would have lost your child."

"I could have married him. What then?"

"My mother and Mrs Perincall liked the boy for what he was, but as a husband, never. Unthoughtful, the pair of you. Thank heaven Mrs Kymmerly and Vela were ignorant of it all."

Morgan thought how late she was in understanding the ramifications of the affair. She had been enclosed in a bubble of self-absorption. "My mother spoke about it . . . elsewhere?"

"The shame of it stopped your poor mother talking to anyone. It's hard enough now, but I see clouds ahead."

"How did *you* know? Did your mother tell you?"

"She never could hide much from me."

Morgan pulled a pillowcase into shape. "I wasn't ashamed."

"So you went to your aunt because you fancied a holiday? And stayed there six months enjoying the scenery while your mother and mine worried themselves sick?" Mrs Retchen stopped turning the mangle. "The way you behaved afterwards makes me certain they did the right thing. I still wonder why you were so set on having that baby."

Her life, Morgan felt, was peeling like an orange. Hiding at Aunt Pandora's in Hackney hadn't been fun. And she would never tell Mrs Retchen she had only wanted to have the baby because nearly everyone was so keen on her losing it. Nor what pain it caused her to part with him. How young she was.

"It hastened your poor mother's end, keeping a child that she knew wasn't rightly hers."

How could this woman say such things? The doting look on her mother's face when she held the baby Morgan had never been allowed to cradle. And for whom she must erase all feeling.

The reality of her father saying, "I have always wanted a son, so some good has come of it." It was doubtless he who had persuaded Dr Chilling to arrange the birth certificate.

They continued with the laundry in silence, both aware of a noise within the house.

It was Charlie, entering through the back door, carrying his coat by the collar like a dead hare. "What were you talking about?" The women had a conspiratorial look.

Morgan said they were talking about his mother. Behind him Parclay, in R.A.F. uniform, came limping, his arm in a sling.

Charlie went to wash, saying, "I didn't invite him to lunch." Mrs Retchen gathered her girls and left for home.

"Where have you been, Peter?" Morgan was relieved to see him.

"In hospital again. They dug another bullet out of my shoulder. Poor me, eh? My leg's complaining. Does that call for extra sympathy?"

"Will you stay to eat? Only liver and bacon, I'm afraid."

"Thank you. I saw your grandmother at her gate. She says your aunts are home. 'The Nazi threat has been exaggerated'!" He was amused. "I tried some history. Left out why we attacked the French fleet at Oran. Had to explain why our pilots are getting younger!" He was trying to help lay the table. "She said that your other aunt, Winifred, has been taken to the asylum."

"What!"

"She was 'succumbing to too much doleance', whatever that means."

Morgan wondered what her pa would do if he knew his favourite sister had been put away because of melancholy.

Florence joined them at the table, saying the river was delicious. Even the dog had paddled. Charlie came late to the table, his attitude wavering between curiosity about the airman's injuries and annoyance at his presence.

Flo cut up Parclay's food for him. With one eye on Charlie, she was encouraging the pilot to talk. Asking why the bombing might escalate. What were the comparative bomb loads of Heinkels and Dorniers? She seemed fascinated by the new Supermarine Spitfire.

Charlie remained challenging, almost rude. He asked Parclay why he hadn't rid them of the Nazi nightmare. Would the war go on forever because the air force had let them down?

"You haven't heard Churchill's 'human conflict' speech?" Peter sounded more light-hearted than he looked. "So many of you owing so much to us, the few?"

"The R.A.F. has saved us all and we can stop worrying!" The cause of Morgan's interjection was Charlie, sitting with a look near hatred on his face.

"Our squadron only has six Blenheims, Morgan. We're dangerously exposed. Your mill's a prime target. You must consider the danger."

"Their aim is bad, that's all." She sighed. "Why is this beastly war forcing me to think? I don't want to think."

"If we pilots stopped to think, we'd stay on the ground."

Florence started, "Fools rush in . . ."

The conversation lapsed as lunch progressed. The only one who ate heartily was Flo. Her offer to accompany Charlie to work "just for fun" was rejected out of hand. Nonetheless, she followed him outside, and saw how furiously he shook off the twins in front of their mother.

In the dining room, Peter told Morgan he was to be called back to combat. Lack of pilots. No refusals. He grabbed her hand. Did she not know by now that he loved her as he'd never ever loved anyone?

Not this. Not after Archie. And Patch. But a rarity had entered her life, someone who could be more than a lover. Here was a genuine friend, the loss of whom dismayed her as much as the risk of falling in love with him.

"Peter, you've seen too many pictures. Two people fall in love, overcome all sorts of hurdles, there's the usual happy ending." She began stacking plates. "In real life there is never a happy ending." She was thinking of the war's effect on them all. "The only ending that's good is the one that ends in death." She wasn't sure if she believed what she was saying. "Yes . . ." she was making it up ". . . in the cinema, if lovers die, they die together romantically. But in reality people love, then separate. There is always separation."

He had stood up, frowning.

"Some separate because they are bored or tired," she went on. "They have found a cause. Or committed some crime." She was thinking of Archie, of her father, of Cat. Then it came to her that she was doing the same, out of boredom, fear, fatigue, any which one. She was angry with herself for trying to prove what she didn't want to believe.

"Isn't it enough for you, that I might be shot down?" Peter's hand was on her shoulder. "So marry me, Morgan, and have your cake and eat it!" She could feel his warmth. "We love one another. Well, I love you more than you love me. We get married. I fly one too many missions and my death, that unhappy ending you much prefer, is yours!"

"You talk such foolishness. You know you're safe from me because of Cathcart and the children."

"Yes. I've been struggling with that, I admit. Your man is a casualty of war and I'm sorry for him. But he doesn't want you." He gripped her arm. "You do know that." She could feel he was in pain. "But I will care for his children, and try not to take them too far from him."

"Cat wouldn't let them go!" The words were out before she could stop them.

"I shall try to love them, because I love everything that's part of you." He sank into a chair. "I sound like one of Patch's songs!"

He was too close and vulnerable. Morgan walked to the window.

"Have you never felt the fear that comes with loving someone utterly? It's like a physical sickness. The whole body is involved."

Morgan stared through the lattice. When he had spoken it was with Archie's same intensity. But he had been talking about another woman. She put her hand to her chest. A catherine wheel of questions sparked in her head and died.

Peter followed her into the kitchen, where she poked the coals, straightened the pot of chats, smoothed her fringe. There was her heart beating, his shoes on the lino, the rustle of the passiflora on the wall. She thought she could hear ducks on the ponds. It struck her hard that Archie had been saying she must know how much he loved his wife. Yet he had felt no guilt, not like the guilt that was flooding into her about him.

What use was a conscience when it might be too late for one? It was not Cat she was feeling guilty about. He had chosen a military career before wife and children. Yet she was certain he would never relinquish either, should she try to escape. And everyone would be on the side of the hero.

"I love you." Peter winced, as if the pain of her was greater than his injuries. "We must look ahead."

Like her father, who saw in Charlie the Perincalls' future. If she had ever looked ahead, it had been during the nine months' wait for that first child. Afterwards she had looked for distraction, because Archie had gone, and with him her keenest desires.

"We must talk of something else," she replied, wanting to tell him of her past, but unable to risk it. Of mindless escapades with compliant boys. Of why she had chosen Cathcart, leaving her child's destiny to someone else. At the time it had seemed the only option.

To carry in her womb Billy, then Teresa, had not been so arduous. She had settled into bovine certainty that Cathcart would always shoulder their problems. Now another man was asking her to look ahead with him. Yet there might be no Ahead to look forward to. It was making her head swim.

War had freed her from a home and life she had not known she did not want. It had returned her to a house and land she loved and hadn't known how much. It had parted her from her children, whom she had relinquished willingly but now feared she might be losing.

The war had given her lovers, taken them away as the wind snatches autumn leaves. And it had left her with the realisation she had been waiting for something not prepared for, something that might finish with a single sound, like a gunshot or a bomb. The fear was that it might, after all, be this particular flying officer.

She gathered the tablecloth. "Why aren't we all searching for peace?" Mr Chamberlain and half the country hadn't wanted war. Even Ronnie Talbott was opposing it. The wireless, newsreels, the papers were adding to the perplexity. Peter said a pilot's goal was of necessity a simple one, to obey orders.

What would her pa have thought had he seen the pitiful survivors on his lawn? But he must have seen them at Dunkirk, dying in the water, shot down on the beaches. German soldiers too. Were there absolute rights and wrongs?

Her doubts had to be put aside, Peter told her. She said the only person she knew who dealt in certainties was Grandma Perincall. And hers were suspect.

He left her at last and reluctantly, warning not of the danger of rejecting his love but the vulnerability of the Villa Rouge.

That afternoon she took the car from the garage. The dog stayed tethered and barking. She drove off, unable to shift her thoughts far from Peter's proposal, from Archie's revelation. From how marginal her husband was. From the disquiet that Charlie induced.

That morning she had again asked him about his lodging in London. She knew he was capable of inventing a story about a woman shaking a teddy bear out of a glassless window. His monosyllabic replies had done nothing to aid his deception.

The enormity of the loss of her home came like a hammer on the road to the Gormsons. With it an exhilarating fear of freedom. Could she stay at the Villa? Should she go back? How to harmonise her life with that of the children, when there was no harmony? What about Charlie?

On the road, airmen shouted at her from lorries. She carried on, thinking she would head towards the undemanding flat lands, where marshes were infiltrated by the open sea.

Yet the greater demand was that of knowing Coral Floster's true intentions. From the day of the parachutist's death, Morgan had suspected she would deny any involvement in his murder. She had to know where she stood, before any potential public exposure. So Iverdon must be her goal.

Mrs Floster, although not welcoming, gave her barley water. She was cheerful, if slightly on edge, her gaze constantly on the camp entrance opposite. "Flossie said the loss of his best pilots is serious. But Herr Schicklgruber has given them breathing space."

After some minutes of forced conversation, she was impelled to ask why her visitor had come.

Morgan said, "Talking of pilots brings to mind a recent event." Mrs Floster's focus was wavering. She was looking over her shoulder at someone outside. Too late Morgan tried to continue; her hostess was leaving the room.

Her footsteps in the hall, the front door slamming. From the window Morgan watched her run along the path with as much energy as she had crossing the potato field. Saw a tall R.A.F. officer coming to meet her. He saluted her. She took his arm.

Morgan stood outside the house, watching the couple conversing excitedly. As they walked down the road she flapped an unacknowledged goodbye at them. Coral Floster stepped into an M.G. tourer. They drove in the direction of Iverdon village, leaving Morgan no alternative but to drive back the way she had come.

Aunt Harriet, who was standing at her mother's gate, saw Morgan about to pass by and flagged her down. Her aunt spoke about the incident in St Margaret's as if it had just happened. "There cannot be any excuses for such outrageous behaviour. Especially on consecrated ground."

"Yes, what that soldier did was unspeakable."

"You will never salve your reputation, Morgan, such as it is, after that display."

Aunt Maud's greeting was, "Why aren't you in black? Your father would have wanted it."

"Is Pa dead? Have you heard something?"

"No. But if he were here, he would wish you to be."

She listened with apathy to her aunts' experiences in Nottinghamshire. They had seen such sights. The war was lowering standards. Here there was talk of goings-on at the R.D.F. camp. Neither aunt asked how she was, nor mentioned their incarcerated sister.

During the visit her grandmother remained unusually silent, breaking it only once to enquire from whom Charlie had managed to obtain Swiss rolls. It wasn't a question Morgan intended to put to him. The unease she had been feeling about him had not left her.

At the Villa, alone after dinner, she waited for the questions he was bound to put. Why had she and Mrs Retchen been talking about his mother? No reason. What did his mother die of?

"A terrible illness," Morgan replied. Known only to her doctor and her husband, to whom it was whispered the moment she expired.

"Did mother die giving birth to me?" No. "Did she die at home?" Yes.

He was sceptical. "What did mother look like in her coffin? Was she in white like Greta Garbo?"

"That's just morbid."

He thought she was being evasive. "Where were you when mother died?"

"Here at the Villa."

"Why didn't you go to her funeral?"

She had been detailed to look after him, she replied. Neither could she face the finality of watching earth drum the coffin lid.

"Why wasn't Rhoda looking after me?"

"She came to live here later. Mrs Retchen and her mother were at the funeral. The nurse had gone, so I had to stay."

Charlie was a cat about to pounce. "You and Mrs Retchen were talking about a baby." He was fixed on Morgan. "I think it was your baby."

"Yes." She didn't say that when her pregnancy began to show she was sent to Aunt Patch, wearing her mother's wedding ring. By her return with the baby her mother's fingers, like her body, were wasting away. Morgan married with Cathcart's ring. And kept Archie's.

"Did it live?" Charlie asked quietly.

"Yes, it lived." There wasn't time to do other than go for the truth.

"What happened to it?" Even with clouds in his head, Charlie knew that neither Billy nor Teresa was that infant. "Later? Did it die later?" He was grasping at straws.

"No, it didn't." She said slowly, "She took him."

"Who is 'she'?"

"The cat's mother!" It was a last foolish attempt to divert him.

He waited, his eyes fixed on the floor.

"My mother, Berenice Perincall, took him." She was willing Charlie to look at her.

"I don't believe you. It was already dead." He wanted it to be so. "Was she dead too?"

"No."

Why, near the end, had Montague refused to enter his wife's room if he loved her so much? How could he have sent Morgan, at fifteen, into the room with the putrid smell that no lavender could disguise? Mrs Retchen's mother had remonstrated with him.

"Not quite yet." Morgan could still remember the over-bright eyes of the woman in constant pain. "There was a plate of melon beside the bed."

What use to tell Charlie how she had coveted the beautiful orange fruit? She was told to throw it away, and had gobbled it secretly in the lavatory. Tried in vain to flush away the rind. Desperately fishing it out, she threw it in the Lodbrook. For a time she wondered if death came from eating infected melon. "The sight of melon always makes me queasy."

"How old were you?"

"I was fifteen."

There had been the sounds of aircraft taking off, competing with the evening song of thrushes and blackbirds. The alert came whining through open windows. They heard the familiar drone of enemy bombers. It was seven o'clock, the light still good. Neither moved to the shelter.

"London will get it tonight," she said.

Charlie, white-faced, was gripping the back of a chair. "So you, my mother, gave me, your son away."

"Pa always wanted a son so I gave him one, didn't I?"

He had a moment of shock. "You don't mean to say that you and Pa . . . ?"

It was her turn to be shocked. "No! Great merciful heavens, no! How can you think such a thing?"

They stood looking at one another. Charlie plunged on. "If you are my mother, then who is my real father?"

She was thinking fast. "Oh, some boy. From beyond Struttleigh."

"Is that all?"

She was trying to foresee his reactions. "He was a delivery boy." The memory of Archie's telegram pouch under her head, sharp straw piercing her shoulders when he removed her blouse. He was not adept, but it hadn't mattered.

"A delivery boy on a bike with a basket in front!"

"He was someone who happened to deliver . . . groceries."

"Well, at least I know my father delivered groceries!" He didn't know if he was feeling anger or jealousy, disappointment or relief. "How long ago? Nineteen years it must be. Where is he now, my father?"

"Dead." She lied without hesitation. What was another lie after all the dissimulation? "Got himself killed." The picture came clearer. "In Libya." Silence. She wished she could faint.

"What was his name? Did he know about me? Why didn't you marry him? What did his parents say? What did our mother, sorry . . . *your* mother, think? And Pa? No, I know what he thought." He was clenching his fists. His thoughts were spinning. "Why did nobody tell me before? Who knows?" There was the far thud of gunfire. "Does Cathcart know?"

"Of course not." How to explain to a nineteen-year-old boy about a fiancé's expectations of virginity?

"Rhoda, does she know?"

"She was never told. Mother died before Rhoda. Soon after you were brought here."

"So at least that's true." He was feeling unwell. "What about before that?"

"I went to stay with Aunt Pandora in Hackney until you were born. When I came home with you, Mother was already very ill."

"So, Aunt Patch knows."

"She is in that institution. She's Granny Dorp's daughter." She was watching him closely, his breathing looked strange. Finally, "Grandma Perincall knows."

"Which means Aunt Harriet, Aunt Maud *and* Aunt Winnie." For the first time he realised the bombers were echoing the beat of his heart. That the wind in the chimneys mimicked his own wheezing breath. And, for the first time, he saw clearly how, on all the visits to Grandma

Perincall's, they had been monitoring a bastard from a suspect liaison. "The whole world knows except me!"

He had begun tapping his knuckles on the kettle, the chickens' pot, the warming pan. Tap, tap, tap, all around until she had to ask him to stop.

Tap, tap. "You left me!"

"You were safe here with Pa. You had Rhoda to look after you. And Mrs Retchen and her mother, before I married Cat."

"You left your seven-year-old son!"

She was suddenly weary. "I came back, didn't I?"

"Only because of the war. You'll go again, I know it. Women are all the same."

"I can't. There's no house to go back to."

"You'll find somewhere. Some man or other. If you haven't already!"

Strange that he wasn't mentioning Cathcart.

His rage was rising. Grabbing the hod, he rattled some coal into the stove, the noise echoed the ack-ack guns starting up.

For two days cheerlessness lay upon the Villa. Even Florence, who had not gone home, was affected by it. She couldn't fathom Charlie. Each night over their heads heavy bombers moved in formation, bringing death to London and the docks. He didn't seem to care. The occasional thud of a bomb, released by a disabled Junkers, shook the shelter where all but he and Myrtle cowered.

Looking for damage to the garage one morning, Morgan noticed the dog was missing.

"Where's your dog, Charlie?" They were in the hall, lit by the stained glass like angels. "What have you done with it?"

His expression was cold. "It wasn't my dog."

"You killed it!" She knew. "Why?"

"You said you didn't like it." The conversation seemed to bore him.

"But *you* liked it, Charlie," she called after him. "You liked it!" It was as if she were trying to force him to feel.

Charlie left the Villa, a slight smile on his face.

In the ensuing days he had no problem telling Florence how the dog had followed him from London and come back with him. Morgan more than suspected he was trying to hurt her.

All night, at work, Charlie's mind spun. How could Morgan be his real mother when his love for her was not a son's love? She had always been more to him than a sister. What were those feelings now? Had she not killed them?

Sleeping with Maya had added confusion. For many weeks Charlie's thoughts of her had centred more and more on her body, his memories rapidly descending to that most important region of gratification, until he could hardly remember her face. Night after night he relived that encounter with her, leaving him exhausted and, like his handkerchiefs, wet.

He knew so little about Maya he could only invent her response to his discovery. Would she tell him that his mother had freed him by not being one? And that losing two fathers was a lucky escape from the parental trap? But she was just another woman with a woman's suspect reasoning. There was nobody to share this terrible discovery with, not even Rhoda.

Charlie left, taking his National Savings book with him.

He had made for Prittend because it was the first bus to arrive. The same irresolution found him in Oban Street. Uncle Herbert was behind the counter, lonely and pleased to talk. Raids on Merseyside and the docks were increasing. The wireless said that airfields and radar stations were under attack.

"Our Frank has been called up for secret work, after some tests. What kind of test is it to do the *Telegraph* crossword in five minutes?" Frank had never been known to joke. "He's gone to Buckinghamshire. For heaven knows what. He's an enigma."

Charlie had nothing to say. His uncle asked if he would do some deliveries on the bike, the one with the basket. Charlie left in a temper. People used him. He had been stabbed in the heart, like the parachutist, by a woman. He was a killer of animals. His mother, his real mother, was a murderer whose blood ran in his veins. She, like Maya, had pushed him away. Had deserted him just like Rhoda.

Morgan went to the Talbotts' house in search of Charlie. Grace Talbott answered the door. She looked somehow different.

"I hit him," she said. "He dared me to and I did."

"Hit whom? Who dared you?"

Without answering, she stood triumphant.

"Have you heard from Charlie?"

"Who?" The woman's mind was on other matters.

Morgan hesitated. How could she involve this poor person whose problems far surpassed hers? Charlie had been gone only a short time. But she needed to share her disquiet. "Charlie's missing," she blurted out. "Just like my father." Tears welled and wouldn't stop.

Mrs Talbott had her in her arms. Ashamed, Morgan freed herself. "Forgive me. It's the fatigue."

"It was you, really, what made the difference." Mrs Talbott was nodding. "What you said the day of that cricket match, sunk in. And him too." Whoever the "him" was, Morgan knew for certain it wasn't Bernard Talbott.

Florence, sun bathing by the river, noticed Charlie creeping towards her. She watched him clamber through the barbed wire, then called a halloo that he ignored. He headed towards the boathouse. Flo watched him emerge in a dinghy. He rowed out to the *Clara*, climbed aboard and tethered the dinghy.

After observing him moving about on deck, folding tarpaulins and untying ropes, Florence decided to swim out.

By the time she had reached him, Charlie had started the *Clara*'s engines. Impervious to her shouts, he was hauling up the anchor. She reached the pulpit rail, and with an effort heaved herself up to flop on the deck. Charlie shouted that she'd better get off. He was heading for open sea.

Florence went to squat in the bow, where bloodstains were still visible, saying she had never been seasick. What kind of trip was it? Was there enough fuel to get anywhere interesting? What was the weather forecast? Would there be food?

Ignoring her, Charlie steered the *Clara* into mid stream, straight ahead. They passed some soldiers in a pillbox, whom she waved at. No other signs of life, only drifting terns and gulls, and the ever-present planes. He was taking the cruiser downstream as fast as her engines would allow. The waves in her wake were lifting bunched seaweed on the shores.

Florence decided to cure Charlie's black mood with conversation. She raised her voice over the engine. There was no response to the subjects of Spitfires, or wheat. He wished she would shut up. Behind them the mill was diminishing from view, the river widening.

Florence tried the cinema and "Goodbye, Mr Chips!" She was standing and shouting about sacrifice. He didn't like it. Didn't like the way she was coming nearer, trying to keep her balance. She didn't know he hated school pictures. The cruiser was rocking against the increasing tide. Now she was closer, tottering from one leg to the other. He was fixing on the open water, trying to ignore her chatter. Now she was on about hares and field mice and horses' hoofs.

Her voice was right at his elbow. He didn't like her asking where they were going. Didn't like the expanse of flesh he glimpsed from the corner of his eye. He had never liked her bathing costumes. He didn't like fat women. He hated Flo.

They were approaching that section of the dyke where the pilot was stabbed, when he asked if she'd ever seen a dead body.

She was standing next to him, her fingers hovering over his on the wheel. She said she'd seen a man who had tied himself and a gun to a tree and shot himself through the chin. "Why? Who knows? He was just a labourer."

Flo's next move caught Charlie by surprise. Her arms went around him. She was trying to kiss him, on his cheek, his neck, anywhere. He was ducking and feinting, attempting to cling on to the wheel. He didn't want her. All women were the same, untrustworthy and cruel, slicing one's heart.

Flo had the tenacity of an octopus. They grappled and fought. She was tough and he needed both hands. The *Clara* began to swing to starboard. Flo was yelling as he pushed and pushed. And pushed.

Her screams as she went overboard were drowned by the engines' noise.

Morgan was preparing to search for Charlie on her bicycle when Ronnie Talbott delayed her. His father had sent him to ask the whereabouts of his wife, Grace. He said it was only to save face. His dad knew full well she'd run off with a quartermaster sergeant. Who could blame her? His sister Dora who was staying at the Groumings – too posh, but she wouldn't come home – kept on about disgracing the family. Ronnie said that had always been the trouble. At his house, he told her, war had been going on a long time.

He handed Morgan a crumpled note, taken by one of the flour baggers from a wireless message. She could make little sense of it except the word *Liverpool*. He said he had no idea where Charlie was.

Granny Dorp's cottage was deserted. Charlie wasn't in the Three Tuns. How easy it had been to make a mess of things. Now she wanted the chance for some kind of redress. She owed it to her son. But first she must find him.

The moon was visible in a daylight sky by the time she returned from scouring the neighbourhood. Along the drive she met Mrs Retchen who, in her need to tell, was choosing to ignore their previous skirmish. Group Captain Floster had been murdered.

"He was found last night, his throat sliced by a wire stretched across his path. He was riding a motorcycle." She paused. "Somebody else's motorcycle. Nobody knows who did it or why."

In her opinion, there being a war on, nobody would investigate it properly. Mrs Coral Floster was out of her mind with grief, and being

376

comforted by an R.A.F. officer! "Where will it end?" If Mrs Retchen had seen that Morgan was distracted, she said nothing.

Nineteen years of subterfuge had been negated in one afternoon. Now Morgan knew, without doubt, she was in Charlie's hands. He wanted her to love him, not realising that for nineteen years all the admonitions had been not to do so. At that very moment he was somewhere trying to make sense of a shocking revelation. In his present state he was capable of anything. And she was incapable of preventing it.

She went to the water's edge. No sign of him. There was no time to do more than wonder why the *Clara* wasn't at her moorings, and why Flo's plimsolls were lying in the mud, when she heard cries coming from the dyke.

It was Flo, a dark figure stumbling towards her along the sea wall, supported by some man. He was not Charlie, but a soldier staggering under her weight. Morgan lost sight of them for a minute and feared for their safety. They reappeared, locked in a bizarre embrace. They advanced on the last stile, negotiating it in a tumble of arms and legs. The soldier landed first, Flo falling into him with howls of pain. Morgan waited while they crawled through the last barrier across the dyke. Joined together they slid down the grass to the beach.

Florence was covered in mud. At close quarters her hair was black. The soldier, a corporal, was caked with it too. She threw herself on Morgan, who had to clasp her slippery body in her arms. Florence then began seriously to cry.

Her story of what Charlie had done, interspersed with the soldier's, lasted all the way back to the Villa. Charlie was the most frightful crazed criminal and should be locked up. The corporal was keen to point out that it was he alone, with his binoculars, who had rescued the young lady from a slow death. He had followed the party's movement from water to asphyxiating quagmire, from which he had extracted her.

Morgan gave them tea. She treated Flo's wounds, wrapped her and tried to quieten her. But Flo kept on crying, about her legs all bruised and scratched; her face. She might have drowned. Been dragged under the boat. Charlie was a monster. Charlie should be locked up. He had absolutely no feelings.

The corporal had begun telling of drowned merchant seamen and dismembered airmen, of soldiers trapped up to their necks in quicksand. The young lady was lucky to be alive. With each account Florence began to wail afresh and wouldn't be comforted.

On the table lay a parcel tied with string. No name or address. In an effort to distract her, Morgan decided to open it. Might not Jerky have left them something like, for instance, chocolate? The corporal thought it might be a bomb, starting Flo's tears again. Morgan asked if he would be needed in his bunker. He said that his mate could manage.

First from the parcel was a packet of Capstan cigarettes. Then a box of Swan Vestas, Oxo cubes, dentifrice, razor blades, letter cards and a pencil. Florence fingered them, tears still dropping.

Lastly Morgan retrieved a packet of Weston biscuits, the sight of which induced mild hysteria in Flo. Between sobs she said she was starving. The soldier began describing a lieutenant's reactions to discovering weevils in his digestives. Florence's cries grew louder as he moved on to the story of an army captain, expired in agony from eating Spam. Florence was bawling now. Morgan put her hands to her ears and shouted and shouted for them to stop. In a slight lull she thought she could hear someone on the stairs.

They waited, Florence whimpering, but listening.

"Charlie! Is that you?"

There were footsteps in the hall. The door opened. Someone said, "What's all the hullabaloo?"

It took Morgan a second to realise that the bearded stranger coming into the kitchen was her father, Montague Perincall.

To be continued . . .

MAGGIE ROSS' first novel *The Gasteropod* (Cresset Press) won the James Tait Black Memorial Prize. Her second novel *Milena* was published by Collins. Her work has been published in short story collections (Penguin, Michael Joseph, Macmillan, Hutchinson), and her stories and plays for radio and television have been broadcast and televised. She worked briefly in television as a drama script editor and was fiction critic for the *Listener*. She lives in London.